# Shafted

# MANDASUE HELLER

# Shafted

HODDER &
STOUGHTON

Copyright © 2007 by Mandasue Heller

First published in Great Britain in 2007 by Hodder & Stoughton
A division of Hodder Headline

The right of Mandasue Heller to be identified as the Author
of the Work has been asserted by her in accordance with the
Copyright, Designs and Patents Act 1988.

A Hodder & Stoughton Book

I

A CIP catalogue record for this title is available
from the British Library

Hardback ISBN 978 0 340 89950 2
Trade Paperback ISBN 978 0 340 89951 9

Typeset in Plantin Light by
Palimpsest Book Production Limited, Grangemouth, Stirlingshire

Printed and bound by
Clays Ltd, St Ives plc

Hodder Headline's policy is to use papers that are natural, renewable
and recyclable products and made from wood grown in sustainable forests.
The logging and manufacturing processes are expected to conform to the
environmental regulations of the country of origin.

Hodder & Stoughton Ltd
A division of Hodder Headline
338 Euston Road
London NW1 3BH

For my wonderful children, Michael, Andrew, and Azzura. And my precious granddaughters, Marissa and Lariah.

# Acknowledgements

As ever, my sincerest love and gratitude go to my family: Wingrove Ward – my partner in life *and* music (the album's sounding great, babe; can't wait to hear it when it's finished!); my lovely mum, Jean Heller; my sister, Ava; Amber & Kyro, Martin, Jade, and Reece; Auntie Doreen, Pete, Lorna, Cliff, Chris & Glen; Natalie, Dan, & Toni.

Not forgetting Uncle Michael, Aunt Paulette, and the rest of our new-found Heller family, USA. And the Wards: Mavis & Joseph, Valerie, Jascinth, Donna (& Ronnie), and their respective children.

Heartfelt thanks to Betty & Ronnie Schwartz, Martina Cole, Norman Fairweather, Wayne Brookes, Faye Webber, Sarj Duggal, and the rest of our friends past & present, for being so supportive. And a big hello to the authors we were lucky enough to meet or reacquaint ourselves with on the roadshow – you were all fantastic!

As are all the Hodder guys; not least my delightfully quirky editor, Carolyn Caughey; Emma Knight; Isobel Akenhead; Ron Beard; Auriol Bishop; Lucy Hale; etc, etc . . . (Far too many to mention by name, but you're all brilliant.)

Same to my lovely agent, Cat Ledger.

Gratitude, as ever, to Nick Austin.

And thanks to Bill Woan for the police info.

Hi! to the reps, buyers, and sellers who we had the pleasure of meeting in Gloucestershire, Manchester, and Glasgow – we had some great nights with you guys, and really appreciate your efforts for getting the books out there. (And the readers for buying them, of course.)

And, lastly, the lovely library ladies for ordering all those extra copies.

Thank you all so much!

# PART ONE

# I

'*Aaaand* cut!'

'Thank fuck for that!' Larry Logan muttered, pulling a tissue from his pocket and wiping his handsome face. Tossing the crumpled wad onto the floor, he said, 'I thought there was supposed to be flaming air-con in here?'

'There is,' the floor manager replied curtly, sick of Larry's moaning and whining – like *he* was the only one suffering. Snapping her fingers at one of the runners now, she barked at him to dispose of the tissue properly. Then she strode out onto the studio floor, yelling, 'Quiet in the audience, please! We're back on air in ten minutes, so no clever ideas about nipping to the toilet or opening noisy sweets, or you're out!'

Sticking two fingers up at her back, Larry sidestepped the make-up girl who rushed forward to repair his face and made a dash for the heavy soundproofed studio door. Yanking it open, he stepped out of the stifling heat and shivered as the contrasting iciness of the corridor bit into him.

Heading towards his dressing room, he glanced back to see if anyone was following, and groaned when he saw the assistant director barrelling out of the studio door.

'Christ's sakes, Gord,' Larry complained, knowing full well that he'd come to keep an eye on him. 'I'm only going to the fucking loo.'

'I'll come with you,' Gordon told him firmly. 'You know what Jeremy said.'

'Tell him I gave you the slip,' Larry flipped back defiantly, walking on.

'No can do,' Gordon said, catching up.

'Give me a break,' Larry moaned. 'I've got the trots, man.'

Stopping in his tracks, Gordon frowned. He'd been ordered to watch Larry like a hawk to stop him getting his hands on any booze, and that was exactly what he *had* been doing – all bloody day, despite having a heavy workload of his own to be getting on with. But there was no way he was standing outside the cubicle while Larry took a dump. That was *way* above and beyond.

Nodding, he said, 'Okay, go on, then. But I'm waiting here. And if anyone asks, I was with you all the way.'

'I'll tell 'em you wiped my arse if you want,' Larry quipped.

'Fuck off! And hurry up. We've only got a few minutes.'

'Thanks, mate. I owe you one.'

Taking off again, Larry turned the corner and ran straight past the toilets. Letting himself into his dressing room, he closed the door firmly and dragged his holdall down from the top of the cupboard. Taking out the bottle of Scotch that was stashed at the bottom of the bag he twisted the cap off and took a long drink, exhaling with pleasure and relief as the liquid seared his parched throat.

Taking another long slug, then another for the road, he put the bottle away again and gave himself an approving once-over in the mirror before heading back to the set.

Concerned that Larry wasn't going to make it back in time, Gordon was just contemplating going to get him when he came hurtling around the corner, making an exaggerated show of zipping up his fly.

'Sorry, Gord . . . took a bit longer than I expected. And there was no paper in my cubicle, so I had to run down the line with my kecks round my ankles. Thought I was gonna have to mop up after myself, as well. Still, better out than in, eh?'

'Too much information,' Gordon grunted, yanking the studio door open and waving Larry back in. 'Better hurry up,' he warned then, nodding towards the floor manager who was standing in the middle of the stage, hands on hips, tight-lipped scowl on her face. 'Looks like she's on the warpath.'

'Fuck her,' Larry scoffed. Then, laughing, he nudged Gordon in the ribs and said, 'Then again, maybe not, eh? I mean, you wouldn't, would you?'

Getting a full blast of Scotch fumes, Gordon grimaced. But it was too late to say anything, because Anne was already waving Larry over, hissing, 'Get a move on! We've got exactly twenty seconds.'

'Keep your knickers on,' Larry called back, blithely strolling towards her – and infuriating her some more when he decided to waste a few more seconds saying hello to the pretty girls on the front row.

Biting down on her irritation, Anne held up her hand when Larry finally sauntered into position.

'Three . . . two . . . one . . . *aaand* action!'

Back under the blistering heat of the lights, the Scotch began to kick in and Larry swayed slightly as he turned to camera six to welcome the viewers back. Burping loudly when he opened his mouth to speak, he gave the audience a mock-sheepish grin.

'Oops! Pardon me for being rude, 'twas not me, it was my food.'

Up in the editing suite, watching the action on a high-tech bank of monitors, Frank Woods gave Jeremy Hislop an accusing look, hissing, 'He's pissed! I thought you said Gordon was watching him?'

'He was.'

'So how the fuck did it happen, then?'

'I don't know,' Jeremy admitted, frowning as he studied

Larry's face on the monitor. Logan was definitely under the influence: cheeks flushed, eyes beginning to glaze over.

'Idiot!' Frank snarled, slamming his fist down on the console. 'How could you let this happen? It's the *Kiddie Kare Telethon*, for fuck's sake. You knew how important it was to keep him in line. You should have handcuffed yourself to him.'

'You wanted me up here with you. I can't be two places at once.'

'You won't be *any* bloody place if he cocks this up, I can promise you that.'

'I *warned* you this would happen,' Jeremy argued, swivelling his chair around to face Frank now. 'But you ignored me, so . . .' Leaving the rest of the sentence hanging, he shrugged, his meaning quite clear without him having to spell it out.

Annoyed as much by the intimation of blame as by the knowledge that it was rightly placed, Frank said, 'What choice did I have? It's the first time they've put a game show in the line-up, and they chose ours. I'd have been crazy to turn it down.'

*Crazy to agree to it, more like*, Jeremy thought scathingly, shaking his head as he turned his attention back to the screens. Only a fool would let a loose cannon like Larry Logan front a live show. He might be Mr Gorgeous, with the ability to charm the knickers off any woman at fifty paces – as he seemed intent on proving, going by the number of times he'd been papped coming out of clubs with different tarts hanging off his arm. But for those who had to suffer him on the dark side of the screen, he was rude, arrogant, and completely incapable of sticking to the format. Working with him had been the longest, most stressful six months of Jeremy's career to date.

And it didn't help that *Star Struck* was the biggest piece

of TV crap Jeremy had ever been unfortunate enough to direct. But a job was a job, and this one paid well enough for Jeremy to bury his personal opinions – for the most part.

Back on set, Larry was taking the two surviving contestants into the final head-to-head. They were both female, but while one was middle-aged and plump – and, therefore, of no interest to Larry whatsoever – the other was young and pretty, with small, pert breasts, full glossy lips, and a sleek, jet-black bob. Just how he liked them!

'The Bat' – as Larry had mentally been referring to the older woman throughout the show – was first up. Making a concerted effort not to stare at the mole on her cheek that was beginning to look suspiciously like a couple of money spiders mating, Larry cleared his throat and peered down at the question card in his hand.

'Right, Elaine . . . for a chance to win tonight's jackpot . . . can you tell me the real name of the former girl-band member known as Baby?'

'Oh, I really didn't want a pop question,' Elaine moaned, biting her lip. 'Oh, damn! I can't think of *any* girl groups.'

'Gonna have to hurry you along there, sweetheart.'

More lip biting and frowning. Then, shrugging hopelessly, 'Is it The Supremes, Larry?'

''Fraid not.' Mock-sympathetic smile. 'I was looking for Emma Bunton from The Spice Girls.'

Turning to tonight's shag now, Larry gave her a conspiratorial wink and slipped an arm around her slim waist.

'Okay, Cindy, my darling, get this right and you'll steal the money. Ready?'

'I think so,' Cindy gasped, her heart thudding in her chest as Larry's hand slid from her hip to the curve of her buttock. She'd loved him from the moment she'd first laid eyes on him, and she couldn't believe that she had finally made it onto his show. And not only was she in with a real chance of winning, but she just *knew* that he fancied her, because he'd been winking at her all day and giving her that super-sexy grin of his. And now he was actually touching her bum!

Stumbling slightly as an alcohol rush threw his head out of whack, Larry dropped his question cards. Muttering 'Shit!' when they landed question-side up on the floor at Cindy's feet, he reached down and snatched them up. 'Sorry!' he said, waving them at the camera. 'But don't panic, she didn't see them . . . You didn't, did you, darlin'?'

'No.' Cindy shook her head innocently.

Feigning a cough to bring himself under control as he felt a sudden urge to laugh, Larry said, 'Sorry, folks, frog in the throat . . . better than *cancer*, though, eh?'

Waiting for the smattering of nervous audience laughter to die down, he turned back to Cindy.

'Right, then . . . for a chance to win ten thousand pounds, can you tell me the name of Britney Spears's last husband, Kevin Federline?'

'Moron!' the floor manager hissed, standing in the shadows beside the camera. Stepping forward now, she waved her arms to attract his attention.

Frowning when he saw her, Larry shrugged, and mouthed, '*What?*'

'*You gave her the answer,*' Anne stage-whispered, jabbing a finger at the question card. 'Ask her another! Ask . . . her . . . *another!*'

'Oh, right,' Larry murmured. Then, giving a cheeky grin to camera, 'Sorry 'bout that. Seems I made a bit of a boo-boo. But 's all right. Just gotta ask another question.'

Rifling through the cards now, he pulled one out at random and looped his arm around Cindy's shoulder.

'Okay, my darling, for ten thousand pounds, can you tell me . . . why the hell Madonna picked Guy Ritchie over me?'

Cindy peered up at him confusedly. Then someone in the

audience started laughing, and everyone else quickly followed suit – Larry included.

Alan Corbin, Oasis TV's Head of Light Entertainment, was far from amused. Storming into the editing suite, he yelled, 'Get him off! *NOW!*'

'He's on the last question,' Jeremy said, trying desperately to remain calm even though he knew it could only get worse. 'If we just—'

Corbin wasn't listening. Eyes bulging from their sockets, he stared at the monitor screens and yelped, 'What the bloody hell's he doing *now?*' in a voice several octaves higher than was healthy for a man of his age.

Down below, Larry had totally lost it. Clutching at Cindy with tears of laughter streaming down his face, he'd managed to snap one of her flimsy shoulder straps, revealing one of her bare breasts.

'Oh, my God!' Corbin croaked as the studio audience erupted with male approval and female disapproval. Shoulders slumping, he sank down on a vacant chair and dabbed his handkerchief over his sweat-slick face. 'We're fucked!'

'Not necessarily,' Jeremy muttered, pushing sliders and pressing buttons on the master control panel. 'We've still got time-delay on our side. Any luck, we'll black-screen before anyone spots the tit.'

'Bit late for that,' Frank interjected bitterly. 'They've been watching him for the last half-hour.'

Ignoring him, Jeremy carried on with what he was doing. Then, sighing with relief after a moment, he said, 'We're off air.'

'What about the tit?' Corbin wanted to know. 'Have you caught it in time?'

'Soon know,' Jeremy told him, turning his attention to the live-stream monitor.

Everyone in the editing suite held their breath as, on screen,

Larry reached the point where he'd dropped the question cards. Snatching them up again, he started to ask the Britney Spears question, but just as he reached the point where he unwittingly supplied the answer, the screen went blank, and seconds later a 'Technical fault' warning flagged up, followed by the help and appeal-line numbers, and a pre-recorded voice-over by Matty Kline, the comedian who was compering the telethon, urging people to '*Keep ringing in those donations, guys, 'cos every little helps!*'

Excusing himself now that the worst of the disaster had been averted, Jeremy rushed down to the set to try and salvage what was left of the show. Grabbing Larry, he frogmarched him to the studio door and ordered him to go and get himself sobered up. That done, he asked Matty Kline to stand in and wrap *Star Struck* up.

Frank Woods and Alan Corbin were in the middle of a hushed but obviously heated discussion when Jeremy got back to the editing suite: Corbin was telling Frank that Larry had to go, but Frank was in no mood to be dictated to. Bad as it had been today, *Star Struck* was his baby, and he was proud of its success. And he wasn't about to risk a drop in the ratings by replacing Larry – not on Corbin's say-so, anyway.

'You're overreacting,' he told Corbin now. 'The viewers love Larry, and they won't hold this against him. We'll just issue a statement saying he was doped up on flu medication, or something.'

'Don't be ridiculous,' Corbin snorted contemptuously. 'Any idiot can see he's steaming. And, to be honest, he's not good enough that I need to be putting myself through this kind of stress every time he hits the screen. He goes – that's my final word.'

'With respect,' Frank replied with measured calm. 'This is *my* production company, and *I* decide who goes and who stays on *my* shows.'

'And *I* decide which programmes to commission for *my* station,' Corbin reminded him firmly. Exhaling wearily then, he said, 'I don't want to fall out with you over this, Frank, but if you can't see what a liability Logan is you're not the man you used to be.'

Frank knew that Corbin was right. Logan *was* a liability. But the public didn't know that, and if Frank had his way they never would.

'I know what you're thinking,' Corbin said perceptively now. 'He draws the viewers, so we should give him leeway. But the Kiddie Kare Telethon is *sacred*, and I paid too much for the broadcasting rights to let one man – who, incidentally, I don't even *like* – jeopardise its future. And you're very much mistaken if you think the public won't hold this against him. Jokers, they accept; piss-heads who make *sick* jokes, they do not.' Standing up now, he shrugged. 'Take my advice, get shot of the dead wood and bring in someone reliable like Dennis or Monkhouse before it's too late.'

'Monkhouse is dead,' Frank reminded him, his flat tone disguising the anger simmering beneath the surface.

'So he is,' Corbin conceded. 'Oh, well . . . Dennis, then. Or how about Richie? He's a good-looking lad with a bit of spark about him. And the viewers adore him.' Nodding now, pleased with his vision, he said, 'Get Shane to front it, and we'll talk about keeping *Star Struck* in the schedule.'

'That's blackmail.'

'Call it what you like, but I don't want to see Logan's face in my station again – *ever.*'

'Bastard!' Frank snarled when the door swung shut behind Corbin. 'Who the hell does he think he is, telling me how to run *my* show? His station was on its bloody arse when I gave him *Star Struck!*'

'You've got to admit he's got a point,' Jeremy said. 'You don't realise how bad things actually are, because we've always smoothed everything out by the time the show airs, but it's murder trying to get a good take out of Larry these days.' Shrugging now, he added, 'Might be worth thinking about a replacement – even if it's only temporary; until he's been through rehab, or something.'

'Bollocks!' Frank shot back dismissively. 'Logan doesn't need rehab, he just needs a damn good kick up the arse.'

'If you say so,' Jeremy said, casually easing up the volume on the monitor so that Frank could hear how good a job Matty Kline was doing as a stand-in for his golden boy right now. 'The audience really likes him, don't they?' he commented as the sound of cheering filled the suite.

'They liked the flaming singing *gerbils*!' Frank reminded him caustically. Then, shaking his head, he muttered, 'All you had to do was keep him in line, but if you're not up to it just say the word, 'cos there's plenty more directors where you came from.'

Biting down on the angry reply that sprang to his lips, Jeremy folded his arms. There was no point arguing with Frank when he was in this kind of mood; he would just dig his heels in deeper and lash out at whoever was closest.

Pushing his chair back with a scrape now, Frank stood up and headed for the door, barking back over his shoulder, 'Find Larry and tell him I want him in my office in five minutes. And, while you're at it, sack Gordon!'

# 2

Katy Lowndes was in bed, but she wasn't sleeping; she was grinding her teeth, fuming about the telethon, which she could hear coming to an end on the TV in the lounge below.

She'd enjoyed the first few hours, crying with laughter when the singing gerbils chased Matty Kline around the stage, and mooning over Westlife. But then *Star Struck* had come on, and her night had been ruined when she saw that Tania slaggy-arse boyfriend-stealer Baxter was one of the contestants. Not only because Tania was too young to take part, but also because she'd won the money under false pretences, pretending to be her older sister, Cindy.

It had actually taken Katy a little while to realise that it was Tania and not Cindy, because she hadn't seen Tania since leaving school a few months earlier and her hair had still been long and blonde then. But now, with it cut and coloured black like Cindy's, with her make-up done the same way and wearing the same kind of tarty dress, Tania looked so much like her nineteen-year-old sister that it was spooky. But she'd made one mistake, and that was how Katy had sussed it.

The tits.

Cindy had had a boob job, and not a subtle one but a full-on Jordan-stylie; whereas Tania's breasts were as small as ever. And as soon as Katy clicked on to *that*, she'd spotted all the other things which had confirmed it for her. Like the scar over Tania's right eyebrow from the time she'd tried to look cool by getting it pierced only for it to go septic; and the

stupid way she stood with her hand on her hip and one leg
stuck out, like she was on a corner looking for passing trade;
and that annoying laugh of hers: head thrown back, gob wide
open like she was waiting for a dick to fill it.

It had been Tania all right, and Katy had watched the rest
of the show with her arms tightly folded and her lips pursed,
just *praying* for someone to rumble the bitch. And when the
screen blacked out for a few minutes, she'd been so sure it
must be happening right then that she'd been on the edge
of her seat biting her nails with anticipation. But then the
show had come back on with Matty Kline standing in for
Larry Logan, and Katy had flipped when Tania went on to
win the money.

Storming up to her bedroom to sulk in private, she couldn't
settle down for the rage and envy that was eating her up at
the thought of Tania cosying up to Larry Logan and flirting
with Matty Kline – like she stood a cat in hell's chance with
either of them, the ugly, lying slag! And now she was ten
grand richer, while Katy had nothing but her job-seeker's to
get by on, and she'd be lording it up all over town; probably buy herself a flashy car to drive on *Cindy*'s licence, and
splash out on loads of tarty new clothes to flaunt herself in.
And, seeing as she obviously wanted to *be* Cindy, she'd probably get a matching boob job as well, and strut round
Stretford like some kind of superstar, with all the lads falling
over themselves to get with her just because she'd been on
telly. And there wasn't a damn thing Katy could do about
it.

Or was there . . . ?

Sitting bolt upright, Katy bit her lip. There *was* something
she could do. She could ring the papers and tell them what
was going on. They'd have to check it out, and then everyone
would know the truth, and Tania would be the laughing stock
of England – just like she'd made Katy the laughing stock of

school when she'd nicked her boyfriend from under her nose and told everyone that he'd said Katy was a crap shag.

Fuelled by thoughts of sweet revenge, Katy jumped out of bed and ran downstairs to use the phone.

Across town, in the converted attic of the shabby three-storey house in Chorlton that he shared with two fellow journalists and a photographer, Sam Brady was tapping away at his laptop, writing a scathing piece on Larry Logan's shameful performance, while keeping half an eye on the telethon's digital donation display board, the numbers on which were constantly changing as the money continued to pour in. The telethon itself was reaching its end – at long fucking last! – and Sam had muted the volume, sick to death of Matty Kline's incessant gabbing and cackling, which seemed to have stepped up several hundred notches after his stint on *Star Struck* earlier.

Like most of the journalists he knew, Sam despised this happy-clappy bung-us-all-your-cash type of show. And it wasn't just the blatant attempt by the Z-list celebrities who clamoured to take part to keep themselves in the public eye that pissed him off, but that these shows were even *necessary* in this day and age. Kids still suffering poverty and neglect, while the government wasted the country's cash on bombs and ammunition for other people's wars. He'd have loved to sink his teeth into a down-and-dirty exposé of *that* kind of injustice, but it was a rare reporter who got away with fucking with political issues without finding every door suddenly slammed in his face. So Sam chose to aim his poisoned pennib into the heart of showbiz instead, taking great pleasure from biting the arses of over-paid celebrities – like Larry Logan.

He was just coming to the end of his latest piece now when his phone rang.

It was Hannah, the switchboard operator at the *Herald*.

'Hi, Sam. Hope I'm not disturbing you, but I thought you'd want to hear this . . .'

Smiling slyly as Hannah relayed the details of the call she'd just had from a member of the public complaining that the girl who'd won the jackpot on *Star Struck* had done so under false pretences, Sam felt the tinglings of a juicy scandal coming on. Every other journo in the country would be writing about Logan being pissed on air, so the papers would be saturated with that, come the morning. But this – providing it was true – would blow the rest out of the water.

Jotting down the alleged cheat's name and address as supplied by the caller, Sam thanked Hannah and promised to take her for a drink as soon as he got a minute. Then, disconnecting, he tapped in Angie Rayner's number, praying that she wouldn't have her phone on voicemail.

'Hi there,' Angie crooned, her smiling voice almost drowned out by the music pumping away in the background. 'Long time no see.'

'Sorry, babe, it's been a crazy few weeks,' Sam apologised, raising his voice just enough to be sure that she could hear him clearly without broadcasting his entire conversation to his rivals in their own rooms below. 'Bit loud there, isn't it? Take it you're at the after-show party?'

'How did you guess?' Angie yelled back merrily. 'Shame you couldn't be here, you'd *love* it.'

'Any chance of sneaking me in?'

'Yeah, right. Like they're not gonna notice the press snooping round at a time like this.'

'I'll keep my head down – promise.'

'Sorry, Sam, but it's a total no-go. We've got major security tonight, and no one's getting in unless they're on the list. We're on complete lockdown. No last-minute friends or relatives – not even for the bigwigs.'

'Don't want to risk anyone getting to Larry, huh?' Sam

grunted, disappointed that he'd have to wait outside with the rest of the press wolves and try to waylay the girl when she came out while the others jumped all over Logan.

'You know I can't discuss Larry with you,' Angie was telling him now, her voice suddenly guarded.

'Chill, babe,' Sam said quickly. 'Obviously I'm *interested* in him – who wouldn't be after tonight? But I'm sure there's enough hacks already queuing up outside for a piece of him.'

'Yes, and they're all wasting their time, because they've already gone,' Angie said, sounding more than a little disapproving.

'They?' Sam pounced. 'Are you talking about him and the girl who won? Have they left together?'

'What do *you* think?' Angie tutted. Then, remembering who she was talking to, she said, 'But *I* didn't tell you that, and if you quote me, I'll deny it, because the boss is already on the warpath.'

'Fair enough,' Sam said. 'Just tell me where they've gone, and I'll be out of your hair.'

'I genuinely don't know,' Angie told him. 'But I'd say it was a fair bet they've gone clubbing.'

'Sure they won't have gone straight back to his place?' Sam asked. 'They'd want privacy, wouldn't they?'

'He's too much of a show-off,' Angie snorted. 'He won't go home until he's been seen by everyone in town.'

Telling her she was an angel, Sam disconnected and rubbed his hands together with glee. It was a godsend having an insider like Angie to keep him up to date about the goings-on at Oasis, and he'd have to remember to send her some flowers if this turned out as good as he expected. Sure as hell none of the other journos would know what he knew yet, and the shit would hit the fan big time when he put it out there. The public might adore Logan, but while the women who made up the bulk of his viewers might tolerate the kiss-and-tells from the fully grown women he'd shagged and dumped, the slightest whiff of an involvement with a child was guaranteed to turn them against him. And – legal or not – sixteen still meant a child in most people's eyes.

If it was true.

Calling his photographer housemate Fred Greene, he told him to get his gear together and meet him at the car – but to make sure that their other housemates didn't see him taking his stuff out.

'What's going on?' Fred wanted to know, already pulling his shoes on in his room directly below.

Telling him that he'd explain on the way, Sam slotted new batteries into his Dictaphone and gave it a quick one-two test. Satisfied that it was working, he looked around for his keys and his wallet. Then, waiting a few minutes to give Fred time to get the car running, he headed out and tiptoed down the stairs.

Blowing on his hands as he waited for the car's heater to kick in, Fred nodded at Sam when he climbed in beside him and said, 'Where to?'

'Dane Grove, Stretford,' Sam told him, pulling his seat belt on. 'We just need to do a quick verification of facts to make sure this isn't a hoax – then it's off to town to catch a rat.'

Peering up at the Baxter house when Fred pulled up to the kerb opposite ten minutes later, Sam was disappointed to see that it was in total darkness. But, just as they were about to set off again, another car turned the corner and drove up to the closed gates.

Switching on the Dictaphone that was nestling in his pocket as a woman climbed out of the passenger side, Sam got out of the car and approached her, calling out, 'Mrs Baxter?'

Turning, Judith Baxter peered at him uncertainly. 'Yes.'

'Sam Brady from the *Herald*.' He extended a hand. 'Sorry for bothering you so late, but I'm covering the Kiddie Kare Telethon and wondered if you'd spare a moment to give your reaction to your daughter winning the jackpot on *Star Struck* tonight. You must be very proud.'

'Sorry?' Judith looked as confused as she actually was. 'I've got no idea what you're talking about.'

'Your daughter, Cindy,' Sam persisted, watching her face closely. 'You *did* know she was taking part, didn't you?'

'I think you've got the wrong family. My daughter's in Majorca.'

*Bingo!*

'Are you sure?' Sam asked, knowing full well that it *was* the right family. Right family, wrong daughter – just as the caller had claimed.

'I think I'd know where my own daughter is,' Judith replied, a bemused expression on her face now as she pulled both gates wide for her husband to drive through.

Scratching his head, Sam frowned. 'Strange. It was definitely a Cindy Baxter from *this* address who won.'

Taking her house keys out of her handbag and reclosing the gates, Judith shrugged. 'They're either lying, or somebody's made a mistake, but it definitely wasn't *my* Cindy.'

'Black hair,' Sam blurted out when she began to walk towards the house. 'Nineteen; very pretty – like yourself; slim; five five-ish; works at a beauty salon called Glamoreyes; wants to be a model . . .'

Turning back, Judith frowned. 'Where did you get all that from?'

'The description's mine, but the info's what *she* gave out,' Sam told her. 'Sorry if I seem pushy, but I can't see there being two girls with the same name, address *and* personal details. Maybe she was planning to surprise you?'

'She's not due back for another week yet,' Judith said

confusedly. 'She wouldn't have come home without telling me. She tells me everything.'

Getting out of the car just then, Phil Baxter looked from Sam to Fred to the camera in Fred's hands, and said, 'What's going on?'

'They're from the *Herald*,' his wife told him, folding her arms. 'They reckon our Cindy's been on some game show tonight.'

'And she won,' Sam added, smiling at the husband now. 'Ten thousand pounds.'

'Nah.' Phil shook his head. 'You've got the wrong house, mate.'

'That's what I said,' Judith told him quietly. 'But it does sound like her from what he's just said.'

'Er, she's out of the country,' Phil reminded her with a sarcastic edge to his voice.

Gritting her teeth, embarrassed that he seemed intent on continuing in front of strangers the argument they'd been having on the way home, Judith said, 'I know that, thank you very much. But he's just described her to a T, and he even knows where she works, 'cos she's supposed to have said it on the telly.'

'It isn't her,' Phil insisted. 'I phoned her at the hotel before we went out, and there's no way she'd have made it back here that fast.'

'Well, how else do you explain it?' Judith demanded.

'How do *you*?' her husband retorted.

Sam and Fred exchanged an amused glance when the couple glared at each other. Then, suddenly, a spark of realisation flared in the father's eyes and, gritting his teeth, he muttered, 'Tania!'

'It can't be,' Judith said, frowning. 'She's only sixteen, and he said this girl was our Cindy's age.'

'Yeah, well she's getting pretty bloody good at lying these

days, isn't she?' Phil snapped. 'If this is why she's been copying her, so she could pretend to *be* her, I'll take her bloody head off!' Snatching the keys out of his wife's hand now, he marched towards the house.

'Don't do anything stupid,' Judith called after him. Then, casting a nervous glance at Sam, she said, 'Sorry, I've got to go. He's . . .' Trailing off, she shrugged, then turned and ran after her husband.

Staying put at the gate for a few moments as lights went on inside the house, Sam heard the sound of heavy footsteps running up the stairs, then shouting when Phil Baxter discovered that his youngest daughter wasn't in her bed. Armed with all the proof he needed to know that Hannah's caller had obviously been telling the truth, Sam jerked his head at Fred and quick-marched back to the car.

Tania Baxter was having a whale of a time. She'd been to Bone a few times with her friends and had thought it was okay, but now that she'd discovered what it was like on *Larry*'s side of the fence, she could see why he loved it. There was no waiting in line for the stars, being looked up and down by the doormen like you were a lesser life form; or waiting an hour to get anywhere near the bar only to find yourself ignored by the bar staff. It was all first-class treatment and free champagne for the stars, and she was loving every single second of it.

And she especially loved being here with Larry, who had caused quite a stir when they'd arrived, giving Tania her first sweet taste of the life she'd always known she was born to live as people in the queue started whistling and yelling his name. Smiling her best film-star smile, she'd welded herself to his side, determined to let it be known that she was his woman now. She'd been a bit miffed that nobody had called *her* name, considering they must have all seen her on *Star*

*Struck*. And it pissed her off *big* time when three tarts at the head of the line flashed their tits at him. But – fortunately for them – Larry didn't notice, or they'd have still been picking their teeth up off the floor.

Clinging tightly to Larry's arm when the doormen waved them inside, Tania had noticed the envious looks she got from a group of clubbers who she'd previously have bent over backwards to be noticed by: the cool crowd, who swanned about Bone like they owned it, acting like celebrities just because they dressed more freakily and necked more drugs than anyone else. But *thinking* you're a celebrity and actually *being* one were very different kettles of fish, as Tania now knew, and she'd felt more than a little smug as she and Larry left them behind in the cold night air.

Still gloating when they reached the VIP lounge, her jaw had dropped to her knees when she'd seen all the famous people who were already there. She'd thought she was in heaven mixing with the celebrities who'd taken part in the telethon, but they'd been small fry compared to this collection of footballers, soap stars, top chart singers and musicians. And they all seemed to know Larry, which just blew her mind, especially when they all said hello to *her*, too, as if she was already one of them.

But if *that* had thrilled her, it was nothing to the knicker-wetting experience of finding herself face to face with the three guys from Unreal when they reached the bar.

Unreal were *the* hottest rap group on the planet, and Tania and her friends had been watching them on MTV just the night before, fantasising about which one they were going to marry. Her choice – after Larry, who was quite simply the god of all gods – was the baby-faced lead singer, Alonzo, who had the sexiest jet-black eyes and the most dazzling smile she'd ever seen. And now here he was, in the flesh, dripping gold and diamonds, and wearing the most expensive sports gear she'd ever seen – and hugging Larry like they were brothers, telling him that he'd caught the show in his hotel room earlier and thought he'd been amazing.

Tania almost fainted when the rappers invited her and Larry to join their party. But she managed to dredge up a modicum of cool from somewhere, determined not to be mistaken for one of the numerous one-night stands that Larry was forever being photographed coming out of clubs with. But calm as she appeared on the outside, she was screaming with excitement on the inside – wishing that her friends could see her now, because they were never going to believe this when she told them.

With the champagne flowing as the night wore on, the VIP lounge was jumping by twelve, the stars letting their hair down and partying hard, safe in the knowledge that they were hidden from the public gaze. And in a corner booth off to the rear of the room, the Unreal crew were having a party all of their own; their table was brimming with bottles of alcohol as glistening, finely chopped lines of coke were passed around on one of their CD covers.

Larry was so pissed, he didn't even notice the coke. But he wouldn't have been interested even if he *had* seen it, because nothing could have elevated his mood any higher right now. Still buzzing about the positive response he'd received when he arrived, he'd mentally rewritten his shambolic perform- ance on the telethon, convincing himself that it couldn't have been anywhere near as bad as everyone back at the studio had tried to make out. Jeremy and his fellow dinosaur Frank were no doubt shitting bricks back there, panicking about the public's reaction to tonight's show and bemoaning the demise of the old-school stars who knew their place and did as they were told. But they were so far out of touch with the reality of today's brand of celebrity that it wasn't even funny, and

Larry wished he'd invited them along to the club so they could see what was *really* what.

Still, he'd have time enough to bring them up to date tomorrow. For now, he was just happy to be seen with Unreal – the *real* big boys of the business. As well known as everyone else in the VIP lounge was in little old England, they were nothing compared to these American superstars, and Larry was amused by how many footballers and sexy starlets kept drifting by their table trying to get themselves noticed. But Unreal weren't interested in socialising with small-timers like them. They were only interested in the big hitters, like Larry.

Closing his eyes now as his umpteenth glass of champagne carried him into oblivion, Larry reminded himself to swap numbers with the guys so he could keep in touch with them after they went home. He might even fly over for a visit in a month or so; set up meets with some producers while he was there and see what they had to offer. The US market was notoriously difficult to penetrate, but he didn't think he'd have any trouble getting his foot through the door now that he had such high-powered friends to help him.

Shocked out of his stupor when bright lights suddenly started flashing in front of his face, Larry's eyes snapped open. Struggling for breath as the girl – whose name he couldn't even remember – jumped on him and clamped her mouth over his, he shoved her off and gazed confusedly around as Unreal's minders leapt to their feet, sending glasses and bottles flying off the table. Screaming girls ran for cover as the bodyguards made a dive for the two men who had sneaked up to get shots of the party.

Too bleary-eyed to recognise them before the minders manhandled them out through the fire-exit door, Larry assumed they must have been a couple of Z-list chancers trying to steal money shots of Unreal at play. Grinning at their audacity, he shook his head and slumped back in his seat. It was one thing having paps waiting outside to take pictures of you with your latest shag, but if this was what you had to put up with when you were in the big league, he supposed he'd best get used to it.

And maybe he'd best start thinking about hiring himself a minder, too, because he was bound to get this kind of shit all the time when he hit the States. He couldn't wait!

# 3

Frank Woods woke in a foul mood. Larry had already skipped out of the station before Jeremy had had a chance to tell him that Frank wanted to see him last night and, furious that he'd been denied the chance to give him a roasting, Frank had tried ringing him numerous times to tell him to get his arse straight back, only to find that the little shit had turned his phone off.

Reaching for the bedside phone now, Frank tried both Larry's mobile and landline numbers, only to find one still switched off and the other engaged. Slamming the receiver down, he cursed under his breath. He'd been nothing but good to that boy, and the contempt he'd received in return was a real kick in the teeth. Larry had been unknown when Frank had handed him his first big break, and when his star rose and his drinking started to grow in line with his ego, Frank had given him chance after chance to sort himself out. He'd fobbed the crew off when they complained about his on-set behaviour, and had given Larry fatherly talking-tos when pictures of him and his whores falling out of night-clubs began to appear almost every day in the papers. And Larry always promised to curb his ways. But words were obviously cheap because he just carried on as usual, no matter what Frank said. And that angered Frank more than anything, because it gave everybody the impression that he was a pushover – which he most certainly was *not*.

Still, everyone had their limits, and Frank had just about

reached his. If he could find an excuse to terminate Larry's contract without giving Alan Corbin the satisfaction of thinking it had been done on *his* say-so, he'd dump him like a hot brick and bring in Matty Kline without pausing for breath.

The idea had been growing on him throughout the night, and he was convinced that it was the perfect solution to the problem of saving *Star Struck*. But his pride was still smarting too much to put his plans into action just yet. Not only because he couldn't bear giving Corbin cause to gloat, but also because he didn't want Jeremy Hislop thinking that it had been *his* suggestion which had swayed him, either. Everybody was just too damn full of their own self-importance these days, and it galled Frank that they all thought they had the right to butt into his business.

Still stewing, having failed to reach Larry after several attempts, Frank got out of bed and stomped down to the kitchen. Snapping at his wife when she handed him a cup of coffee and accidentally spilled a tiny drop onto the sleeve of his dressing gown, he immediately turned his frustrations onto the dog, yelling at the poor thing for getting under his feet when all it was doing was giving him its usual good-morning greeting.

Muttering under his breath when the dog slinked away to mope in its basket, he turned his back on his wife's disapproving face and snatched up the kitchen phone. One last chance, and if Larry still didn't answer, pride be buggered, he was history.

The newspapers dropped onto the hall mat with a dull thud. Lips pursed, Brenda Woods stalked past her husband and went to get them. She didn't know what his problem was, but he'd better snap out of his mood before he even *thought* about leaving for his precious office today, or he'd find himself with a mutiny on his hands when he came home tonight.

Bringing the papers back into the kitchen now, she dropped them on the table, sending a cloud of soot from Frank's ashtray up into the air.

'Bloody hell, woman!' he complained, snatching his cup up before the ash landed in it. 'Watch what you're doing, can't you?'

'Don't you *woman* me,' Brenda retorted indignantly. 'I don't know what's eating you today, Frank, but whatever it is, it's none of my doing, and I won't have you taking it out on me. It was bad enough putting up with you tossing and turning all night. I hardly slept a wink.'

Muttering 'Sorry,' because she was right that this wasn't about her, Frank clicked the still-unanswered phone off and swept the ash off the table with the back of his hand. But just as he was about to blow the residue off the newspapers, the main headline of the *Sunday Herald* caught his eye and, snatching the paper up, he spread it out to read the article.

'*LOGAN'S LOLITA!*' the headline screamed, followed by the sub-heading: '*Read the exclusive account of what happened when* Herald *reporter Sam Brady caught game-show host Larry Logan seducing the* 16-YEAR-OLD *girl who tricked her way to the £10,000 jackpot on Star Struck last night!*'

Turning from her washing-up when Frank uttered a strangled gasp of horror, Brenda asked him what was wrong. Tutting loudly when he brusquely shushed her, she turned back to the sink and clattered the plates into the rack with venom.

Ignoring her, Frank read on.

*Larry Logan surely lost any shred of credibility when he appeared drunk during live filming of the Kiddie Kare Telethon last night, prompting the organisers to ask Matty Kline to stand in for him. The official explanation – released post-broadcast, in what some may consider an attempt by*

*Oasis TV to cover for their golden boy's indiscretions – cited an adverse reaction to flu medication as the cause of Logan's bizarre behaviour. But, whatever the truth, Logan's shameful display of contempt for one of the country's most sacred causes won't easily be forgotten – or forgiven – by a nation already weary of his antics as, week by week, he drags Star Struck into territory more befitting a late-night slot on a dodgy cable channel than prime-time family viewing.*

*And now we can exclusively reveal an even* darker *side to the Logan saga, having caught him in a steamy clinch with the winner of last night's jackpot – 16-year-old TANIA BAXTER!*

*Masquerading as her 19-year-old sister CINDY – who is currently out of the country and unavailable for comment – TANIA duped the producers of both Star Struck and the telethon into allowing her to take part, despite being two years too young. Then she tricked her way into trendy night-club Bone, in Manchester's fashionable Northern Quarter, where, surrounded by alcohol, drugs, and some seriously dodgy company, we caught her sharing an illicit embrace with 27-year-old Logan.*

*Questions must surely be asked as to how a 16-year-old got through Oasis TV's supposedly rigorous security pro-cedures to waltz off with a cheque for £10,000. But love-rat Logan must come under scrutiny too, because this isn't the first time a female contestant has caught his eye only to go on to win the jackpot. And while his Romeo reputation has been well documented since his sudden – and, some might say, undeserved – rise to fame on Star Struck, this latest foray into the murky underworld of barely legal bed-mates is a new, more sinister twist, and must surely serve as a warning to every parent whose little girl has a picture of the handsome heartbreaker on her bedroom wall.*

*There's no way of knowing if Logan and his Lolita left*

*Bone together at the end of their passion-fuelled night, because
reporter Sam Brady and photographer Fred Greene were
chased from the club in fear of their lives by the vicious bodyguards of American rap group Unreal who are currently
touring the UK to promote their latest – and aptly titled –
album, Baby Ho! But we think the photographs paint a clear
enough picture for people to draw their own conclusions about
the outcome of the sleazy clinch. And, while Tania Baxter
may be just about legal, Logan will feel the cold winds of
suspicion blowing his way from here on in – and we can
rest in the knowledge that we've done our duty in raising
the public's awareness of the evil that may well be lurking
behind that seductive smile.*

Looking now at the two photographs attached to the story,
Frank gritted his teeth. Eyes glazed, body slumped like a sack
of wet spuds in the first shot, Larry seemed to be sucking
the face off the girl, who was more or less straddling him,
with only the edge of the table and the bottles cluttered on
its surface covering what was most probably going on below
decks. The second shot clearly showed just how drunk Larry
had been as, shocked out of the clinch by the flashing lights
and fracas that had reportedly followed, he gazed out with
unfocused eyes, not seeming to know what was happening
or where he was.

The girl, however, not only looked absolutely aware of her
surroundings, she'd even managed to locate the camera's lens
and was staring straight into it like a seasoned pro, with a
mile-wide smile on her lying face – no doubt hoping to launch
her future modelling career off the back of this amazing photo
opportunity.

And the gold-digging, publicity-seeking little slut would
probably succeed, too, Frank thought, furiously skimming
through the rest of the papers now. The *Herald* was the only

one carrying *this* story, but the rest were full of Larry pissed out of his head live on air, which was just as bad.

Shoving the papers angrily away when he'd seen enough, Frank lit another cigarette and snatched up the phone again. This was the worst publicity he'd faced in twenty-three years as a producer, and – pride be damned – he'd rather eat Corbin's shit-caked underpants live on the six o'clock news than have the public think he was standing by Logan after this.

He would demand an internal investigation, of course – to find out how the girl had managed to slip through the net in the first place, and to nail the stupid bastard who'd let it happen. And he would stop the cheque immediately, before the girl managed to cash it. And – for face-saving's sake – he would then publicly donate the prize money to the Kiddie Kare fund.

And then he would murder Logan with his bare hands!

'I take it you've seen the papers?' Jeremy said when he answered – further incensing Frank, who sensed more than a hint of *I told you so* in his flat tone. 'Doesn't look too good, does it?'

'Get everyone in for a meeting,' Frank barked, letting Jeremy know from the off that he was still in control and wouldn't tolerate any bullshit. 'And get hold of Matty Kline while you're at it.'

'Do you want Larry there, too?'

'Only if you want to see me go down for murder! Just ring the little fuckwit's agent, and tell her to tell him that if I see him anywhere near the studio again in this lifetime, I will personally rip his fucking face off. Got that?'

'Loud and clear,' Jeremy replied, sensibly keeping his opinions to himself: that this could have all been avoided if Frank had only taken his advice and kept Larry Logan well away from a live broadcast.

★

Over in the city centre just then, the sun was casting an orange glow through the uncurtained floor-to-ceiling, wall-to-wall window of Larry's penthouse apartment. Hanover Towers boasted some of the finest views, and some of the richest, most famous inhabitants of Manchester – the latter being the major reason why Larry had bought the apartment. No point being a star if you couldn't show it off to the world, and all that.

Waking up in his bed now, Tania stretched her arms out above her head and gazed around the unfamiliar room, sleepily studying the designer furniture and the funky artwork decorating the walls. She hadn't noticed too much after falling through the door in the early hours, but now that she could see everything clearly she was far more impressed than she'd expected to be, because the whole place screamed of money and style.

Switching her gaze to the window after a while, she sighed longingly as her eyes danced over the few building tops that were visible from up here, imagining what it would be like to live here permanently.

Turning to look at Larry when he made a soft noise beside her, Tania inhaled softly and bit her lip. He always looked amazing on screen but here, in the naked flesh, with his usually perfect hair tousled, his eyes closed so that his long dark lashes rested on his cheeks, and his lips parted to reveal a sliver of white teeth, he was so breathtakingly beautiful that she could have cried.

Just wait till her friends heard about this! They'd think she was lying, because they all knew how much she idolised Larry. But they'd soon know she was telling the truth when they saw the pictures those men had taken at the club last night. It was just a shame that Unreal's minders had chased them off before she'd had a chance to get her pose exactly right, but at least they should have got a good one of her and Larry kissing, which was fantastic. And any picture was better than no picture, so there would be plenty of opportunities to get into modelling now that the world was going to see how gorgeous she was. And being Larry Logan's girlfriend wouldn't hurt her future prospects, either. She could just see the headlines now:

*Larry Logan and mystery lady only had eyes for each other at Bone last night . . .*

*Larry and lover at premiere of Ritchie's latest movie . . .*

*Larry and supermodel girlfriend Tania Baxter spotted looking at diamond rings . . .*

*Wedding bells for Larry and—*

'What the *fuck*!' Larry squawked, opening his eyes to find Tania peering glassily down at him. 'Who the hell are *you*?' Sitting bolt upright, he dragged the quilt up over his stomach to cover his need-a-piss hard-on.

'Morning,' Tania purred. 'Sleep well?'

Jerking away from her, Larry glared at her with suspicion, convinced that she was a whacked-out stalker who'd broken in while he was sleeping. At least she was naked, so she obviously didn't have a concealed weapon on her. But, knowing his luck, she'd probably have something heavy close at hand – to beat his face to a pulp when he rejected her.

Tempering his tone now, in case he alarmed her and made her do something stupid, he said, 'How did you get in here?'

Giving him a quizzical smile, wondering how he could have forgotten, Tania reminded him that he had invited her back here last night.

Muttering 'Did I?' Larry ran a hand over his aching eyes, damned if he could remember.

'Do you want me to get you anything?' Tania asked, thinking he looked a bit pale and wanting to make him feel better.

'Coffee,' he croaked, replacing the phone which had somehow been knocked off its stand and reaching for a cigarette. Lighting up, he lay back against the pillows and peered at her through the swirling smoke screen as she climbed out of bed. She did look vaguely familiar, he supposed. But then, she had tits and a pussy, so she could be literally anybody.

Stretching languidly, hoping that the sight of her naked body in the sunlight would inflame Larry's desires and cement her place in his heart, Tania tipped her head to one side and smiled coyly down at him.

Eyebrows puckering with irritation, Larry said, '*What?*'

Smiling knowingly, she said, 'You've got a hangover, haven't you? I'm not surprised, with all the champagne you drank last night. You were wrecked enough before we left the studio, so God knows how you managed to—'

'The studio?' Larry repeated. Then, with a flash of recall, he clicked his fingers. 'You were one of the contestants.'

'The *winner*,' she corrected him, grinning proudly as she reached down for her handbag and pulled out the cheque.

Nauseated by the rocking motion of the mattress when she jumped back onto the bed to show the slip of paper to him, Larry muttered, 'Congratulations.'

'I thought they were going to cancel everything when you went off,' she told him. 'But Matty Kline stood in for you, so it was all right.'

'Matty Kline?' Larry's eyebrows knitted together. 'What was *he* doing on my show?'

'That snotty director with the bushy hair brought him on after he sent you off,' Tania explained, adding loyally, 'But he's nowhere near as good as you. No one was laughing at his jokes – not like they were at yours. Especially when you gave me the answer to the Britney Spears question. That was *classic*. Everyone was cracking up over that.'

'Oh yeah?' *No recollection.*

'Then you had to ask me another one, and it was so funny.'

'Uh-huh?' *Still nothing.*

'Then you snapped my strap and my boob fell out, and all the guys in the audience started cheering and whistling.' Giggling now, Tania's eyes were lit with satisfaction as she added, 'The women went mad, though. You should have *seen* them, slapping their boyfriends for looking, and everything!'

'Well, you *have* got nice tits,' Larry murmured, feeling the hard-on that had died creeping back to life as he eyed her jutting nipples.

Spotting the movement beneath the quilt, she gave him a catlike smile. 'Still want that coffee, or would you rather—'

The phone started to ring before she had a chance to finish the sentence. Glancing at the clock, Larry groaned when he saw that it was only nine-thirty. No one with any sense would disturb him at this time of the morning, so it had to be Jeremy Hislop calling to give him a bollocking. He had half a mind to ignore the phone but decided he might as well get it out of the way so that he could get on with shagging *thingy* here in peace.

'Do us a favour and get us that coffee while I take this,' he said, waving her towards the door. 'You'll find everything you need in the kitchen.'

Blowing him a kiss, ecstatic that everything seemed to be going so well between them now that he'd remembered who she was, Tania slid off the bed and sashayed out of the room.

Reaching for the phone when she'd gone, Larry started speaking immediately, intent on depriving Jeremy of the pleasure of lecturing him.

'Yes, Jez, I know I was a twat, but I'm really, really sorry, and I promise it'll never happen again.'

'You're right there,' his agent, Georgina Wise, replied coolly. 'You're sacked.'

Frowning because he hadn't expected to hear her voice – or to hear what she'd just said – Larry said, 'What are you talking about?'

'You're sacked,' she repeated. 'I've just had Jeremy on the phone, and he says Frank's absolutely had it with you.'

Sure that it was a wind-up – Frank's way of punishing him for taking off before the after-show party – Larry said, 'All right, Georgie, you can quit now. We both know I'm worth way too much for Frank to want rid of me.'

'Not any more,' Georgie countered, her serious tone making Larry wonder if this was actually for real. 'As of now, your contract is terminated.'

'He can't do that,' Larry blustered. 'And if he tries, I'll have him in court so fast for unfair dismissal his head will explode.'

'He can, and he has,' Georgie replied. 'And if I were you, I'd read the papers before you make any threats about suing anybody, because you've given him more than enough rope to hang you with this time. And you can't say you weren't warned. I mean, did you *really* think you'd get away with being drunk on air?'

'Christ, trust Frank to overreact,' Larry snorted. 'All this fuss over one little drink.'

'You were pissed as a fart,' Georgie reminded him. 'And I don't even want to *know* what you thought you were playing at when you exposed that girl's breast.'

'So I like tits,' Larry drawled unconcernedly. 'Shoot me, why don't you.'

'This is not a joke,' Georgie told him irritably. 'And Frank's adamant that he's not going to change his mind this time. He says it's bad enough having to justify putting you on the telethon in the first place, but what you did with that girl—'

'Exposing one stupid tit?' Larry interrupted. 'Do me a favour! It'd be the highlight of the show, if the public had even seen it – which we both know they didn't, because Jeremy would have edited it out as soon as it happened. What's the big deal?'

'The big deal,' Georgie echoed, 'is what you did *after* you left the studio.'

'Stop right there,' Larry warned her sharply. 'What I do in my free time is nobody's business. Not yours, not Frank's – *nobody's.*'

'It is when you're doing it with a child,' Georgie snapped, the disapproval ripe in her voice.

'What the fuck's *that* supposed to mean?' Larry demanded.

After telling him to read the *Sunday Herald* and see for himself, Georgie said, 'But you'd better prepare yourself for a shock, because it's pretty bloody damning.'

Rubbing at his temples as the headache deepened into a dull, sickening throb, Larry said, 'Okay, cut the cryptic shit and just tell me what it says, 'cos I haven't got a clue what you're going on about.'

'The girl who won the show,' Georgie said quietly. 'You took her to a club after you left the studio, right?'

'Yeah. So what?'

'So, she's not as old as she made out. In fact, she's only just turned sixteen.'

'Fuck off!' Larry croaked, his stomach flipping as his world slipped out from under him.

'It's true,' Georgie assured him. 'Apparently, the reporter checked it out with the family before he came after you, and Jeremy told me that Frank had it confirmed this morning. Her name's Tania, and she used her older sister's ID to get past the security checks. The real Cindy's in Majorca and knows nothing about any of this. And our girl would have got away with it if her friend hadn't spotted her and called the *Herald.*'

'Bitch!' Larry spat, shoving the quilt aside and dropping his feet to the floor. '*Sixteen?* Christ! Everyone's gonna think I'm a fucking paedophile!'

Guessing from his reaction that he and the girl *had* finished the night together, Georgie sighed. She was tempted to point out that Larry wouldn't have got himself into such a compromising position if he wasn't such an out-of-control piss-head, but she held her tongue. The girl had obviously fooled the whole production team, so Larry could hardly be blamed for having been taken in by her too.

But the tabloid-reading public wouldn't see it like that, and Jeremy had told her that the studio switchboard had already been flooded with complaints from disgusted viewers demanding that Larry be sacked. So even if Frank had *wanted* to excuse him, he wouldn't have been able to without risking losing viewers – and there wasn't a producer in the land who was stupid enough to support the star at the expense of the show.

'What are they saying about me?' Larry asked now, a vague image of flashing lights and scuffling men flitting through his clouded mind. 'Are there any pictures?'

'The big Sundays are full of you reeling about on the telethon set,' Georgie told him. 'But the *Herald*'s the one you need to see. And they've got two pictures: one of you and the girl kissing, the other of you a bit the worse for wear, while the girl's grinning like she's hit the jackpot all over again.'

Muttering, 'Shit!' Larry stubbed out the burned-down cigarette and immediately lit another.

'Shit, indeed,' Georgie agreed disapprovingly. 'Oh, and they're all saying it's nonsense that you were high on flu medicine, by the way.'

'Flu medicine?' Larry repeated numbly. 'Did someone slip me something?'

'No, that was just Frank's explanation for the state you were in. But nobody believes it – not now they've seen the pictures of you doing drugs.'

'*What?*' Larry squawked. 'No way! I haven't been near drugs in months. *You* know that.'

'The pictures say different. There's coke all over the place.'

'Well, if there was, I didn't know about it.'

'Maybe you've forgotten?' Georgie suggested quietly. 'You know what you're like when you're drunk. You can't even remember where you've been or how you got home some nights.'

'I always knew if I'd done coke,' Larry argued. 'And I know I definitely didn't do any last night. This is a *booze* hangover – period!'

Jumping up now, he paced the length of the bedroom, his mind ticking over painfully as he struggled to remember what had happened the night before.

'It's a set-up!' he declared after a minute. 'You know what those paps are like – they'll do anything to discredit you when you're at the top, and they're always gunning for me. I'll bet the bastard who did this got himself a nice pay-off. But let's see what he's got to say when I sue him for libel! And I'll have a blood test to prove I didn't touch any drugs. They'll have to retract the story then, and Frank will have to give me my job back.'

Instinctively believing him – about the drugs, at least – Georgie said, 'Okay, Larry, I'll arrange a blood test if that's what you want. But it won't change anything as far as Frank's concerned. He is absolutely not going to change his mind this time.'

'He will if he knows what's good for him,' Larry shot back, looking around for his jeans. '*Star Struck* is *my* show, and when I prove I'm innocent he'd *better* reinstate me or I'll sue *him* as well. There's nothing in my contract that says I'm not allowed to have a couple of drinks when I'm working, so he's got no justification for sacking me.'

'No one who saw the telethon will ever believe you'd only had a couple, so you're onto a loser with that argument,' Georgie told him firmly. 'Even without the subsequent drug stuff, and the girl's age, Frank is well within his rights to fire you, because you made yourself incapable of performing the work you're contracted to do.'

'It was a one-off,' Larry said, pulling the jeans on without bothering with underwear. 'I'm not letting this go without a fight. Where's Frank now? At the studio?'

'I believe so. But he really doesn't want to see you.'

'Only because he's believing the shit in the papers. Soon as he realises it's a set-up he'll—'

'He's already signed up your replacement,' Georgie cut in, sounding genuinely sorry for him now. Larry was a pain, but she knew how much he'd loved the show. Unfortunately, just not enough to make him pull himself together before it got to this.

Slumping down onto the edge of the bed, Larry said, 'You've got to be joking. He can't do this to me.'

Assuring him that it was true, Georgie closed her eyes when Larry demanded to know who had been signed in his place, and murmured, 'Matty Kline. Sorry, Larry, but it's a done deal.'

'I'll kill him!' Larry snarled, the blood boiling in his veins. 'I will fucking *kill* him!'

Sensing that he'd taken as much of a kicking as he could stand right now, Georgie said, 'Look, go and clear your head with a cold shower before you do anything stupid. I'll get onto the doctor to arrange that blood test. And when you're feeling better, we'll sit down and talk about finding a new show for you. But, whatever happens, you've got to knock the drinking on the head, Larry. You might think you've got it under control, but the fact that you can't even remember what you were doing last night should tell you that you haven't.'

It was good advice, but Larry didn't hear a word of it; he was too busy staring at Tania, who had just come back into the room. Disgusted that she was parading around naked with a stupid smile on her face while his whole world collapsed around him, he felt the rage welling up inside him.

'Larry . . . ?' Georgie's distant voice drifted out of the phone. 'Are you still there?'

Switching the phone off without responding, Larry followed Tania with his stare as she slinked over to the other side of the bed and placed the coffee cups on the table.

Pretending not to notice his intense gaze, Tania strolled to the dressing-table and leaned provocatively forward to smooth her hair in the mirror. If there was one thing she knew about boys, it was that they were natural voyeurs who got turned on by watching girls who didn't know they were being watched. Laughable, really, when you considered that girls *always* knew when they were being watched.

'Get dressed,' Larry spat, sickened by the sight of her preening herself.

Turning, Tania gave him a questioning smile. 'Sorry?'

Barking 'You heard!' Larry got up and marched out of the room.

Staring after him in disbelief, Tania winced when the front door slammed a couple of seconds later. Chilled by his angry tone, she rubbed at her arms, wondering what had happened to make him bite her head off like that. She'd heard him raise his voice a couple of times when he was on the phone, and wondered if it had been a woman – one of his girlfriends, maybe – who'd found out about him taking Tania to the club and had rung to have a go at him about it. If so, it hadn't sounded like he'd been begging for forgiveness, which had to be a sign that he wanted Tania more than he wanted the girlfriend. And it would certainly explain his sudden mood swing, because he was too nice to dump a girl without feeling even a little bit guilty about it, so she wouldn't hold it against him for taking it out on her.

Just as she'd managed to convince herself that everything would be okay, Larry marched back into the room, with the *Sunday Herald* he'd just borrowed off a neighbour clutched tightly in his hand.

Flapping the paper in Tania's face, he said, 'Just tell me one thing . . . were you in on this from the start, or did they persuade you to do it after we got to the club?'

'In on what?'

'Don't play the innocent with me! This what you wanted, was it? To make me lose my fucking job?'

'I haven't seen the papers,' she reminded him, stepping nervously back because he looked like he was going to hit her. 'I've only just got up. What's wrong?'

'Like you don't know!' Marching away from her to put distance between them – because he *did* feel like throttling her – Larry threw the paper down onto the bed and snatched up yet another cigarette with shaking hands.

Hardly daring to move in case he shouted at her again, Tania tilted her head and peered at the paper. She couldn't see the headline, but there were two pictures: one of her and Larry kissing; the other of her smiling and Larry looking confused, while the guys from Unreal looked shocked and angry as their minders scrambled to their feet. She couldn't see details, but she genuinely didn't see anything wrong with what she *could* see – nothing to make Larry so angry, anyway. In fact, she thought she looked particularly pretty.

'I don't know why you're looking so proud of yourself,' Larry spat, noticing the way she was studying the photos. 'You've destroyed my life with that little stunt of yours.'

Looking up at him, Tania frowned. He was being absolutely horrible about this, and she really didn't understand why. He'd been photographed with thousands of women, so why get so mad about two little shots with her? He certainly couldn't be ashamed of her, because she was *way* better looking than half the women he'd been seen with. And none of *them* had been celebrities, either, so it couldn't be that Tania didn't match up in *that* department.

'Was that the point of coming onto my show?' Larry demanded now, his tone cold and accusing. 'To get me drunk and manipulate me into taking you out, so that your friend could take pictures of us?'

Stunned that he was trying to blame her for whatever was eating him, Tania gasped and said, '*I* didn't get you drunk. You were already plastered. That's why they sent you off.'

'Convenient,' Larry muttered, knowing full well that she was right – about that bit, anyway. But she'd definitely had a hand in setting him up, he was sure about that. Scowling at her now, he said, 'For Christ's sake, get dressed. I feel sick enough without having to look at *that*!'

Humiliated by the contempt in his eyes, Tania scooped her dress up off the floor and pulled it over her head. It was badly creased, but that hardly seemed to matter in light of how disastrous this date was turning out to be. Slipping her panties on when Larry turned his back on her and marched across to the window, a surge of anger reared up through the emotional pain. All she'd ever wanted was to be with him, but he was being so nasty that she wasn't sure she wanted to see him again – not until he apologised, anyway. He might get away with treating his other women like this, but not her. There was no way *she* was going to roll over and let him walk all over her just because he was a star.

Hands on hips when she was dressed, Tania faced Larry's rigid back and said, 'Look, I'm sorry you're so upset about having your picture taken with me, but *I* don't see the problem. And I certainly don't deserve to be shouted at for it.'

'I thought you'd have been used to being shouted at,' Larry retorted coldly. 'You must get it all the time off your parents and teachers.' Turning to face her now, he folded his arms. 'Isn't that what adults do to naughty children?'

Cheeks flaming, Tania raised her chin. 'I don't know what you're talking about.'

'Come off it!' Larry snorted. 'Did you really think you'd get away with it? I know *every*thing, you stupid little girl. Everybody knows.'

'Everybody knows what?' she demanded, trying to front it out, sure that whatever he *thought* he knew, she could still talk her way out of it.

'That you're *sixteen*,' Larry told her slowly, making sure that she heard it loud and clear. 'That your real name is Tania, and that you lied your way onto my show by pretending to be your sister Cindy – who is in Majorca as we speak. That enough for you?'

The tears came now; a slow trickle which quickly became a torrent. 'I'm sorry,' Tania wailed, looking at him with pleading eyes. 'But does it really matter? I'm old enough to sleep with anyone I want to, so nobody can stop us if we want to be together.'

'Are you *mad*?' Larry gasped incredulously. 'Do you really think I'd want anything to do with you after this?' Laughing without humour now, he shook his head. 'Christ, I didn't even know who you were when I woke up – that's how forget-table you are.'

'Larry, please . . .' Tania begged, the burst of righteous indignation gone now as she took a step towards him. 'I know I could make you happy. Just let me show you.'

'Stay right there,' he ordered, amazed that she seemed to think she could make everything all right by getting him back into bed. The very thought that they had already done *any*thing sickened him to his stomach, and he was just thankful that he couldn't remember a single thing about it. But whatever *had* happened, it most definitely would not be happening again.

'Please don't be like this,' Tania persisted tearfully. 'I didn't do anything wrong. I know I lied about my age to get on the show, but I *had* to – to meet *you*. The first time I ever saw you I knew we were meant to be together. And you like me too, so I wasn't wrong, was I?'

Shaking his head with disbelief, Larry said, 'Have you any idea how childish you sound? You're like a twelve-year-old with a crush on a pop star.'

'I'm old enough for sex,' Tania reminded him desperately. 'And I'm not at school any more, so my mum and dad can't tell me what to do. We could even get married if we wanted to, and nobody could stop us.'

'Behave yourself!' Larry snapped, feeling more nauseous by the second. This had to stop – now. It was sick, and he could understand why the public would have a problem with it. If *he* heard about a man of his age sleeping with a sixteen-year-old, he'd call him all the perverts under the sun – even if the girl looked older, like this one did.

Sidestepping her now, he snatched up her handbag and thrust it into her hands, telling her to go home and forget that any of this had ever happened.

'I can't forget it,' Tania wailed, clutching at his hand. 'You're everything to me.'

Wrenching himself free, Larry said, 'Christ, you've already lost me my *job*. Don't you get it? Your silly little crush and stupid lies have *destroyed* me. I don't want you, and I never will. I just want you to disappear like you never existed!'

'Stop it!' Tania cried, throwing her hands over her ears. 'Stop it, stop it, stop it!'

Afraid that the neighbours would hear her and think that he was beating her up, Larry rushed towards her and gave her a gentle shake, hissing, 'Pack it in, for God's sake.'

Sobbing loudly, Tania fell against him and buried her face in his shirt. Everything had been going so well before he'd found out about her age, but she genuinely didn't think she'd done anything wrong. And she'd have told him the truth eventually – when she was sure that he was as deeply in love with her as she was with him.

Pushing her away gently when the sobs began to subside at last, Larry looked down into her swollen eyes and sighed. She was just a child, and he couldn't put her out of his apartment in this state. But he couldn't let her stay, either. Now he'd seen the pictures and knew that Georgie had been telling the truth about the drugs, he was terrified that the police would come crashing in at any minute, and the last thing he needed was for her to still be here. Knowing his luck, he'd get done for drugging and date-raping her, or something ridiculous like that.

Tempering his tone now, because Tania seemed to be calming down and he didn't want to set her off again, he said, 'Look, I'm sorry for shouting, but you've got to go before anybody realises you're here and makes something out of it. I'm going to call you a cab, but we'll have to sneak you out through the underground car park in case any photographers are hanging about. And I need you to promise that you'll keep your head down. Okay?'

Nodding, glad that he was being nice again, Tania said, 'I didn't mean to get you in trouble.'

'Yeah, well, let's try and avoid any more scandal, eh?' Larry took another step back. 'And can we agree to say that nothing happened if anyone does catch up with you?'

'Nothing did happen,' she admitted, with more than a tinge of regret in her voice.

Peering down at her with a confused frown, Larry said, 'Sorry?'

'Nothing happened,' she repeated, taking a tissue out of her bag and wiping her nose. 'You were too drunk to do anything by the time we left the club, so I got your keys out of your pocket. It was just lucky the taxi driver knew you, so he already had your address, 'cos I don't think my dad would have been too happy if I'd had to take you back to mine.'

Heart racing as the clouds of gloom began to disperse, Larry said, 'Is this for real? You're not lying again?'

'It's the truth,' Tania insisted, adding, 'I would have if you'd wanted to, but you were practically unconscious. So, I . . .' Trailing off, she dipped her gaze as flames of embarrassment seared her cheeks. 'I got you undressed. But I didn't look at – *you* know. I just wanted you to be comfortable.'

Exhaling loudly as the last of the tension floated away, Larry gazed at the ceiling and murmured, 'Thank you, God!' Then, moving towards Tania – but not *too* close – he inclined his head and kissed her on the cheek. 'And thank *you* for telling me the truth. Now, let's get you out of here before anyone realises you stayed the night.'

'What should I tell my mum and dad?' Tania asked, the fear in her eyes displaying exactly how young she really was. Her parents would have seen the papers by now, and they'd never believe that nothing had happened if they found out she'd slept in his bed with him. It wouldn't have been such a problem if he'd been willing to stand by her, but she wasn't brave enough to face that on her own. Her dad had a vicious temper when he was angry, and she was bound to get battered – and not just for this, but for stealing his precious Cindy's ID, too.

Larry hadn't even considered how Tania's parents might react to the news that their daughter had spent the night with him. But now that she had mentioned them, it struck him that they would probably be even more scandalised than the rest of the country about him supposedly corrupting their little girl. Worried that they might decide to take the matter further, he asked if she thought they were likely to go to the police.

Shaking her head, Tania said, 'No chance. They wouldn't want the neighbours gossiping. They'll probably just put me on total lockdown till I'm *thirty*, or something.'

'Oh well, that's good.'

'For *you*. But what about me? They'll kill me if they find out I stayed here.'

'Can't you tell them you stayed with a mate?'

Face lighting up, Tania said, 'Yeah! I can say I kipped in Joanne's garage – they'll deffo believe that.'

'They'd believe you slept in a garage?' Larry gave her a doubtful look.

Assuring him that she did it all the time, Tania said, 'It's more a sort of den than a garage, with beanbags and cushions, and that. Me and my mates always doss there when it gets too late to go home. And Joanne and her mum are at her nan's in Scotland this week, so no one would know if I'd really been there or not. I'll just say I got a taxi from Bone. And if they ask about you I'll say you told me to get lost when you found out how old I was.'

Smiling, grateful that she was willing to put herself on the line for him, Larry gave her a fatherly pat on the arm, and said, 'Good girl. That'll really help me out.'

'It's all right,' Tania said, her own happy smile fading when Larry slipped his jacket on, because she knew that she would have to leave him now. Biting her lip nervously, she said, 'Can I ask you something?'

'Shoot,' Larry said, looking around for his keys.

Dreading a negative answer, Tania looked at her feet and said, 'You do like me, don't you?'

'Course,' he replied, magnanimous in the face of relief. 'What's *not* to like?'

'I mean in *that* way,' she persisted, blushing furiously, but determined to take this one last chance to salvage something from the disaster. 'Only, I'll be eighteen in two years, so, I just thought . . . well, maybe I could see you again – when nobody can say anything bad about it?'

'Tell you what I'll do,' Larry said, herding her towards the door. 'I'll take you out to dinner on your eighteenth birthday. How about that?'

'Really?' Eyes glowing, Tania gazed up at him lovingly.

'Really. Now, where did you put my keys?'

Winking at her when she said she'd left them on the hall table, Larry reached for the phone and ordered two cabs, then led her out.

'My cheque!' Tania squealed when he picked up his keys and opened the front door. 'I left it on the bed.'

Reaching out to stop her as she made to go back for it, Larry said, 'Forget it, sweetheart. They've probably already cancelled it. You won't get a penny.'

'But why?' she gasped. 'I won it fair and square.'

'You lied about your age,' he reminded her, pushing her gently but firmly into the communal corridor and stepping out after her.

'It's not fair,' she complained, folding her arms as he locked the door and led her down the stairs to the car park. She might have lost him for the time being, but that money would have really helped to soften the blow.

'Yeah, well, life ain't fair,' Larry said simply – blissfully unaware of just how true that statement would prove to be for *him* in the coming months.

# 4

Larry's life fell apart. And not gradually, which he might have been able to work his way through, but swiftly and completely.

True to her word, Tania had gone home that morning and done a fine job of convincing her parents that she'd spent the night in her friend's garage – alone. Relieved that their daughter, who had already been branded a cheat for entering the show in her sister's name, was at least absolved of the 'slag tag', they had immediately contacted the press, resulting in numerous interviews with the tearful girl, who doggedly stuck to her story throughout.

That, coupled with the blood-test results which proved that there had been nothing but alcohol in Larry's bloodstream, should have been enough to clear his name and win him back his job – especially after the police declared that he had no case to answer.

But it didn't.

He might have been proved innocent, but Frank Woods had already made an appearance on the local evening news by then, naming Matty Kline as the new host of *Star Struck*, and citing Larry's continuous drunken behaviour as the real cause of his dismissal. And, pre-empting Larry's threat to sue him for slander, libel, defamation of character, unfair dismissal – or anything else he might choose to throw into the mix – he'd backed up his claims with out-takes from the *Star Struck* archives, showing Larry in the worst possible light: reeling drunkenly around the set, forgetting his lines, being abusive to the crew, and groping the female contestants.

His professional reputation in tatters, Larry had to accept that there was no going back as far as *Star Struck* was concerned. But he consoled himself with the belief that something bigger and better would soon come along. He was a major star, after all, and his fans would demand that *somebody* get him back on screen as soon as humanly possible, because everybody knew that there wasn't another host in Britain who could hold a candle to him when it came to looks, charm, and personality.

Wrong again.

The rumoured alcoholism and teeny-bopper sex scandal lingered around Larry's head like a toxic cloud. Producers wouldn't touch him, and his showbiz so-called friends shunned him because they were afraid of being tainted by association. But if all that was humiliating enough, it was nothing to the knock his pride took when he discovered that he'd been left off the guest list for the annual TV awards ceremony.

For five years solid, since exploding onto the screen and into the female population's hearts with *Star Struck*, Larry had been invited to the awards and had always come away with a symbol of his success: Best Newcomer; Best Host; Most Popular Male Star; Most Downloaded Pin-up . . . Accolade after accolade, seemingly forgotten in the flash of a viciously penned news story. And he couldn't even sue Sam Brady, because the bastard had worded the original story so carefully – and implication, according to Larry's solicitor, was not the same as accusation, so he had no case.

Battered and bruised, and tortured by the injustice of being barred from Oasis TV and overlooked by the awards' organisers, Larry ventured out to the clubs in search of women, intent on fucking away the pain of rejection – only to find himself blacklisted from every VIP lounge in town as word got out that he was no longer considered a celebrity. And he wasn't even afforded the respect of being informed about this via a quiet word in the managers' offices, which was the least he'd have expected given how much money he'd spent in their establishments in the past. Oh, no . . . it was left to the doormen to inform him that he was no longer welcome – in full view of the everyday punters, who jeered him from the queues as his old still-celebrity friends sailed past him as if they didn't even know him.

Upset and frustrated that, despite being cleared, nobody wanted to give him a chance, Larry slid ever deeper into despair. Unable to show his face outside without some smart-arse picking a fight or calling him a pervert, he hid away by day, only venturing out at night to stock up on booze, cigarettes and takeaways. Holed up in his apartment, with the blinds closed to keep prying eyes at bay – and he was *sure* that he was being watched, despite being too high up for anybody to see in unless they used a helicopter – days rolled into nights into weeks into months, with no company except for the TV.

It killed Larry to hear the *Star Struck* music every Wednesday evening, and he despised the sight of Matty Kline's smug grinning face on screen. But, perversely, he couldn't *not* watch it. It was an open wound which needed to be picked and scratched and poked and prodded – and that was exactly what he did, until the poison festered in his heart and soul. *Star Struck* was *his* show and always would be, and he spent that weekly thirty minutes of agony tearing Kline's performance to pieces and wishing him a slow, painful death. And then he would ring his agent, Georgie, demanding to know why she hadn't lined him up any new projects yet – and calling her every fat, useless bitch under the sun when she told him that there was nothing in the offing, even though she was the one and only person who had stood by him throughout that terrible time.

Larry knew he should be grateful to her for that, and in his rare moments of lucidity between waking up and getting pissed again, he would berate himself for being such a bastard. But guilt didn't sit too comfortably with self-pity, so every time he had an attack of remorse after abusing Georgie over the phone, he would drown it with even more alcohol.

Which was precisely what he did when, after almost a year in the showbiz wastelands, *she* actually called *him* for a change.

Already halfway through his latest bottle of Scotch despite it being only five in the afternoon, and in a foul mood because there was a noisy party going on in the apartment next door – to which, surprise, surprise – he hadn't been invited, Larry bit Georgie's head off when she told him he'd had an offer of a job.

'What is it? And it'd better be good, 'cos I'm not just taking any old shit.'

Sensing from his tone that he was spoiling for a fight – as he always seemed to be lately – Georgie sighed. Any other agent would have dumped him after the telethon scandal, but her instincts had prevented her from buying into the witch-hunt. Pain in the arse that he undoubtedly was when he was drunk, Larry had been a nice, sober young man when she'd met him, fresh off the cabaret circuit where he'd been muddling along playing host in a strip venue in Blackpool. She'd never for one minute believed that he was a paedophile and, sensing that the sweet, ambitious boy he'd once been still lurked behind the raging ego, she'd stuck in there, sure that when the rumours eventually fizzled and died and he got a grip on his drinking, some smart producer somewhere would remember his appeal to the female viewing population and give him a fresh start.

And it had finally happened, but not in the way she'd hoped, and Georgie just knew that Larry was going to kick off when he heard what was actually being proposed. In fact, she was so sure he would turn it down flat that she'd spent a good ten minutes after speaking with the producer chewing her nails, wondering whether there was any point even telling him about it. But her conscience hadn't allowed her to keep it from him, and there was always a chance, albeit slim, that he might just surprise her and jump at the chance to get back in front of the camera – like any sensible person would if they had been out of work for as long as he had.

'Oi!' Larry barked suddenly, snapping her out of her thoughts. 'Spit it out, or I'm hanging up. I've got better things to do than sit here listening to you panting down my ear like a knackered old dog.'

Gritting her teeth, Georgie said, 'It's such a joy speaking to you, too, Larry, and if we can forgo the insults for a moment, I'll happily tell you. But before I do, I should point out that I'm not expecting you to like it. I *do*, however, expect you to be sensible enough to at least think it over before you say no, because the money is quite excellent for what it is.'

'Whatever,' Larry muttered, sounding thoroughly unimpressed. 'And what *is* this marvellous thing you've got lined up for me, pray tell?'

'It's a game show,' Georgie told him, adding quickly, 'along the lines of a McIntyre sting,' in the hopes that the mention of the heavyweight of undercover exposés might draw him in for long enough to hear her out. 'The production company are US-based, and they assure me that they were doing this kind of thing over there long before McIntyre got into it, so there's no problem with copyright, or—'

'Bollocks to copyright,' Larry interrupted. 'Who are they, and what's the deal?'

Crossing her fingers, because he actually sounded interested,

Georgie said, 'They're called Shock-Wave, and they're over here filming a documentary series about the differences between US and UK police forces. It's quite—'

'They want me to front it?' Larry cut in again, wondering why on earth she'd assumed that he wouldn't like it. He'd had nothing for a year, and now he was being offered a whole series – and everyone loved those American cop shows. This could be the start of something huge!

'Not exactly,' Georgie said, bringing him back down to earth with a resounding thud. 'Apparently, the officer they've been liaising with for the series asked if they'd consider doing this as an offshoot to the main programme, and *that*'s what they want you for. Unfortunately, it's only been commissioned for the States at the moment, but there's always a chance it'll be picked up over here if it's a success. And they're really keen to have you on board,' she added, wanting to boost him back up before he completely switched off on the idea. 'They delayed going back to the States just so they could work with you.'

That last bit was a blatant lie, but Georgie crossed her fingers, praying that Larry wouldn't question it too closely. He'd always believed that he could make it in the States given half a chance, and with any luck he'd be so flattered at the thought of an American company actually having heard of him that he wouldn't dig too deeply.

And Georgie wouldn't disillusion him by telling him that they *hadn't* actually heard of him. That it had in fact been the police inspector's idea to have him as host, claiming that a well-known presenter with a history of falling foul of the law himself might be better suited to luring in the criminals they were targeting than the goody-goody presenter whom Shock-Wave had originally had in mind.

'The money's fantastic for a one-off,' she repeated now. 'But I do have to warn you that this might be because the project contains a certain element of risk.'

'Risk?' Larry lit a cigarette and sucked wetly on it. 'So, what we talking here? Danger money?'

'Only inasmuch as you'll be dealing with criminals. It's what they call a sting, you see: a fake show to lure in offenders that the police are finding it hard to get hold of by conventional means. But I'm assured there's no danger of you being left alone with them. You'll have the full protection of the company's own security team, and if you saw the McIntyre shows you'll know that the place will be crawling with police, so I really can't see anything going wrong.'

Amazed that she had thought he would give this the time of day, Larry said, 'Fuck that! And fuck *you*, if this is the only shit you can come up with. What use is it to me if no one will even *see* it, you stupid bitch? And you think it's all right to put me in danger, too! Christ, call yourself an agent? I'd get better service off a fucking *chimp*!'

'I really wouldn't advise you to dismiss it out of hand,' Georgie told him calmly, refusing to rise to the insults. 'There's huge potential here if you look at the bigger picture.'

'Potential for what?' Larry snorted. 'Getting myself fucking shot by some psycho crack-head carjacker?'

'For getting yourself back on screen, and shaking off the scandal once and for all. And for showing that you're still a serious prospect. McIntyre hasn't looked back since he—'

Yelling 'McIntyre's a wanker!' Larry slammed the phone down, livid that Georgie was lumping him into the same category as that loser. If she knew anything about Larry Logan, she'd know just how much he despised the jokers who sprang out of nowhere and got famous for shitting themselves in front of a hidden camera. Larry had achieved *his* status through hard work and actual talent, but these idiots had done nothing to justify *their* so-called fame in his opinion. And it wasn't even *them* that the public wanted to see, anyway. It was the criminals whose worlds they could never otherwise infiltrate that they were lusting to watch. And, popular as that kind of show might be, there was no way Larry was reducing himself to taking part in a poxy one-off – no way, no how!

Stewing over the indignity of being asked to demean himself with such a shite job, Larry drank and slept, drank and slept, hoping to drown the self-pitying voices in his head. Life sucked, but the worst was yet to come.

Roused by the sound of heavy knocking on his front door a few days later, he opened his eyes and gazed groggily around the room, trying to remember where he was. It was dark but for the flickering static coming from the TV, which had lost its channel thanks to him lying on the remote, and it took several moments before he realised that he was on the couch in the lounge.

Sitting up, Larry groaned when he felt the material of his jeans pressing cold and damp against his inner thighs. Shoving the jacket he'd been using as a blanket aside, he peered at the dark patch with a grimace of disgust. Great! He'd pissed himself – *again*.

Dropping his feet to the floor, he cursed through gritted teeth when the empty bottle he'd been nursing rolled off the cushion and landed on his bare foot. Snatching it up, he hurled it across the room, where it landed and smashed on a pile of empties in the corner.

Another burst of knocking jarred his head, followed by a man's voice yelling, 'Open up, Mr Logan . . . It's the bailiffs.'

Shocked out of his stupor, Larry jumped up and stumbled out into the hallway, wondering what the hell was going on. It was the middle of the night. Since when did bailiffs get permission to hassle people at night? And why were they here, anyway? He didn't owe anybody anything.

Reaching the front door just as the man knocked again, he leaned against it, and yelled, 'What do you want?'

'It's Mike Flood from King and Johnson's debt recovery agency,' the man announced. 'We've got an order to remove property.'

'Why?' Larry demanded indignantly. 'I've paid for everything I've got.'

Sighing wearily on his side of the door, Flood said, 'Come on, now, sir. We went through all this last time we called.'

'What are you *talking* about?' Larry said confusedly. He had no recollection of any visits from anyone, let alone a bailiff.

Heart racing now, he leaned even harder against the door when it suddenly occurred to him that this must be one of those cons he'd heard about, where gangs of men tricked people into opening their doors by pretending to be policemen or utility-company workmen so that they could gain entrance without making noise or leaving evidence of a break-in. Then they'd beat the shit out of the occupants until they gave up their cash cards and PIN numbers.

'Let's not play games, Mr Logan,' Flood said, his voice so close to Larry's ear that Larry actually jumped. 'You had your chance to resolve this last time we saw you, and I told you we'd be back in a month if you didn't make the first payment on the instalment plan.'

'I've got no idea what you're talking about,' Larry protested, struggling to remember what he'd done last *night*, never mind a month ago.

On the other side of the door Flood rolled his eyes at his partner, and said, 'Told you he was too pissed to take in what we said last time. He hasn't got a fucking clue who we are.'

'Boot it in,' Pete Baron grunted, cracking his knuckles loudly. 'I can't be doing with going through all that shit again. Whatever you say, it just goes in one ear and straight out the other. I hate fucking alkies!'

Amused by his younger colleague's lack of patience and

compassion – qualities he would eventually have to acquire and embrace if he hoped to survive in this stressful line of work – Flood grinned and shook his head.

'I wouldn't go applying to work with the Samaritans any time soon, Bazza. You're a right unsympathetic little bastard.'

'And you're a right soft twat,' Baron shot back with a grin of his own, knowing full well that, polite and professional as Flood might be on the job, he was more than a match for any man if push came to shove.

Giving Logan one last chance to get his head around the facts before they were forced to call in the law to help them execute the warrant, Flood gave another little rap on the door, and said, 'Come on, Mr Logan – the courts don't pass these things on to us unless they've already given you ample opportunity to sort it out with them first. Now, I told you we'd be back, and we are, so why don't you just let us get on with it, eh?'

'I've called the police,' Larry lied, shaking furiously, because he'd heard them talking quietly between themselves and was convinced that they were planning to rush him. 'They'll be here any minute.'

'Fine by me,' Flood replied calmly, his jacket making a swishing sound on the wood as he leaned against the door. 'Makes it easier for us in the long run.'

Confused by Flood's lack of concern, Larry narrowed his eyes. Either the man was calling his bluff, or he genuinely wasn't bothered if the police came. And, given that he didn't seem in any hurry to leave, it was probably the latter, which meant that he probably *was* who he'd said he was. But Larry still couldn't remember them calling round before.

Just then, a door on the opposite side of the communal corridor opened. Larry panicked when he heard his neighbour – a well-known TV chef with a habit of gossiping about his fellow celebrities on his weekly show – asking the bailiffs if everything was all right. Scrabbling to open the door before they blurted out the shameful nature of their visit, he waved Flood and Baron inside.

Gazing up at them when the door was shut he panicked all over again, because both men were absolutely huge and looked like thugs in their leather jackets and with their close-cropped hair. Now that he could see them, he *did* vaguely recognise them, but he still didn't remember speaking to them, or coming to any sort of payment arrangements with them.

'Glad you've decided to cooperate,' Flood said, his polite tone at odds with his brutish appearance. 'Never like having to force entry. But you haven't got kids, if I remember right, so this shouldn't be too difficult.'

Resigned to getting this over and done with now that they were actually inside, Larry said, 'I'm not being awkward, but have you got any ID? Only you can't be too careful these days, can you?'

Reaching into his pocket, Flood took out his official badge and showed it to him. Peering at it for a moment, Larry nodded. Then, blushing when he saw Flood's gaze dip to the wet patch on the crotch of his jeans, he excused himself and rushed to his bedroom to change.

Exchanging a smirk with Baron, Flood sauntered over to a heap of newspapers and unopened letters lying behind the front door. Using the toe of his boot to sift through them, he reached down and picked up several envelopes bearing the King & Johnson stamp. Showing them to Baron before placing them on the hall table, he said, 'No wonder he didn't expect us, eh?'

'Lazy bastard wants to try cleaning up once in a while and he'd have known,' Baron grunted, wandering into the lounge and peering around in disgust. 'He hasn't lifted a finger since last time we were here. It smells like a fucking toilet.'

'Yeah, well, that's his business, not ours,' Flood said, sliding his hand across the wall and flicking the light switch, only to find that the bulb had blown. 'We're not here to judge,' he went on, picking a careful path through the debris to the window. 'So let's just do what we've got to do and leave the man in peace.'

Having changed his wet jeans for a fresh pair, Larry slinked back into the lounge like a dog with its tail between its legs. Flood had opened the blinds so that he and Baron could see what they were doing and, confused by the bright daylight streaming through the windows, Larry glanced at the clock. Having thought it was the middle of the night, he was shocked to see that it was actually nine in the morning. He'd been living in virtual darkness for months, drifting from day to night in a fug of Scotch and bad TV and, now that he could see the filthy hovel that his once-pristine apartment had become, he was so ashamed he could have crawled under a rock and died right then and there.

'You know those letters we sent telling you we were coming?' Flood said over his shoulder just then, as he concentrated on removing the screws from the panel securing the flat-screen TV to the wall. 'We just found them in the hall. There's a fair few, so you might want to look through the rest when you get a chance – make sure you haven't got any more nasty surprises like this lined up.'

Grunting a grudging thanks, because he really didn't see what business it was of theirs if he chose not to open his mail, Larry was further irritated when the other thug pointed out the heap of broken glass in the corner, saying, 'You want to clear that up before someone gets hurt, mate. Must have been a hell of a party, though, eh?'

'Yes, it was actually,' he lied, running a hand through his hair. Recoiling at the stench from his underarms, he folded his arms tightly. 'So, what happens now?'

'Remember we made a list of assets last time we came?'

Flood replied – pretty sure that Larry didn't remember, because he'd been so off his head at the time. 'Well, now we remove them.' Pausing, he turned to look at Larry. 'Unless you'd rather settle up? Only it'll have to be in full, I'm afraid, because you've already forfeited the right to instalments. Better than losing all your stuff, though, eh?'

Backed into a corner, Larry sighed and flapped his hands. 'Don't suppose I've got much choice, have I? It'll have to be a card, though, because I don't carry cash,' he added point-edly, letting Flood's dodgy-looking mate know that he'd be wasting his time if he had any thoughts about trying to rip Larry off.

Assuring him that cards were fine, Flood took a small card-reading machine out of his pocket and asked if it would be debit or credit.

'Debit,' Larry muttered, lifting cushions and sifting through the clothes that were scattered all over the furniture in a bid to locate his wallet. 'How much is it?'

'Three thousand, six hundred and twenty,' Flood told him, giving a small sympathetic shrug as he added, 'Sounds a lot, but these things tend to grow like wildfire if you leave them.'

'*What?*' Larry squawked, finding the wallet and turning back to Flood. 'Am I paying the electricity bill for the whole fucking block, or something?'

'This isn't an electric bill,' Flood told him patiently. 'It's council tax.'

'You're joking.' Larry frowned, suddenly sure that they had got him mixed up with someone else. 'How come? I pay it by direct debit.'

'Apparently not,' Flood said, shrugging. 'You'd have had letters telling you that there was a problem, so you could have sorted it out before it got to this. And you're welcome to appeal, but our order still stands, I'm afraid. You'll either have to pay, or we'll have to take goods. Your choice.'

'Oh, I'll appeal, all right,' Larry muttered, incensed that the authorities were allowed to raid people's homes like this when it was obviously their mistake. 'I still don't see why it's so much, though. The council tax is never three grand.'

'No, but they lump the court costs on top of that. Then you've got late-payment fees, plus admin charges. And then the bailiff's fees get whacked on, and every visit we have to make adds a couple of ton.' Pausing, Flood gave another little shrug. 'Just the way it works, sir.'

'Jeezus! Talk about a rip-off,' Larry sniped, taking his debit card out of his wallet and thrusting it at the bailiff.

Face impassive, Flood slotted it into the machine. He couldn't count how many times he'd heard those exact same words from disgruntled debtors, and it never ceased to amaze him that people couldn't seem to grasp that they wouldn't be in this position if they'd just pay their bills on time. And this guy had less excuse than most, because he was a TV star and must be worth a fortune.

But then again . . .

Taking the card out of the reader, he handed it back to Larry.

'Sorry, sir, can't take this. It's coming up as insufficient funds.'

'*What?*' Larry yelped, frowning deeply. 'No way! Your thing must be faulty.'

Assuring him that the machine was in perfect working order, Flood asked if he wanted to try a different card.

Thrusting a credit card at him now, Larry said, 'Try that. And if it doesn't work, it's definitely your machine.'

Slotting it in, Flood extracted it after a moment and shook his head.

'You're kidding me!' Larry murmured, the blood draining from his face. 'Look, do me a favour and wait while I ring the bank, will you?'

'As long as it doesn't take too long,' Baron piped up, glancing pointedly at his watch. 'We haven't got all day, you know.'

Giving him a dirty look, Larry went into the bedroom and closed the door to make his call in private.

'I'm sorry, Mr Logan, but the figures are perfectly correct,' the bank's branch manager told him patiently, after ten minutes of Larry arguing that they had made a mistake at their end, or that somebody must have been illegally accessing his account. 'I have the full read-out of this years' movements on the screen, and there is nothing out of the ordinary about it. Apart from your mortgage repayments – which, incidentally, I was about to write to you about, because I'm concerned that you won't be able to meet them after this next one, given that you've had no money paid into your account for so long – you seem to have spent the bulk of the rest in . . . let me see now . . . ah, yes, here we are . . . Bargain Booze; Oddbins; The Balti Palace; and Asda 24.

'Now, about the mortgage repayments,' he went on, as Larry sat on the bed in stunned silence. 'Shall I pencil you in for a meeting on the third of next month . . . ?'

Coming back into the lounge at last, Larry's face told a clear enough story for the bailiffs to know that he'd been unsuccessful.

'Is there someone who could pay it for you while you get it sorted?' Flood suggested as Baron immediately resumed his efforts to remove the TV's holding panel. 'A friend, or a family member?'

Larry shook his head. He had no friends, and he'd disowned his family years ago when his rise to fame had turned them into a pack of vultures, forever trying to get their dirty, lazy hands on his money. So they wouldn't help him out even if they'd been able to – which they wouldn't be, because they were such a bunch of losers.

There was absolutely nobody he could turn to, and the realisation of just how alone he was hit him harder than he would have imagined it could. Overcome by a sudden urge to cry, he went back into the bedroom, calling over his shoulder for Flood and Baron to take whatever they wanted.

Staying there until he heard the front door closing, Larry waited a few minutes to make sure that they had really gone. Then, wandering back into the lounge, he slumped down on his chair and gazed around to see what damage they'd done. They had taken everything of value, from the TV to the studio-quality stereo system, right down to the paintings off the walls. It was a wonder they hadn't taken the cushion from under his arse as well, he thought miserably. But that would have been too much of a piss-take, considering that they'd get far more than the three and a half thousand he supposedly owed for what they *had* taken.

Searching without success for alcohol to numb the pain, Larry held his head in his hands, wondering how the hell he'd managed to piss five years' worth of earnings up the wall in one short year. He'd always been extravagant, splashing it about in the clubs and casinos, often picking up the tab for his fellow drinkers and whichever bird he was wooing at the time, and taking taxis and even chauffeured cars here, there and everywhere. But he'd never thought it was a problem, because he'd been paid enough to sustain the lifestyle and hadn't concerned himself with trivialities like checking his account to see what a dent it was really making. Obviously, he'd been riding close to the line all along, though, so when the pay stopped coming in to top it up, it hadn't taken long to erode the rest.

Larry was broke now, and with no job to replenish his funds he had no means of getting out of the pit he'd fallen into – or, rather, *jumped* into, because he'd done this with his eyes wide open. He couldn't even sign on to get him through, because they'd laugh him out of the benefits office. And he had nothing of any real value left to sell. He was already in danger of losing the apartment if he couldn't meet the next mortgage payment – which, obviously, he couldn't. But even if he'd wanted to sell it, he doubted that the bank would allow him the time it might take to offload it without heaping penalty payments and interest on his head, leaving him with nothing but more debt for his troubles.

It infuriated him that he even had to *think* about selling his home. He'd worked bloody hard for it, and resented that he might be forced to move into some small tatty place – like the hovels his scummy family called home. And how could he live among the public again, anyway, now they'd made it so clear what they thought of him? He'd be dead within a week – if he hadn't killed himself first!

Left with no other option, Larry reached for the phone.

'Well, well,' Georgie said coolly. 'This is unexpected, I must say. Was there something you forgot to say last time we spoke? Because I'm pretty sure you covered everything when you told me to go and fuck myself.'

Like a spoiled child being taken to task by a disapproving parent, Larry wanted to scream at her to get off his back. But she had the upper hand right now, and if he was to have any hope of crawling out of the hole that life and ill fortune had landed him in, he knew he'd have to swallow his pride and throw himself on her mercy.

Muttering 'Sorry,' he gritted his teeth when Georgie asked him to speak up because she *didn't quite catch that*. 'I said I'm *sorry*,' he repeated tersely. 'I know I was out of order the other day, but you caught me at a bad time. Anyway, I really am sorry if I offended you, but I've had a good think about what you were saying, and I reckon you could be right about giving that job a go. But I'm only doing it for you,' he added quickly, as if she ought to be grateful. 'And it's got to be on my terms.'

'Too late,' Georgie said when he'd finished. 'I've already told them you don't want it.'

'Well, tell them I've changed my mind,' he blustered, a note of desperation sparking in his voice. 'Christ, Georgie, I thought you knew me better than that? A job's a job, so why the hell would I turn it down?'

*Because you're an arrogant little bugger who still thinks he's calling all the shots*, Georgie thought.

Sighing, she said, 'Okay, I'll see what I can do. But don't hold your breath, because they've probably found somebody else by now.'

'Just try,' Larry said, his tone defeated now as he added, '*Please*.'

Sensing that it had taken a lot for him to climb down like this, Georgie said, 'Okay, leave it with me, I'll see what I can do.' Then, seizing the rare opportunity that his humility had presented her, she said, 'Just one thing, Larry . . . if you get lucky and they haven't already filled the slot, don't be turning up drunk and looking ghastly, or that really will be the end of you and me. You know I love you dearly, but it's time you stopped feeling sorry for yourself and quit the drinking before you lose everything. And I'm not just talking material possessions, I'm talking looks and personality. Alcohol destroys them both, and before you know it you'll have nothing left to offer.'

'I'll sort it,' Larry said, having no intention of doing any such thing but wanting to shut her up because she was depressing him.

# 5

Terri Lawson was the producer of *Cops 'n' Bobbies*, Shock-Wave's first foray into the transatlantic market. Sitting in the plush office they were using while they were in England, she and her assistant Jon Street were checking over some stills from a shoot when Julie, the Mancunian temp receptionist-cum-secretary, burst in.

'He's here!' she announced, her eyes alight with an excitement that Terri wouldn't have imagined she was capable of feeling, given that she usually sighed her way through the day as if life was a burden. 'D'y' want me to send him in?'

'In a minute,' Terri told her firmly. 'And please knock next time. We could have been doing anything.'

Giving a disparaging *I doubt that very much* snort, Julie closed the door and sashayed back into the reception office to tell Larry and his agent that the boss would see them in a minute.

Thanking her, Georgie wandered over to the window to take a look at the view.

Taking her mobile phone out of her bag, Julie whispered, 'Could you do me a massive favour and say hello to my friend, Larry? Only she'll never believe I really met you otherwise.'

Telling her that he'd be delighted, Larry trailed a fingertip over her thumb when she handed her phone to him and smiled when he felt the tremor pass through her.

'Her name's Emma,' she gasped, her pretty face flushed. 'And I'm Julie.'

'Nice name,' Larry drawled silkily. 'Had a girlfriend called Julie once. Lovely-looking girl – bit like yourself.'

Almost wetting herself, Julie gazed up at him with adoration in her eyes, murmuring, 'I can't believe you're actually here. I used to watch *Star Struck* all the time, but it's not the same without you. And me and my friends thought it was disgusting when they sacked you like that.'

'Don't worry about it,' Larry said. Then, holding up a finger when the phone was answered, he said, 'Is that Emma? Hi, this is Larry Logan. Julie asked me to say hello.'

'Don't lie!' the girl at the other end of the phone squealed. 'No *way* is that you! Say that thing you always said at the end of your show.'

Chuckling, Larry said, 'Join me next week for another round of *Star Struck* – the only game where *you*, the public, can win big money for knowing the secrets of the stars!'

Jerking the phone away from his ear when the girl literally screamed, he winced and handed it back to Julie.

'God, thanks!' She grinned. 'She'll be made up. Well, you can *hear* how chuffed she is, can't you? But she'll be so jealous that I got to actually *meet* you.'

Turning round when she heard a buzzing sound, Georgie saw that it was coming from the desk phone. Clearing her throat to snap the girl out of her trance, she nodded towards it.

Sighing, Julie said, 'Looks like she's ready for you.'

Winking at her, Larry put his hand in his pocket and followed Georgie into the producers' office, filled with renewed hope for the future. He'd been wallowing in self-pity and injured pride for so long now, thinking that the public had turned their backs on him. But judging by Julie's reaction to seeing him just now – and her friend's at having simply heard his voice – it was clear that he still had that certain *something*. And, better yet, they weren't blaming him for the disastrous telethon or the shit that followed. Fingers crossed, his luck might actually be about to turn around.

Terri and Jon exchanged a surreptitious glance when Larry walked in. As Terri had confessed to Georgie when she'd made the initial call, she'd never actually heard of him before. But she had made it her business to view old tapes of his show since, in order to judge his hosting abilities. But, good-looking as he undoubtedly was on screen, she was unprepared for the presence he exuded in the flesh. Even with the extra weight, and the small number of stress lines around his eyes, he was extraordinarily handsome.

Sober and showered, and having made a real effort to clean up his act in the week since telling Georgie that he wanted this job, Larry knew that he looked great. He still resented being forced to take a one-off show, but beggars couldn't be choosers so he'd had his best suit dry-cleaned and had booked himself in for a haircut with his favourite stylist – which had cost him far more than he could really afford. But, catching the look that passed between the producer and her assistant, he figured it had been worth it.

Extending his hand now when Terri stood up to greet him, he gave her the same kind of once-over she'd just given him. She had too much black eyeliner framing her wide-spaced eyes, and her lipstick was too garish a red for her pale complexion, but she had the dark glossy hair that he liked, and her figure was pretty good for her age, which he esti-mated to be somewhere around the mid-thirties. Bit old for his taste, but she might be worth a second glance – if it helped get his career back on track.

Turning to the man now, Larry smiled as he shook his hand. Jon was obviously younger than Terri, but his receding hairline and misguided attempt at dressing trendily made him look older. And Larry recognised the glint of envy in his eyes all too well, because it was the same expression that less handsome men always got on their faces when he walked into a room. Oh, he was back on form, all right.

'Great to meet you both at last,' Terri said, waving them to take a seat. 'We were so pleased when Georgie told us that you'd reconsidered, Larry.'

'Me, too,' Georgie murmured, settling in her seat and gazing around the office.

'Can we get you guys anything before we start?' Terri asked now, perching prettily on the chair opposite Larry's and indicating the table between them, which was stacked with nibbles and a variety of alcoholic and soft drinks.

Larry felt a tugging sensation in his gut as he eyed the bottle of Scotch that was crying out to him from the centre of the table. But Georgie would be leaving from here to go to a family funeral and she was upset enough without him stressing her out by taking a drink before the contract was signed. And much as he'd have loved a glass or three of the hard stuff right now, he just couldn't do that to her, so he asked for a fresh orange juice instead.

'So, here's the deal,' Jon said when they all had their drinks in their hands. 'As you might have guessed from the accents, Larry, we're from the States, and we're over here shooting a series about US versus UK cops—'

'Georgie's already given me the background.' Larry cut him short, his gaze focused firmly on Terri, who was leaning forward in her seat giving him a bird's-eye view of creamy cleavage.

'Okay, good . . . well, that saves a bit of time, I guess,' Jon said, sitting forward in his own seat to draw Larry's attention back to him. He could almost see the sparks flying between the two of them, and felt an urge to intervene before they ignited into a flame. Terri was no easy lay by any means, but this guy was too handsome by far, and Jon wanted to remind them that this was a business meeting, not a blind date.

'Can I take it you're familiar with this kind of programme, Mr Logan?' he asked now, switching to formality to keep things on a professional footing.

Giving Jon a knowing smile, sure that he was trying to warn him off his woman, Larry said, 'I've seen a couple, yeah.'

'And you're not intimidated by the thought of being involved with criminals?'

'Should I be?'

'Not at all,' Terri said, frowning at Jon, because they were meant to be welcoming Larry to the project, not putting him off it before they'd even started. 'We have a fantastic security set-up, and we don't anticipate any trouble.'

'But we obviously can't offer a watertight guarantee on that,' Jon countered, irritated that Terri seemed intent on letting her pussy do the talking instead of adhering to the correct protocol for protecting the company in a worst-case scenario.

'I'm sure I'll be fine,' Larry drawled, exchanging a hooded glance with Georgie, amused by the friction that seemed to be developing between the producer and her uptight assistant.

'Right, then,' Terri said firmly. 'Let's move straight to the terms of the contract, shall we? I know you've already talked it through with Larry, Georgie, so we can—'

'Sorry,' Jon interrupted, giving Terri a piercing look. 'But can we just have a little chat before we proceed?'

'Can't it wait?' Terri asked, wondering why he was interrupting things at this stage for a chat.

'No.' Jon shook his head, casting a surreptitious glance at Larry. 'Sorry, but it can't.'

Sighing, Terri gave Georgie and Larry an apologetic smile, and said, 'I'm so sorry about this, but could you just give us a moment? I'm sure Julie will take good care of you while you're waiting.'

Frowning, because she really didn't have time for messing around today, Georgie said, 'Sorry, but is there a problem? Only I thought everything was set for Larry to sign?'

'Oh, it is,' Terri assured her. 'And I promise we won't keep you any longer than necessary.'

Flapping his hands, Larry said, 'No problem. Just give us a shout when you're ready.' Getting up then, he jerked his head at Georgie, and sauntered out of the office.

Waiting until Georgie had followed and closed the door behind her, Terri turned to Jon and hissed, 'What the hell is *wrong* with you?'

'There's nothing wrong with me,' he replied stiffly. 'I'm just not sure he's the right guy for us.'

'Why? He's charming, laid-back, good-looking.'

'Some might say *too* good-looking. And I'm a little concerned that his face might be more of a hindrance than a help.'

'Are you serious?' Drawing her head back, Terri peered at him. 'How can you be too good-looking?'

'Oh, I've no doubt women probably idolise him on sight,' Jon sniped. 'But we've been working on this kind of thing for long enough to know that men despise guys who are prettier than their girlfriends – especially the kind of men we'll be targeting here.'

Mulling this over for several moments, Terri said, 'You've got a point, and ordinarily I'd probably agree with you. But that's back home, and we already know how different everything is over here. And Inspector Keeton mustn't have thought it would be a problem or he wouldn't have suggested him. And let's not forget *why* he chose him.'

'Which is the other thing that's bothering me,' Jon said. 'That whole under-age sex thing was wrong, and I'm not sure I can work with someone who's into that kind of shit.'

Reminding him that it hadn't been proved or Larry would

have been prosecuted, Terri said, 'Mud sticks, but that doesn't make it true. Anyway, I prefer to go with my instincts, and they're telling me that he's not the type to do something like that.'

'He's not going to be obvious about it, is he?' Jon argued. 'Decent people are disgusted by that kind of thing, which is why it's such an underground issue.'

'Well, now you've met him, do *you* think he's a child abuser?' Terri challenged.

Folding his arms, Jon pursed his lips. Shrugging after a moment, he said, 'Probably not. But you can never be sure, can you? Take that guy last year: fucking every grown woman he could get his hands on, just to deflect suspicion from the fact that he had all those kids locked in his basement.'

'You can't compare *him* to Larry.' Terri laughed. 'Anyway, I told you it was him from the start, but *you* thought it was that kid from down the block.'

'Yeah, well, there was something wrong with the kid, too,' Jon muttered, knowing that he'd used a bad example. 'He had the shiftiest eyes I've ever seen.'

'Because he was terrified the cops were going to stumble across the grass he was growing in the attic,' Terri reminded him. 'Anyway, we're getting off track here. This is about Larry, and I really think he's our guy.'

'I don't.' Jon shrugged again. 'But you're the boss, so it's your call. Just don't say I didn't warn you if anything goes wrong.'

'It won't,' Terri stated with certainty. Then, smiling, she said, 'Right, let's call him back in and get this contract signed before he runs out on us.'

Reaching for the Scotch that Larry had resisted, Jon poured himself a stiff shot. He'd respect Terri's decision, but that didn't mean he had to agree with it. He was professional enough to push his personal feelings aside for the sake of his work, and he just hoped that Terri would do the same, because he'd hate for her lust-life to jeopardise their project.

Still, if she fucked it up, Shock-Wave would have to see that it had been a mistake putting her in charge, and Jon might just get the chance to show what he was made of – at last.

Calling Larry and Georgie back in, Terri signed her part of the contract and pushed it across the table to Larry, mentally crossing her fingers in the hope that Jon hadn't put him off – because *she* thought that he was absolutely perfect.

Giving it to Georgie, who took one last look over it to make sure that it hadn't been altered in any way since she and Terri had agreed the terms, Larry signed it and pushed it back to Terri.

Reaching out to shake first Georgie's, then Larry's hand, Terri said, 'Great to be working with you. And now we've got that out of the way, I'd love to take you both over to see the location.'

Glancing at her watch, Georgie said, 'I can't, I'm afraid. But I'm sure you can manage without me, can't you, Larry?'

Patting him on the arm when he said he'd be fine, pleased with him for behaving himself, Georgie said, 'Okay, well, I'll speak to you when I get back. And it was very nice to meet you both, Terri and Jon.'

'Nice lady,' Terri said when Georgie had gone. Then, back to Larry, 'Right, well, shall we set straight off, then? Or would you rather have a spot of lunch first?'

Frowning, because he'd just picked up the scent of the Scotch that Jon was cradling, Larry shook his head and said, 'I'd rather just go straight there, if you don't mind.'

*Then I can cut loose and get blasted.*

Handing the signed contracts to Jon, Terri stood up and reached for her jacket. 'Come on, then. Let's get you over there to meet everyone. Do you want to hang on here in case that call comes through, Jon?'

Guessing that it wasn't a question, Jon smiled tightly. 'Yeah, why not,' he said, getting up to put the paperwork in the safe. 'I'm sure you'll manage without me for an hour or two.'

Saying 'Call me on the cell if you need me,' Terri opened the door and waved Larry out of the office ahead of her.

Passing Julie as they went through the outer office, Larry flipped her a wink and said, 'Later babe.'

Smiling as they took the elevator down to the ground floor, Terri said, 'I think you've got yourself quite a fan back there.'

'Who, _Jon?_' Larry quipped, feigning surprise. 'Well, I must say, I'm shocked. I got the distinct impression he didn't like me.'

Telling him that she'd been talking about Julie, although she guessed that he already knew that, Terri stepped back to let him out when the elevator stopped. Following him out into the foyer, she hesitated when she saw how many young women were milling about there. She recognised most of them as secretaries and receptionists from the various businesses located in the block, but she had never seen so many of them in the same place at the same time before. Word that Larry was here had obviously spread.

Most of the girls were trying to act cool, but when one rushed forward just as Larry reached the street door and asked him for his autograph, the rest quickly followed, and Terri had to wait almost ten minutes while he obliged.

Stepping out onto the pavement at last, she hailed a cab and rushed him into it, in case any of the women who were already doing double takes as they passed on the street decided to delay them further. It was an amazing reaction, she thought, given that Larry had supposedly been off the scene for so long and out of the public's favour. But it all boded well for her project because, if the British women were so taken with him, then the girls back home were bound to fall for him, too.

Terri had chosen an almost derelict Victorian warehouse in the undeveloped section of Trafford Park's otherwise flourishing industrial estate as the location for her mock-studio. Gazing out at the building as the cab pulled up at the kerb, Larry wondered what on earth had possessed her. It looked in serious danger of crumbling to dust if too many more rats trod its mouldy boards, and there was no way anyone was going to be fooled into thinking it was a genuine TV station – especially not the notoriously paranoid Mancunian criminals they were hoping to lure in. They'd take one look at the place and run for their lives.

'I know it looks awful,' Terri said, paying the driver and climbing out. 'But it's a lot better inside. And when we're done, the exterior will be just as good, I promise.'

Doubting that very much, Larry wasn't holding his breath as she tapped on the ancient shutters which were drawn almost all the way down over the entrance. But he got a shock when someone hauled the shutters up a few seconds later and he found himself walking into a modern reception area, complete with a long polished desk, over which two men were busy erecting a neon sign reading *INDIGO TV*.

'Good, isn't it?' Terri said, smiling because he looked so surprised.

'Great,' Larry agreed, gazing around. 'It's a lot like Oasis, actually – the studio I used to work at.'

'So I heard,' Terri said, nodding her approval to the workmen when they stepped down to view their handiwork. 'But then, most station receptions look like this, so it wasn't hard to set it up. And it will look even better when we put the finishing touches to it. A few potted palms, and maybe a coffee machine. Oh, and do you get the name, by the way?'

Shrugging, Larry said, 'It's a colour, isn't it?'

'In-di-go,' Terri said, punctuating each syllable. When Larry still looked blank, she said, 'In *dey* go – to prison. Get it?'

'Ah . . .' Larry drew his head back. 'Very clever.'

'Thought you'd like it,' Terri said proudly. 'And we're calling the game show *Gotcha!*, by the way.'

'Right,' Larry murmured uncertainly. 'And you don't think that's a bit obvious?'

'Not at all,' Terri replied, smiling coyly as she added, 'Mind you, I'm bound to say that, considering it was my idea. But everyone else seems to like it, so I guess it must be okay. Anyway, come on . . . let me show you around.'

Leading him to a door marked PRIVATE at the far end of the reception area now, Terri thanked Larry when he held it open for her, and wondered as she passed him – as she'd been doing since she'd first laid eyes on him – how one man could have been blessed with such an extraordinarily beautiful face. She'd worked with some of the most handsome men in the States during her time in TV, but none had been quite as stunning in the flesh as Larry was. She just prayed that his year away from the camera hadn't dulled his on-screen magic or she'd have some serious explaining to do, having practically forced Jon to dismiss his own instincts in favour of hers.

Smiling to himself, sure that Terri was thinking hot thoughts about him, Larry followed her into the heart of the old warehouse. Having expected it to be a cold, cavernous shell, littered with the remnants of old machinery and resonating with the echoes of a long-gone Victorian workforce, he was surprised to see how much work Shock-Wave had done to transform it into a credible-looking TV studio, complete with sound-proofed walls and hush-foot flooring. A large stage-floor had been laid to the rear of the hall, and several set-builders were busy hoisting a glitzy backdrop into position as he watched. And rows of audience seating were being installed, the workers creating a cacophonous din with their hammers and screeching drills; while, overhead, metal clanked on metal as technicians moved huge banks of studio lights into position.

Watching Larry raptly as the light of something indefinable began to shine in his eyes, Terri said, 'Impressed?'

'Very,' he murmured, his heart singing a sweet song of joy at being back where he belonged – despite it not being real. 'Seems a lot of expense for a one-off show, though. Hope the owners aren't letting you foot the bill for the work *and* charging you rent?'

'Actually, we got a very reasonable deal,' Terri told him. 'And we were already using it as our base for *Cops 'n' Bobbies*, so it made sense to use it for *Gotcha!* as well. It's cost more than we originally intended to convert it into a realistic-looking studio, of course, because we were only actually using it for editing and equipment storage before. But if we get a fantastic show out of it, I don't think anyone's going to complain about a few extra thousand.' Smiling now, she gazed around with satisfaction. 'Everything's coming along fantastically so far, and Inspector Keeton's been a huge help, because he knows your laws and regulations so much better than we do.' Chuckling softly, she added, 'I actually think he's been bitten by the showbiz bug, because we can't seem to keep him away from the place. He's always offering help and making suggestions. Like the commercial – that was one of his.'

'Commercial?' Larry repeated, giving her a quizzical look.

'Oh, sorry, did I forget to mention that?' Terri gave him an *I'm so ditzy* smile. 'Yeah, we're planning a twenty-second ad to air at prime time for two weeks, running up to the actual day of filming, with a Freepost address for anyone who wants to apply to be a contestant. Bit of a shame for those who never hear back from us, I know, but at least it won't have cost them anything.'

Wondering how they would get away with that, given that there *was* no show – not of the kind that they'd be advertising, anyway – Larry said, 'Isn't that entrapment, or whatever you call it?'

'Not if you word it right,' Terri told him. 'And our legal guys are the best, so I don't anticipate any problems. No one will be out of pocket, and we won't be promising replies, so the ones who don't hear back will just assume they were unsuccessful, while the targets will believe that they *were* successful.'

'And what if they never entered in the first place?' Larry said, thinking he'd stumbled onto a pretty major flaw in her seemingly perfect plan.

'Oh, you'd be surprised how gullible people can be,' Terri said, reaching into her pocket for her mobile when it began to ring. 'And the smarter they think they are, the easier they are to fool. Show them a golden ticket with their name on it, and they don't tend to question how we got hold of them. Greed is a terrific tool of persuasion, in my experience.'

Glancing down at her phone, she sighed when she saw the name on the screen. 'My mother,' she said, switching it off. 'I keep telling her not to call me on the cell because it's so expensive, but she won't wait till I get back to the hotel. And it'll only be something trivial, like the kettle won't boil, or the cat won't come down from the tree, or something.'

'Right,' Larry murmured, sure that it had actually been a man, and that she'd ignored it because she hadn't wanted Larry to hear her talking to him. Probably that dipstick Jon, checking up on her.

'What was I talking about?' Terri said now. Then, clicking her fingers, 'Oh, yeah, the commercial . . . Right, well, we're planning on shooting later today – if that's okay with you?

We can reschedule if you've got something else to do, but I'd really appreciate it if you could fit us in. You're the bait, after all, so we need to get your face out there as soon as possible.'

Assuring her that he had nothing to rush away for, Larry forgot all about the drink he'd been so desperate for when they'd left her office. He was ecstatic to hear that his face *would* be back on screen over here, after all – and at prime time, too, putting him right back where he belonged come Wednesday night: smack in the middle of Matty Kline's inferior version of *Star Struck*. And what a kick in the bollocks *that* would be for the slimy bastard!

Thanking Larry for jumping in at such short notice, Terri spotted Inspector Keeton arriving just then. Waving to him, she linked her arm through Larry's as she said, 'Come and meet Bill. He's adorable, and he's got a great sense of humour. But I guess you need one in his line of work, don't you? The cops we work with back home sure do. They call it morgue mirth, or something like that.'

Looking the inspector over as they approached him Larry thought that 'adorable' was the *last* tag he'd have ever given him, because Keeton had a face like a grumpy old bulldog's. And he didn't like the way the man was looking at him, with his eyes narrowed – like he was sizing him up for a prison cell.

Bill Keeton was indeed studying Larry. He'd seen him before, of course, but only on screen or in the papers, never in the flesh. Face to face now, he knew he'd made the right choice when he'd suggested him as host, because Larry Logan was a very handsome lad. And Keeton would bet his own untainted reputation that he wasn't a kiddie-fiddler, either – and he'd met enough of *them* to know.

Extending a hand now when Terri introduced them, he said, 'Pleased to meet you, Mr Logan.'

'Likewise,' Larry said guardedly. 'But please call me Larry.'

'Will do,' Keeton agreed, a small but seemingly genuine smile lifting one side of his thin lips as he added, 'But only if you call me "sir".'

Relieved that the glint of suspicion had left the inspector's eyes, Larry was about to make a witty comeback when a loud crashing sound came from the stage area, followed by a string of expletives.

Frowning, Terri said, 'Sorry, guys, think I'd best go see what's happened. Will you be all right by yourselves for a minute?'

Assuring her that they would be just fine, Keeton waited until she'd gone. Then he turned back to Larry and said, 'Doing a grand job, isn't she? I don't think we'll have much trouble convincing the jumpers they've hit the jackpot when they cop for this lot. Given you the low-down, has she?'

'Er, yeah,' Larry replied uncertainly. 'Sorry, did you say jumpers?'

'Bail jumpers,' Keeton explained, folding his arms across his chest. 'That's the bulk of what we're after with this, and I've a feeling we'll net a fair few once the ad's airing and the flyers are doing the rounds. Good to have you on board, by the way,' he said now, giving Larry a sympathetic smile as he added, 'Any luck, it might help to put all the troubles you had last year behind you, eh? Can't have been easy holding your head up with all that nonsense going on.'

Touched that yet another person – and a police inspector at that – had expressed support for him after the living nightmare of being shunned and vilified for the best part of a year, Larry thanked him. Then, feeling awkward as they lapsed into silence, he stuck his hands deep into his trouser pockets and looked around as if he was suddenly really, *really* interested in the activity of the workmen. He'd never been good at small talk. Not with men, anyway – and definitely not when he was sober.

Rushing back just then, Terri said, 'Sorry about that. Just a little hitch with some guy ropes, or something, but it's fine now. Anyway, this is for you.' She passed a two-sheet script to Larry.

'And these are for you.' She handed Keeton a thick wad of gold tickets. 'Just back from the printers, so be careful they're not still damp.'

'Oh, they're good,' Keeton murmured approvingly, looking them over and handing one to Larry. 'What do you think, son?'

'They look great,' Larry agreed. 'I reckon I'd be fooled if one landed on my doormat.'

Chuckling softly, Keeton nudged him. 'Me, too. Good job I'm in on it, or I'd have probably sent in for an application form.'

'You're not that stupid,' Terri purred, giving him a fond smile. Then, taking a sheet of paper from the stack she was holding, she said, 'Oh, and before I forget, look what just got faxed through.'

Taking it, Keeton gazed at the printed picture and whistled softly between his teeth. 'Bloody hell, that's nice.'

'What is it?' Larry peered over his shoulder.

'Range Rover Sports, with full body-kit,' Terri told him. 'One of the guys who works at our head office in LA ordered it for his British wife, and he gave us permission to use it for the shoot before he ships it over. Trouble was, he ordered so many extras to be added to it that I was starting to think it was never going to be ready. But it's done now, so that's one less thing to worry about.'

'Until it gets here,' Keeton said, his tone serious now. 'You'll need armed guards to keep the ringers away when they hear you've got this on the premises. There's firms in Manchester who specialise in stealing and exporting luxury vehicles, and they wouldn't think twice about hitting an out-of-the-way location like this to get their hands on it.'

'Good thing you and your men will be on hand to stop them, then.' Terri smiled, seeming not to grasp the seriousness of what Keeton was saying. Then, letting him know that she was actually *fully* aware of the risks, she said, 'Don't panic, Bill, it's not actually going to *be* here. I had a chat with our guys back home, and we figured we'd need so much extra insurance and security to keep it safe that it wasn't worth the risk, so I'm having a couple of life-size picture boards made up instead.'

Still gazing at the picture – and seriously thinking about ordering one for himself when he'd built his savings back up – Larry asked what they were planning to do with it.

Telling him that it was a bogus bonus prize, Terri said, 'We're going to flash it up on screen at the end of your ad – kind of like an added incentive for the targets to accept our invitation.' Glowing with excitement now, she hugged the papers she was holding to her chest. 'This is going to be so *good*! Larry Logan, a gorgeous car, and the best crime-buster in Manchester. How can we possibly go wrong?'

'Don't say that,' Keeton scolded her softly. 'You know what they say about tempting fate.'

Amused that this upstanding figure of authority was driven by the same superstitious fears as most showbiz folk, Terri smiled again and promised not to even *think* it in future. Then, glancing at her watch, she said, 'Wow, lunchtime already. I know you said you didn't want any, Larry, but can I persuade you to change your mind and join us? I'm *starving*, and Bill is bound to be ravenous, because – between you and me – he's a bit of a pig.'

'That supposed to be funny?' Keeton said dryly, frowning down at her.

Grinning guiltily, she said, 'Sorry, Bill. Didn't mean it like that.'

'I'll let you off this time,' he said mock-sternly, winking at

Larry as he added, 'But don't let it happen again, or I'll have to arrest you.'

After lunch, which he'd barely been able to keep down because he was so nervous about getting in front of the cameras again, Larry holed himself up in his makeshift dressing room and tried to learn the script. It was mercifully short, being just commercial length, but he'd never been good at memorising lines so he just couldn't seem to get it right. And the harder he tried, the worse it got.

After an hour in front of the mirror, grinning like an idiot, his once sexy wink cheesier than a chunk of Cheddar as he tried to deliver the words with conviction, he tossed the script aside in disgust and lit a cigarette. It was hopeless. He was *never* going to get it right and didn't know why he'd thought he could, because it was quite obvious that he'd lost whatever he'd once had. He was utter shit, and it was no wonder nobody had wanted to give him another chance after *Star Struck*. And he had half a mind to go and tell Terri that she'd made a massive mistake.

But then he'd have to relinquish the money, and he absolutely couldn't afford to do that. So, picking up the script, he tried again.

Still plagued by doubts when Terri brought the make-up artist in a little while later to get him ready for camera, Larry was shaking from head to toe by the time she led him out to the set. Standing on the X-spot with the entire crew facing him, he silently cursed whichever gods had put him in this terrible position, pleading with them to quit fucking with his head and whisk him out of here so that he could die in dignity, because he just knew he wasn't going to remember a single word he was supposed to say.

Then, suddenly, the lights came up, and almost as if they had triggered a switch in his head, Larry felt a surge of

Super-Host blood course through his veins. Eyes twinkling, feeling as if he'd come home after being lost at sea for a thousand years, he looked into the camera when he received the cue and delivered a word-perfect take – and that was an absolute miracle, given how long it had used to take him to get it right when he was still fronting *Star Struck*.

Commercial for *Gotcha!* in the can, and his photo taken for the flyers, there was nothing left for Larry to do but go home and wait for the big day to come around.

He was under strict orders from Terri to relax so that he would be on top form when he went back in front of the cameras for real. But he was far too excited for that, so he cleaned the apartment from top to bottom, then waded through the backlog of mail that he'd been ignoring – intent on clearing his debts while he had the upfront half of his fee sitting in his account. That done, he sat back and twiddled his thumbs, willing the time to hurry up and pass.

The advert was airing every evening – and it was brilliant, even if he *did* say so himself. And now that he'd had his first sweet taste of the limelight after so long out of it, he was itching to get back to work.

He just didn't want to think about what he would do when it was all over.

# 6

Larry barely slept a wink the night before the big day. He tried, but it was impossible, and he tossed and turned all night, filled with a sickening mixture of terror and excitement. He knew he could have dropped off in minutes if he'd given in to temptation and downed enough Scotch to drown the voices of the gremlins in his head – who were trying to convince him that it was all going to go horribly wrong. But he'd done so well in cleaning himself up over the last few weeks that there was no way he wanted to risk sliding back down that slippery slope for the sake of a bit of sleep.

There would be plenty of time for that when it was all over and he was slung back onto the scrap heap – as the gremlins insisted he would be.

Climbing into the white stretch limo which Terri had sent for him in the morning, pale, exhausted, and in desperate need of an expert make-over, Larry closed his eyes and rested his head against the cool glass of the blacked-out window, praying that nothing would go wrong.

Keeton was standing outside the back door when the limo pulled into the studio parking lot fifteen minutes later. Dressed in slacks, open-necked shirt and buttoned-up cardi, with his thinning red hair combed neatly over his freckled pate, he looked more like a benevolent grandfather than a respected police inspector when he opened the door to let Larry out.

'All set?' he asked, giving Larry a pumping handshake.

'Bit nervous,' Larry admitted, shivering as the cold morning air bit at his fragile body.

'You'll be fine once we get you inside and warm you up,' Keeton assured him, clapping a fatherly hand on his shoulder. 'Come on, let me give you a quick tour before we kick off.' Pulling the door open now, he waved Larry in, saying, 'You won't recognise the place since last time you saw it. You'd never guess it was just a front, it's that good.'

He wasn't wrong, Larry soon discovered when, instead of the mass of activity and cacophonous noise which had been going on all around him last time, he found himself in a fully kitted-out TV studio with the calm, hushed-air quality that was peculiar to professional recording areas.

Following Keeton out through a heavy stage door behind the set and into a long corridor, which ran the entire width of the building, Larry saw that there were several offices already in operation, and the sounds of ringing telephones, typewriters, printers and fax machines drifted out as Keeton led him past.

Stopping at the far end, Keeton pushed open a door and waved him in. Telling him that this was the mail room, he nodded towards a stack of sacks piled high in one corner, and said, 'They're all applications. Pity most are from ordinary folk who could probably really use a shot at the money, but you have to cast a lot of sprats to catch a mackerel, don't you? Or, in this case, *shark*.' Grinning now, he folded his arms and gave a proud sigh. 'Must say, I never expected it to be this much of a hit when I put the idea to Terri. Almost makes me think a career change might be in order if I can pull something like *this* off in such a short time. I'm obviously wasting my talents, eh?'

Amused that Keeton was crediting himself for how well things were going, Larry decided not to burst his bubble by pointing out that it was more likely Larry's involvement that had tipped the scales and persuaded people to put pen to paper. It took time to build up this kind of interest from the public, and it certainly didn't happen for new shows – not unless the host was already a hit. And, judging by this, it was obvious to Larry that he still *was* a hit – which just proved how wrong Frank Woods had been when he'd insisted that the show was always bigger than the star. And could it be any coincidence that *Star Struck* was reportedly losing viewers? Larry didn't think so, somehow.

Satisfied that he'd seen enough, Keeton now jerked his head for Larry to follow him through to the greenroom, telling him as they walked that they had received confirmations from most of the targets they were after.

'We'll probably have a few no-shows,' he concluded, pouring two coffees from the urn and carrying them over to an empty table. 'But I'm expecting most of them to turn up, so I'm not overly concerned about losing the odd one.'

Frowning, because it hadn't even occurred to him that somebody might *not* turn up, Larry tore open a sachet of sugar and tipped it into his cup. He hoped to God they all *did*, though, because no criminals meant no show – putting him right back where he'd started. *Nowhere.*

Answering Larry's unspoken fears as he poured three sachets of sugar into his own cup and stirred it, Keeton said, 'They'll come, or they wouldn't have bothered replying. But even one out of ten would be a result, so, like I say, I'm not worried.'

Taking a pack of Bensons out of his cardi pocket, he passed one to Larry. Then, squinting at him across the table when they'd both lit up, he said, 'Not about them, anyway. But there *is* one we haven't heard back from, and I've got an idea I wanted to run by you.'

'Oh?' Intrigued by the sudden seriousness of Keeton's tone, Larry sat back in his seat.

'Dex Lewis,' Keeton said, his eyes taking on a cold light at the mention of the name. 'If I could get my hands on *him*, I'd happily let the rest of them walk. But we haven't heard back from him since we sent him the ticket, and we sent two follow-up letters warning him that he'll miss his big chance if he doesn't confirm, but still nothing.'

'He's obviously not interested, then,' Larry said simply, wondering why Keeton was bothered about one man if he was so convinced that the rest would come. One more or less wasn't going to make or break the show.

'I *want* him,' Keeton replied darkly, the gleam in his eyes unnerving Larry. 'And this might be my best shot at getting him, so I'm not letting it go without a fight. That's why we've decided to give him the full VIP treatment – which is where *you* come in.'

Peering back at him through the smoke, Larry felt his heart rate step up a pace. Something told him he wasn't going to like this.

'We want you to go to Lewis's house and schmooze him,' Keeton explained, adding quickly, 'but you won't be alone, so there's nothing to worry about. One of my men will be acting as your chauffeur, and I'll have plenty of back-up scattered around the area, so we'll be right on it if there's any trouble.'

'You *are* joking, right?' Larry drew his head back, his brow puckering with concern. 'He must be bad if you're this keen to get him. So what is he? An armed robber, or something?'

'Pardon my French, but Lewis is a cunt,' Keeton said bluntly. 'And the worst kind of cunt at that, because we know he's got his nose in all sorts. But we can never pin him down. He's either got an alibi, or he just isn't where we think he's going to be when we go looking for him. But I've had a tip-off that he's been seen at his mother's place recently.'

'So why don't you just go round there and arrest him?'

'Not that easy,' Keeton muttered, tapping his cigarette agitatedly on the rim of the ashtray. 'It's not his house for starters, so we'd have a problem getting a warrant to enter when all we've got to go on is hearsay. Anyway, the mother's as bad as him, so she'd hide him down her knickers if she thought he'd fit. And even if we got in and found Lewis there he's guaranteed to kick off and I can't put my lads in danger, because he seriously injured a couple of them last time we pulled him – and only got fourteen months for the privilege, which is nothing for someone who's spent half their life behind bars.'

Eyebrows creeping steadily upwards, Larry gazed at the inspector in disbelief. He didn't want to endanger his own men, but it was all right to sacrifice Larry?

'You don't seriously think I'm going to agree to this, do you?' he croaked when Keeton looked back at him expectantly. 'Can you imagine what would happen if my face got damaged? I'd never work again.'

Assuring him that he wouldn't be in the same danger as his men would be, Keeton said, 'One thing you've got to understand about criminals . . . they might hate uniforms, but they *love* being associated with fame, 'cos they all think they're fucking superstars already. And in their own little underworlds I suppose they are, which is why they get away with so much, because no one will dare grass them up. But if someone like *you* gets in with Lewis, he'll be your best mate – I guarantee it.'

'Er, I'm not sure I want a best mate like that.' Larry gave a nervous little laugh. 'Anyway, if he hasn't responded to the letters, he's obviously not interested, so I can't see me making any difference.'

Peering at him across the table, Keeton said, 'I honestly think you would. And I'm not just saying that because I want you to do it – I'm saying it because I know you'd walk it.'

Flattered that the inspector seemed to have such faith in him, Larry sat back in his seat and exhaled loudly. The sensible, life-preserving part of his brain was screaming at him to say an emphatic no. But, perversely, the same terror was weaving a seductive spell on the rest of his body, giving him a tingling sensation of excitement at the thought of being involved in something so dangerous. It would make for shit-hot TV if he pulled it off. And why wouldn't he? He was Larry Logan.

*Which was precisely why he shouldn't even be thinking about it.*

Watching Larry for a good few minutes and seeing the emotions – from terror to excitement to panic – flicking through his eyes, Keeton said, 'Look, I can see you're not sure about this, so I'm going to lay it on the line. Truth is, if I thought it would work I'd steam into his mother's place and take him out. But even if we got the warrant, we'd need so many men to tackle him, everyone in Manchester would know we were there before we got out of the van, and he'd be on his way to Spain before we got through the door. That's why I need *you*.'

Stubbing out his burned-down cigarette, Larry shifted uncomfortably in his seat, wishing that Keeton would quit staring at him.

Taking the hint, Keeton finished his coffee and slid his sleeve back to look at his watch.

'Right, well, I'd best go and see how Terri's getting on.' Standing up, he looked down at Larry with a hopeful smile, saying, 'No pressure, son, but I'd appreciate it if you'd think it over and let me know as soon as, so I can shuffle a few things around. Okay?'

'What's Lewis done?' Larry asked, folding his arms defiantly to let Keeton know that he'd by no means decided yet.

Pursing his lips, Keeton looked down at him, weighing up

how much he should actually reveal, given that Larry was, in effect, just an ordinary member of the public. But he needed his cooperation right now, and if that meant telling him things that he was not really entitled to know, so be it.

'We're after him for jumping bail on a charge of TDA at the moment,' he said.

'Is that all?' Larry frowned, sure that TDA was something to do with cars. 'Bloody hell, the way you were talking, I thought he was a drugs baron, or a mass murderer, or something.'

'That's all we've actually got on him at the moment,' Keeton admitted. 'Which is another reason why it's not worth trying to get a warrant for his mum's place, because there's no real justification for heavy-handedness on a minor charge like that. I honestly couldn't tell you how many more things he's done and got away with, though – but it's a fair bet they involved violence, because that's the kind of guy he is. We've pulled him for numerous violent incidents in the past, but he must have some sort of charm hanging over him, because he always manages to get off more lightly than he deserves.'

Gazing back at him, Larry sensed that the inspector's interest in Lewis was far more personal than professional. Keeton obviously hated the guy and would do anything to put him away – no matter who he had to sacrifice to achieve it, apparently.

'Look, our powers have increased since the last time we had our hands on him,' Keeton told him now. 'And if I can just get hold of him for long enough to get a DNA sample, I'm sure it will lead us to something more serious than the TDA. You'd be doing me and the rest of Manchester a huge favour if you helped me,' he said now, gazing down at Larry earnestly. 'And I'd stake my reputation that you'd be in no danger. But it's your decision, so just think it over and let me know one way or the other before it gets too late. Okay?'

Nodding, Larry's spirits sank as he watched the inspector walk away. Keeton obviously believed that he could do this or he wouldn't have asked him, and Larry didn't want to disappoint him. But was wanting to please the man a good enough reason for putting himself in danger? He didn't think so.

But then again, if Keeton was to be believed – and he seemed pretty straight to Larry – there wouldn't *be* any danger, so would it really hurt to give it a shot? It *would* be amazing to front it out and be the one who brought this Dex Lewis person to justice.

But there wouldn't be any cameras there to witness Larry's heroism – so would there really be any point?

Christ, what a dilemma!

# 7

Nora Lewis's eyes were narrowed to crinkly slits as she peered at her oldest friend Hilda Jones across the kitchen table. It was only eleven in the morning – hardly the most atmospheric time to have your tea leaves read. But Hilda could turn it on at the flick of a switch, so Nora had thought *What the hell?* when she'd turned up claiming to be on a strong psychic vibe. And, tearing open five of her best pyramid bags, she'd brewed a pot and downed a cup, then let Hilda loose on the dregs.

That had been over an hour ago now, and Hilda's psychic vibe had been one big wash-out. She'd been way off the mark, so far, babbling on about horses and chariots like they were still in the flaming Middle Ages, or something. And if she didn't start coming up with something better than this shite pretty quick, she needn't think she was getting her tenner, because Nora had no intention of shelling out one single penny. If anything, *she*'d be charging Hilda – for all the tea she'd supped since she got here, and the two slabs of cake she'd stuffed into her fat gob.

Keeping her eye on Hilda when the doorbell rang now, Nora yelled, '*Molly! Get the door!*'

Upstairs, in the small bedroom she shared with her mongy little cousin Lyla, Nora's fourteen-year-old granddaughter Molly turned the stereo up a couple of notches, increasing the pounding bass that was already rattling the teeth in Nora's head below. She was sick to death of the lazy old bitch forever yelling at her to come do this and go do that.

'I'll bleedin' swing for her one of these days,' Nora snarled, pushing her sleeves roughly up her arms, revealing the faded blue tattoos of various men's names which swam in and out of the wrinkled flesh. 'Our Dex wants to take a belt to her lazy backside; lying in bed all day like a dog, and out all night doing God knows what. It's a wonder she ain't got ten kiddies sucking her tits off by now, it really is.'

Keeping her opinions to herself as her friend scraped her chair back and grumbled her way out of the room, Hilda waited until she was out of sight. Then she reached over and slid two cigarettes out of the pack that Nora had left on the table. Slipping one into her pocket for later, she lit the other and dangled it from her lips as she poured herself a fresh cuppa from the pot. Nora might well scoff, but Hilda knew what she'd seen, and if her friend had any sense she'd tell their Patrick to get that car shifted off the path before the coppers clocked that it was nicked. And as for that little madam upstairs, Nora would do well to get *her* down to the clinic pronto, because she *was* expecting if Hilda was any judge – and it was anyone's guess what colour it'd be when it popped out, 'cos Hilda had it on good information that Molly Lewis liked her internationals. Horses and chariots: cars and prams. As God was Hilda's witness, Nora Lewis had surprises of a not-so-pleasant nature hurtling her way.

The bell chimed again just as Nora reached for the latch. Wrenching the door open, all set to give whoever it was a ticking-off for being impatient, her jaw dropped when she saw who it was.

'Good bollocking Christ!' she gasped. 'What are *you* doing here?'

Larry was crapping himself but, all too aware that Dave, the sneering police 'chauffeur' who'd driven him here was probably laughing at him from the safety of the limo parked up at the kerb beyond the gate, he swallowed hard and forced himself to smile. At least the woman recognised him, so he didn't have to embarrass himself by doing the whole 'Don't you know who I am?' routine. But whether or not she was pleased to see him was a different matter. And if *she* wasn't pleased, how would Derek Lewis – whose scary mugshot Keeton had shown to him just before he'd left, almost making him change his mind – respond to him calling round un-announced?

Taking a deep breath now, aware that time was pressing on, Larry switched into genial-host mode, and said, 'Good morning, Mrs Lewis . . . Or –' cheesy grin '– should that be *Miss*, because you *must* be Derek's younger sister?'

Laughing out loud, Nora clapped a hand over her mouth, suddenly wishing she'd thought to slot her teeth in. 'Get away with you,' she cackled. 'I've seen you on that show of yours, flirting with all the young lasses. But don't be trying it on me, you bugger, 'cos I'm old enough to be your mam!'

'Me, flirting?' Larry placed a hand on his chest, affecting innocence. 'Never! I just appreciate a beautiful lady, that's all.'

Laughing again, Nora glanced out over his shoulder to see if the neighbours were watching. They were, of course, although most had actually ventured out onto their doorsteps rather than just twitching the nets like they usually did when something was happening over here – which was pretty bloody often, Nora had to admit, although not usually good stuff like this. Larry Logan ringing *her* doorbell, with a bottle of champagne in his hand and a white stretch limo parked outside her gate, with a chauffeur and everything. Would you credit it!

'Is Derek in?' Larry asked now.

'Oh, sorry, pet, he's not,' Nora replied, wondering how on earth her son knew a famous man like this – and why he hadn't bothered telling her about it.

'That's a shame,' Larry murmured, an expression of disappointment on his face despite the raging relief in his heart that he wouldn't have to confront the man. Although, now that he was actually here, he was beginning to suspect that Keeton might have exaggerated the dangers, given that he'd described the mother as being just as bad as her son, when, as far as Larry could tell, she was just a nice old lady.

'What did you want him for?' Nora asked now, lowering her voice because she didn't want the neighbours listening. Eyeballing was one thing, but earwigging on the Lewises' business so they could bandy it about to all and sundry was another matter altogether.

'My new show,' Larry told her, grinning proudly as he added, 'You must have seen the adverts?'

'Oh, aye, 'course,' Nora affirmed. 'Ever so good, they are, too. Looks like it's going to be a much better one than that *Star* thing you used to do. Not that *that* wasn't good,' she added earnestly. 'Highlight of me week, that was – after *Corrie* and *EastEnders*. Oh, and *Emmerdale*, obviously.' Pursing her lips now, she shrugged. 'Don't watch it no more, mind. Can't abide that Matty fella. Too far up his own arse for my liking.'

Larry wanted to kiss her. Instead, he winked and leaned towards her, whispering conspiratorially, 'Don't tell anyone I told you this, but it wasn't his *own* arse he went up to get the job – if you get my drift?'

'Well, I never!' Nora gasped, shaking her head. Then, knowingly, 'Still, it figures he'd be a puff with all that hair. You wouldn't catch none of my lot dead with a mop like that. But they're like you, my lads – nice and respectable. Still, I expect you'll already know that if you know Dex?'

Larry raised an eyebrow. 'Nice' and 'respectable' were hardly the words he'd have used to describe the shaven-headed, mean-eyed thug in the mugshot.

'I haven't actually met him,' he admitted. 'But I was really hoping to – so I don't suppose you'd know where he is, or when he'll be back?'

'No, pet, I don't. Could be ten minutes or ten days, knowing him.' Giving a disappointed shrug, Nora folded her arms – then quickly unfolded them and dragged her sleeves down to cover her tattoos. Larry Logan didn't look the sort to appreciate that kind of thing, and – call her a vain old fool if you liked – she didn't want him going away with the impression that she was some rough old tart.

Just then, one of the kids from the crowd who were watching from the front yard of the house opposite came over to the gate, and yelled, 'Oi, mister . . . you're that Larry Logan off the telly, aren't you? What you doin' round here, then?'

Barking, 'Piss off out of it, you cheeky little bastard – and tell your mam to mind her own business before I mind it for her!' Nora glared at him until he'd fled back to his own side of the road. Turning back to Larry then, she shook her head, saying, 'Sorry about that, pet, but you can't move round here without some bugger knowing where you're going before you get there.'

Shocked by the viciousness of her tone when she'd yelled at the kid and thinking that maybe Keeton *hadn't* been exaggerating, after all, Larry gave her an uncertain smile. 'Sorry . . . I didn't mean to cause a disturbance.'

Assuring him that it wasn't his fault, Nora stepped back into the hallway and jerked her head at him, saying, 'Come in and have a cuppa while you're waiting. I'll give our Dex a ring on his mobile.'

Reluctant to enter the lion's den, Larry glanced at his watch, and said, 'That's very kind of you, Mrs Lewis, but I really haven't got time.'

''Course you have,' she insisted, already setting off up the hall. 'You'd have been here longer than this if he'd been in, 'cos he can talk the bollocks off a dog, him.'

Turning, Larry gave the police officer a helpless shrug. Then he followed her inside.

The hallway was jam-packed with stacks of cardboard boxes, the top ones of which were open, revealing that they were full of car stereos and SatNav systems. Guessing – correctly – that they were stolen, Larry edged past them, terrified of leaving his fingerprints on anything.

Following Nora into the kitchen, he nodded at the woman who was sitting at the table. She was of a similar age to Nora but, unlike Nora who was wearing no make-up and had obviously never put a bottle of dye anywhere near her wispy grey hair, this woman had a full face of slap, and vivid orange hair which clashed horrendously with the crimson lipstick smeared over her flabby mouth.

Giving her friend a gummy grin, Nora said, 'Look who's called to see our Dex, Hilda . . . It's only Larry Logan.'

'I know who he is,' Hilda replied tartly, irritated that Nora was trying to make out like she was stupid, or something. 'What's he want with *him*, though?'

Telling her to mind her beeswax, Nora switched the kettle on, then grabbed the floor brush and gave the ceiling a couple of whacks. Tutting when the pounding music went up in volume yet again, she said, 'Sorry about this, Larry. Just give me a minute to shut her up, and I'll get you that tea.'

Taking another cigarette from Nora's pack when they were alone, Hilda lit up and gave Larry a sickly smile. 'So, you're here for their Dex, are you?' she asked, in her best posh voice.

'Er, yeah, that's right,' Larry said, wincing when the sound of raised voices came from above. 'Hope I haven't got anyone into trouble.'

'Oh, they're always like that,' Hilda assured him, flapping her hand dismissively. 'So, what do you want with him, then? You and he friends, are you?'

Repeating what he'd already told Nora about not having

met Dex yet, Larry followed the sound of running footsteps across the ceiling with his eyes.

Before Hilda could pry any further, a far younger, prettier version of Nora, with long honey-blonde hair, and large breasts which strained at the tight blouse she was just about wearing, burst into the kitchen and gaped at Larry as if she couldn't believe her eyes.

'My God, it *is* you, an' all! Me nan said you was here, but I didn't believe her. Jeezus! Wait till me mates hear about this!'

'Never mind your bloody mates,' Nora snapped, coming back into the room and shoving the girl out of the way. 'And don't even think about ringing none of 'em up and having me house filled up liked a flaming doss-house – 'cos he's here to see your dad, not you and your mates.'

'Me dad?' Molly's pretty brow creased with disbelief. 'What d'y' want *him* for?'

'Have *none* of you got the manners you was born with?' Nora snapped, putting her hands on her hips. 'If he wants to see your dad, it's *his* business. And I don't see why you're all so surprised, anyway, 'cos my Derek's as good as anyone else.'

Muttering, 'Yeah, *right!*' Molly continued to eye Larry with curiosity. 'You haven't come for a weed, have you?' she asked suddenly – squealing with shock when she got a resounding slap across the face from Nora, whose hand shot out with a speed that was totally at odds with her elderly appearance.

'Idiot!' Nora hissed, her eyes flashing with a look that Larry would have mistaken for hate if it hadn't been her own granddaughter she was directing it at.

Holding her cheek, which was smarting enough to have brought tears to her eyes, Molly's nostrils flared. But she kept her mouth shut. If anyone else had pulled a stunt like that she'd have kicked the living crap out of them, but she'd never dare raise a hand to her nan, because she knew what she'd get off her dad and his brothers if she did. Nora was a nasty, spiteful old cow, but her lads treated her like the bloody Queen Mother, and woe betide anyone who crossed her.

'Kettle's boiled,' Nora said now, jerking her thumb at Molly to go and finish making the teas. Sitting down, she reached for her cigarettes and slid one out of the pack. Narrowing her eyes when she saw how many were left, she gave Hilda an accusing look. 'You been helping yourself to my fags?'

Blushing, Hilda shook her head, her gaze flicking guiltily to Larry. ''Course not. You know I always ask first.'

'So what's that?' Nora indicated the cigarette Hilda was holding. 'Scotch mist?'

'You gave me this,' Hilda lied, praying that Larry wouldn't contradict her. Nora would kick her out in a heartbeat if he did, and she didn't want to miss out on this celebrity visit.

Grunting, 'I don't remember giving you nowt, but even if I did, you wanna try buying some for a change, 'cos I'm sick of you scrounging off me all the time,' Nora handed a cigarette to Larry without bothering to ask if he smoked.

Taking it because he sensed that she'd be offended if he didn't, Larry gave Hilda a tiny, sympathetic smile as he reached into his pocket for his lighter.

'Ooh, that's nice,' Nora said when she saw it. 'Look at this, Molly. Isn't it nice?'

'Yeah, it's lovely,' Molly agreed, folding her arms and giving Larry a shy smile.

'Have it,' he said, feeling sorry for her. 'I've got another one at home.'

'Don't be daft,' Nora protested. 'She don't need no fancy lighter.'

'I want her to have it,' Larry insisted, handing it to Molly over Nora's head, amused by the glint of envy in the older woman's eyes. Served her right for smacking the girl around the face like that.

The front door opened just then, rattling the glasses and cups that were standing on the draining board when it slammed shut again.

'You seen that car outside, Mam?' a man's voice called out as heavy footsteps headed their way. 'Looks like someone's getting married, or something. Can't be none of these cunts round here, though, 'cos none of 'em could afford a bleedin' chauffeur.'

Giving Larry a conspiratorial grin, oblivious to the fact that his heart was pounding with fear in his chest as he prepared to come face to face with Dex, Nora whispered, 'Watch when he sees you sitting here. He'll have a fit.'

Hoping to *God* that she didn't mean 'fit' in the bad sense, Larry tensed as the man walked into the room.

'The driver best not get out for a piss, though, 'cos I'll have them wheels off in a flash.' Still talking, Patrick Lewis shrugged out of his jacket and hung it on the back of the door. 'They cost about a grand each, them, so I'd easy get a couple of ton apiece. And them wing mir—' Noticing Larry just then, he stopped dead in his tracks and stared at him.

Still grinning, Nora waited for the light of recognition to enter her son's eyes. When it didn't after a moment, she said, 'You know who it is, don't you?'

'Seen him somewhere,' Patrick murmured. Then, clicking his fingers, 'Larry Logan! Christ, mate! Nice to meet you.' Reaching for Larry's hand, he pumped it firmly. 'Shit, man, I never expected to find a star sitting in me kitchen, I can tell you *that* for nowt! That your motor outside, is it?'

Giving a sheepish shrug when the man finally let go of his hand, Larry said, 'It belongs to the studio, actually, but they let me use it for special occasions.'

'And *this* is a special occasion? Popping in for a cuppa

with me mother?' Patrick grinned. 'Bloody hell, Mam, you're coming up in the world, ain't you? What you done to deserve this, then? Been doing secret charity work on the side, or something?'

'He's come to see our Dex,' Nora told him, getting up to finish making the tea which Molly, who was leaning back against the sink still staring at Larry, seemed to have forgotten about.

'Dex?' Patrick repeated, frowning now. 'What d'y' want with *him*?'

Wondering why Nora hadn't told *this* one to mind his own business like she had everyone else so far, Larry cleared his throat, and said, 'He, er, applied to be a contestant on my new show. And he got through, but he didn't reply to confirm his place when we wrote to him, so I've been sent to give him the good news in person.'

'You've *got* to be kidding me,' Patrick snorted. 'I didn't even know he could *write*!'

'Don't be cheeky,' Nora scolded, carrying the teas over to the table and placing Larry's down in front of him. 'Our Derek's very smart. He's the only one of you buggers who came out of school with certificates, anyhow.'

'For *swimming*,' Patrick reminded her scathingly. Rolling his eyes at Larry now, he pulled a chair out from under the table and sat down. 'So what's this show our kid's entered himself for?'

'It's called *Gotcha!*' Larry explained, wishing that Terri had chosen a better title because this one *still* sounded shit. 'It's just a regular type of game show, really. Contestants answer different categories of questions through three rounds, knocking each other out along the way until there's only two left.'

'Sounds just like your other show, that.'

'Kind of, but there's a twist at the end when the last two

go head to head. Instead of just answering straight questions at that point, they have to convince their opponents that they know the answer even if they don't. And the one who makes the other one fold is the winner.'

Mulling this over for a moment, Patrick said, 'I'm sure I've seen something like that before with Ant and Dec. Sounds all right, though. And our Dex would be pretty good at it if it's a case of blagging your way through, 'cos he can bullshit like no one on Earth, him.'

'He's certainly got the gift of the gab,' Nora agreed, quickly adding for Larry's benefit: 'But he's not malicious with it. He's just a bit of a joker, that's all.'

Exchanging a wry smirk with Molly, Patrick said, 'When's he on, then? 'Cos I'll have to get all the lads round for a laugh.'

'Actually, we're filming it today,' Larry told him. 'But it won't be shown over here just yet, because it's only a pilot at this stage.'

'A what?'

'A kind of practice run – to see if it gets a good enough response to merit commissioning a full series,' Larry explained. 'It'll only be broadcast in the States to start with,' he went on, the disappointment in his voice genuine as he added, 'Bit of a bummer for me, because I could really do with getting back on my feet over here. But it will be good for the contestants, because there's a good chance they'll get a fee for agreeing to let it be shown over there.'

'You mean the jammy twat will get paid even if he doesn't win?'

'Absolutely.'

'And what if he *does* win?'

'Twenty grand, and – potentially – a Range Rover Sports with full body kit.'

'No way!' Patrick gasped. 'Are you shitting me?'

Smiling, Larry said, 'No, I'm not *shitting* you. We want the pilot to be as good as, if not better than the real show.' Shaking his head when Nora offered him another cigarette, he took out his own pack and offered these round instead, saying, 'We knew the contestants would be disappointed about not seeing themselves on TV over here, so we decided to throw in the car to soften the blow – *and* to make us look better, of course. You know what those Yanks are like for having to have everything bigger and better than anyone else. We're pretty sure it'll be a hit, though, because we've been careful to choose only big characters for the pilot – like your Derek.'

'I wish *I*'d known about it,' Patrick said disappointedly. 'I'd be great on something like that, me. Any chance of getting me on instead of him, or what?'

Giving him a mock-regretful smile, Larry shook his head. 'Sorry, not this time. But you can always apply for the proper show – *if* it gets commissioned.'

'Oh, it's bound to,' Nora piped up confidently. 'What, with you *and* our Dex on this pilot? It'll be bloody marvellous.'

'Mmm,' Larry murmured, glancing pointedly at his watch. 'Only if we can find him in the next hour and make sure he hasn't changed his mind about appearing.'

'Oh, bloody hell,' Nora said, looking around for the phone. 'I said I'd ring him, didn't I? Got a head like a flaming sieve, me.' Clicking her fingers at Molly now, she pointed at the phone on the ledge and told her to pass it over. Tapping in the number, she listened for a moment, then tutted loudly. 'Switched off.'

'Oh, dear,' Larry said, as if he was really disappointed. 'Be such a shame if he misses the deadline and loses out on the chance to win that twenty grand.'

'*And* the car,' Patrick reminded him.

'He won't go for it,' Molly said quietly, startling Larry because he'd forgotten she was still here.

'Don't be thick,' Patrick sneered. ''Course he will, or he wouldn't have applied.'

'I don't think he *did* apply,' Molly persisted, looking at Nora now. 'Come on, Nan . . . can *you* honestly see me dad sending off for something like that?'

'Summat like what?' Dex Lewis asked, striding in through the back door just then.

Stomach flipping at the sight of him, Larry swallowed hard and prayed that Nora and the others would protect him if Dex went for his throat. Because the man was absolutely enormous, with the broadest shoulders Larry had ever seen, and the thickest, most muscular thighs.

Standing behind his brother's chair now, Dex peered down at Larry with dark, unreadable eyes. Giving an upward jerk of his chin after a moment, he said, 'You who I think you are?'

'Er, I don't know,' Larry replied, his face frozen in a grin as he made an effort to stop shaking. 'Depends if you're thinking along the lines of Brad Pitt or Leonardo Di Caprio. Common enough mistake, either way.'

Giving a tiny, crooked smile, Dex slid the hood down off his head, revealing a closely shaved map of battle-trophy scars. 'What you doing round here, then?'

Laughing, because it was the first thing everybody had asked so far when they'd seen Larry, Nora got up and went to pour Dex a cup of tea, telling him over her shoulder, 'He's come to give you the surprise of your bloody life, that's what. And if you didn't keep switching your bloody phone off all the time, you'd have known, wouldn't you, 'cos I'd have told you.'

'Oh aye?' Taking her vacated seat and helping himself to one of her cigarettes, Dex peered at Larry with curiosity. 'What's going on, then?'

'You've been picked to go on that new show of his,' Patrick

blurted out before Larry had a chance to open his mouth. 'Twenty grand and a kitted-out Range Rover Sports, and all you've got to do is blag some fucker that you know the answer to a question even if you don't.'

'I've been picked?' Dex frowned suspiciously. 'From what?'

'From the application you sent in,' Patrick reminded him, grinning as he added, 'Bet you thought we wouldn't find out, didn't you, you crafty shite? Scared I'd go in for it an' all and beat you, were you?'

His gaze still fixed on Larry, Dex pursed his lips and shook his head. 'I didn't enter for nothing.'

'*Told* you,' Molly declared, giving Nora a triumphant look. No one knew her dad better than she did – and she didn't care *who* they thought they were.

Ignoring her, Nora said, 'You sure, son? You don't reckon you might have done it when you was a bit –' pausing, she cast a surreptitious glance at Larry before adding '– *drunk?*'

Knowing full well that she meant stoned, Dex shook his head. You forgot a lot of shit when you caned as much weed as he did, but not something like this.

Flapping her hand, Nora said, 'Oh, well, whatever. You liked his other show when you and me used to watch it, didn't you?'

'I only watched it with you 'cos you was sick and I was looking after you,' Dex muttered, hoping that Larry didn't get the impression that he was a fan, or anything, because that would be too fucking gay for words. 'But I still didn't enter myself for nothing.' Turning to Larry now, he said, 'No offence, mate, but it ain't my kind of thing.'

'Are you off your *head?*' Patrick piped up. 'You could win twenty grand and a Range Rover *Sports*. Addy would bite our *hands* off for one of them! Shit, man, we could send it straight to the Dam without involving him, 'cos we wouldn't even have to worry about the paperwork. We'd be minted.'

'*We?*' Turning his head slowly, Dex gave his brother one of the coldest stares Larry had ever seen. 'I didn't hear no mention of *your* name, so how comes you're trying to claim a slice?'

'I was only saying,' Patrick muttered sulkily. 'No need to bite me head off.'

Afraid that Dex would turn on him next, Larry almost jumped out of his skin when his mobile began to ring in his pocket. Hands shaking, he pulled it out and glanced at the screen. Seeing the name 'Inky', which told him that it was Inspector Keeton checking that everything was all right, he bit his lip then switched it off. He was having enough trouble keeping up the pretence without having to chat to a policeman in front of these people as well. He just hoped that Keeton didn't take it as a sign of trouble and come rushing in, because Larry was sitting too close to Dex for comfort, and was bound to be first in the firing line if he kicked off.

Everybody was peering at him when he glanced up again, curious to know why he'd ignored the call. Thinking on his feet, he shrugged, and said, 'My producer. She'll only be bugging me to see if I've had any luck with Derek, but she can wait till I get back to the studio. No point embarrassing myself having you guys hearing me get an ear-bashing.' Grinning sheepishly now, he stood up. 'Anyway, thanks for your hospitality, Mrs Lewis, but I'd best get moving.' Then, smiling at the rest of them, 'Nice meeting you all. And I'm sorry it didn't work out, Derek, but you know where we are if you change your mind.'

'Do I?' Dex looked amused. 'And how's that, then? 'Cos I sure as hell ain't psychic.'

Reminding him that the phone number was on the letters they'd sent him, Larry saw the blank look in his eyes and frowned. 'Don't tell me you didn't get them? Christ, no wonder you didn't know what I was talking about.' Exhaling wearily now, he ran a hand through his hair. 'We sent you the gold ticket to let you know that you were through, and then wrote twice after that asking you to confirm that you were coming. I can't *believe* you didn't get them. And here's me, turning up with the car, expecting you to hop right in it and come to the studio with me.'

'You know what?' Dex said thoughtfully. 'I *did* get something gold the other week, but I thought it was one of them "You've won the Dutch lottery" bollocks, so I binned it. Don't remember getting any letters, though.'

'Did they come in official envelopes?' Nora asked Larry now. 'Only, if they did, he'd have binned them an' all, knowing him.'

'I'm not sure,' Larry admitted. 'But I wish I'd thought to check, because I'm exactly the same. I got so many bloody solicitors' letters and what-have-you when I was going through all that shit last year, I just stopped opening them in the end.'

'We heard about that,' Nora said sympathetically. 'But we never believed none of it. Everyone likes a drink or two, but that don't make them an alkie. And as for all that stuff with the lass, it was obvious what *she* was after from the start. But even if you *had* done something with her, she was old enough, so it was no one's business but yours and hers.'

'Christ, *I*'d have given it one if she was offering it up to me on a plate,' Patrick chipped in with a dirty chuckle. 'I was more surprised that you *didn't*, to tell you the truth.'

'She wasn't my type,' Larry muttered, sickened by the lustful look in the other man's eyes. 'Anyway, I got tons of stick from the pigs, threatening me with this, that and the other even though I'd been proved innocent, and I got so sick of it I stopped opening my letters – which isn't the smartest thing I've ever done, because I've just had the biggest nightmare trying to sort out all the bills I ignored. I've got those bastards down at the police station to thank for that, and I wouldn't mind but they made most of it up.'

'You don't need to tell us about the pigs,' Patrick sneered. 'We know all about them in this house—'

'Maybe we do, but we don't need to bore Larry with the details,' Dex interrupted, giving Patrick a warning glare before he started blabbing all their personal dodgy business to the world and his wife. Turning to Larry now, he said, 'One thing, though, mate . . . who gave you my name? And how did you know to come here looking for me?'

Shaking now, sure that Dex was about to rumble him and kick the teeth right out of his mouth – or worse – Larry frowned. 'Well, I thought *you* did when you sent in the application form, but obviously not if you don't know anything about it. Maybe one of your mates did it for a laugh?' he suggested. 'Shame they didn't let you in on it, though, because the laugh would have been on them when you walked out with the money and the car. And, between you and me, I think you'd have stood a really good chance of winning. But if you don't want to do it, you don't want to do it, so I won't try and persuade you.'

Giving Dex a disapproving glare, Nora got up and came around the table to Larry. Patting him on the arm, she said, 'I am sorry, pet. I do hope we haven't ruined it for you.'

''Course not,' he assured her. 'And it's *me* who should be apologising – for turning up unannounced like this. You must think I'm a right pushy so-and-so.'

'We most certainly do not!' Nora protested earnestly. 'I've bloody loved having you here – we all have. And it's given them nosy buggers out there something to gossip about, an' all.' She jerked her thumb towards the door. 'I'd have *paid* you to come round if I'd known what a fuss it'd cause. I'll be like flaming royalty round here after this.'

Winking at her, Larry squeezed her hand and thanked her

again. Then, picking up the champagne which had been sitting on the table the whole time, he handed it to Dex, saying, 'This was for you – to celebrate you coming on the show. But I guess you might as well have it anyway – compensation for me bending your ear when you didn't even know what I was talking about.'

Taking it, Dex handed it to Molly to put into the fridge. Holding out his hand then, he said, 'Cheers, mate. And any time you need a favour, you know where I am, yeah?'

Feeling the power of the other man vibrating through his body as they shook hands, Larry remembered Keeton's warning about Dex becoming his new best friend and felt an overwhelming urge to run for his life before the Lewises sucked him any deeper into their murky little world.

Showing him out a few seconds later, Nora stepped out onto the path and pulled the door to behind her. Glancing back at the house to make sure that no one was spying, she took Larry's arm and walked him to the gate, whispering, 'How long have you got before he needs to be there, pet? Only I was thinking, it seems a shame for him to miss out just because he wasn't ready. Specially after you went to all this trouble to fetch the car over for him, an' that.'

'It's not a problem,' Larry assured her, wishing she'd let go of his arm so that he could escape. 'We start filming at two, but we'll just rejig it so the stand-in takes his place.'

'But I don't want you to do that,' Nora said, peering up at him. 'I want my Dex to go in for it. I don't care who entered him for it, and I know you said it won't even get shown over here, but at least I'll know he's been on telly for something good, won't I?'

Feeling bad for lying to her, Larry smiled down at Nora guiltily. She'd obviously had to adopt the hard-as-nails approach to survive amongst the scum who lived around her, but there was no denying how dedicated she was to her family.

It saddened him that she was so desperate for at least *one* of them to make something of themselves.

'Can you wait?' she asked now, her eyes pleading with him. 'If you're not filming till two, you've got time to hang on here for another few minutes, haven't you – give me a chance to work on him; see if I can't make him change his mind.'

'I don't know,' Larry murmured, biting his lip. 'I really should be getting back.'

'Please?' Nora tightened her grip on his arm.

Feeling the sharpness of her gnarly old nails through his jacket, Larry winced. Nodding, he said, 'Okay. I shouldn't really, but I suppose I can wait ten minutes.'

Reaching up, Nora pinched his cheek and gave him a gummy grin. 'Thanks, pet. I owe you one.'

Watching as she waddled back up the path, Larry opened the gate and strolled to the limo.

'Well?' Dave asked, peering at him in the rear-view mirror when he slid onto the back seat. 'Was he there?'

'Not at first, but he came in the back way just after I went in,' Larry told him, snatching one of the bottles of alcohol out of the rack and twisting the lid off. Taking a long swig, he grimaced when he realised it was brandy, not Scotch.

'*And . . . ?*' Dave persisted impatiently. 'Did he go for it, or what?'

'Not exactly,' Larry admitted. Then, relaying what had happened about Dex not receiving the letters and saying he wasn't interested, he said, 'But his mum reckons she can persuade him to change his mind, so I said we'd give him ten minutes. That's all right, isn't it?'

'I'd wait all fucking day if it meant getting my hands on that bastard,' Dave snarled, glancing at the house now as he reached for the radio to let Inspector Keeton know what was happening.

★

Back inside the house, Hilda was busy telling Dex that she'd go in for that show if she were him, because he was guaranteed to win.

'Oh aye?' he sneered. 'And who told you that, then? One of your spirit guides? Big Chief Knock-on-the-fucking-'ead!'

'I seen it in the tea, smart-arse,' she informed him tartly, changing her previous interpretation to fit the new situation. 'Horses and chariots – gift-horses and cars. As God is me witness, you'll regret turning your nose up at this chance, 'cos you'll be losing out on a—'

'Belt up, you!' Nora snapped, coming back into the room just then. 'I've listened to enough of your bloody shite to last me a lifetime.'

'I'm only telling him what I saw,' Hilda protested. 'And you can't deny it's what I said, can you? And you can't get much closer to the mark than that.'

Casting a scathing glance in Hilda's direction, Dex said, 'Can't you tell her to sling it, Mam? She does me head in, coming round every bleedin' day talking shit.'

'Oi!' Nora scolded, giving him a slap on the back of the head. 'Don't be so bloody rude, you. Do I complain about *your* mates?'

'No, but *my* mates don't talk to dead people or look like fucking clowns,' Dex retorted, chuckling softly.

Adopting a martyred air – secretly loving that her friend had defended her against her precious son – Hilda said, 'Don't mind him, Nora, love. If he don't want to know that the tea's urging him towards riches, that's his business.'

Sharing a piss-taking smirk with Patrick, Dex said, 'So, what's this week's lottery numbers, then, Hilda? Only if the tea wants me to be rich, I might as well go straight for the biggie, eh?'

'It doesn't work like that, *actually*,' Hilda informed him primly. 'I'm not meant to know things like that, because my gift is to help others, not to bring me personal gain.'

'Who said I was gonna *share* it with you?' Dex snorted, finishing his tea and shoving his cup towards her. 'Go on . . . knock yourself out.'

'Mock if you must,' Hilda said wearily, pushing the cup back across the table to him. 'But I know what I saw, and it's your lookout if you want to ignore it.'

'You wanna watch yourself,' Patrick told her. 'They *drown* people like you.'

Laughing, Dex said, 'Yeah, but usually at birth, not this close to death.'

'Pack it in,' Nora muttered, superstitiously crossing herself because she was actually a few years older than Hilda and was terrified by the thought of dying any time soon.

Sparking the single-skin spliff he'd rolled while she was showing Larry out, Dex sat back in his seat and peered up at his mother with a questioning smile on his lips.

'What?' Frowning, Nora turned a full circle, like a dog seeking its own tail. 'What you looking at me like that for?'

'Just wondering how come it took you so long to see Logan out, that's all. Sure you weren't setting up a date with him?'

'Don't be so bloody soft!' she snapped, giving him a clip round the ear.

Chuckling softly, Dex leaned back in his chair and blew smoke rings into the air, aiming them at the fire alarm to see if he could set it off and really wind her up. She had a razor blade for a tongue, his mother, but she was a soft-hearted old bird when it came to her boys, and he'd always been her favourite.

Temper dissolving as suddenly as it had come on, Nora reached for a cigarette, wondering how to bring Dex round to the idea of going on Larry's show while making him think it had been his own decision. Gazing off into the distance now, she said, 'Aw, but he's a lovely lad, though, isn't he?

Beautiful skin, and *gorgeous* hair. Did you see it how shiny it was? Proper expensive cut an' all, that was.'

'Behave,' Dex snorted. 'Why am I gonna be checking out another bloke's fucking hair?'

'I wasn't talking to *you*, I was talking to our Molly and Hilda,' Nora informed him, using her free hand to sweep the bits of tobacco and weed that he and Patrick had spilled on the table onto the floor. 'Anyway, I don't see what you've got to be so sarcastic about. I notice you didn't object to him giving you that champagne, did you? And he didn't have to, you know – not after you went and wrecked his chances of sorting his life out. All he wanted was for you to help him out,' she went on, sighing heavily now. 'But you couldn't do that for him, could you, you selfish sod? No. You've got to send him away with a flea in his ear – snatching the bottle out of his hand on his way out the door!'

Looking up at her, Dex shook his head and said, 'You don't half talk crap sometimes, Mam. He's lucky he's *got* another show after the way he fucked up his last one.'

'That weren't his fault, as you well know,' Nora countered defensively. 'And don't tell me you've never done nothing wrong, 'cos I'll eat me bloody frying pan if you're trying to deny all the stunts *you*'ve pulled over the years.'

'Make us a bacon butty first, though, eh?' Dex shot back, grinning now. 'Me belly feels like me throat's been cut.'

'Should've thought about that when you was busy turning your nose up at twenty grand,' Nora muttered, folding her arms. 'You could have hired yourself a maid to make your sodding butties with that, couldn't you?'

'Got three of them already,' Dex quipped, winking at Molly.

'Don't be including *me* in that,' Molly grunted, snapping out of her daydreams and pocketing the lighter that Larry had given her in case her dad spotted it and took it off her. 'I'm no man's slave, me.'

'Get her,' Nora sniped. 'Anyone would think she was someone special.'

'She is,' Dex said proudly. 'And let me catch any cunt treating her any different when she starts dating, and they'll soon know about it.'

Tutting softly, Nora shook her head. *When* she starts dating, indeed. For a man who claimed to be so smart, his eyes and ears were shut tight when it came to that girl. But if he didn't open them quick-smart, Molly was going to end up just like her whore of a mother – and God only knew what Dex would do then, because he couldn't put *her* in hospital like he had Jane, that was for sure. Not that Jane didn't deserve it, though, for grassing him up to the coppers like that, and all because she'd caught him in bed with another lass. Some women were just too damn precious for their own good. Couldn't accept that they weren't the entire universe with jam on, and freaked out when their man fancied a change of menu. But Jane had messed with the wrong one trying to put their Derek on a short leash – and messed with him even worse by throwing her hand in with the pigs over him. And dropping her knickers for his so-called mate the minute his cell door banged shut behind him had been her biggest mistake of all – the treacherous slut.

'Don't you reckon he should go in for it, Mam?' Patrick asked suddenly, interrupting her thoughts – and earning himself a rare pat on the head from her for unwittingly helping her out.

Adopting a weary expression now, Nora sighed and flapped her hands, saying, 'Aye, I do, son. But it's his decision, not ours, and he don't want to do it.'

'Yeah, but look at all that money he's missing out on,' Patrick persisted. 'If it was me, I'd go for it like a shot.'

'Specially when you know he's gonna win,' Hilda interjected, getting dirty looks from everyone for interfering in family business.

'I don't want to do it,' Dex told them – slowly, to make sure they got the point. 'In case you've forgotten, I'm on the run – so how smart is it going to look if I go and splash me face all over the telly? The pigs would be all over me like a rash.'

'But no one would even see you over here,' Nora pointed out. 'It's a pilot, and it's only being shown in America.'

'She's right,' Patrick affirmed, telling his brother exactly what Larry had told them before he'd come in. 'So, there's no danger of you getting nabbed because of it,' he concluded. 'And you won't just get the money and the car – you'll get paid for going on the show, an' all.'

'You sure about that?' Dex asked, frowning thoughtfully. 'The last time I saw Logan, he was live on that crap charity thing. I thought this would be the same.'

'No, it's definitely not being shown here,' Nora told him, reaffirming what Patrick had said. 'That's what he told us – isn't it, Molly?'

Shrugging when her dad looked at her, Molly said, 'That's what he said, yeah. But I didn't think you'd go for something like that, Dad. Not exactly *cool*, is it?'

'Who cares about cool?' Patrick sneered. 'No one's gonna see you, and just think what we can do with that kind of money, man. If you win, we export the car and pocket the money along with the twenty grand. Lose, we just find out where the winner lives and do the fucker over. It's a total win-win situation.'

'I don't know,' Dex murmured, relighting his spliff.

Refusing to let it go if there was even the slightest chance of making his brother change his mind, Patrick said, 'Come on, Dex . . . this is the best chance we're ever gonna get to make some serious money and get ourselves out of this shit-hole. Even if it's only a month in Spain, or something, I don't care. I just want to be able to pay off my debts and chill for a bit. And you can have your tattoos lasered off so you'll be less recognisable next time you get pulled.'

'I'm not *gonna* get pulled, and the tats are going nowhere,' Dex snapped.

'You should invest in a nice toupee,' Hilda told him. 'I know you lads say you like it short, but that's just an excuse because you're going thin, isn't it? You'll look like that man off the telly soon, if you're not careful – him what has that daft bit combed over the top what lifts up in the wind.'

'Don't talk to my dad like that,' Molly snapped indignantly. 'If anyone needs a new wig, it's *you*, 'cos you've probably got all sorts living in that mess of yours.'

Wanting to keep Dex's mind on the subject at hand, Nora told Molly to button it, then said, 'What d'y' reckon, son?'

Shrugging, he said, 'Our Pat should do it instead, seeing as you all think it's such a good idea.'

'They won't let me or I would,' Patrick told him, his eyes showing how much he'd have loved to do exactly that. 'It's you or nothing, our kid. You're the only one who can give me mam a better life – and God knows she deserves it after all the shit she's put up with off us over the years.'

Frowning at him, Nora said, 'All right, no need to lay it on so thick.' Then, back to Dex: 'Your decision, son, but you'd make me *that* proud if you did it, you really would.'

Reaching out when she took a tissue out of her pocket and dabbed at her eyes, Dex put his arm around her waist and gave her a hug. 'Don't start blubbing, you dozy auld cow. I'd do it for you if I could, but it's too late now, 'cos he's gone, isn't he? And I don't know where they're doing the filming.'

Smiling, Nora looked down at him. 'You'd really do it for me?'

'Too right.' He winked at her. 'I don't usually agree with our kid, but he's right about this – you *do* deserve something good after all the shit we've put you through.'

'Good,' Nora said, all trace of teariness gone now. ''Cos he's waiting outside. You'd best get a move on, though, 'cos he won't be there for much longer.'

'You kidding me?'

'Do I look like I'm kidding? Now, get yourself up the stairs and put something nice on, 'cos I'm not having you going on telly in your scruffs and showing me up – even if I won't get to see it.'

Laughing, amused that he'd just been manipulated by the crafty old girl, Dex stood up and went to do as he was told.

'Result!' Patrick crowed, jumping up and giving his mother a kiss. 'Just wait till he comes back in that Range Rover, Mam. Then you really *will* be proud!'

'Horses and chariots,' Hilda piped up, her face a picture of smug satisfaction.

Too excited to be annoyed with her, Nora took a cigarette out of her pack and chucked it at her, saying, 'Here . . . get that in your gob and belt up, for gawd's sake!'

Even Molly laughed now. She hadn't thought her dad would go for a game show, but she had to admit that she was chuffed to bits that he'd decided to do it. None of her mates' dads could lay claim to being on first-name terms with a big star like Larry Logan! Just wait till they heard about this.

'Bloody hell, he's coming,' Larry said, his eyebrows arching with genuine surprise when the Lewises' front door opened a few minutes later and Dex walked out, looking much smarter than when Larry had left him, in a shirt, trousers and a black leather jacket. 'I can't believe she managed to persuade him.'

'That's mothers for you,' Dave grunted amusedly. 'Wish I could be a fly on the wall to see her face when she realises she's sent her precious son to the gallows, though. And I wouldn't like to be in *your* shoes when she does, 'cos she's gonna be after your blood.'

Grinning because he was so pleased with himself for netting Keeton's most-wanted, Larry said, 'Tough. She'll be too late to do anything about it, won't she.'

'Best get out and open the door for him,' Dave said now, watching Dex out of the corner of his eye as he came towards the car with his head down.

'That's the chauffeur's job,' Larry reminded him.

'Only if you want him to do a runner before we even get moving,' Dave hissed, pressing the button to slide the mirrored panel across to shield him from view.

Tutting softly when he found himself staring at his own reflection, Larry opened the door and climbed out. Ushering Dex in, he waved to Nora, Molly and Hilda, who were standing together at the gate now, and called, 'Promise I won't keep him out too long, Nora, but you'd best not wait up – just in case.' A grin now. 'You know what it's like when lads get together to celebrate – hard to keep track of time.'

Delighted that the neighbours were still out to witness this, Nora called back loudly, 'You keep him out as long as you like, Larry, love. Only don't go getting him *too* pissed, or I'll have to tan your backside for you!'

Laughing, Larry climbed into the car with Dex and said, 'She's a character, your mum, isn't she?'

'You can say that again,' Dex agreed, rubbing his hands together as he scanned the booze. 'Do we help ourselves, or have you got a servant stashed away somewhere to come and pour it for us?'

Waving for him to help himself, Larry said, 'Knock yourself out. It's all free.'

Reaching for a glass, Dex filled it with neat brandy, then offered the bottle to Larry. Grinning when he refused, he said, 'Bit of a lightweight these days, are you?'

'Only in public,' Larry said, intimating that he was just as much of a hard-drinking man in private as ever, because he sensed that Dex would respect him more for that. In actuality, he'd cut down dramatically since securing this contract, disgusted with himself for letting it get so out of control in the first place and almost losing everything.

Settling back in his seat, Dex stretched his legs out and gazed around the lush interior of the car. 'No wonder you're so desperate to get yourself back on telly if this is what comes with it. Get to ride round in one of these all the time, do you?'

'When I'm working,' Larry said, reaching for the remote and switching on the small plasma-screen TV. 'What do you fancy?'

'It's the business this,' Dex said, looking thoroughly impressed. 'Stick it on Q, or something – see if they've got any of them rock bands on with the birds in hot pants.'

'Wouldn't have taken you for a rocker,' Larry said, scrolling through the menu to find the channel that Dex wanted. 'Thought you'd have been more of an Eminem guy.'

'Won't catch me listening to that shite,' Dex sneered, swigging on his drink. 'Pure metal merchant, me.' Sitting up straighter as they turned out of his mother's street onto the main road, he peered out of the window, saying, 'Hey, there's some of me mates. Watch their faces when they cop me in this!' Pressing the button to lower the window, he climbed halfway out and waved his glass in the air, yelling, 'Yo! Mark . . . Reidy . . . Chinko! Check me, you cunts!' Laughing when the men started yelling back, asking what he was doing in a motor like that, he gave them the wanker sign and flopped back onto his seat. 'They'll be straight round me mam's to find out what's going on, you watch.'

Closing the window again from his side, Larry smiled, amused by Dex's boyish excitement because it was such a stark contrast to the mean, moody macho act he'd put on in his mother's house. Listening as he chattered on about how jealous his mates were going to be when they saw him in his *own* new car, and how he was going to treat his mother to a cruise with the money, and buy his daughter a whole new wardrobe of clothes and shoes, Larry wondered if Inspector Keeton had been talking about the same man. Dex wasn't the kind of person Larry would choose as a mate, but he definitely didn't seem as bad as he'd been painted, and Larry actually felt a bit guilty for setting him up.

But only a bit. Definitely not enough to let him off the hook and warn him what was coming.

Which reminded him . . . he needed to talk him through the show before they got there; make sure he knew there could be delays in case he got jumpy and thought about taking off before Keeton got around to him, because his arrest would be the money shot of the show if they got it right.

'I'll run you through the schedule before we get there so you know what's what,' he said. Then – to make Dex feel really privileged – he added, 'But don't tell any of the other contestants that I personally came to get you, because we don't want them thinking I'm playing favourites, or anything.'

'Secret's safe with me,' Dex drawled, tapping the side of his nose with his finger. Then, 'So, who am I up against? Bet they're all dead posh, aren't they?'

'I haven't actually met any of the others, but I imagine there'll be a fair mix,' Larry said. 'I'd prefer not to have posh ones, 'cos I reckon if they've already got money they should leave things like this to the people who really need it. But if there are any, I'll just take the piss out of them – and that's always fun, 'cos they never catch on. You've got nothing to worry about, though,' he said now, giving Dex a conspiratorial smile. 'I reckon you're gonna do really well.'

Grinning, convinced that his new mate Larry was going to make sure that he won, Dex said, 'Cheers, mate. And fuck the posh cunts, 'cos us working-class heroes are coming to snatch back some of the money they've been sitting on!'

'Too right,' Larry murmured, wondering where people like Dex got the idea that they were any kind of heroes when the only work they ever did usually involved ripping off honest workers. He knew the type only too well, because his brothers, his dad, and even his mum to some extent had been like that. They all thought nothing of stealing what they couldn't afford to buy – even from him. Bastards!

'Anyway, the schedule,' he said now, shaking the thought of his family away because they annoyed him even from a distance. 'You'll get a champagne reception when we get there, and then you'll be introduced to your team.'

'Team?' Dex repeated, not looking quite so pleased suddenly. 'I thought this was an every-man-for-himself kind of thing. I don't want to be on a *team* and end up having to share the prize with some cunt.'

'It's not that kind of team,' Larry assured him, grinning slyly as he added, 'This is more of a personal-escort type of thing. And I guarantee you'll like it, because I saw the girls before I left the studio this morning, and they are *hot*.'

'Girls, eh?' Dex was all ears again. 'Oh, well, that's different. And what are they gonna be doing?'

'Keeping you happy,' Larry told him. 'And they will, because they're all models, and they've got tits like you wouldn't believe.' Flapping his hand now, he said, 'But you'll see them for yourself when we get there, so I'll shut up before I end up walking in with a fucking flagpole sticking out of my pants.'

'That good, huh?' Dex leered.

'Better,' Larry said. Then, 'Anyway, all the contestants get their own team, and they stay with you all day till you go on set – to make sure you're not too nervous, and keep you supplied with drinks and food, and what have you. You'll all have your own rooms just in case there's any trouble, because some contestants can be a bit *competitive* when there's so much at stake, and it can get a bit nasty.'

'That don't bother me,' Dex said unconcernedly. 'I'll just knock the fuckers out if they try pulling any shit like that on me.'

Chuckling softly, Larry said, 'Good job we're keeping you away from them then, eh? I'd hate to see you lose your chance at getting that car just because someone's said something bitchy and wound you up. Anyway, the girls will make sure no one gets into your room, and if you want anything just ask and they'll get it for you. But you won't be able to go walkabout, I'm afraid, because the producers don't want to risk anyone getting hold of the question-and-answer sheets.'

'That's me fucked, then,' Dex snorted amusedly.

'You'll be fine,' Larry said, giving him yet another hint that he had it in the bag.

'How long's it gonna take?' Dex asked now, wondering when he'd be getting his next smoke, because he'd only had one little spliff before leaving and he was already coming down off that.

Telling him that it was in the hands of the technical-equipment gods, Larry said, 'We're scheduled for a two o'clock start, but every show I've ever done has had delays of some sort or another, so you're best looking on it as a day-long thing. Not got plans for tonight, have you?'

*Because you won't be keeping to them if you have.*

'Nah, I'm cool,' Dex said. 'Just fancied a bit of puff, but I've left mine at the house. Don't suppose you've got any?'

Shaking his head, Larry gave a surreptitious nod towards the mirrored panel separating them from the driver. 'Can't risk it with these company chauffeurs. They'll either run straight back to the boss and grass you up, or sell the story to the papers. Best just leaving it till you get home.'

*In three years or so, in your case.*

'Plenty of booze, though.' He waved for Dex to help himself. 'And with any luck, there'll be champagne coming out of your ears by the end of the night.' Smiling slyly, he said, 'Anyway, let me talk you through the procedure before we get there – make sure you know everything you need to know so we can wipe the floor with the bastards.'

Back at the studio just then, Terri was panicking. For a show like this to work, timing was everything, but Keeton had already thrown the schedule out when he came up with the bright idea of sending Larry out to Dex Lewis's house in one of the two limos this morning. And, then, to make matters worse, Keeton himself had been called back to the police station across town to deal with some sort of emergency. And with Jon busy assisting with the editing of the first cut of *Cops 'n' Bobbies*, getting it ready to send back to Shock-Wave's LA office, she was having to cope with all of this alone – and was beginning to feel way out of her depth.

Larry had been out for far too long already, so the second car was having to do all the collecting and delivering, and they were way behind now, with only five targets here when there really should have been ten. Although that was actually a mixed blessing, because Terri was already running round like a maniac trying to make sure that their paths didn't cross, so it would have been worse if there had been twice as many to deal with. The entire crew were equipped with radio head-sets so that they could let each other know where they were at all times, but if one target happened to spot another and suss what was going on it would blow the whole thing apart. And the longer Larry and Keeton were gone, the more chance there was of something like that happening.

The teams, which consisted of three gorgeous, busty models – and one gorgeous, busty undercover cop, who would check

IDs to make sure that the targets really were who they claimed to be, and keep control if anything untoward happened – were doing a great job of entertaining their subjects so far, but what if—

*What if . . . what if . . .*

That was all Terri could think about at the moment, and it was driving her crazy. She just wished Keeton had left well enough alone. If he hadn't let his obsession with arresting Dex Lewis run away with him, Larry would be here and they'd be well on their way with filming now. But when Larry got back there would be even more time wasted, because he'd need to go into make-up and get changed, *and* be brought up to speed about the targets – to make sure he didn't give the game away when he was introducing them by saying the wrong name. All stuff that he *should* have been concentrating on in his dressing room this morning, never mind going AWOL.

The targets were all so horrible and rough-looking, swaggering out of the limo and into reception with the same *don't-fuck-with-me* expressions on their faces, wearing the same uniform of tracksuit, trainers, and obligatory hoodie – to disguise themselves with should anybody see them who wasn't supposed to. But, proud as they all were of their street-smarts, they were clearly too stupid to realise that it was those who lay in wait *inside* who posed the real threat, not those who might happen to spot them outside.

Carjacker Mark Thompson had been the first to arrive, followed by Colin Leach, a shoplifter and bag-snatcher with the worst teeth Terri had ever seen on a living person. The third was Steve Brightman, a feral-faced heroin addict who was wanted for stealing and selling prescription pads and chequebooks; then Gary Hutchinson, who was wanted for burglary – but who needed a psych ward rather than a cell, in Terri's opinion. And lastly, Rachael Gold, the first of the three females on the list, who, like her name, was dripping with cheap gold chains and had both hands crammed full of gaudy rings and both ears weighed down with heavy gypsy loops – probably spoils from the numerous muggings she'd apparently been responsible for.

Rachael had been given a team of men to keep her occupied, but she'd done nothing but moan since she got here, acting like some sort of visiting superstar, demanding to know why Larry hadn't been in to see her yet. She was annoying the hell out of everyone, but it was Steve Brightman who was causing Terri the biggest headache. He'd obviously had a hit before the car picked him up, and every time he nodded out she was worried that he might not wake up again. But then, when he did, she was even more worried, because he kept trying to sneak away to the toilets by himself, claiming that he had a weak bladder.

Suspecting that he was actually trying to get himself deliberately 'lost' so that he could search the building for things to steal, Terri went to her office to phone Keeton and beg him to hurry up, because she was convinced it was all going to fall apart at any minute.

'If Brightman gets too much for you, just have him brought straight in,' Keeton told her, saying that it was better to lose one minor player like him than to lose the chance of taking a major piece of shit like Dex Lewis down. 'Whatever you do, don't let Lewis out of your sight when he gets there, though, because he'll be off like a shot if he gets one whiff of what's going on.'

'How about if we put him through first?' Terri suggested. 'At least he'd be out of the way and we could get back on track.'

'Do *not* try to take him without me being there,' Keeton warned her sternly. 'This one needs particularly careful handling, and I don't want anyone getting hurt.'

There was a tap at the door just then, and one of the runners stuck his head round to say that Larry's limo had just pulled up out front.

Feeling sick, Terri relayed the news to Keeton.

'I'll be there as soon as I can,' he said, his voice cold and clipped. 'Just keep him well away from the others, and try to keep him occupied.'

Promising that she would do her best, Terri put the phone down. Then, taking a deep breath, she left the office and rushed back to reception to make sure that Brightman had been moved out of sight.

Strolling through the doors with Dex Lewis at his side, Larry looked like the cat who'd got the cream. Waving to members of the crew who were milling around, he nudged Dex and nodded towards the poster-board of the Range Rover, whispering, 'What d'y' reckon?'

'It's a fucking beast,' Dex replied, grinning widely – sure that now he and Larry were such good mates the motor was as good as his.

Coming in through the staff door just then, Terri inhaled nervously when she saw the size of Lewis. Even with his back to her she could feel the vibe of danger streaming off him, and she suddenly understood why Keeton had urged such caution around him: he would obviously be capable of doing immense damage if he were to get physical.

Glancing quickly around now, to make sure there were at least two police officers at hand should she need assistance, she took a deep breath and approached Larry and Lewis.

'About time!' she said, opting to play the harassed producer with deadlines to adhere to so that she could whisk Larry away. 'I was just about to send all the contestants home and reschedule filming for when you actually had time for us.'

Instinctively playing along, Larry said, 'Sorry. It took a bit longer than I expected to persuade Dex here to join us. But it's our fault, not his. Seems he didn't get our letters, so maybe it's your secretary you need to be having a go at.'

'Oh, don't worry, I will,' Terri muttered, running a finger down the list on her clipboard. 'Sorry, who did you say this was?'

'Dex Lewis,' Larry told her, giving Dex a conspiratorial side-glance as if to say *See what I have to put up with?*

'Funny.' Terri frowned. 'His name's not here.'

'Because he didn't get our letters,' Larry repeated wryly. 'But he's here now, so do you think we could get him a drink?'

Looking up at Dex, who was smiling down at her, Terri saw something dark and vicious behind his eyes and shuddered. No wonder Keeton was so desperate to get him off the streets.

Keeping her nerve with difficulty, she held Dex's gaze as if she was totally in control and said, 'Do you have your ID?'

'ID?' Frowning, he turned at Larry. 'You never said nothing about that.'

Saying, 'Oh, shit, I forgot,' Larry clapped a hand on his forehead. 'Sorry, mate. I was supposed to tell you to bring three forms of ID to verify that you're the real contestant – otherwise anyone could walk in off the street and take your place, couldn't they? Don't suppose you've got a driving licence, or a bank card, or something?'

Pursing his lips, Dex shook his head. 'Nah. I don't carry shit like that around with me.'

'Oh, well, I'm sorry,' Terri said coolly. 'We can't proceed without it.'

'Oh, come on,' Larry said, wondering what she was playing at. 'Can't we bend the rules just this once?'

'Tell you what, let's just give it a miss, eh?' Dex said, giving Terri a hooded look. 'You never said nothing about ID or I wouldn't have bothered coming.'

Sensing that he was getting set to walk, Larry turned his back on Terri and said, 'Come on, man, don't throw it all away. You're here now. Just chill.'

'Nah, it don't feel right,' Dex muttered stubbornly. 'I can't be doing with official shit, it mashes me head up.'

Determined not to see his efforts go to waste over something stupid like this, Larry said, 'Look, just leave it with me and I'll sort it out, yeah? You're the only contestant I've met so far, and I want *you* to win, man. But if you walk, I'll have to let some fucker who doesn't even deserve it take the lot. Look at the car, man. Are you gonna walk away from that when you *know* it's got your name on it?'

Breathing in deeply, Dex cast a glance at the poster-board. It really was an impressive set of wheels, and it was his for the taking if he could just shake off the weird feeling that had just come over him. Reminding himself that it was probably just a bit of paranoia, he told himself to get a grip. If he could just stick it out for a few hours, he'd be driving home in his new car – stopping off on the way to buy himself an ounce of the white stuff out of his twenty grand.

Looking at Larry again, he said, 'All right, I'll stay. But only if you sort this ID shit out, 'cos I'm not showing no one nothing.'

Winking at him, Larry turned back to Terri and jerked his head for her to follow him into a quiet corner out of earshot.

'What are you *doing*?' he hissed when she reached him. 'Have you any idea how long it took me to get him here?'

'I'm sorry, Larry,' she whispered, 'but it could mess everything up if we don't follow procedure.'

'That's for the targets Keeton doesn't personally know, to make sure it's really them,' Larry argued. 'But he *knows* Lewis.'

'Yes, but he's not here to verify it. And, with respect, Larry, *you*'ve never met him before, so there's always a chance that you might have brought the wrong man in.'

'I haven't,' Larry insisted. 'Keeton showed me his mugshot before I went over there, and I *know* it's him. If I'm wrong, Keeton can sort it out later, can't he?'

Looking up at him, Terri bit her lip. The ID issue was one of the strictest no-ifs-or-buts rules on this project, but Larry was right: Keeton would know soon enough if they'd got the wrong man. And she'd rather risk keeping the wrong one unnecessarily than letting the right one get away.

'Okay, we'll drop the ID,' she said. 'But we need to keep him occupied until Keeton gets here, and I don't know how long that's going to be.'

'Leave him to me,' Larry said confidently. 'I'll just get him tanked up – that'll keep him quiet.'

'Not *too* drunk,' Terri warned, worried that Lewis would be hard enough to contain without alcohol. 'But you won't be able to stay with him, because we've already got the first five targets here, and Keeton wants them off the premises before he tackles Lewis. You've not even been to make-up yet, and you still need to get changed.'

'Stop panicking,' Larry told her, giving her a reassuring pat on the shoulder. 'It's all going to work out fine.'

'Not if we don't get moving in the next five minutes,' Terri said, glancing at her watch. 'We're cutting it really close now.'

'All right – just let me get him settled and I'll be right with you,' Larry said, rubbing his hands together as the excitement of getting the show on the road stepped up a notch.

Jerking his chin up when Larry strolled back to him a couple of seconds later, Dex said, 'What's she saying?'

Assuring him that it was sorted, Larry said, 'She's just flapping because I'm late and they need me to do the camera and sound checks before we can start filming. I'll have to go get ready in a minute, but let me get you that drink first and introduce you to your team.'

Leading Dex out of reception and along a corridor now, Larry held a finger to his lips and pointed to a red light over one of the heavy studio doors, telling him to stay quiet because something was being filmed in there. In actuality, it was just one of the many spy-cams they had set up all around the building, to catch the contestants' every move and word throughout the day, the footage of which would later be edited together with the footage of them on their best behaviour on set, before the inevitable kick-offs when they were arrested.

Opening the door to Dex's allotted room now, which was way on the other side of the studio from all the other targets' rooms, he waved him inside.

'*This* –' he said, smiling when Dex's mouth almost dropped open at the sight of the girls '– is your team.'

'Jeezus!' Dex hissed, gazing at them like a kid in a sweet-shop. 'Look at the *tits* on 'em, man!'

Larry couldn't disagree. They *did* all have gorgeous tits, which was precisely why they'd been hired: to keep the targets' minds off everything else while they were here.

'They'll be looking after you today,' he told Dex now. 'Anything you want, just ask and they'll get it for you.'

'*Any*thing?' Dex leered.

Chuckling softly, Larry said, 'Within reason, yeah. But try to resist temptation till we've got the show over with, 'cos there'll be time enough for getting numbers when we're out on the town celebrating tonight.'

Leaving Dex with the gushing girlies now, Larry jerked his head at Carla, the undercover policewoman who was over-seeing this particular team.

Large breasts jutting out invitingly, and a sexy smile on her glossy painted lips, she said, 'Hi there, Larry . . . glad you could join us.'

Fully aware that she was making it look like she was flirting with him for Dex's benefit, Larry took her aside and quickly brought her up to date.

'Keeton's trying to get back a.s.a.p. but he says to keep Dex occupied till he gets here – and not to let him out of your sight under any circumstances. I've got to go and get ready so we can get the rest of them out, but someone will let you know when it's all clear. Any problems, just . . .' Pausing, he flapped his hands. 'Well, I'm sure you'll know what to do.'

'I'm sure I will,' Carla assured him, fluffing her long red hair now.

Wondering for a moment if she actually *was* flirting with him after all, Larry narrowed his eyes and peered into hers.

No. Definitely nothing but steel and ice.

Saying, 'Okay, well, I'll leave you to it,' he gave Dex a wave, then hurried back out to the reception area where Terri was waiting for him.

Going back to Dex, Carla's long, heavily mascara'd lashes concealed the disdain in her dark eyes. She'd never actually met him before, but she knew all about him from his files and had requested that she be assigned as his team leader when she heard that he was coming in. She figured that she was the only one who would stand a chance of keeping him in line if he got out of hand.

For safety's sake, the models hadn't been told what was really going on today. They truly believed that they were helping to host a real game show. Consequently, they also believed that Carla really was one of them, and that was driving her absolutely crazy: all they'd done all morning was twitter on about clothes and make-up, which footballers they'd dated, and how many expensive presents they'd been given for their stupid services.

A bit older than them – and infinitely more sexy, being a

real woman, not a vacuous air-headed bimbo tart – Carla had no trouble snatching Dex's attention away from them now. Ignoring the resentful looks they tossed her way, she said, 'So, Derek . . . Larry tells me you're our special contestant, and I'm to keep you *really, really* happy.'

Grinning, Dex said, 'Yeah, that's right. Me and Larry are good mates.'

Purring, 'Any friend of Larry's is a friend of mine,' Carla linked her arm through his and led him to the table-top bar for a glass of champagne.

She'd be his friend, all right. And then she'd wipe the smirk right off his surprisingly handsome, thoroughly villainous face with a nice pair of handcuffs!

# 8

'And . . . *action!*'

Looking into camera one as the theme music came to an end and the canned applause faded, Larry smiled and, reading from the autocue, said, 'Good evening to all you lovely folks at home, and a warm welcome to those of you who've joined us here in the studio for this fantastic new show of mine . . .'

*Pause for more applause, perfectly cued in by the sound engineers.*

Beaming, as if there really were members of the public filling the seats and not just a row of police officers shielded by the bright lights, Larry rubbed his hands together and said, 'Now, as you might know if you've seen the ads over there, this is a game show with a difference. Not least because it's got the best *host* –' waggle of eyebrows; cheeky wink '– but also because we've got the best prizes. Twenty thousand pounds – that's *forty thousand dollars* to you guys at home there in the States . . .'

*Canned gasps of appreciation.*

'And one of the nicest cars I have ever seen in my life!'

*Burst of music. Spotlight on second poster-board of Range Rover.*

'And all our contestants have got to do is wait to hear the fateful word *Gotcha!*, and they'll walk away with the prize of their life!'

The words were for the benefit of the target who was currently waiting in the wings for his introduction. But the sly smile and knowing look to camera as yet more applause echoed around the set were for the viewers, who would know exactly what was really happening by the time they got to see this.

Even if it *was* just Americans who'd be getting the privilege.

'Anyway,' Larry said now. 'Without further ado, let's get this show *started*!'

*Another burst of theme music.*

Waiting impatiently in the shadows off to the left of the set, Mark Thompson was hopping from foot to foot like Rocky waiting to get into the ring. Giving a shake of his shoulders and a roll of his head on his neck when the floor manager asked if everyone was ready, he said, 'Yeah, *I* am. But I can't say the same about this one – eh, mate?' Grinning, he nudged the man beside him, who he'd met a short time earlier, having finally been let out of the room he'd been holed up in all day and taken to meet his 'fellow contestants' in the greenroom – all of whom, he was about to discover, were undercover policemen and policewomen.

Playing the part of the nervous-wreck contestant who was *ever* so grateful to Thompson for taking him under his wing, PC Pete Silcock gave a sickly smile, and muttered, 'I'm all right.'

Holding up a hand for silence as Larry called for the contestants to come on out, the floor manager pushed Thompson and Silcock out into the light. Striding onto the set like a conquering hero back from the war, Thompson held up his hands in a pre-victory salute to the audience – even though he couldn't see them for the bright spots that were blinding him.

Introducing him, Larry said, 'So, Mark Thompson, how's it going? I hear you made yourself a bit of a friend back there.'

'Yeah, Larry.' Thompson grinned, nodding at Silcock. 'He's a bit nervous, like, so I've been helping him chill, and that.'

'Ah, that's nice,' Larry said, flashing a sly side glance to camera. 'Anyway, let's get on with the introductions, shall we?' Reading from the cards in his hand now, he said, 'It says here that you're quite a Jack the lad?'

'You could say that,' Thompson agreed, grinning broadly.

'And you like nothing better than a good old booze-up with your mates, a gorgeous girl on your arm, and a pocket full of money.'

'Yeah, man!'

'And a nice car to take you from A to B.'

Grin widening, Thompson rubbed his hands together and said, 'That Range Rover will do me just fine, Larry. Bring it on!'

Stepping forward just then, PC Silcock cleared his throat and said, 'Mark Matthew Thompson . . .'

Laughing, Thompson jerked his head at Larry. 'Eh up, mate, looks like someone's after your job.'

'Hey, I'm cool,' Larry drawled, holding up his hands and taking a step back. 'Not me you need to be worrying about – *mate*.'

Confusion flickered through Thompson's eyes, followed by a spark of realisation, then an awareness of betrayal. 'Aw, man!' he groaned, giving Larry a disbelieving look. 'You set me up, you cunt!'

Smiling unconcernedly as Thompson was handcuffed and read his rights, Larry turned back to the camera and said, 'Mark Thompson, ladies and gents . . .'

*Canned applause.*

'And, just in case you're thinking he's nothing but a cheeky chappy who's gone astray, take a look at him earlier when he didn't know he was being filmed by our spy-cams, busy telling anyone who'd listen how "feared and respected" he is, and how he only has to snap his fingers for people to do whatever he tells them. And if you still think he's a good guy after *that*—'

Calling 'Cut!', the floor manager hurried over to him and whispered, 'Just stick to the script, please, Larry. Personal opinions could seriously jeopardise things at this stage.'

Winking at him, telling him that he'd try to remember that, Larry waved to Mark Thompson who was complaining loudly as he was led off stage by two uniformed officers. Then, turning to Terri, he said, 'Next one ready?'

Holding up a hand, Terri pressed the earpiece of her radio headset deeper into her ear to hear what one of the team leaders was saying. Tutting then, she called the floor manager over and said, 'Sorry, Carl, but we're going to have to switch the order. Rachael Gold's causing problems and we need to get her out.'

Yelling at one of the runners to have Colin Leach taken out of the greenroom and back to his holding room, Carl told another one to go and tell the autocue operator to switch segments.

Thanking him, Terri got on the radio to let Rachael's team leader know what was happening. Then, taking Larry aside, she said, 'That was fantastic. And I love that sly look you give to camera. It's so effective, and the viewers will get a real sense of intimacy from you – like they're right in there with you.'

She didn't add that it was so sexy and smouldering a look that she'd actually felt a bit weak-kneed when she'd watched it on the monitor. But she couldn't wait for her bosses back home to see the finished version, because she just knew it was going to be wonderful. More fool the British producers for not keeping hold of him when they had him.

Oblivious to what she was thinking beside him, Larry glanced at his watch, itching to get back out there. He was buzzing big time, and couldn't wait to get through the next few contestants, so that he could finally get round to Dex Lewis. Knowing that they would have to wait until Keeton and his extra back-up were here before they could even think about proceeding with Lewis, though, he asked if there was any word yet.

'Not yet,' Terri told him, a small cloud of worry darkening her eyes. 'I didn't want to ring him again in case he thinks I'm harassing him, but I think I'm going to have to chase him up soon, because I've had one of the drivers on asking when they're supposed to go ahead and start picking up the next batch of targets.' Chewing her lip now, she said, 'This is all going to fall apart, I can tell.'

'Stop stressing – it's going to be great,' Larry said, grinning as he looped an arm around her shoulder and gave her a reassuring squeeze. 'Now get that lovely ass of yours moving and see what's happening out there,' he said then, slapping her playfully on the backside.

Blushing, because it was the first time he'd actually touched her like that, Terri said, 'Right . . . I'll go and hurry them up. You just keep doing what you're doing, because it's fabulous.'

Winking at her, Larry watched as she scuttled away, then strolled back into the spotlight to let the make-up girl touch up his face and re-comb his hair before the next target got her comeuppance.

'How's it going?' Keeton asked, rushing in through the back door some time later.

'Fantastic,' Terri told him, feeling a whole lot better now that he was here. Keeping her voice low now as they passed the greenroom, where the last contestant before Dex Lewis was waiting for his moment of glory, she said, 'The first four went through without a hitch, and the editor reckons we've got some amazing secret footage – although I can't *believe* how awful your criminals are. They're so disgusting when they don't know they're being watched. I've heard some of what they've been saying, and it made my skin crawl. They're all so homophobic, and racist and sexist. How do you guys cope with it?'

'By getting them off the street and putting them behind bars where they belong,' Keeton grunted, glad that she understood why he'd been so keen to do this project in the first place. Her bosses hadn't been too eager to part with the extra money, from all accounts, but Terri had persuaded them that it would be a good addition to the main show. And Keeton was grateful to her for that, because he'd never have managed this without her.

'Where's Lewis?' he asked now, holding the heavy studio door open for her and waving her through.

'Still in his room, but we'll have him brought up as soon as we get Steve Brightman on set.'

'He's still with us, then, is he?' Keeton said. 'Not OD'd yet?'

'No, but I think he's starting to withdraw,' Terri said, waving to Larry, who was having the sweat mopped off his face and a fresh dusting of matt-powder applied, to let him know that Keeton was back. 'I shuffled the order and put the girl and the other guy through before him, but I'm wondering if I shouldn't have left him where he was, because he's looking quite sick now. Maybe we should get the doctor to take a look at him?'

'Bugger that,' Keeton muttered dismissively. 'He'll get seen by the station doctor soon as he gets there, and a bit of shivering and shaking won't hurt him till then.'

Trusting that he was more experienced in these matters than she was, Terri nodded, and said, 'Okay, whatever you think best. If you'd like to go and sit down I'll have him brought out.' Standing on tiptoe now, she peered out into the auditorium. Then, pointing towards the dark left-hand corner at the back, she said, 'I think your extra men have been put over there if you want to join them.'

Thanking her, Keeton made his way off into the shadows. When she could no longer see him, Terri called out to Larry to see if he was ready. Giving him the thumbs-up when he said yes, she radioed the greenroom and told them to bring Brightman out. Then she contacted Carla, and told her to bring Dex Lewis over to the greenroom in ten minutes.

Just as Dex and his team were heading for the greenroom, a policeman masquerading as a runner slipped out through the studio door. Theme music flooded the corridor. Above the noise Steve Brightman could be heard complaining loudly as he was hauled off-set in cuffs, while Larry's gloating voice proclaimed: 'And another one bites the dust!'

It was only a few seconds before the door closed and there was silence again, but Dex had heard enough to make him stop in his tracks. Peering down at Carla, he demanded to know what was going on.

Thinking on her feet, she linked her arm through his and said, 'They're probably just having a mess-about while they check the equipment. They always do that before they bring the contestants out.'

Dex hadn't caught what Larry had actually been saying. But he wasn't convinced by Carla's explanation and alarm bells started to ring in his head.

Guessing what he was thinking, Carla gave him a re-assuring smile and tugged on his arm to try to get him moving, saying, 'Come on, Dex, we really need to hurry. The green-room's just down here, and everybody's waiting for you.'

Jerking his arm out of her grip, Dex muttered, 'Something ain't right here.'

'There's nothing wrong,' she assured him, staying cool even though she could sense that he was about to kick off. Keeping her gaze fixed firmly on his eyes, she used her peripheral vision to locate the PC who had caused all this by coming out while the red recording light was still glowing, and gave the tiniest of flicks of her wrist to alert him that they had a situation brewing.

Pretending to have things to do elsewhere, the PC hurried off down the corridor. As soon as he was out of earshot, he put out an alert call over the radio.

Back inside the studio, Terri felt a chill trickle of dread snake down her spine when she heard the alert. Waving to Larry from the wings, she gave him the wind-it-up signal, then chewed nervously on her fingernails until he came to her. Dex Lewis was an awesome presence, and she'd known as soon as she saw him that his arrest would be the highlight of the show, but she didn't want it to come at the expense of anybody's safety.

Wiping his brow on a tissue, Larry strolled over to her. 'What's up?'

Relaying what she'd already heard, Terri held up her hand for him to stay quiet as she listened to something else on the radio. Then she said, 'Right, they're giving the policewoman a couple more minutes to try and persuade him, then they're going to rush him in the corridor, so we've all got to stay in here till we get the all-clear.'

'No chance!' Larry blurted out indignantly. '*I* got him here, so I should be there when he gets arrested. It'll mess the whole show up if I'm not.'

'I know it's disappointing,' Terri replied quietly. 'But if he won't come on set, they'll *have* to take him out there. And I can't risk letting you go out and getting caught up in the crossfire.'

'There won't be any crossfire if I talk to him,' Larry said

confidently. 'Carla's obviously cocked it up and made him nervous, but he trusts me. Just get one of the lads to bring a camera out in case we miss anything.'

'No, I'm not putting anyone in danger,' Terri told him firmly.

'Fine, I'll do it by myself,' Larry said, already setting off for the door. 'There are hidden cameras in the corridor – we'll just use that footage.'

'No, there aren't,' Terri called after him. 'There's only CCTV, and the quality's too poor for broadcast, so it's not worth it.'

Stopping, Larry turned back, a frown of disbelief on his face. 'I thought you said you'd put cameras all over?'

'I didn't think we needed one out here,' she admitted. 'It's so close to the greenroom, and the targets wouldn't be talking or doing anything worth filming out there, so I figured it was a waste of money.'

'I thought money was no object?' Larry reminded her sarcastically.

'Well, I'm sorry,' Terri said, shrugging defeatedly. 'But there's nothing we can do about it now. I can't send anyone out there, so if Carla can't persuade him to come in we'll just have to let it go.'

'No.' Pursing his lips, Larry shook his head. 'I'm *not* letting it go. He's mine, and I'm having him.' Turning, he marched towards the door again.

'What are you *doing*?' Terri gasped, almost tripping over a bundle of wires as she rushed after him.

'Making sure we've still got a show worth watching,' Larry told her. 'Just tell Keeton to hold fire till I've had a shot.'

'It's too dangerous,' Terri insisted. But it was too late – Larry had already yanked the door open.

Dex was stalking the opposite way down the corridor, looking like a man possessed as he rattled door handles in search of an escape route. Mentally crossing himself, Larry called his name and rushed after him.

Catching up with him at the end of the corridor where he found himself trapped, Larry said, 'What's wrong, man? I've just been calling for you to come on set. I know it's taken longer than we said, and you're probably pissed off with all the hanging about. But we're sorted now, so why don't you come back with me?'

'Nah.' Shaking his head, Dex set off back down the corridor. 'It don't feel right. I'm out of here.'

Glancing up to make sure they were in view of the CCTV cameras, Larry went after him, telling him that nothing was wrong; that delays were par for the course on shows like this, where everything was being filmed in front of a live audience.

'Don't take me for some kind of fucking mug,' Dex growled, the veins throbbing in his thick neck as his temper rose. 'If I don't get out of here I'm gonna fucking blow. So do your-self a favour and get the fuck away from me before you get hurt, yeah?'

'I thought we were mates,' Larry persisted, adrenalin propelling him on even though he could clearly see that Dex was close to the edge. 'Come on, man, don't give up now. Think what you're gonna lose if you walk out. The money, the car . . .'

Breathing hard, Dex stopped and turned to face Larry. Peering down at him, he searched his face for signs of duplicity or guilt. At the very least he'd have expected fear, but Larry just looked confused and that, in turn, confused Dex. His instincts were still telling him to get the fuck out of there, but he couldn't help but wonder if it was just another burst of para-noia. Surely no one could be stupid enough to stand right in front of him and lie to his face like this – definitely not a wuss like Logan. So was he making a huge mistake here? Missing out for nothing on the chance to win the money and the car?

Before Dex had had a chance to convert these thoughts into a decision, the studio door burst open and the corridor was suddenly swarming with uniformed police officers. Striding to the fore, Keeton said, 'Derek John Lewis, I am arresting you for—'

'Fuck you!' Dex cut him off, his eyes narrowed to slits as he glanced at the officers, assessing who to take out first if he was going to make it through them.

'Raise your hands and face the wall,' Keeton ordered him sharply, gesturing for his officers to move in.

'I wouldn't if I was you,' Dex snarled, reaching down and pulling a flick knife out of his sock.

Hyped with the excitement of being in the middle of something he'd only ever seen on TV before, and conscious of how amazing he was going to look if he talked Dex down, Larry held up his hands in a calming gesture and said, 'Hey, come on, Dex . . . don't be stupid. Just put the knife down before someone gets hurt.'

'Stay out of this, Larry!' Keeton barked, furious that Logan was out here in the first place when he'd been told to stay out of harm's way.

'*Larry?*' Dex repeated darkly, the final pieces clicking into place in his head.

Larry's excitement turned to icy fear when Dex turned and glared at him. But before he could even think about running, Dex grabbed him by the lapels of his jacket and, flipping him round, dragged him up against his chest. Looping a thick arm around his throat now, he pressed the tip of the blade against the soft skin under his chin.

'Back off – *NOW!*' he snarled to Keeton. 'And get your dickheads out of the way, or he's dead!'

'Don't be stupid, Lewis,' Keeton said calmly, holding up a hand for his officers to stay put.

'*I*'m not the stupid one here,' Dex spat back at him. '*You* are if you think I'm sticking around to let you stitch me up again. That TDA was nothing to fucking do with me, and you fucking *know* it wasn't! Now, back the fuck off and let me out, or he's dead, and I'm not messin' around here.'

'*Don't!*' Larry croaked, feeling light-headed as blood began to trickle down his neck. 'This has got nothing to do with me, Dex.'

'You think I'm some kind of fucking idiot?' Dex growled down his ear. 'You're the cunt who got me here, and you're the cunt who's gonna pay for it if they don't back off.'

'Let him go,' Keeton ordered, giving a covert signal to one of his men to get the Taser ready.

'Fuck you!' Dex retorted defiantly. 'He's coming with me, so get that lot shifted. And I want an unmarked car, an' all.'

Unable to breathe as Dex started forcing him forwards toward the wall of officers, Larry kicked back with his heels to make him loosen his grip. But it had the opposite effect – bright sparks exploded behind his eyes when Dex increased the pressure on his throat. As the darkness enveloped him, Larry dimly heard Keeton shouting, 'Go, go, go!'

# 9

'I need a smoke,' Larry said irritably, struggling to sit up.

'Just keep still and let them finish doing what they're doing,' Georgie scolded him sharply, reaching out and giving him a gentle but firm push on the shoulder to make him lie down.

Sighing loudly, Larry did as he was told. Yelping when the nurse resumed her stitching, he gave her an evil look and said, 'Christ, watch what you're doing! I thought this was a hospital, not a flaming butcher's shop!'

Apologising, the young nurse blushed. She'd never had a patient as famous or as drop-dead gorgeous as Larry Logan before, so it wasn't easy trying to stitch him up when her hands were shaking so badly. And she was much closer than she'd ever imagined she would get to him, which was making her doubly nervous: knowing that he could probably smell her breath and the sweat that was pouring off her.

Telling Larry to stop being so bloody rude when people were only trying to help him, Georgie tutted when her mobile phone began to ring in her pocket. Taking it out, she switched it off and tossed it into her messy handbag.

'Who was it?' Larry asked through gritted teeth, trying not to move his chin as the nurse picked up the syringe to give him another shot of anaesthetic.

'Probably more well-wishers,' Georgie murmured, peering at him worriedly as the nurse swabbed up a fresh trickle of blood. 'They haven't stopped since word got out what happened. You'll be the only headline in the papers tomorrow, that's for sure.'

'That's good,' Larry said, exhaling through his teeth as the numbness crept up his chin, making him feel like Desperate Dan.

'Yes, well, I'm more concerned about you right now,' Georgie told him sincerely. 'So will you please stop talking and let the nurse patch you up?'

Winking at her, because he could see that she was genuinely shaken, Larry said, 'Okay, *mum*, stop worrying. I'm going to be right as rain.' Turning his head slightly to look at the nurse now, he said, 'Sorry for shouting, sweetheart. You're doing a great job.'

Almost melting off her stool, the nurse dipped her gaze, unable to look into Larry's green- and gold-flecked eyes because they were just too beautiful and sexy.

Another nurse tapped on the door just then. Popping her head in, she gazed at Larry for a moment, then turned to Georgie, saying, 'Sorry to disturb you, but there's about a hundred photographers outside, and now some TV news vans are pulling in and blocking the ambulance bays. My manager's freaking out, and she said to ask if you can do something about it.'

Sighing wearily, Georgie flapped her hands. 'I don't really know what I can do, but I'll try.'

Thanking her, the nurse held the door open for her.

'Your mum's nice,' the first nurse said when she and Larry were alone, needing to fill the silence in case he heard how loudly her heart was thudding.

'She's all right,' Larry said, aware that he was slurring as the anaesthetic began to affect his tongue. 'Think I look like her?'

'Not really,' the nurse said diplomatically, thinking that he was utterly gorgeous, whereas his mum had a really big nose and her eyes were dark and droopy. 'She really loves you, though, doesn't she? She was so worried when she came into reception looking for you.'

Amused that the nurse believed that Georgie *was* his mother despite the fact that she was obviously Jewish and he obviously wasn't, Larry said, 'Yeah, she's always fussing over me, my old mum. Can't complain, I suppose. But she's a terror with my girlfriends. Scares the bloody life out of them when I bring them home.'

The nurse bit her lip, wishing that *she* would ever get lucky enough to go home with him. And she'd make damn sure his mum liked her if she did.

'I think she's lovely,' she murmured now, carefully inserting the last stitches into the small but fairly deep wound under Larry's chin. The last thing she wanted was to be responsible for scarring him any more than could be helped.

'She is, isn't she?' Larry agreed quietly, actually meaning it. Even after all the shit he'd given Georgie over the last year, she'd been at the hospital almost before they'd finished unloading him from the back of the ambulance and had stayed with him while he was being examined, holding his hand and telling him he was going to be fine.

Outside the hospital at that moment, Georgie shielded her eyes as cameras flashed all around her. Holding her hands up for quiet when the questions started coming thick and fast, she introduced herself as Larry's agent and spokeswoman. Then she said, 'I can't tell you too much at the moment, because I haven't heard the full story myself yet. But I can assure you that Larry is being extremely well looked after, and his injuries seem reasonably minor, so we're hoping for a full and quick recovery.'

'Any news on Dex Lewis?' one of the reporters called out.

'Is it true he was admitted to hospital for burns caused by the Taser?'

'I have no information about Derek Lewis,' Georgie informed the crowd coolly. 'But I'm sure the police will be happy to help you with your enquiries.'

'When will we get to see the show?' another reporter wanted to know now. 'Or will it be held as evidence against Lewis?'

'Again, I have no information about that,' Georgie answered. 'But I can tell you that the programme wasn't scheduled to be shown in England anyway, so I imagine you'd have to speak to the producers to see if they're planning on releasing any extracts.' Holding her hands up again, she said, 'That's really all I can tell you at this stage, so I'll leave you with that, because I want to get back to Larry. Thank you for your interest, and I'll keep you informed about his condition.'

'Did you ask them to clear the ambulance bays?' the nurse whispered when Georgie came back to the door.

Admitting that she'd completely forgotten, Georgie turned back and called out to the reporters, asking them to please respect that normal hospital business must be allowed to continue as usual, and could they take care not to block the entrances.

Awed by her aura of authority, the nurse almost curtsied when she let Georgie back into the hospital. Thanking her when the reporters started moving further back, she asked if there was anything she could get for her.

'A very strong coffee would be wonderful,' Georgie said, smiling gratefully and wearily. She'd been riding along on a tide of adrenalin since she'd heard that Larry had been attacked and injured, but now that she knew he was alive and reasonably unscathed, her body was beginning to close down on her.

'Are you okay?' the nurse asked, thinking she looked a little too pale.

Georgie opened her mouth to say that she was perfectly all right, but the ground gave way beneath her feet before a word came out.

Calling for assistance, the nurse made sure that Georgie was in safe hands, then rushed back to the small private room where Larry was being treated.

'Don't be alarmed,' she said, going in and closing the door behind her, 'but your mum's had a little turn, and we're having a doctor take a look at her. I just need to know if she has any conditions we ought to be aware of, or if she's taking any medication we should know about?'

'I want to see her,' Larry said, sitting up far too quickly. Shaking his head to clear the dizziness, he tried to get off the bed but stumbled back against it. When both nurses rushed forward to steady him, he pushed their hands away, saying, 'I'm fine – really. I just need to see her.'

'I'll get you a chair and take you to her,' his original nurse said, reluctant to let him out of her sight because they'd been getting on so well.

'*I'll* get it,' the second nurse said, backing quickly out of the room before her rival had a chance to beat her to it. Coming back seconds later, she helped Larry into the chair and wheeled him out.

Georgie was lying on a trolley in the A&E department, waiting to be seen by a doctor. The curtains were pulled only partially across the bay, and the other patients could clearly see her as they passed, which annoyed Larry.

'Why have you got her in here?' he demanded. 'Why didn't you bring her straight to my room? She's not a bloody sideshow.'

Apologising, the nurse explained that Georgie'd had to be brought into this section because she'd collapsed in the reception area.

Saying, 'I want her moved to somewhere better. And get

a doctor to see her – *now!*' Larry pulled the curtain aside and wheeled himself into the small room.

Opening her eyes, Georgie looked round at him and shook her head. 'What have I told you about being rude? And what are you playing at, anyway? You should be in bed.'

'Never mind me,' he said, gazing up at her worriedly. 'What's with you and all this collapsing nonsense, you dozy cow? Trying to steal the limelight, or what?'

'I'm diabetic,' Georgie told him. 'But I'm fine now. One of the nurses gave me a shot of insulin. They just want a doctor to take a look at me before they okay me to leave.'

'Since when have you been diabetic?' Larry frowned. 'And why didn't you tell *me*?'

'It's none of your business,' she told him, mock-sternly. 'You don't think I tell you everything, do you?'

'Yeah, well, you should have told me about *this*,' he muttered. 'What if you'd collapsed when you were driving me around? You'd have killed us both, you selfish bitch.'

'For your information, I have been managing my condition quite successfully for nigh on thirty years,' Georgie informed him tartly. 'So I neither need nor appreciate a lecture from someone who knows less than nothing about it.'

Coming back in time to hear this, the nurse raised an eyebrow, shocked that anybody would speak to Larry like that, never mind his own mother. But he obviously didn't mind, because he was holding her hand and looking up at her like he really loved her.

Smiling at Georgie now, so that Larry would see that she was treating his mother with the deference she deserved, the nurse said, 'I've arranged for you to be moved to a private room, and a consultant will be coming to see you as soon as possible. I'm very sorry you weren't seen immediately, but it's hectic in here tonight.'

'No need to move me,' Georgie told her, flapping her hand

to silence Larry when he opened his mouth to object. 'And I'm quite happy to wait my turn to see the duty doctor, thank you. I've already been treated, so I shouldn't have another episode just yet. In fact, I'm feeling a little guilty for taking up a bed, because I'm perfectly all right now. You could do one thing for me, though . . .' She jerked her head in Larry's direction. 'Take him back to his room before I strangle him.'

Exhaling wearily, Larry held up his hands in a gesture of surrender. 'Okay, I'm going. But you'd best do as you're told while you're here. And I'll be waiting for you out there, so don't even think about sneaking out and jumping in a cab, because I'm taking you home to look after you.'

'I think you'll find that it's *you* who needs looking after, not me,' Georgie informed him in clipped tones. 'So you're coming home with me tonight. Now scoot.'

Waiting until the nurse had taken Larry away and the curtain had been pulled all the way across, Georgie laid her head back and pressed her thumbs onto her eyelids to prevent the tears that were burning the back of her eyes from escaping. *That* was the Larry Logan she knew and loved. Not the egomaniacal little swine he'd morphed into over recent years, who flirted and demanded his way through life not seeming to really care about anyone or anything. She'd always known he was still in there somewhere, but it was so touching to actually see him again – and all the more touching that it should be in *his* hour of need that he'd chosen to resurface to care for *her*. That made all the irritations and hurt feelings of the last year evaporate as if they had been nothing but a bad dream.

All the way across town on the south side of Manchester, having escorted Dex Lewis to Wythenshawe Hospital – personally, to ensure that no more cock-ups occurred before

they got him safely back to the station and into a cell –
Inspector Keeton was pacing up and down outside the exam-
ination room, waiting to hear the prognosis.

Lewis had looked pretty rough when they'd brought him
in, but injuries were unavoidable when prisoners resisted arrest
as vigorously as he had. The Taser had laid him out
temporarily, giving the police a chance to rescue Larry and
get him seen to, but Lewis had been back on his feet in record
time, and then it had taken a whole battalion of men to bring
him under control. As Keeton had expected and wanted to
avoid, Lewis had managed to inflict a fair bit of damage on
a few of the uniforms before they managed to subdue him.
Most just had minor cuts and bruises, but two of the lads
were still under observation back at the MRI, and at least
one of them was looking quite serious, having taken a savage
kick in the head.

But, much as he regretted what had happened to his own
lads, and, worse, to Larry Logan – awkward questions were
bound to be asked about *that* – Keeton was still glad that
he'd finally got hold of Lewis. He just hoped that the bastard
hadn't sustained any serious injuries of his own during the
battle, because he'd be bound to put in a claim for compensation, and the increasingly crazy human-rights brigade would
no doubt back him up and make sure he got a huge pay-
out.

Stopping mid-pace when the examination-room door
opened, Keeton jerked his chin at the doctor.

Frowning at him over the rim of his glasses, the medic
walked away from the door, forcing Keeton to follow him
down the corridor. Stopping when he thought he'd put enough
distance between them and the patient, the doctor said, 'He's
a very lucky man, inspector. Given his external appearance,
he has remarkably few injuries. No internal bleeding, breaks
or fractures. No significant trauma at all, in fact. Just a great

deal of bruising, which should fade within a matter of weeks, I would imagine.'

'Are you sure?' Keeton asked, having prepared himself for the worst. 'What about the after-effects of the Taser? He took quite a hit.'

Shaking his head, the doctor shrugged. 'Nothing to cause alarm. Appearances to the contrary, the man seems to be in perfect physical order.'

'I'll be buggered,' Keeton murmured, running a hand over his face. Then, 'Right, well, good. I'll take him, then.'

Peering at the inspector, the doctor said, 'Might I ask if this man has ever had a psychiatric evaluation?'

'No idea,' Keeton said brusquely, immediately suspecting that Lewis might be trying to pull a fast one and get himself off the charges by claiming diminished responsibility. 'And to be honest, doc, I'm not interested. If you can just give me the discharge, we'll be on our way.'

Nodding, the doctor said, 'As you wish.'

Thanking him, Keeton exhaled tensely as the doctor walked away. Lewis wasn't seriously hurt – that was all Keeton cared about. But he *had* seriously hurt at least one copper, *and* stabbed Larry Logan – which should bring a hefty sentence all of its own. Attempted murder, if Keeton got his way.

# IO

'What do you mean, you can't get me bailed?' Dex hissed, peering at his solicitor across the interview-room table. 'What the fuck do I pay you for?'

'It's not that easy,' Keith Hall hissed back, his brow deeply creased as he looked at the cuts and bruises covering Dex's face. It was a week since Lewis had been arrested at the sham game show, and he still looked terrible. But rather than make him look like a victim of police brutality, it just made him look even more villainous than usual, and Keith was worried that the judge at his client's pre-trial hearing would take one look and label him a worthless thug.

'What have they actually got on me?' Dex asked now.

'You're already wanted for jumping bail on the TDA,' Keith reminded him, 'so there's no chance you'll get bail this time. But that's the least of your worries, because they're going after you for aggravated assault of several police officers – which you've already got a history of, so *that* won't look good either. And then you've got the attempted murder of Larry Logan as well.'

'He deserved it,' Dex spat, his eyes flashing with a lust for vengeance.

'Maybe he did,' Keith retorted impatiently. 'But not in front of the entire fucking police force *and* a CCTV camera. How the hell am I supposed to get you out of *that*?'

'You don't get it,' Dex said quietly. 'I can't stay here. They took my DNA.'

'I know,' Keith murmured, his gaze darting to the door when he heard a movement outside. Lowering his voice even further, he said, 'Look, just give me time to get my stuff together, and let me see if I can get a reduction, if not a dismissal, on the grounds of provocation and entrapment. The TDA's minor compared to that, so we could be looking at only two to three if the other charges get chucked out. But you've got to stay cool while I'm working on it, or you won't stand a chance.'

Slamming both fists down on the table top, Dex said, 'How the *fuck* am I supposed to stay cool with these cunts jeering at me through the cell door, telling me what they'd do if they could have two minutes alone with me. Pussy cunts won't come into the cell alone, though, 'cos they know I'd break their spineless backs in half!'

'And *this* is exactly what I'm talking about,' Keith told him firmly. 'Carry on like this and you'll be playing right into their hands. They're on dodgy ground with the methods they used to effect arrest, and they know it, so they're going to do their damnedest to wind you up while you're in custody to make you really lose it.'

'If you don't pull your finger out and get me bailed, they'll get what they're looking for,' Dex growled. 'But it won't just be assault or *attempted* murder, it'll be the real fucking deal. You've got to get this sorted *now* so I can disappear.'

Resting his elbows on the table, Keith clasped his hands together and peered at Dex. He'd known him for almost ten years, and had actually been a mate of his before qualifying and becoming his solicitor, so he knew enough about him to realise that he was hiding something. Dex was smart enough to usually stay a couple of steps ahead of the police, so they'd only had him on relatively minor charges so far. But Keith guessed from his demeanour that there were worse things to be uncovered than the present charges they were levelling at him. And now that the police had his DNA it would be only a matter of time before they found them.

Needing to know what he was dealing with, he said, 'What are we talking here, Dex?'

'No details, but it's bad,' Dex replied evasively. 'So just do what you've got to do to get me out on bail. Leave the rest to me.'

Nodding, Keith said, 'I'll do what I can. But it might take time, and they're not going to make it easy.'

'I pay you to *make* it easy,' Dex reminded him, giving him a long meaningful look.

'I said I'll do what I can,' Keith repeated tersely.

Nodding, Dex said, 'Go see me ma when you leave here and make sure the lads have cleared the house out, 'cos I don't want her dragged into this. And tell our Pat to stay low and get some tickets for somewhere hot, yeah?'

'Anywhere specific?' Keith asked, gathering his paperwork together.

'He'll know.'

'Anything else?'

'Yeah, tell me ma to tell Gaynor to pull all my money in and keep it safe till I get out. She knows where it's at. You got all that?'

Nodding, Keith stood up. 'I'll do my bit, Dex. But you've got to do *yours* – just take it easy till I get back to you, or you're screwed.'

'So long as these cunts lay off with the lip,' Dex replied coldly.

Shaking his head, because Dex truly was his own worst enemy, Keith tapped on the door and told the officer who was standing guard outside that he was leaving.

'Make it quick,' Dex called after him, glaring at the young PC as if he'd like to rip his head off his shoulders and stick it as far up his arse as it would go.

★

An attractive young policewoman was walking hurriedly along the corridor when Keith came out of the interview room. Nodding at her as they passed, he walked on a couple of yards, then stopped when he heard her asking the PC – who was now waiting for back-up to come and help him take Lewis back to his cell – if he'd seen Inspector Keeton. Instincts prickling, Keith casually squatted down and unzipped his briefcase, then rifled through it as if he was looking for something among the papers that it contained.

Telling her that he thought he'd heard the inspector say that he was going to the canteen, the PC tilted his head to one side and watched her as she walked away.

'Nice arse,' Keith commented amusedly.

'Nice everything,' the PC agreed, with a laddish grin. Then, looking down at the case, 'Lost something?'

'Just checking I've still got my mobile,' Keith said, re-zipping the case and straightening up. 'Can't be too careful with this lot, can you?' He cast a meaningful glance at the interview-room door.

'Not with the likes of him,' the PC grunted quietly.

Amused that he'd lowered his voice, probably scared that Dex would hear him and kick off, Keith smiled. It was a myth that solicitors and police officers treated each other like enemies. TV coppers and briefs might circle each other like dogs trying to sniff out each others' weaknesses without revealing their own, but it was just wordplay in reality, and there was rarely any actual animosity. In Keith's experience, it was better to appear to be leaning more towards the police side of the line, because you learned far more that way.

Glancing at his watch now, he ran a hand through his hair, muttering, 'Oh, great, I've missed my train. Anywhere I can grab a cup of tea in here while I'm waiting?'

'Canteen's down there,' the PC told him, pointing the way.

'Round the corner, second left. Anyone asks, just tell them Mick Dillon okayed it.'

Thanking him, Keith set off at a casual pace. But he speeded up as soon as he turned the corner in the hopes of being in time to eavesdrop if the woman was telling Keeton anything pertinent to Dex's case.

Keeton was shovelling the last forkful of lamb curry into his mouth when Keith walked into the canteen, and Carla was just sitting down at his table with the coffee she'd bought herself. The table was situated close to the sandwich bar so, keeping his face turned in case the inspector recognised him, Keith walked over to it and pretended to be looking at the display.

'Gawd, that was hot,' Keeton said, putting his fork down and wiping his face on a napkin. 'But you can't beat a good curry for clearing the sinuses.' Smacking his lips now, he patted his belly with satisfaction. 'Right, I'm all yours.'

'Nothing definite, but we might have a hit,' Carla told him, sipping on her coffee. 'Harry flagged up a cold case in Salford from seven years back, and – fingers crossed – Lewis might be a match.'

'Yes!' Keeton hissed jubilantly. 'Is it big enough to nail him, or just something trivial?'

'Big enough,' Carla replied, smiling at the look of triumph in his eyes. 'Remember the gang who broke into the house and tortured the guy who lived there?'

'Then raped his mother when she heard noises and went to investigate,' Keeton said, the gleam in his eyes turning to ice. 'You saying that was him?'

'Could be.'

Shaking his head, Keeton exhaled loudly. 'I always knew he was a bastard, but I didn't think even *he* was capable of something like that.'

'Yes, well, we'll soon know,' Carla said quietly. 'But we'll still have to find the rest of the gang if it was him.'

'Shouldn't be too hard to trace them.'

'From seven years ago?'

'Old habits die hard,' Keeton said simply. 'And we can start with his brothers, because they're bound to be involved.' Glancing irritably around now when somebody moved past his chair and brushed his head with their elbow, he glared at Keith's retreating back and called out sarcastically, 'Yeah, you're all right, son, apology accepted.' Tutting when he got no response, he turned back to Carla. 'So, when does Harry reckon he'll know for sure?'

'Normal speed, or complete rush job?' Carla asked, smiling again because the inspector had that bit-between-the-teeth look in his eyes.

'What do *you* think?' he said, already mentally rolling up his sleeves in preparation for wiping the Lewis family off the crime map.

Nora Lewis's hand was shaking when she put the phone down. Her whole body was shaking, in fact, and she felt the ham sandwich she'd just eaten churning in her stomach. Shoving her chair back from the table, she got up and rushed out into the hall, yelling, '*Patriiiick!*'

Flying down the stairs, Patrick saw how pale her face was and thought she was having a stroke or a heart attack or something. Reaching out to her, he said, 'What's wrong, Mam? What is it?'

Slapping his hands away, Nora pointed at the boxes of stolen gear that were still stacked in the hall, and said, 'Shift this.'

'Jeezus!' Patrick exhaled loudly. 'Is that it? I thought you was fucking dying, you silly old cow.'

'What's up?' Nora's youngest son Jason asked, running down the stairs with Molly close behind.

'I thought she was snuffing it,' Patrick told him, rolling his eyes. 'But she's only narking about the bleedin' boxes.'

'Don't take the piss out of me,' Nora snapped, in no mood for games. 'I want it shifted *now*! I've just had Keith on the phone, and he says they're gonna hammer our Dex. So, no more messing about, just move it. And you . . .' She jabbed a finger in Molly's direction. 'Get your shoes on and go tell that bitch of his to collect his money from wherever he's got it stashed, 'cos he needs it all there when he gets out.'

'Don't see why *I*'ve got to tell her,' Molly grumbled, stomping back up the stairs. 'She's got no business knowing where his money is, anyway. None of *us* know, so why does she?'

'None of us is happy about it,' Nora shouted after her. 'But now's not the time to play funny buggers, so just do as you're told.' Turning to Patrick now, she said, 'Keith says you're to go and buy tickets for somewhere hot.'

Patrick stopped in his tracks. For Dex to say something like that, he had to think that he was going to get charged with something heavy and was planning on doing a runner. And if it was coming on top for *him*, then Patrick would no doubt be getting a tug as well, because he'd been involved in everything that Dex had ever done.

'Did Keith say what they're charging him with?' he asked, needing to know how urgent this was.

'No idea,' Nora said, yanking Jason down off the last step and shoving him towards the boxes. 'He just said it's bad, and you've to clear the house out before we get raided. So quit yakking and get on with it.'

'Where are we supposed to put it?' Jason asked, picking up the first stack, a sulky look on his face. He hated being the youngest, because the others used him as a joey and he always got the least when it came to divvying up the money.

'Shove it in the car,' Patrick told him, rushing back upstairs. 'I'll drop it at Mark's on me way out.'

'Mark's a thieving cunt,' Jason yelled after him. 'Why don't you take it to Keith's instead? The coppers can't go searching a solicitor's gaff.'

'He ain't there,' Nora said, lighting a cigarette and letting it dangle from her lips as she rolled up her sleeves. 'He's passing the case over to one of his colleagues, 'cos he's going on holiday.'

Stepping aside to let Molly pass when she came back down just then, Jason dropped the boxes. 'What do you mean, he's going on holiday? He can't. Our Dex needs him here.'

'Yeah, well, I thought it was a bit funny an' all, but that's what he said,' Nora muttered, more concerned about clearing the house out than arguing over details. 'Hurry up and get that bloody car loaded up before I have a flaming stroke, will you? I can't be doing with all this bother at my age.'

Coming back just then with his and Dex's passports in his hand, Patrick gave Jason a shove. 'What you been saying to upset her, dickhead?'

'I ain't said nowt,' Jason replied defensively, stooping down to pick up the boxes again. 'It's *her*. She reckons Keith's going on holiday and passing our Dex on to some other cunt.'

'Don't start,' Nora snapped when Patrick asked her what was going on. 'You want to pick a fight, give *him* a ring, or go see him, but don't keep questioning me, 'cos I'm only the bleedin' messenger.'

'I'll see him, all right,' Patrick muttered darkly, yanking his jacket off the hook and pulling it on. 'If he thinks he's taking off for a fucking sunbathe and leaving me and our Dex in the shit, he's got another think coming.'

'You?' Nora peered at him questioningly. 'What's it got to do with you?'

'Leave it, Mam,' Patrick muttered, zipping up his jacket.

'Don't you try and fob me off,' Nora snapped, blocking his path as he made to move to the door. 'I need to know what you've been up to so I know what to say when the coppers turn up.'

'The less you know, the better,' he said, taking her by the shoulders and moving her gently but firmly out of the way. Pulling his hood up now, he eased the door open and peered out to see if the house was being watched. Satisfied that it was all clear outside, he ran to the car, calling back over his shoulder for Jason to get a move on.

It took Molly twenty minutes to reach her dad's flat, and she was in a foul mood by the time she got there. She didn't see why she'd had to walk when her uncle Patrick could have dropped her off. And why did *she* have to come, anyway, when everyone knew she hated Gaynor's guts?

She'd never understood what her dad saw in the slag. She was a right vain bitch, always checking herself out in the mirror like she was Miss Fucking World, or something. But she was nothing special in Molly's opinion: all make-up and expensive clothes – expensive clothes that Molly's *dad* had paid for, because Gaynor was too bleeding lazy to earn her own money.

Molly resented her for that, almost as much as she resented her living in the flat while Molly had to share a tidgy room with her cousin at her nan's. Still, at least her dad had been spending more time at her nan's since he'd jumped bail, so Molly got to see more of him than Gaynor did. And her nan had refused to let him bring the slag with him, which showed her exactly where she stood with the family – *nowhere*.

Jamming her key into the lock now, Molly went in and slammed the door behind her. Barging noisily into the living room, she sucked her teeth when she saw Gaynor curled up on the couch, wrapped up in the duvet, watching TV with the curtains shut.

Sighing when she saw who it was, Gaynor reached for the remote and turned the TV volume down. Molly was a living nightmare, and she wished Dex hadn't given her a key because it was horrible to have someone walk into your home whenever they felt like it. But you couldn't say a word against Dex's precious little princess without him kicking off, so Gaynor had no choice but to grit her teeth and bear the little madam. Sometimes she really regretted having given up her own flat to move in here.

'Your dad's not called,' she said now, hoping that Molly would turn round and walk straight back out.

'I know *that*,' Molly spat, not even attempting to keep the hatred out of her voice or eyes.

Frowning, Gaynor sat up. 'Has he called you?'

'None of your business,' Molly sniped, stalking across the room and picking up a bundle of unopened letters that Gaynor had left on the table. Leafing through them, she said, 'He says you're to get all his money together as soon as poss and bring it to me nan's.' The last bit was a lie, but she didn't care. If her dad was getting sent down, there was no way this bitch was getting her mitts on his dosh.

'Leave the mail alone,' Gaynor told her irritably, swinging her feet down to the floor. 'It's private.'

'It's me dad's, and so's this flat, so I'll do what I want,' Molly retorted, eyeing Gaynor's pyjamas with contempt. It was three in the afternoon, and the dirty cow wasn't even dressed yet. Defiantly pocketing the letters, she walked back to the door, shouldering past Gaynor who was standing up now.

Resisting the urge to give Molly a long-overdue slap, Gaynor folded her arms. 'Has he said what they're charging him with yet?'

'Don't ask me,' Molly said tartly. 'All I know is it's supposed to be bad. So I'd get packing if I was you, 'cos there's no way you're staying here if he gets banged up.' Giving Gaynor a last dirty look, she yanked the door open and marched out.

Gaynor exhaled loudly. Molly was too rude for her own good, and if Dex didn't do something about her she was going to get on the wrong side of the wrong person one of these days.

But that was their problem, not hers. Gaynor had more important things to think about right now – like trying to round up Dex's money. And that was going to take ages, because she'd have to go round to all of his mates to pick up the bits and pieces he'd stashed with them, then work her way through his book collecting the debts he was owed. And, knowing his skanky debtors, it wasn't going to be easy to get them to cough up if they'd heard that he was off the scene. But she had to try, or Dex would blame her for letting them take the piss.

It annoyed Gaynor that Dex had landed this on her, especially when he hadn't even bothered to ring her to let her know what was happening. He could find the time to ring his precious bloody mother, though, and that really pissed her off, because he was always putting his family before her. Still, it was nothing less than she'd come to expect of him lately.

What she *hadn't* expected was for him to demand that she get all his money together. It must mean that they had something heavy on him, and it worried her that she had no idea what it was, or even if she might somehow be implicated in it because she lived with him. But she doubted his family would enlighten her, because his mother seemed to hate her as much as his daughter did. And his brothers weren't much better, although at least they just ignored her for the most part – which was fine by her because she didn't particularly like them, anyway.

Truth be told, she didn't like Dex much, either, at the moment. He'd been so sweet when she met him, always taking her out and paying her compliments. But that had soon stopped when she moved in with him. From charmer to bad-tempered pig in one fell swoop, and if she complained he thought nothing of giving her a slap. So now she kept her mouth shut and got on with doing his cleaning while he took off for days at a time, doing God knew what with God knew who. And she didn't even have anyone to talk to when he was gone, because his family hated her and her own family and friends had turned their backs on her because *they* hated Dex.

But not liking Dex and not *loving* him were very different beasts, and her heart always overruled her head when she thought about leaving. So she stayed, praying for the day when the real Dex would reappear. And now that he'd gone and got himself banged up, she saw a glimmer of a chance that, with time to sit and think instead of always running, he might just re-evaluate his life and stop taking her for granted.

And it wouldn't hurt him to be away from his interfering mother for a while, either. He'd been more distant than ever since he'd been staying with her, and Gaynor was sure that the old bitch had been slagging her off. She wouldn't have minded if she'd actually done something to warrant it, but it seemed that just being another woman in his life was enough.

But there was time enough to worry about them and their stupid jealousy when she'd sorted Dex's money out. So, taking a quick shower, Gaynor got dressed and made her way out to make her first pick-up. But she wouldn't be taking the money to Nora's when she got it – and Molly could kick off as much as she liked, because if Dex had wanted them to have access to it he'd have told *them* where it was.

Patrick went home a couple of hours later with two open-ended tickets to Amsterdam. He'd called in at Keith Hall's office on the way back, to find out what was happening and make the cunt change his mind about the timing of his holiday. But he'd been too late, because Keith had already gone, and Dex's case had been passed over to a woman.

Patrick wasn't impressed by the thought of having a bird for a solicitor, but Kay Morgan soothed his nerves a little when she took him into her office and told him that she was well aware of Keith's 'special relationship' with the Lewises and would endeavour to maintain it in his absence. She talked poncy but there was something ballsy about her, and Patrick came away with a grudging respect for her. He still wasn't convinced that she'd get their Dex bailed when he went to court tomorrow for his preliminary hearing, but she was the only chance he had, so all they could do was cross their fingers and pray that she pulled it off like she seemed to think she could.

Sitting at the kitchen table now, with his mother and his older brother Jimmy, Patrick was chewing his nails to the quick, waiting for Kay to call. She'd set off for her first meet with Dex after talking to Patrick, and had promised to call them as soon as she was clear, to bring them up to speed and pass on any messages. All Patrick wanted to know was whether he needed to disappear *now*, or wait to hear if Dex had got bail tomorrow.

Their only other option was to intercept the vehicle transporting Dex to the court and spring him. But that would be major risky, and the police would no doubt be planning on stepping up their security in anticipation of them doing just that, so it wasn't really feasible in any case.

At least the house was clean, so they didn't have to worry about Nora getting caught up in anything if it went pear-shaped. And Molly had been sent back to her mother's to keep her out of the way, while Molly's little cousin Lyla had gone to stay with one of Nora's nieces. With their Jason keeping an eye on Gaynor in case she tried to pull a fast one with the money that she'd refused to hand over, they were as sorted as they could be, so they just had to wait now and see what happened next.

And that was torturous – especially for Patrick, who felt like an animal trapped in a cage while the hunters moved in silently from the shadows.

Everyone jumped when a heavy knocking came at the front door.

'I'll get it,' Jimmy said, waving his mother to stay put.

'It'll probably be Hilda,' she said, reaching for yet another cigarette. 'She said she might be popping in, and I forgot to tell her not to.'

'Tell her to piss off if it is,' Patrick called after Jimmy who was already making his way to the door. 'I can't be doing with her today.'

Nora tutted softly. She didn't particularly want to see anyone right now, either, but she couldn't half do with having her tea leaves read – just to set her mind at ease.

It wasn't Hilda, it was Dex's ex-wife Jane.

'What do you want?' Nora grunted when she saw her.

'A cup of tea would be nice,' Jane said, giving her ex-mother-in-law a sarcastic smile. 'If you can manage it.'

Grumbling under her breath about uninvited visitors always pushing themselves on her when they were least welcome, Nora got up and filled the kettle.

Sitting down, Jane took a cigarette out of her bag and lit it, saying, 'How's it going, lads?'

Still chewing his nails, Patrick shrugged. He didn't like Jane any more than he liked Gaynor. But then, he didn't particularly *dis*like them, either. Truth be told, he felt nothing for either of them – other than a bit of dick interest, because they were both good-looking and sexy: Jane fair, like Molly, with the same big tits and sassy attitude; Gaynor dark-haired and quiet, with smaller tits and longer legs. He'd have given either of them a seeing-to if Dex weren't around, but Dex would kill him without blinking if he as much as looked at one of his women. Maybe if Dex went down for a long stretch . . .

'What do you want, Jane?' Jimmy asked her coolly, having no such interest in her. She was nothing but his brother's skanky ex, as far as he was concerned, and he didn't trust her as far as he could throw her.

'Just visiting my family,' she replied nonchalantly, as if she didn't know that she was about as welcome as a vulture at a plane crash. 'Thought you'd want to know how Molly was getting on now she's back home where she belongs.'

'She's only been gone a week,' Nora snapped, bringing the teapot and four clean cups to the table and banging them down.

'Yeah, and she's already eaten all the bloody food I had in,' Jane said, flicking her ash into the overflowing ashtray. Licking her fingertip when some of the ash landed on the table top, she picked it up and deposited it with the rest, saying, 'So I need some money.'

'You what?' Nora gasped disbelievingly. 'She's *your* kid.'

'And Dex's,' Jane reminded her tartly. 'And I don't see why I should be out of pocket just 'cos he's had enough of playing happy families with her.'

Incensed, Nora shoved her sleeves roughly up her arms and jabbed a finger down on the table. 'Now you just listen here, madam. We've had that girl for the better part of a year, and we ain't had one single bloody penny off you, so don't come here with your hand out expecting us to subsidise you, 'cos you're not on.'

Sitting forward, Jane calmly poured herself a cup of tea. Stirring sugar into it, she said, 'If you want me to keep her, you'll have to help me out, that's all I'm saying. The benefits don't cover nothing these days, and I can't afford a greedy teenager. Especially not one like her, who seems to think she deserves hundred-quid trainers every other week. I don't know what you lot have been filling her head with, but she's not the kid I used to know, I can tell you that for nowt. I've never met a more spoiled brat in me life.'

'Yeah, well, maybe if you'd been a better mother we wouldn't have had to give her stuff to make up for what she never got off you,' Nora retorted.

'Dex tell you I was a bad mother, did he?' Jane asked calmly, smiling with her lips while her eyes blazed with anger. 'That his version of why he took her off me, was it? Not that he put me in hospital and *had* to take her or she'd have been on her own?'

Gazing back at her, Nora shook her head. 'You're a piece of work, you are, Jane. You know full well why he did that, and you had no one but yourself to blame, so don't come it with the poor little victim routine.'

'So I shagged his mate.' Jane shrugged. 'Big deal. It wasn't like *he* wasn't doing it with every other bird in Manchester.'

'He's a *man*,' Nora reminded her, as if that made all the difference.

'Yeah, and I was his woman.'

'Not enough of one, obviously, or he wouldn't have had to get it from them other lasses.'

Sitting back now, Jane narrowed her eyes. 'You call *me* a piece of work, Nora, but you're ten times worse. It's no wonder your Dex turned out the way he did with you filling his thick head with poison.'

'And it's no wonder your Molly's turning into a slut, with you showing her how it's done!' Nora spat back.

'Don't you call my daughter a slut.'

'Well, you keep your dirty gob shut about my son, then!'

'Shut it, the pair of you,' Jimmy barked, slamming his hand down on the table.

Reaching out to steady the teapot, Nora pursed her lips.

Looking at Jane now, Jimmy said, 'Sling your hook, Jane, you're getting nowt off us.'

'Fine,' Jane replied coldly. 'Well, I'll just send her back then, 'cos I can't keep her on fresh air.'

Getting up now, Jimmy came around the table and leaned down so that his face was just inches away from hers. 'Don't play games with me, you slag. She's your responsibility, so get your arse home and be the mother you're supposed to be.'

Drawing her head back, Jane glared up at him defiantly. 'Don't you threaten me, Jimmy Lewis, or I'll scream my head off, and all them coppers will come bursting in and—'

'Coppers?' Patrick squawked. 'What coppers?'

'Them what's sitting in the van at the top of the road,' Jane told him, still glaring at Jimmy.

Jumping up, Patrick rushed out of the room and ran up the stairs to look out of the bedroom window.

'What are they doing?' Nora asked Jane when he'd gone. 'Are they watching this house or someone else's?'

Shrugging, Jane said, 'How do I know? They were just sitting there when I drove past. I didn't stop to ask them who they were after. But knowing this lot round here, it could be anyone, couldn't it? Anyway, they've already got Dex, so what you worrying for?'

When Patrick came back just then, Jimmy gave a questioning jerk of his chin. 'They still there?'

'No,' Patrick muttered, going to the back window and closing the curtains. 'I don't like it. Why would they be sitting there one minute, then take off as soon as *she* clocks them? And they haven't gone to anyone else's gaff, so they must have been watching us. I've got to get out of here.'

'We've to wait for that solicitor to call and let us know what's happening,' Nora reminded him. 'Anyway, they might not have been watching us. They could have just been checking out a car, or anything. Just sit down and chill out. We'll know soon enough.'

'I can't chill out,' Patrick snapped, pacing the floor now. 'They could be coming after me.'

'The solicitor would know if they were and she'd have told us,' Nora said, more to convince herself that everything was all right than to convince him.

'You can wait if you want, but I'm off,' Patrick said, reaching into his pocket to check that the tickets and passports were still there. 'I'll stop round at Mooky's, so ring us on me mobile soon as you hear anything. And if they keep our Dex, I'll leave his ticket there.'

'Wait,' Jimmy said sharply when he headed for the door. 'If they *were* watching us, they'll have backed off 'cos she saw them, but they won't have gone far. And they'll be watching the back as well as the front in case you do a runner.'

'So what am I supposed to do?' Patrick yelled.' Just sit here and wait for them to bust us for fucking murder?'

'Murder?' Nora squawked. 'No one mentioned fucking murder to me!'

Chuckling softly, Jane shook her head. 'Oh, come on now, Nora, don't tell me you don't know what your lads get up to behind your back. Why do you think I was so glad Dex got sent down that time? I love the bones of the bastard, but when he starts threatening to kill *me* – and I *know* he's capable of it – I'd have been an idiot not to be glad he was nicked.'

'You shut it, you!' Nora yelled at her, wondering why she was still here.

'If you insist,' Jane said, folding her arms. 'But I *was* about to suggest a way for your Pat to get out of here without the coppers seeing him.'

That got everyone's attention.

Swallowing hard because it stuck in her craw that she might have to be nice to Jane if this suggestion involved her smuggling Patrick out in her car, or something, Nora said, 'How?'

Smiling slyly, Jane reached up and pulled the wig off her head. 'He can wear this.'

'What the fuck are you wearing *that* for?' Nora said, looking at it like it was about to bite her. 'It's exactly the same as your own.'

'Exactly,' Jane said, shrugging nonchalantly. 'I always wear it when I can't be arsed washing my hair. And no one's ever sussed it, so why not?'

Jimmy gave a rare laugh. 'You know what, I think it might work.' Turning to Patrick now, still grinning, he said, 'Shove it on, our kid, and let's see if you can pull it off.'

'You can put my clothes on as well,' Jane said, standing up now and slipping her pink faux-fur jacket off. 'Some of them coppers clocked me when I passed them, so they'll think you're me if they see you in this. You'll have to leave me skirt unzipped 'cos you're too much of a fat bastard to fit into it. And you'll have a bit of a problem getting your feet into my stillys, 'cos I'm only a six.'

'Fuck off!' Patrick snorted, tossing the wig onto the table. 'I'm no fucking tranny.'

'You are if you want to get out of here before they come for you,' Nora said in a no-nonsense tone. Looking at Jane now, she nodded. 'Thanks, love. You've done us a big favour here.'

'That's what family's for,' Jane said, already stepping out of her skirt, unconcerned that Patrick and Jimmy were getting an eyeful of her sexy knickers. Dex hadn't cared about all the men ogling her when she'd been lap dancing, so why would he care about his brothers ogling her now?

Looking thoroughly sulky, Patrick took off his jeans and

slipped the skirt on. Reaching for Jane's blouse when she pulled it off, he dipped his gaze, trying not to stare at her nipples which were clearly visible through the silky sheerness of her bra.

The stilettos were far too tight, but Nora had an idea and bustled up to Molly's room. The girls these days liked the toes of their shoes to be wider than the pointed jobbies their mothers preferred, and Molly had about a million pairs to choose from. Picking out a pair of open-toed slip-on's with a middling heel now, she carried them back down and told Patrick to try them.

'They fucking hurt,' he complained when he'd wedged his feet into them.

'At least you got into them, so shut it,' Nora scolded unsympathetically. 'Now shove the jacket on, and let's have a look at you.'

Laughing loudly, Jimmy said, 'Fucking hell, man, you've got hairy legs for a bird. Don't you think you'd best give 'em a shave?'

'Just shove some tights on,' Jane suggested, taking her make-up out of her handbag and laying it out on the table. 'But let me do this first.' Pulling a chair out, she pushed Patrick down onto it. 'I'll put some foundation on to cover your spots, and I've got some bright red lippy that should suit you. No one will ever guess you're a bloke when I've finished with you.'

Breathing hard as Jane stood in front of him painting his face, Patrick gritted his teeth to keep the hard-on at bay. Dex had paid for her to have a boob-job before it all blew up between them, and they were jutting out at him like twin beacons of pleasure. He could smell her perfume, too, and it was bloody nice. Why the hell their Dex was bothering with boring Gaynor when he could be shafting this one, he didn't know. But, then, Dex *did* still shaft her when he felt like it – he just didn't let Nora know about it, because she'd only give him earache about diseases.

'There we go,' Jane said, stepping back when she'd finished. 'You look like Marilyn Monroe.'

Looking at himself in the mirror, Patrick grimaced. 'More like Danny fucking La Rue.'

'Hey, don't knock it,' Jimmy teased. '*I'd* shag you if I saw you in a club.'

'You'd shag a fucking *dog* if its hair was long enough,' Patrick retorted angrily.

Telling them both to stop talking dirty, Nora flapped her hand at Jane, saying, 'Give him your keys.'

'He can't take my car as well as me clothes,' Jane snorted, folding her arms. 'I'm not running a bloody charity here.'

'You can take his till you get yours back.'

'I'm not driving that fucking death trap. I'll take Dex's, or forget it.'

'Dex would kill us if we let you take his Jag,' Nora said. 'He don't let no one drive that.'

Pointing out that Dex wasn't in any position to give orders, Jane shrugged. 'Your choice. Oh, and I want a grand, as well. And don't tell me you haven't got it, 'cos Molly told me that bitch he's shacked up with has got all his money.'

'You'll get your money,' Jimmy said, no longer smiling, because this was the Jane they all knew and hated – give with one hand, snatch back with both. 'But you'll have to wait, 'cos it's round at his place. And you ain't getting Dex's car, so forget that.'

'Okay,' Jane conceded, giving him a satisfied smile. 'But don't even think about forgetting the money, or I might just have to play dirty.'

'And you might just wind up getting exactly what you're asking for,' Jimmy said quietly, his eyes flashing a clear warning.

Pulling Jane's jacket on now, Patrick flapped his arms. 'Well?'

'Brilliant,' Nora told him, circling him to look him over. Up close, it was obvious that he was a man, but from a distance it would be really hard to tell. And the coppers would only get a brief glimpse from wherever they were hiding as he walked to the car, so he should get away with it.

Exhaling nervously, Patrick said, 'I hope to God this works, 'cos if they pull me and take me to the nick looking like this I'll get fucking gang-banged.'

'Get the walk right, and you'll be fine,' Jane called after him as Jimmy herded him towards the door. 'Just think like all them strippers you've seen over the years.'

Hanging back to give Nora a quick hug, Patrick said, 'Right, I'm off then. Keep your fingers crossed, and I'll give youse a ring when I get to Caroline's.'

'I thought you said you were going to Mooky's,' Nora said, peering up at him.

'Yeah, 'cos I don't trust *her*,' Patrick hissed, nodding back towards the kitchen. 'Don't be telling her *nothing*, Mam.'

Promising that she wouldn't, Nora gave him a last kiss, then pushed him out of the door.

Sitting in an unmarked car at the end of the road, Carla saw the Lewises' front door open and a woman come out. Sliding lower in her seat, she clicked her radio on and whispered, 'Someone's leaving the house.'

'One of the lads?' Keeton replied from the van, which was out of sight around the corner now.

'Blonde woman. Want me to pull her?'

'No, it'll be that tart Lewis used to be married to. She drove past us before. She's nothing. Just keep your eye on the house, make sure no one slips out with her.'

'Will do,' Carla said, settling back down to watch.

The woman drove past a minute later. Shaking her head

in disgust when she saw the pink jacket, Carla wondered how come unattractive women always wore the most garish colours to draw attention to themselves when they really should be doing their damnedest to fade into the background. And, considering Dex Lewis prided himself on his ability to pull fit birds, he'd sure picked an ugly one to mother his child.

Keeping his cool, Patrick kept an eye on the unmarked car in the rear-view mirror as he reached the corner. He'd clocked the stupid bitch who was almost lying down in the front seat, and knew that she'd clocked him, too. But she wasn't moving, so it was looking pretty good so far.

Spotting the tiniest glimmer of white in the mouth of the alley to his left when he turned onto the main road, he kept his gaze firmly to the front and, sticking his little finger out like women did, flicked at the fringe of the wig as he drove past the hidden police van, as if he was preening himself.

Laughing with relief when the van didn't come after him either, Patrick waited until he was well clear. Then he put his foot down and bombed to his part-time shag Caroline's house.

# PART TWO

# 11

Inhaling deeply through his nose when the video came to an end, Larry crossed his legs and clasped his hands together in his lap as gasps of shocked disbelief and admiration rippled through the audience.

It was three months since he'd filmed the sham game show, and his career was back on with a vengeance. He was something of a national hero, in fact; everyone was clamouring for his story since it had emerged that Dex Lewis was guilty of far worse than the original charges that the police had wanted him for. The whole thing had exploded into something huge and crazy, and Georgie had been working her backside off as offers of new shows and requests for interviews poured in. Larry had even been offered a seven-figure deal to write his memoirs – which he would give serious consideration to, if he ever got a spare minute between interviews. But the way it was going right now, it didn't look like he ever *would*, because his diary was absolutely chocka.

He was back where he belonged, and loving every single second of it!

Shaking her head beside Larry now, Raine Parker's diamond rings sparkled like firecrackers as she moved her hand away from her mouth. Still gazing at the screen, on which the last shot of Larry slumped unconscious in Dex Lewis's arms had been frozen, with a dark trail of blood zigzagging down his throat from the cut beneath his chin, she said, '*That* . . . must have been the most *terrifying* moment of your entire life?'

Grinning wryly, Larry said, 'Can't say it was the most fun I've ever had.'

Laughing incredulously, Raine turned to the audience. 'Is this just the bravest man you've ever met?'

'Believe me, I wasn't being brave,' Larry chipped in modestly. 'It was kind of out of my hands – if you know what I mean. He wasn't exactly giving me the choice to stay or go.'

'As we saw,' Raine said admiringly. 'But I doubt you would have escaped even if he *had* let you, because we all saw what happened. And you put yourself right in the middle of the action without any concern for your own safety, just to bring that awful man to justice. That deserves a medal, in my book – don't you agree?'

She turned to the audience again, who immediately applauded.

'Yeah, well, I wasn't looking for glory,' Larry lied when the noise died down enough for him to be heard. 'I only did what anyone else would have done in that situation. He was a dangerous man, and I couldn't just stand back and watch him get away – not when I'd made him trust me enough to turn up in the first place. I had to see it through to the end.'

'Well, you certainly did that,' Raine said, elegantly crossing her legs. 'So, let's talk about how dangerous this man actually was, Larry. Because burglary was just the tip of the iceberg, wasn't it?'

'Oh, yeah,' Larry chuckled, nodding.

'You see, it turned out that this man,' Raine told the audience, 'had far worse crimes to answer to than simply jumping bail. And if it hadn't been for Larry, he would have got away with it.' Back to Larry now. 'Tell them what the police discovered when they checked Lewis's DNA.'

Taking a slow deep breath, Larry said, 'Kidnapping, false imprisonment, GBH, rape—'

'Rape,' Raine jumped in, glancing slowly around the audience for effect. 'This *animal* and his gang *raped* an old lady whose son they were holding hostage in his own home. They'd already beaten him to within an inch of his life, and were in the process of *torturing* him when his mother heard noises and went to investigate . . .' Pausing for several beats to let the horror of what she was saying sink in, she added, 'And they *raped* her. And if Larry hadn't been brave enough to go to Lewis's house and persuade him to take part in the game show that day – putting his *own* life in danger, as we clearly saw from the video – nobody would ever have known that Lewis was involved. And not just Lewis, but one of his brothers as well.'

'Yeah, but the other one got away,' Larry said, shrugging, as if to say, '*Not my fault; I did my bit.*'

A suitably serious look in her pretty grey eyes – an expression which didn't quite touch her perfectly painted face – Raine said, 'And that was a pretty major concern, wasn't it? Not only because he's on the loose when we all know he's capable of such heinous crimes; but also because you were actively threatened, weren't you, Larry?'

'Yeah. Dex Lewis made a point of telling me he was going to "get me" when they sentenced him.'

'Weren't you absolutely terrified?' Raine asked, shaking her head incredulously when Larry gave another casual shrug.

'Not really. I mean, he's not exactly going to be able to *get* me any time in the next fifteen years, is he?'

'What about when he gets out?'

'I'll be an old man,' Larry chuckled. 'I'm sure he won't recognise me by then. Probably no one will. I'll just be a sad old fart, shuffling round with my cats in my cabin in the hills.'

'Rubbish!' Raine scoffed, smiling flirtatiously. 'You, Mr Logan, will *never* be a sad old man, because you're far too handsome.' To the majority-female audience: 'Don't you agree, ladies?'

Smiling coyly at the roar of agreement, Larry nodded when Raine said, 'Let's just hope the police catch up with the missing brother soon, so we can all sleep easy in our beds. But I think we can safely say that he's not an immediate danger to you, Larry, because the police are pretty sure that he's out of the country, aren't they?'

It was true that Patrick Lewis had supposedly fled the country, but Larry was nowhere near as nonchalant as he was making out. In fact, he'd been so scared by Dex Lewis's threat that he'd stayed with Georgie for almost a month after the court case, claiming that he was worried about her because she hadn't been as well as she'd made out after her collapse at the hospital.

He'd enjoyed his stay, because Georgie lived in a secluded little house off the beaten track, and nobody knew where it was, which made him feel safer. And she'd fussed over him like a doting mother while he'd been there, feeding him real food instead of the convenience shit he usually favoured, and doing all his laundry. But he'd eventually tired of it, and had gone home to get some breathing space – preferring to suffer the nagging fears rather than Georgie's incessant smothering.

She still insisted on driving him to every interview and appearance, though, which wasn't too bad. But he'd have to tell her to back off soon, or people would start to wonder what was going on with them. And he wouldn't mind being free to have a shag without her continually vetting the women who approached him, either.

Yes, he definitely had to cut the apron strings before it got too late.

Snapping out of his thoughts when Raine's voice filtered

through, Larry blinked several times to bring himself back to the here and now. He hoped he hadn't missed anything, because it would be really embarrassing if she asked him a question and he couldn't answer it.

Saying, 'And even the *mother* was charged with handling stolen goods after Larry alerted the police to the haul he saw in their home,' Raine sat back in her chair as if she was exhausted, and shook her head. 'Thanks to Larry, that is one family who won't be terrorising our streets for some time to come.'

Modestly lowering his gaze as the audience erupted into applause again, Larry said, 'I only did what anyone would have done.'

'Well, I think you went well above and beyond,' Raine countered firmly. 'And I for one would like to see you get the recognition you deserve.' To camera now: 'So, if the police are watching tonight, give . . . this . . . man . . . a . . . *medal*!' Pausing to allow time for the renewed applause to die down, she said, 'So, when can we expect to see the full version of the show, Larry?'

'Wednesday the fourth,' he told her, unable to stop himself from smiling now, because he was still chuffed to bits that a British station had snapped it up. He'd been gutted to think that it would only be seen by Americans who didn't know him from Adam. But now everyone would see it. It couldn't have worked out better if he'd personally orchestrated it.

'Can't wait,' Raine said enthusiastically. 'And it's great to have you back, Larry, it really is. Just one thing I wanted to ask before you leave us, though . . .' Pausing, she gave him another flirtatious smile. 'How's the love life?'

Snorting softly, Larry shook his head and grinned. 'Don't even go there, Raine. I'm *so* not interested.'

'Oh, but that's such a waste,' she purred, her gaze boring sexily into his eyes.

'Hey, I'm not saying never,' Larry assured the audience who were loudly proclaiming their disappointment. 'Just not yet. I'm still a bit fragile after all that rubbish last year.'

'Ah, yes, *that*,' Raine said, a serious note in her voice. 'It must have been terrible, but I think I speak for the nation when I say I never believed a single word of it. So you can hold your head up high, because everybody knows you were completely and utterly innocent of any wrongdoing.'

Thanking her for her support, Larry smiled at the audience who were showing theirs by cheering and whistling.

Standing up now, Raine gave a theatrical wave of her hand. 'Larry Logan . . .'

Getting up to a standing ovation, Larry went to Raine and kissed her on the cheek. Smiling slyly when she whispered, 'Don't forget my party later,' he said he'd try to make it. Then, giving one last wave to the audience, he walked off set, smiling again when he heard Raine saying, 'How fantastic was *he*? . . . And didn't he look *amazing*?'

Oh, yes . . . he was back, all right!

Georgie was waiting in the corridor when the stagehand eased the door open and let Larry out of the studio. Handing him a towel, she gave him a quick hug, and said, 'You were wonderful, darling. I told you they'd love you. You're England's new superhero, don't you know?'

'Aw, shucks, it was nutt'n!' Larry drawled, grinning broadly as he followed her into his dressing room.

'Oh, *please*!' Georgie chuckled, taking the towel from him and handing him a comb. 'But, seriously, I agree with Raine – you *were* brave, and I'm very proud of you.'

'The two-faced bitch has invited me to her party tonight,' Larry sneered, turning to the mirror to straighten his hair. 'Can you believe that? Last time I saw her, she completely blanked me – like all the other bastards round here. Didn't want to be associated with me when I was being accused of fucking child abuse. But now that I'm a *hero*, she's making out like we're long-lost lovers, or something.'

'So, what time's the party?' Georgie asked, smiling playfully at him in the mirror, because they both knew that he *would* go – whatever he thought of Raine Parker.

'Ten.'

Glancing at her watch, Georgie said, 'Plenty of time, then. Anyway, hurry up and get yourself sorted out, because we've got exactly twenty minutes to get to the BBC. Oh, and when you've done the Radio Two interview, they've asked if you'll pop in for a chat with James Fletcher on Four.'

'Aren't I supposed to be going straight over to Century?'

'Yes, but they've agreed to delay for thirty minutes, so there's no panic.'

Looking at himself in the mirror again while Georgie gathered his things together and threw them into his bag, Larry fingered the scar beneath his chin. Despite the blood he'd lost at the time, it had turned out to be fairly superficial. But he wore it like a badge of honour nonetheless, and was a little disappointed that it was already fading. Still, the grainy black-and-white footage from the CCTV camera had made the incident look much worse than it had actually been, so at least he'd have that to remind people of how close he'd come to death. Even *he*'d been shocked when he saw it played back for the first time, so it was guaranteed to stay in the nation's collective memory for some while to come.

'All set?' Georgie asked when she'd finished packing up his things.

Nodding, Larry took one last look around, then followed her out into the corridor – just as Frank Woods was passing.

'Ah, Georgie,' he gushed, reaching out to air-kiss her on each cheek. 'How are you, my dear? Did you get my message?'

'Yes, I did,' she said. 'And I'm sorry I didn't get back to you, but I haven't had a single moment to myself in months.'

'Not to worry,' Frank murmured. Looking at Larry, he gave him an uncertain smile. This was the first time they had actually seen each other since the telethon, and he wasn't sure how the boy would react to him trying to be friendly now.

Returning the smile as if there were no hard feelings, Larry slipped a hand into his trouser pocket and said, 'How are you, Frank?'

'Fine,' Frank said, feeling very awkward. 'So, how does it feel to be a national hero?'

'Oh, you know.' Larry shrugged. 'Can't complain.'

'So I hear,' Frank said, folding his arms, wondering whether, while he had them both here, he should broach the subject of why he'd rung Georgie.

Glancing at her watch before he had a chance, Georgie said, 'Sorry, Frank, I don't mean to be rude, but we really can't hang around. We've three more interviews to get to tonight.'

'Oh, sorry, I should have realised. Will you, um, give me a ring sometime soon? Because I really need to speak to you.'

Smiling warmly, because she and Frank had always got along okay, Georgie linked her arm through Larry's and said, 'Of course. I'll call you tomorrow.'

Saying goodbye, Frank watched as they hurried away down the corridor. Larry was looking a whole lot better than he had last year. And he'd been as sober as a judge, which was very good, because Frank hadn't seen him like that for a good long time before their split. And now that he was back on form and solidly re-established in the affections of the public, Frank really needed to talk to Georgie about getting Larry to return to the show. Matty Kline was doing okay, but he just didn't have the same mass-market appeal, and it had to be said that *Star Struck* hadn't been the same without Larry at the helm.

Heading out to the parking lot at the rear of the studio just then, Larry was smiling like the cat who'd got the cream. All the way from his dressing room people had been stopping to congratulate him and tell him that they'd missed him, and he was lapping it up. Not only because it felt good to be back among his peers, but also because this was the first time he'd been allowed into Oasis since the telethon. It was like a grand homecoming, because this was where he'd got his first break. And knowing that, in view of his renewed popularity, Alan Corbin had been forced to retract the lifetime ban he'd slapped on Larry was particularly sweet.

Thanking the security guard when he held the door open for them, Georgie stepped out into the icy evening air and shivered. Pausing to wrap her coat around herself, she noticed a group of women gathered on the street side of the barrier. Nudging Larry, she nodded in their direction.

Following her gaze, Larry saw the women at the same time as they spotted him and started yelling his name. Grinning, he said, 'That's a sight I didn't expect to see again this time last year.'

'Well, don't keep them waiting,' Georgie teased, giving him a gentle push in their direction. 'But please be quick, because we really do have to get moving.'

Strolling towards the women as Georgie raced off to fetch the car, Larry smiled to himself when he recognised some of them from Raine's audience. Her show wasn't even over yet, but they'd deserted it to come out here and stand in the cold on the off chance of catching him before he left. He was truly back on the crest of the wave – and this time there would be no fuck-ups to knock him back into the water.

Laughing as the women tussled to get closer to him when he reached the barrier, Larry stayed a couple of steps back to avoid being mauled. He grinned at the familiar old security guard who came out of the booth to assist him, saying, 'Just like the old days, eh, Don?'

'It is that,' Don agreed with a chuckle that turned into a hacking smoker's cough. 'Can't say anyone else has caused a ruckus like this since you've been gone. But it doesn't make my job any easier, so don't make a habit of it.'

Laughing, because he knew that Don was only joking, Larry took a pen out of his pocket and set about signing the programmes that the women were thrusting at him.

Working his way through the crowd, he heard a strangled cry of pain from somewhere at the back. Unable to see over the other women's heads, he craned his neck and called, 'Everything all right back there?'

When the rest of the women turned to see what was going on, Larry was able to see that one of them had fallen over and was clutching at her leg, grimacing as if she'd really hurt herself.

'Are you okay?' he called, dipping under the barrier and going to her.

Blushing as he held out his hand to help her up, she nodded quickly. 'Yes, I'm fine. I just tripped over. Sorry . . .'

'Hey, don't apologise,' he said, peering down at her concernedly. 'You're the one who got hurt, not me. Are you sure you're okay?'

Nodding again, she winced.

Frowning, Larry said, 'What hurts?'

'I banged my knee,' she said, dipping her gaze and swiping at the dirt on her trousers. 'But it's fine now, honestly.'

Unconvinced, Larry said, 'Come to the security booth. Let me take a look at it in the light.'

Glancing up, the woman shook her head as if she were horrified, and said, 'No, really, I'm fine.'

Before Larry could argue, Georgie beeped the car horn. Turning his head, he saw her waving for him to get a move on. He shrugged, telling the woman, 'Sorry, I've got to go. Will you be okay to walk on it?'

Smiling now, she nodded. 'It's feeling better already, thanks. And I don't need to walk, because I'm getting picked up.'

'If you're sure,' Larry said, smiling at her. She was really quite attractive, with dark, glossy hair – which made her stand out in the sea of blondes he was surrounded by – and equally dark eyes, which was a very sexy combination.

Contrary to what he'd just told Raine – and her nine million or so viewers – he wasn't averse to hooking up with a woman again. He just didn't want to risk landing himself with another gold-digging, demanding diva who would sell him out to the papers as soon as he'd shot his load. This woman didn't look the type to do something like that. But then, it wasn't smart to judge a book by its cover, and he didn't have the time to waste finding out.

Honking the car horn again, Georgie rolled the window down and shouted, 'Come on, Larry. We're going to be late.'

Saying, 'Sorry, ladies,' when the women groaned disappointedly, he blew kisses to them all, then ducked back under the barrier and climbed into the car.

Waving through the window when Don raised the barrier and Georgie began to ease the car out, he winked at the dark-haired one, getting a tiny shy smile in return before she turned and walked away in the opposite direction.

Watching him out of the corner of her eye as he gazed after her, Georgie said, 'Don't even think about it. We're not picking up waifs and strays, so just sit back and relax, and think about what you're going to say if you get asked any tricky questions in your next interview.'

'You know, you really should quit acting like my mother,' Larry grumbled, lighting a cigarette and rolling the window part-way down.

'When you learn how to behave yourself, I will,' Georgie said mock-sternly.

Shaking his head, Larry sat back as she manoeuvred the car through the evening traffic and headed for the BBC studios. He shouldn't complain, because she'd been amazing over these last few months. And, truth be told, he wouldn't have been so well now without her help. After Dex had attacked him, he'd found himself slipping back into his old drinking habits. But Georgie had nipped that in the bud, and he really felt as if he'd conquered the booze now, too.

But while he was undoubtedly grateful, he thanked *God* she hadn't been invited to Raine's party tonight, because she'd probably want to whisk him out of there and home to bed by eleven. So, off the hook for the first time in ages, he would go to the party. And if he happened to fancy shagging some lucky lady at the end of the night, then that was exactly what he would do.

It just wouldn't be Raine Parker – no matter how obvious she'd made it that she wanted into his pants!

Larry was knackered by the time he'd finished the last of his three radio interviews. They had gone really well, though, and he was pleased with his performance. Particularly on the second, unscheduled one, when James smart-arse Fletcher had tried to get him to admit that he really *had* known that the girl from the *Star Struck* scandal was almost under-age, and that he'd helped her to win the jackpot with the express intention of fucking her brains out – or words to that effect.

Georgie, who'd been sitting on the other side of the studio glass, had jumped to her feet, all set to pull him from the interview. But Larry had kept his cool, figuring that this was as good an opportunity as any to get his version of events out there. And he must have made a good job of it, because Fletcher had done a complete about-turn by the time the interview came to an end, shaking his hand and inviting him to come back next month to sit on the panel of the Radio Book of the Year Awards.

His interview with Dixie Dean on Century had been a breeze after that and, despite being exhausted, he was still buzzing about the volume of listeners who'd rung in to chat to him – which, Dixie had told him, far outweighed what any of her previous guests had managed to attract.

If the night had been slightly less successful, he probably would have given Raine's party a miss. But he knew he wouldn't sleep if he went straight home with all the positive comments still swirling round in his head, so he had Georgie drop him there on her way home.

Not that it *was* on her way but, oh, well . . . maybe she'd think twice about sticking to him like glue in future.

Raine had changed into a flowing evening dress, which plunged in all the right places and caressed her womanly curves like a stroke from a velvet glove. With her shoulder-length honey-blonde hair loosed from its chignon and held in place at the nape of her neck by a diamante clasp, one tanned arm bare while the other sported an intricate gauntlet-style bracelet of diamonds and emeralds, she looked like a goddess when she opened the door for Larry.

'Darling,' she purred, stepping back to look him over – really a ploy to make *him* look *her* over. 'You look amazing.'

Smiling wryly, because he was wearing exactly the same clothes as earlier, he said, 'You, too, babe.'

Thanking him, she reached up and kissed him flush on the mouth, letting her lips linger softly for several seconds to give him a taste of what was to come before taking his arm and leading him into the already crowded living room.

Announcing, 'He's here!' she smiled up at Larry, thrilled by the look of surprise in his eyes.

He was surprised all right, but not necessarily in a good way. Gazing at all the old familiar faces as the guests raised their glasses and gave him a welcoming cheer, he was struck by the sheer hypocrisy of it all. Unlike the general staff back at Oasis who had seemed genuinely pleased to see him, every one of these stars and fat-cat executives had turned their backs on him when he'd most needed their support. But that all seemed to have been forgotten now – by them, at least.

Refusing to give them the satisfaction of thinking that their behaviour had had any effect on him, he smiled now as if he was as pleased to see them as they seemed to be to see him, and said, 'Wow, this is amazing. Thanks, guys. It's good to be back.'

'Where you belong,' Raine crooned, reaffirming her intention to keep him to herself tonight by giving him another kiss – although this time on the cheek, because everybody was still looking. 'Now, let me get you a drink, then I'll show you around. Still Scotch on ice?' she asked pointedly, letting him know that she'd noticed him *before* his career resurrection. Wouldn't do to let him think that she was just jumping onto the bandwagon now.

'Actually, I prefer dry white these days,' Larry lied, narrowing his eyes surreptitiously as he peered down at her – there was a tiny spot of what looked like blood at the corner of her mouth. And, once he'd noticed that, he was sure he could see several minute pinhole marks in her make-up-camouflaged forehead. Suspecting that she'd had a quick-fix Botox session in the three hours since the show, he struggled not to grimace. Even if he'd been interested before – which he hadn't been – that would have turned him right off. Getting a blow job off a woman with a frozen mouth was about as much fun as sticking your dick into an unripe watermelon.

'Be right back,' Raine purred now, stroking a hand suggestively down his arm. 'Don't you dare move.'

As soon as she'd gone, Matty Kline strolled over. Curls springing out like corkscrews all over his head, he grinned widely at Larry and slapped him heartily on the back.

'Hey, guy . . . long time no see. How's it going?'

'Fine,' Larry replied smoothly, slipping his hands into his pockets to keep them from forming fists. He still felt like punching the man whenever he saw his face on TV but here, in the flesh, the desire intensified tenfold. 'You?' he asked now, determined to stay cool.

'Great.' Matty nodded as if he was truly satisfied with his lot in life. Then, smiling guiltily, he said, 'Look, I know this is probably the wrong time and place, and all that, but I just wanted to apologise for all that shit last year. No hard feelings, I hope?'

'Hard feelings?' Larry gave him a questioning smile.

'Yeah, you know – about me taking over *Star Struck*. I know you weren't happy about it, but we've all moved on since then, haven't we?'

'Christ, yeah,' Larry drawled. 'I'd forgotten all about it.'

'Good,' Matty said, breathing a silent sigh of relief. This was the first time he'd seen his rival since the telethon, but Larry seemed cool as a cucumber, so it looked like they were going to avoid the embarrassment of a showdown. 'So, what's on *your* horizon?' he asked now, taking a sip of his drink. 'Anything good lined up?'

'Oh, you know,' Larry said evasively. 'Loads of offers flooding in, but I'm biding my time to make sure I choose the right thing. Don't want to lump myself with a no-hoper like last time.' Grinning sheepishly now, as if he hadn't meant to say that, he said, 'Sorry, Matt, didn't mean that the way it sounded. You know I enjoyed *Star Struck* while I was doing it, but you don't always realise the bad effect something's having on you till you get a break from it, do you? I mean, take my last performance . . . it's no secret I was pissed.'

'You can say that again,' Matty snorted amusedly, remembering it all too well.

'Yeah, well, that was a symptom of how shit I was feeling,' Larry said, glancing innocently at the large glass of alcohol in Matty's hand. 'Don't know about you, but I tend to drink more when I'm frustrated. But I don't need the crutch these days, 'cos I'm totally cool with life.'

Matty smiled uncertainly. He was sure that Larry had just taken a pop at him, but there was nothing he could say about it, because it hadn't been delivered as an insult – more like sympathy at the fact that he was stuck in Larry's old rut while Larry's own career was soaring to new heights. And it couldn't have escaped Larry's notice that *Star Struck*'s ratings had slipped since his time as host, so he just had to be gloating about that. Matty knew that he would be if the situation were reversed.

Larry *was* gloating, as it happened. And knowing that Matty knew it only added to his sense of satisfaction. That was the price you paid for jumping into someone else's grave – you got buried right along with them. And, judging by the amount of neat Scotch that Matty was nursing, he already had one foot planted firmly in the dirt. Poetic justice, or what?

Frank Woods and Alan Corbin arrived just then, along with their respective wives, Brenda and June. Spotting Larry, Brenda made a beeline straight for him.

'How lovely to see you, Larry,' she said, kissing his cheek. 'Frank mentioned that he'd bumped into you at the studio, and I was hoping I'd get to see you, too. I can't tell you how much I've missed you.'

Giving her an affectionate smile, aware that Matty was looking more than a little put out that she hadn't said hello to him first, Larry hugged her warmly, saying, 'Missed you, too, babe. Still running round like a French maid after the old man, are you?'

'As if!' Brenda chuckled. 'He knows to behave himself if he wants his dinner on time. And don't be fooled by the sophisticated façade. He might pretend to like the fancy restaurants, but he couldn't survive without my steak-and-kidney pud.'

'Oh, don't,' Larry groaned. 'I can still taste that last one you made me.'

Patting his hand, Brenda said, 'Give me a ring when you're free, and we'll get together for dinner.' Turning to Matty now, she said, 'Hello, dear. I hope you didn't think I was ignoring you, but I haven't seen Larry for ages.'

'Don't worry about it,' Matty said, wondering how come she never greeted *him* like that. Not that he particularly wanted her to, but it would be nice to know that the boss's wife had loyalty to the new over the old.

'So, tell me what you're up to?' Brenda said now, switching her attention back to Larry as if Matty hadn't even spoken. 'I hear you've got the drinking under control at last – which is wonderful, because I could have shaken you silly for letting yourself go like that.'

'I wish somebody had,' Larry murmured wistfully, as if a good talking-to was all it would have taken to keep him on track.

'Oh, come now,' Brenda chided softly, cutting through the bullshit in one fell swoop. 'I'm the first to admit that Frank has his failings, but you weren't one of them, my love. He tried his damnedest to bring you to your senses before it was too late, but you were too wilful for your own good. And if *he* couldn't get through to you, nobody else stood a chance. It was down to you to sort yourself out, and I'm delighted that you finally realised that.'

Laughing, Larry looped an arm around her shoulder and

gave her a quick squeeze. 'Frank's a good man,' he conceded, shoving all the bad thoughts he'd levelled at his former boss in the last year to the back of his mind. 'And you don't have to worry about me, because I'm all grown up now, and I can take care of myself.'

'Yes, well, just make sure you don't slip back into your old habits now that things are looking up,' Brenda warned.

'Stop it,' Larry groaned. 'You're starting to sound like Georgie.'

'Oh, is she here?' Brenda asked, glancing around. 'I'd love to catch up with her; she's a lovely girl.'

'She couldn't make it,' Larry lied, not wanting to have to explain why he hadn't wanted to bring her after everything she'd done for him.

Coming back with Larry's drink just then, Raine said a cool hello to Brenda, who, as the mere wife of one of her acquaintances – and not a particularly important one at that, given that Frank had no part in or power over her show – was less than nothing to her.

Brenda couldn't give a toss what Raine Parker thought of her, and felt no urge to make small talk with her, either. So, giving Larry a kiss and reminding him to give her a call when he wanted to come for dinner, she made her way back to her husband and left them to it.

'What a mouse,' Raine sniped when she'd gone. 'Frank must have got himself shackled to her long before he found success as a producer, because he'd surely have gone for somebody with more *oomph* if he'd known what would become available to him.'

'Like you?' Larry asked, with an innocent smile on his face.

'Darling, my charity work consists of helping sick children, *not* pleasuring pensioners,' Raine replied with a soft, throaty laugh, sure that Larry was only teasing her, because he could never believe that a glamorous beauty like herself would be interested in an old man like Frank Woods. And it was quite beside the point that she was currently pleasuring Alan Corbin, who was equally as old as Frank, because Larry wouldn't be hearing about that.

Clearing his throat suddenly to remind them that he was still there, because he was beginning to feel like a spare part in Larry Logan's toolbox, Matty said, 'Did I tell you how lovely you're looking tonight, Raine?'

A flicker of an irritated frown attempted to cross her taut brow at the interruption, but she quickly replaced it with a smile and a purred thank-you. Matty wasn't in Larry's league when it came to looks, but he was still young, virile, and important enough in his own right to warrant her attention. And he was by far the best-looking of the other men who were here tonight, so it was worth keeping him in the loop in case it didn't work out with Larry and she needed a stand-in.

Watching Raine over the rim of his glass as he sipped the wine, Larry wondered why she'd gone to so much trouble to throw this party for him. It certainly wasn't out of the goodness of her heart because, like her show – which she was rumoured to control every aspect of with a passion bordering on obsession – her life was a series of calculated manoeuvres: not one step taken unless it advanced Raine Parker in some way. But if it was simply a means of getting at his dick, she was going to be very disappointed, because it wasn't happening. Still, he'd let her down gently. No point making enemies of the big hitters at this early stage in his career resurrection.

Using the fact that she was talking to Matty as an excuse to get away now, Larry waved as if he'd just spotted some-body, and said, 'Sorry, guys, you'll have to excuse me. There's someone I really need to talk to.'

Clutching at his hand as he made to walk away, Raine

pursed her lips petulantly. 'You're not deserting me already, are you? You've only just got here.'

'I'll be right back,' he lied, squeezing her hand before snatching his own away. Saying, 'Good to see you again, Matty. Catch you later,' he walked quickly away and plunged himself into the thickest group of people across the room.

Shaking hands and kissing cheeks without actually stopping to chat to any of them, Larry made it into the kitchen and headed for the breakfast bar where numerous bottles of alcohol had been placed for people to help themselves to if the actual bar back in the lounge was too busy. Glancing back to make sure that Raine wasn't hot on his heels, he tipped the wine down the sink and refilled his glass with neat vodka. He detested wine and had only asked for it to knock Raine down a peg, because she'd thought she was smart for guessing that he would go for Scotch. And he wouldn't satisfy her by having Scotch now, either, even though he really wanted one. At least he no longer *needed* one – that was the difference.

Taking a handful of penis-shaped ice cubes out of the bucket now – probably Raine's personal design, Larry thought scathingly – he dropped them into his glass and was about to go back into the party when Alan Corbin walked in. Hesitating in the doorway, his face reddening slightly, and ran a finger around the inside of his shirt collar as if it were suddenly too tight.

Smiling, because he'd found that it actually made the people who had done him down in the past feel more guilty when he was nice to them, Larry extended his hand, saying, 'Good to see you, Alan. How's it going?'

'Very well,' Corbin said, shaking it. 'You?'

'Great, thanks.'

'Glad to hear it.'

Letting go of Corbin's hand now, Larry gestured back to the drinks. 'Can I get you something?'

'Um, yes, please,' Corbin muttered uncomfortably. 'Martell. Actually, make that two, because I'm getting one for Frank. And a couple of white wines for the ladies – if it's no trouble?'

'None whatsoever,' Larry assured him, going back to the bar and looking for glasses.

Slipping his hands into his pockets, Corbin wandered over and stood beside him. Watching him from the corner of his eye, Larry saw that he was sweating, and licking his lips as if he wanted to say something.

'Everything all right?' he asked.

'Oh, yes, fine,' Corbin replied. Then, 'Actually, I wanted to congratulate you on the undercover show you did. I had a chance to look over the clip before it aired tonight, and it was really very good. You must be delighted it's going to be shown over here.'

'I wasn't really bothered if it came out over here or not, to tell you the truth,' Larry lied, shrugging nonchalantly. 'It got an amazing reception in the States, so it'll just be a nice little bonus seeing it over here.'

'I'm sure it'll open lots of doors. I believe you've already been getting offers?'

'Yeah, some. But Georgie's sifting through them – cutting the wheat from the chaff, so to speak.'

'Good, well, let's hope you get what you deserve out of it.'

'Isn't that what people were saying last year when I was being ripped to pieces by the press?' Larry said softly. Then, turning to look straight at Corbin, he winked and added, 'But, hey, that's all water under the bridge now.'

Sensing that Larry was still bitter about the aftermath of the telethon, despite the affected nonchalance, Corbin said, 'There were contributory factors which led to all that, Larry.'

'Like me being a piss-head?' Larry quipped, leaning back against the bar and folding his arms.

'Well, frankly, yes,' Corbin replied bluntly, refusing to be made to feel guilty. 'You placed the telethon in jeopardy, and then there was all that business with the girl.'

'Who *was* old enough, despite the rumours,' Larry reminded him. 'Even though I didn't actually *do* anything with her.'

'Yes, well, that's a matter for your own conscience,' Corbin murmured, still not altogether sure that he believed the girl's denial, because it had all seemed a little orchestrated for his liking.

Larry was struggling to maintain the façade of calm. Everybody he'd spoken to since he'd come back on the scene had been eager to let him know that they had been on his side all along, but Corbin obviously considered himself too important to run with the crowd. It irritated Larry that the man seemed to be implying that he still didn't believe him about the girl – because he genuinely *was* innocent.

Walking in just then, Raine said, 'Oh, *there* you are. I've been looking everywhere for you.'

Swallowing hard, Corbin looked from her to Larry as a nervous flush suffused his face. Surely she wasn't stupid enough to make an overt display of her affection in front of Larry of all people? He wasn't ready for that. His wife was in the next room, and she had no idea that anything was going on – and this was not the way he intended for her to find out. When the moment came, it would be in private, and there would be no mention of Raine. *She* would only come into the picture after a suitable period of separation, when she would be unveiled as the replacement, not the cause.

'You're a very naughty boy,' Raine went on, slinking sexily across the kitchen. 'I thought you said you were coming right back to me?'

Blinking rapidly with confusion when she bypassed him and linked her arm possessively through Larry's, Corbin gave her a questioning frown.

Smiling back at him as if he were nothing more than a work colleague, Raine said, 'I think your wife was looking for you, Alan. Weren't you supposed to be getting her a drink?'

'Yeah, and I was supposed to be pouring it,' Larry said, using it as an excuse to extract himself from her clutches. 'Two white wines, you said?'

'Yes, that's right,' Corbin muttered, still peering at Raine. He was waiting for some sort of signal from her to explain her behaviour and let him know that she wasn't trying it on with Logan, as she very much seemed to be doing.

Giving him a defiantly unconcerned look in return, Raine shrugged, and mouthed, *'C'est la vie.'*

Loading the four glasses onto a small tray, Larry handed it to Corbin. Thanking him, Corbin flicked Raine a look which said that this wasn't finished with, then walked out of the room with as much dignity as he could muster. Raine was a proud woman, and he could only assume that she was punishing him for bringing his wife along tonight. But Raine had personally invited her, so what was he meant to do?

Having picked up on the tension between Raine and Corbin, Larry said, 'Am I missing something here?'

'Nothing whatsoever,' Raine lied, reclaiming his arm and giving him a sultry look. 'But *I* missed *you* while you were away, so why didn't you stay in touch?'

Peering down at her, Larry wondered if she was on drugs, or something. What did she mean, why didn't he stay in touch? They'd never *been* in touch – not in the way she apparently meant, anyway. She'd already been established by the time he'd hit the screen with *Star Struck*, and had treated him like an office junior whenever their paths had crossed. She'd been more forthcoming when his star had really started to rise, but they'd barely seen each other to say more than a passing hello, so it wasn't like there had ever been any sort of friendship. Certainly nothing to make her think that they were rekindling something they had once had and lost, anyway.

Taking his silence and the way he was staring at her as a sign that he was nervous, Raine lowered her eyelashes and traced a fingertip over his hand. Poor little Larry might look and act like an experienced man about town, but he'd obviously never had a red-blooded woman like Raine Parker show an interest in him, and he looked completely out of his depth. But he had nothing to fear, because she was about to take him to a whole new level of sensuality.

Inhaling deeply, wondering how the hell he was going to get out of this without offending her, Larry was flooded with relief when the girls from the top R-'n'-B girl-band Teeza walked into the kitchen in search of booze.

Spotting him, Shari, the lead singer, yelped, 'Larry, baby!' and rushed over to throw herself into his arms. 'I didn't know you were already here,' she gushed, planting a big kiss on his lips. 'We only just got here ourselves, but I was just telling Kaylise that you'd better show your ass soon or I was outta here, 'cos I only came to see you!' Smiling at Raine now, with her arms still looped around Larry's neck and her pretty head resting on his shoulder, she said, 'No offence, Ray, but I haven't seen this boy for the longest time, and I just love him to bits.'

'Yes, well, we're all very fond of him,' Raine said smoothly, determined not to let the pushy little bitch see how irritated she was by the interruption. She didn't know why the band had been invited in the first place, because she'd specifically told her PA to only invite the cream of the crop, and surely *Teeza* didn't fall into that category – however many number ones they had been clocking up lately.

Getting a look-in now that Shari had had her fill, the other girls moved in to give him kisses and hugs, and Larry encouraged them with sexy smiles and compliments – more to put

Raine off than to turn them on. Gorgeous as these girls undoubtedly were, they all had huge hip-hop boyfriends, and there was no way Larry wanted any of them thinking he'd been trying it on with their women.

'Hey, come see who's here,' Shari said now, grabbing his hand. 'You'll *die* when you see her.'

Snatching up his glass as the girls surrounded him and hustled him towards the door, Larry gave Raine a what-can-I-do? shrug to let her know that he wasn't being deliberately rude.

Giving him an understanding smile, she nodded, sure that he would find an excuse to come and seek her out when he was done with his fans. She wasn't concerned about them, anyway. As far as she knew, Larry had never been photographed with any black girls, so they probably weren't his type. Pouring herself a fresh drink now, she smoothed her hair down and went back into the party to mingle with her more important guests.

Someone had made the DJ take off the mellow background music Raine had ordered him to play and put Teeza's latest album on instead. Going straight into their routine when they heard the first bars of their latest single, 'Watch Me Now', the girls sang along as people cleared a path to watch them do their thing.

Edging his way around the room when he saw Jooce, the gorgeous American singer the girls had brought to the party, Larry headed over to her. The first and last time they'd met, she'd been performing the final gig of her first British tour at the MEN Arena, and Shari had introduced them at the backstage party. They'd all gone on to Bone from there, where they had partied for a few hours before Larry and Jooce had sneaked off to spend the rest of the night having crazy sex at his apartment. It was one of the few times when Larry had managed to outwit the paparazzi and, if he remembered rightly, Jooce had greatly appreciated that because she'd only just got married. She certainly hadn't wanted her new husband to see pictures of her getting jiggy with a sexy white boy while she was still effectively on honeymoon.

'Hey, *you!*' Jooce drawled now when he reached her, her voice every bit as husky and sexy as he remembered from when she'd whispered dirty nothings down his ear that night. 'I hear you're the man of the moment, huh?'

'So they say,' Larry said, thinking she'd put on a couple of pounds as he gave her a hug – and loving the feel of it. 'That's some booty you got there, girl,' he whispered now, copying her accent.

'You know it,' she giggled, pushing her breasts up against his chest. 'Remember these babies, 'cos they sure remember you?'

'How could I forget?' Larry chuckled, detaching himself in case anyone got the wrong idea. 'So, how's the husband?'

'He's *fine*,' Jooce drawled, smiling up at him coyly. 'I'll introduce you soon as he gets here, 'cos I told him all about you, and I know he'd like to meet you.'

'Hey, I hope you didn't tell him *every*thing?' Larry drew his head back.

'Oh, now don't be stressing on me,' Jooce teased. 'Bo knows you and me is friends, and that's all he *needs* to know.'

'Hope so,' Larry said uncertainly. He'd never seen Bo, but Jooce had told him that he was a pro basketball player, so he had to be at least nine feet tall and built like a rhino.

'How are you, anyway?' Jooce asked now, her wide-spaced eyes glowing like ebony coals of compassion. 'Shari kept me up to date about alla that stuff you went through last year, and I was so mad about it, I was all set to hop on a plane and come rescue you. That ho never shoulda gotten away with fixing you up that way, and I'd have made sure she paid for putting you through something like that.'

'Nice to know you were thinking about me,' Larry said, thinking that it was quite amazing that Shari had bothered telling *her* when she hadn't actually bothered to contact *him* during that time to ask if he was okay.

'Never stopped,' Jooce said, giving him a very pointed smile. 'Any time you wanna catch up, just give me a call. Matter of fact, you'd better take my number before Bo gets here – but don't be telling my girls, 'cos they be leakin' green from their eyes if they hear we hookin' up again.'

Assuring her that he wouldn't breathe a word to them or to anyone else, Larry took her number – just in case he needed it. Who knew when he might get called over to the States, and it'd be good to have a contact when he got there – especially one who was as big a star as Jooce was, seeing as he'd never seen or heard from the rap group Unreal again after unwittingly dragging them into his bad publicity that time.

He'd just put his phone away when Jooce spotted her husband coming through the door. Waving over Larry's head, she said, 'Hey, here's my baby now.'

Turning, Larry gulped when he saw Bo, who was every bit as big and muscular as he'd imagined. He looked like he'd stepped straight off a bad-ass-rapper video set.

'Baby, I want you to meet Larry,' Jooce said when Bo walked over and kissed her. 'Remember I told you about him from last time I was touring here?'

'Ah, yeah,' Bo drawled, giving Larry an easy smile as he reached for his hand. 'Pleased to meet you. I caught you on that undercover cop show a coupla weeks back, and you were cool, man. The way you handled that crazy dude with the knife, that was just *whack*, man.'

Sensing that Bo was a decent guy, Larry felt an unfamiliar twinge of guilt, knowing that he hadn't only slept with his wife but had just taken her number so that he could contact her if he ever wanted to get properly reacquainted. But Jooce obviously wasn't worrying about it, because she tipped Larry a promise-laden wink, even though she was sitting on Bo's knee now, with her arms wrapped around him like they were love's young dream.

Feeling increasingly uncomfortable, Larry thanked Bo for the compliment and told him it had been a pleasure to meet him. Then he made his excuses and left them to make out in peace.

Wandering around the room chatting to his old so-called friends and acquaintances while keeping a couple of steps ahead of Raine who kept trying to catch his eye, Larry wandered out onto the balcony after a while to get a bit of air. He was tired again, and wished he could take off so he could hit the sack. But no one else seemed to be in any hurry to leave, so he couldn't just up and go – not when the party had been thrown in his honour.

Sipping at the vodka, he rested his elbows on the railing and gazed down at the darkly glittering waters of the canal below. It was a beautiful complex consisting of four blocks of apartments, two of which sat on either side of the narrow waterway. The ground floors of each had been leased out to commercial businesses, and there were units displaying everything from shoes to candelabras to exotic deli foods in their darkened windows. There were also several tiny wine bars, which were still brightly lit, their waterfront tables buzzing with customers as tinkling musak filtered out through their open doors. It wasn't a particularly warm night, but Larry could understand why they'd chosen to sit outside with a view like this. And, anyway, alcohol tended to make you feel warmer than you actually were.

Hearing the sound of cheering floating up from the wine bar directly below the apartment, he stepped up onto the bottom rung of the railing and leaned over to see what was happening. There was a birthday party going on, and the man of the moment was being presented with a cake, the top of which was decorated with a circle of flashing sparklers. Smiling when the man started dancing with his cake, almost falling into the canal with it, Larry was about to step back down when a woman sitting alone at a table off to the side of the party caught his eye. It was the almost blue gleam of her dark hair under the lights which rang a bell; that, and the fluffy green scarf wrapped around her throat, which was identical to the one the woman who'd fallen over at the studio had been wearing. But how could it be the same woman? What were the chances of her having been *there* at the same time as him and now *here*?

*Unless she was a stalker.*

But no, that was ridiculous. She would have to have followed Larry, to know that he would be here, and that would have been impossible, because she'd been heading in the opposite direction when they'd left the studio. And she'd been walking, whereas he'd been in Georgie's car. It had to be a coincidence.

Creeping up behind him just then, Raine put her hands on his lower back and gave him a gentle push, whispering, 'Gotcha!'

Jumping, Larry slipped down off the railing and turned to face her. 'Christ, Raine, you frightened the bloody life out of me. You could have pushed me right over.'

'Never,' she purred, the smell of alcohol ripe on her breath as she pressed herself up against him. 'You don't really think I'd let you fall, do you? Not unless you're falling for *me*, of course, because that's entirely different – and utterly allowable.'

Aware that she was teetering on the delicate line between tipsy and outright drunk, Larry was nervous that they might *both* fall over if she carried on leaning against him like that.

It wasn't the most solid of railings, and it was a hell of a drop if it went.

'Look, let's move back towards the doors if you want to talk,' he said, putting his hands on her shoulders and trying to gently ease her away.

Resisting him, she said, 'No, I like it here – in the shadows where no one can see us.'

'Please, Raine, it's not safe,' Larry said, increasing the pressure.

Shivering, Raine bit her lip. 'Oh, your hands feel so good on my skin. So soft, yet so masculine. I'd like to feel them all over my—'

'Oh, damn!' Larry squawked, cutting her off. 'My phone!'

'I can't hear anything,' Raine said, looking up at him blearily. Then, smiling again, she slid her hands down over his buttocks. 'Oh, I see . . . I bet you've got it on vibrate, haven't you? Shall I find it for you and switch it off?'

'It's gone through the railing,' Larry lied, pushing her firmly back a few paces. 'I was checking for messages before you came out, and I mustn't have put it back in my pocket properly, because I just felt it go.'

Saying, 'Oh, well, never mind,' Raine advanced on him again. 'We'll get you another in the morning – after breakfast.'

'I can't,' Larry yelped, horrified at the thought of waking up beside her and seeing her without her camouflage. 'It's too important. I've got numbers in there that I can't afford anyone to get hold of.'

'It'll be in the canal by now.'

'Can't take the risk.' Shrugging, Larry smiled as he edged his way around her. 'I'll just go and see if I can find it before someone picks it up. Shouldn't take too long.'

'Mmm, well, make sure it doesn't,' Raine said petulantly. 'I'm not happy with you; you've been avoiding me all night.'

'Rubbish,' Larry scoffed, reaching the sliding door and stepping back into the lounge. 'See you in a minute.'

Rushing out of the apartment, he tapped the button for the communal elevator, then changed his mind and went for the stairs instead. Running down them so that Raine couldn't catch up with him if she took it into her head to follow, he reached the ground floor and pushed his way through the heavy outer door. Glancing around to get his bearings, he realised that he was on the wrong side of the block and ran towards the pathway separating it from the neighbouring one. Racing right the way around, he skidded to a halt just before he ran straight into the canal. He shook himself to regain his composure. Then, hand in pocket, he strolled casually along past the closed shop units until he reached the wine bar.

The party had moved inside but the woman was still sitting at her table, although she'd changed chairs by now so that she was in semi-darkness, with her back against the bar's wall. She didn't notice Larry as he approached because she was gazing out at the water, seemingly lost in her thoughts.

Checking to make sure that Raine wasn't leaning over the balcony watching him, Larry walked right up to the woman and said, 'Sorry . . . don't mean to disturb you, but are you following me?'

Snapping out of her trance at the sound of his voice, she glanced up at him confusedly. 'Sorry?'

Smiling, Larry said, 'I asked if you're following me?'

Looking utterly mortified, she put her glass down on the table and snatched her handbag up off the floor. Edging out from behind the table, she waited for him to move out of her way.

Sensing that he'd offended her, Larry held up his hands and said, 'Hey, I was only joking. I just thought it was funny that we should be in the same place twice in one night, that's all. You don't have to leave on my account. You haven't even finished your drink yet.'

'I've had enough,' she murmured without looking at him. 'I was about to leave anyway. I was waiting for someone, but . . .'

'Date?' Larry probed when she left the rest of the sentence hanging. Groaning when she immediately frowned, he said, 'Oh, shit, I'm not doing too well here, am I?'

'With what?' the woman asked, looking up at him now with a challenging lilt to her chin.

Struck by the intensity of her dark eyes, Larry gave a sheepish shrug. 'I'm not really sure, to tell you the truth. I'm knackered, and I've just escaped a really boring party, so I'm not back in the swing of things yet. I just saw you sitting down here and thought . . . well, I don't know *what* I thought. I guess I just wanted to say hello.'

'You saw me sitting down here?' she repeated slowly, her eyes narrowing with suspicion. 'From where?'

'Up there,' Larry admitted, motioning upwards with his eyes towards Raine's apartment. 'I was on the balcony.'

'I see,' she said, sounding as if she didn't know whether to be flattered or scared.

Flapping his hands, Larry said, 'Look, I honestly wasn't spying on you, but I *was* looking for an excuse to get out of there, so when I saw you I thought it'd be nice to come and say hello. But you don't need to worry; I'm not a weirdo.'

'I'm sure you're not,' she conceded.

Exhaling with relief, because she seemed to be thawing, Larry said, 'Right, well, thank God we've got *that* cleared up. I was starting to feel a bit stupid there.'

'I guess I didn't help,' the woman admitted. 'But I was in a world of my own, so you kind of took me by surprise.'

'Sorry,' Larry apologised, thinking how beautiful she looked when she smiled. 'Hope you weren't annoyed with me for not signing your programme earlier, by the way, but my agent was rushing me.'

'Programme?' She gazed back at him blankly.

'Yeah, for the show.'

'Sorry . . . I don't know what you mean.'

Peering down at her, Larry frowned. 'Raine Parker's chat show. I was the guest. How's your knee, by the way?'

A spark of realisation flaring in her eyes, she said, 'Oh, right . . . You were at the TV studio. Er, yeah, my knee's fine, thanks. But I think we've got crossed wires here, because I wasn't there to see the show; I was just walking past because I was supposed to be getting picked up at the corner, but then I fell over. I did wonder what all those women were doing there . . .' Her voice trailing off, the woman gave an embarrassed little shrug. 'Guess I'd made enough of a fool of myself by then without asking, though.'

'They'd been in the audience and wanted my autograph,' Larry told her, wondering if it were possible that she didn't actually know who he was, when his face had been splashed across every newspaper after Dex Lewis got sentenced, followed by numerous TV and radio interviews. Not to mention how well known he'd been *before* all that.

Studying his face hard now, the woman suddenly put a hand over her mouth, and said, 'Oh, God, you're Larry Logan, aren't you? I'm so sorry. You probably really *did* think I was following you, didn't you?'

'Not at all,' he said, laughing softly. 'I just thought it was a coincidence – a *nice* one, though.'

Thanking him, she said, 'Well, I'd better go and let you get back to your party.'

'You don't have to,' Larry told her. 'I mean, it's your choice, obviously, but I'm not planning to go back to the party, and I was hoping you might join me for a drink. You'd be doing

me a big favour,' he added sincerely. 'You've already been
better company than that lot up there.'

'I don't know,' she murmured uncertainly. Then, looking
up at him and seeing the hopeful smile on his lips, she nodded.
'Okay, why not?'

'Great!' Larry said, rushing round the table to pull her seat
out for her. 'What are you drinking?'

'Black Russian. But I really don't need another one. I'd
only just got this one when you came over.'

'Okay, well, just let me get myself one and I'll be right
back.' Turning to go inside, Larry hesitated when he reached
the door and said, 'You're not going to run away, are you?'

Smiling, the woman shook her head.

Pushing his way through the revellers inside, Larry felt
giddy as he made his way to the bar. He wasn't sure if it
was because the drinks he'd already had at Raine's party
were starting to affect him, or that it was such a pleasant
change to meet a woman who genuinely hadn't recognised
him – and hadn't immediately started flirting when she did.
Either way, he wasn't complaining, because she was way
more attractive than any of the available women at the
party.

Ordering another Black Russian for her, and two double
Scotch and sodas for himself, he carried them out and placed
them on the table, saying, 'Hope you don't mind, but I thought
I'd better get you another one, because they'll be closing
soon.' Sitting down across from her, he exhaled loudly as if
he'd been running a marathon, then reached into his pocket
for his cigarettes.

Shaking her head when he offered her one, she said, 'No,
thanks. I don't.'

'Sensible,' Larry said, lighting up and blowing his smoke
into the air away from her. Looking around then, he said,
'I've never been here before. It's nice, isn't it?'

Murmuring, 'Lovely,' the woman gazed out at the water, seemingly deep in thought again.

Sitting in silence beside her, Larry felt the tensions of the night evaporate. It was so nice to be with a female who didn't feel the need to chatter incessantly to keep his interest. She was obviously shy, but not the awkward kind of shy that turned him off, and there was an intriguing aura of aloneness about her, as if she'd have been content to sit here all night with or without him.

'I love being near water when it's dark like this,' she said just then, as if she was unaware that he'd been looking at her for the past few minutes. 'There's something really soothing about the sound of it lapping against the wall. That's why I like this bar. It's not so busy that you can't hear yourself think, but not so quiet that you feel unsafe sitting outside on your own.'

'You wouldn't have been on your own if your ride had turned up,' Larry reminded her, liking the soft huskiness of her voice, which was more of a bluesy jazz-singer type than the dirty-sex kind of husky like Jooce's.

'I'm used to it,' she told him quietly, blushing as if she was embarrassed to be talking to a stranger about her personal life. 'My, um, fiancé has a habit of getting distracted and forgetting that he was supposed to meet me.'

'Fiancé?' Larry glanced at her fingers. 'Sorry, I didn't realise. You're not wearing a ring.'

'No,' she murmured, slipping her hand into her jacket pocket. 'Apparently it's too traditional.'

'Interesting,' Larry said, thinking the man was obviously a cheapskate. 'Is he likely to turn up any time soon?'

Shaking her head, she said, 'Not a chance. Wherever he is, he'll be *far* too busy enjoying himself to think about me. Probably won't see him till tomorrow now.'

Peering at the woman when she sighed, Larry wondered

what kind of fool her boyfriend must be to leave her hanging around like this, not knowing where he was or what – or who – he was doing, or even if she could expect him to come home tonight. Larry had only known her for a few minutes, but he already knew that she didn't deserve to be messed around like that. Serve the guy right if she had a little fun of her own in his absence. And not just with some nobody like he was probably shagging while she sat loyally waiting for him, but with a star. *That* was revenge with a capital R.

'What's your name?' he asked now, settling back in his seat.

'Stephanie.'

'And is that what people call you, or do they shorten it to Steph?'

'Sometimes.'

'Which do you prefer?'

'Either's fine.'

Thinking about it for a moment, Larry said, 'I like Stephanie.'

'It's nice when you say it,' she murmured softly.

Their gazes met and held for several long moments. Then, breaking away, Stephanie gazed out over the water again, racked with conflicting emotions – the strongest being guilt, because she shouldn't have been doing this.

Guessing that she was thinking about her inconsiderate dick of a boyfriend, Larry surprised himself by not making an immediate move on her. It was the perfect opportunity, and he'd usually have been going in for the kill round about now. But something was holding him back. Apart from the fact that he'd already nearly scared this woman away once tonight – so she'd probably bolt if he took her by surprise again – she obviously had problems and he wasn't really in the agony-uncle mood. He was too knackered for tea and sympathy.

Finishing his cigarette in silence, he flicked the butt into the water and was just on the verge of drifting off to sleep when the waiter came out to clear the empties from the surrounding tables. Sitting up straighter when the man told them that the bar was closed and they'd be taking the furniture inside in a minute, he downed both of his drinks and handed the glasses over. Glancing at his watch then, he asked Stephanie how she was getting home.

Finishing her own drinks and thanking the waiter, Stephanie said, 'Taxi, I guess.'

'Me, too,' Larry said, reaching into his pocket for his mobile. 'Where are you going to?'

A flicker of a frown crossing her brow, Stephanie reached for her handbag. 'It's okay. I'll just flag one down out on the road. That's what I usually do.'

Telling her that he had to call one for himself anyway, Larry scrolled through his menu to find the company he used when Georgie wasn't around. Pressing 'call', he looked up at her. 'I just need to tell them where you're going to.'

'Fallowfield,' she lied, not really wanting him to know where she lived.

Ordering two cars, Larry pushed his chair back and stood up. 'They're busy tonight, but they reckon at least one should get here soon.' He held out a hand to help her up. 'We've got to wait outside the gates, though, because they won't drive in.'

Reaching for his hand, Stephanie gasped when a tiny crackle of static leapt between their fingers. Blushing, she jerked her hand away and, looping her bag over her shoulder, kept her eyes to the floor as they made their way round to the road fronting the apartments.

It was ten minutes before the first taxi arrived.

Turning to Stephanie, Larry said, 'You take this one.' Then, inclining his head, he kissed her on the cheek, saying, 'Nice meeting you, and I hope your boyfriend makes it up to you for standing you up. But tell him thanks from me, because you've been good company in my hour of need.'

Telling him that she'd enjoyed herself too, Stephanie climbed into the car when he opened the door for her. Dipping his head, Larry asked the driver if he had any idea how long the next car would be.

'You'll be lucky if it's in the next half-hour,' the man said. 'Don't know what's going on in town tonight, but we've been rushed off our wheels for the past couple of hours.'

'Typical.' Larry tutted, swaying slightly as the alcohol he'd just downed rushed to his head. Steadying himself with a hand on the roof of the car, he looked at Stephanie and shrugged. 'Oh, well, I'll just have to wait, won't I? See you later.'

Looking up at him guiltily as he moved back to close the door, Stephanie said, 'Look, why don't we share?'

Hesitating, he peered in at her. 'Are you sure? I don't mind waiting.'

Shaking her head, she said, 'No, that's silly when this car's already here.' Sliding further across the seat to make room for him now, she smiled. 'Please. I'll feel really guilty if I leave you standing here.'

Thinking it over for a moment, Larry flapped his hands and climbed in beside her.

# 12

'Oh, Larry, that wasn't nice,' Georgie scolded, shifting the phone to her other ear to continue rifling through the paper-work littering her desktop. 'I know she's a pain, but you shouldn't have walked out on her party – not when she threw it especially for *you*. The least you could have done was wait until everybody else had gone.'

'And have to fight her off when she tried to make me stay?' Larry replied, sounding more relaxed than Georgie had heard him sound in a long time. 'I don't *think* so! She was already talking about breakfast. And I'm sorry, but there was no way I was going for that. It'd be like waking up in Madame Tussaud's.'

'Yes, well, I agree you didn't have to *sleep* with her,' Georgie said, a mock-disapproving edge to her voice. 'But you shouldn't make an enemy of her. She's a powerful lady, and she could make things very difficult for you.'

'Don't see how,' Larry drawled, stretching out languidly in his bed. 'There's nothing she can do to ruin things for me now.'

'Don't be silly.' Georgie tutted. 'You might be back in favour right now, but what happens when the next big story hits the news and you slide back into obscurity?'

'Not going to happen,' Larry said unconcernedly. 'You've got tons of stuff lined up for me.'

'Yes, and you said that none of it was big enough for you to waste your time thinking about.'

Tiring of the conversation now, Larry said, 'Just stop fannying about and get me something amazing, Georgie. And if it makes you feel any better, I'll ring Raine and tell her I got sick and had to go home. I'll even send the old bag flowers, if you want. But there's no way I'm shagging her – not even for you.'

'Thank you,' Georgie said, with a hint of satisfaction. 'And I'm sure the flowers will suffice. You might not realise it, but it was Raine who got the ban lifted so she could have you on her show last night. Alan Corbin was reluctant to back down, as you can imagine, but I hear she pulled the right strings and got him to reconsider, so I think you ought to be thanking her for that, at the very least.'

'I didn't ask her to put herself out.'

'No, but it's just as well she did, because she's got the highest ratings of any chat show in the country, and I've already had calls from a couple of producers off the back of it.'

'There you go, then.' Larry grinned. 'So, what are they offering?'

'Nothing particularly interesting,' Georgie admitted. 'And I've already turned two of them down. But it's good to know they're sitting up and taking notice, isn't it?'

'So they should be,' Larry said, rolling across the bed to slide a cigarette out of the pack on the table. 'What were they, anyway?'

'One was a cameo on *Judge Joanie*, but it was only two days' work, and they wanted you to play a criminal.'

'Cheeky bastards.'

'My sentiments exactly,' Georgie agreed. 'The other was a guest presenter slot on CBBC's *Garage Gang*, but that's *so* not you.' Pausing now, she cleared her throat. 'But they weren't the only producers I've been speaking to this morning, and I thought you'd be rather pleased when you heard what my last chat was about.'

'Oh, yeah?' Larry said, smiling at Stephanie when she walked into the room. She was wearing one of his shirts, which really accentuated the length of her lovely legs, and she looked gorgeous with her glossy, sleep-tousled hair framing her beautiful face. And it was a refreshing change to see that she hadn't redone her make-up while she was in the bathroom – the girls he bedded usually liked to get their faces perfect before he laid eyes on them the morning after.

'Remember we bumped into Frank when we were leaving the studio yesterday and I promised to return his call?' Georgie was saying now. 'Well, I felt a little guilty about neglecting him, because he'd actually rung a couple of times and left messages, so I rang him this morning to apologise and find out what he wanted.'

'And what *did* he want?' Larry asked, drawing the quilt back for Stephanie to climb back into bed beside him.

'*Well* . . .' Georgie said, drawing it out because she thought he'd be ecstatic when he heard the news. 'He wants to give you your old job back.'

'Are you joking?' Larry frowned. 'What about Matty?'

'I don't actually think he's part of the equation,' Georgie said, chuckling softly. 'It's not a job for two hosts, is it? Anyway, you and I both know that the ratings have slipped since you left, so this is purely good business as far as Frank's concerned. And I'm delighted, because this really marks how far you've come since last year.'

'I hope you told him where to stick it,' Larry said, sounding more offended than impressed.

'Absolutely not,' Georgie replied confusedly. 'I thought you'd be pleased.'

'Well, I'm not. I haven't gone through all this shit to go straight back to square one.'

'But I thought this was what you wanted? You've been

saying it's your show all the way down the line. Don't you even want to think about it?'

'What's to think about? I don't want it, and I'm amazed Frank thought I'd even give it the time of day. No wonder he was being so flaming nice when I saw him at the party last night. He must think I've forgotten what he did to me.'

'I'm sure everybody's got regrets about what happened,' Georgie told him. 'And Frank is a decent man, so I imagine he'll have had his fair share.'

'What about Terri?' Larry asked, abruptly changing the subject. 'Has she been back to you about that American thing she was talking about yet?'

'Obviously not, or I'd have told you,' Georgie said, wondering why Larry still seemed to think that Terri Lawson had any power or influence, given that she'd been dumped by Shock-Wave after the disastrous game show. The woman talked a good game, you had to give her that. She'd been on the phone almost continuously in the first month after she went home in disgrace, telling Georgie that she was concentrating all her efforts on Larry now, trying to get him a vehicle that would secure him his big break in the States. But nothing had happened in the three months since the programme had aired over there, so it was all hot air in Georgie's opinion, and of no real benefit whatsoever to Larry.

'Never mind Terri,' she said now, wanting him to focus on the *real* things which were on offer over here. 'I know you say you're not interested, but would you please just think about Frank's offer. *Star Struck* made you, and I think it would be fantastic for you *and* the show if you went back and rescued it now that it's failing. Frank's proposing a completely fresh start. New theme tune, new set, new – fantastically higher – salary. And you'll have the option of backing out of the contract after a year, so it would give you a real chance to pick and choose where you went from there.'

'See you later,' Larry said, refusing to humour Georgie by agreeing to even think about it when he'd already made his feelings quite clear. Disconnecting the call, he tossed the phone onto the floor and turned to Stephanie, who was still sitting up, with her arms folded around herself.

'Something wrong?' she asked. 'You didn't sound too pleased with that call.'

'My agent,' Larry told her, reaching up and stroking a finger down her cheek. 'Apparently I've just been offered my old job back, and – for *some* reason – she seemed to think I'd be pleased.'

'But you're not?'

'No, I'm not,' Larry murmured softly, pulling her down beside him and gazing into her eyes. 'But I don't want to talk about it, so let's just . . .'

Closing her eyes when he lowered his head and kissed her softly, Stephanie shivered when he slid his hand down over her breasts and slowly unbuttoned the shirt.

'Like that?' he whispered, easing the material aside and lowering his head to tease each nipple in turn with his tongue.

Nodding, she bit her lip and arched her back as he slid his hand down over her stomach. Raising her hips to meet his fingers, she gasped when he slid one inside her. Then she gripped his hair, holding him to her.

Pulling away when he felt her body begin to tense, Larry rolled onto his back and pulled Stephanie on top of him, easing his tongue into her and savouring the sweetness of her juices as she bucked her hips above him. Groaning when she lowered her head and trailed her tongue slowly along the length of his dick, he gripped her thighs tightly in his hands and thrust himself into her warm mouth, holding her fast until the heat in his balls turned to searing flames.

Flipping her over then, he pushed her arms up above her head and peered down into her eyes as he thrust himself into her. She looked so vulnerable and sexy, with her lips parted and her eyes so dark and intense, and he felt as if they were melting into each other as their hips rose and fell in perfect unison.

Throwing his head back when the orgasm tore through his body, he gritted his teeth and rode the waves, feeling the sensation increasing and sucking him in as Stephanie cried out beneath him.

The phone started to ring again. Ignoring it, Larry flopped down and laid his head against Stephanie's sweat-slick breasts, listening to her heart pounding wildly in time with his own.

'Shouldn't you get that?' she asked him breathlessly, swiping damp hair out of her eyes as the phone continued to ring.

Larry shook his head. 'I don't want to move.'

'It might be important.'

'Nothing's that important.'

Exhaling softly when the phone stopped ringing at last, Stephanie gazed down at Larry's head on her naked breast and felt a crushing wave of guilt wash over her. Closing her eyes as a tear trickled slowly down her cheek, she fought to stem the rest that were threatening to follow.

She hadn't intended for this to happen. She'd never in her life slept with a man on a first date before – not that it had *been* a date. But whatever it was or wasn't, it certainly wasn't right, and knowing that she had cheated on the man she loved was the worst feeling in the world.

The drink had obviously played a large part – not that *that* was any excuse. And it hadn't helped that Larry was so good-looking, and charming, and gentlemanly. If he'd been cocky or presumptuous, she'd have found it so much easier to keep him at bay. But he'd made her feel so relaxed. And, even though they hadn't spoken about very much at all, he'd really listened to what she had to say, and she'd found herself enjoying his company far more than she should have.

Standing beside him waiting for the cab, with the drink stirring feelings which had been buried for far too long, Stephanie had found herself wondering what it would be like to have his arms around her – even if it was just a quick goodbye hug. Anything to take the edge off going home to an empty bed again.

Then the taxi had arrived, and she'd been glad, because she was disgusted with herself for getting drunk enough to feel attracted to another man. But when the driver had told Larry that he'd have a long wait for his own cab, she'd felt too guilty to leave him standing there and had offered to share. And he'd accepted. And once they were sitting together on the dark back seat, the drink had really kicked in, so when he made his move she was ashamed to say that she'd been more than ready to let him.

Lying in her arms, Larry was thinking much the same thing – although without the guilt. He'd been determined not to make a move on her in case he offended her, but when she'd offered to share the cab his dick had overruled his sense of decency and he'd gladly accepted. And she'd looked so shy and sweet with the light from the passing street lamps flickering across her face that he couldn't resist kissing her. And when she didn't push him away, there'd been no turning back.

And he was glad he'd gone for it, because it made a nice change to make love instead of just fucking.

Not that it *was* love, of course, because that was something he'd never experienced and had no intention of looking for at this point in his life – not when there were still so many gorgeous girls out there that he was yet to meet and be entertained by. But she'd be a nice alternative to his usual tarts until whatever this was that they had started ran out of steam and she went back to her boyfriend.

The phone began to ring again. Tutting, Larry eased himself

up and reached for it. Hearing Georgie's voice, he was just about to tell her to piss off and stop disturbing him when she said, 'You'll never guess who I've just been talking to? . . . Craig Woodburn! He saw you on Raine's show last night and wants to give you your own chat show!'

'Are you kidding me?' Sitting up now, Larry reached for the shirt that Stephanie had been wearing and wiped the sweat off his face.

'My darling, I *never* kid,' Georgie trilled happily. 'He wants to see you *today*. And he's so confident you'll accept his offer that he's already having a contract drawn up so we can sign there and then.'

'Wow,' Larry murmured, a thrill of real excitement coursing through him.

'Wow, indeed!' Georgie agreed. 'They're proposing a twice-weekly slot, Monday and Friday, at – wait for it – *six-thirty*!'

'No way,' Larry gasped. 'The same time as Raine's show?'

'The exact same time, but on a more popular channel,' Georgie told him. 'And right before the soaps, so there's no way anyone will miss you. You've done it, darling! You've snatched the crown!'

Arranging to meet her outside in half an hour so that she could take him to meet with Craig Woodburn, Larry disconnected the call and turned to Stephanie.

Smiling because he looked so excited, she said, 'Good news?'

'The best!' He grinned, planting a kiss on her lips. 'What are you doing today?'

Glancing at the bedside clock, she frowned when she saw the time. Telling him that she had to be somewhere in an hour, she reached for the damp shirt and modestly pulled it on, saying, 'Would you mind if I take a quick shower?'

Hopping naked out of bed, Larry reached for her hand, and said, 'We'll share one. Then you can cancel whatever you're doing and come with me, because I reckon you just might be my good-luck charm.'

Letting him help her out of the bed, Stephanie closed her eyes when he hugged her. 'I can't cancel it,' she said.

Easing her away and peering down into her eyes, Larry saw the cloud of sadness there and frowned. 'Ah . . . the boyfriend?'

Nodding, she dipped her gaze. 'Sorry.'

'Don't be,' Larry said, tilting her chin up and kissing her softly. 'It would have been nice to have you there, but you've got your own plans, so I shouldn't have expected you to drop them just like that.'

'I would if I could,' she told him, feeling bad for running out on him like this.

'No problem,' he drawled, too happy about his good news to be overly concerned that she was putting her boyfriend before him. 'We'll celebrate later, yeah?'

Nodding, Stephanie smiled.

Putting her into a cab outside his block twenty minutes later, Larry had just closed the door and stepped back to wave her away when he remembered that he hadn't taken her number. Slapping the roof of the car to stop it as the driver started to pull away from the kerb, he yanked the door open and said, 'I need your number.'

Murmuring, 'Oh, right,' Stephanie took her phone out of her bag. Switching it back on, hoping that he wouldn't question why she'd turned it off, she said, 'Sorry, it takes ages for me to find it.'

Telling her he could wait, Larry waved to Georgie, who had just pulled up behind the cab. Taking his own phone out then, he tapped in Stephanie's number when she found it and blew her a kiss, saying, 'I'll give you a call as soon as I'm finished. Make sure you're free.'

Promising to try, Stephanie glanced out of the back window when Georgie beeped the horn.

Seeing her face, Georgie pursed her lips.

'Well, well,' she said when Larry waved the cab off a few moments later and climbed in beside her. 'I see someone got lucky last night. And, unless I'm very much mistaken, wasn't that the young lady who fell at your feet last night at the studio?'

'Jeezus, you've got a good memory,' Larry laughed, pulling his seat belt on.

'Yes, I have,' Georgie said disapprovingly. 'But it appears that yours *isn't* so good, because I'm sure I heard you telling Raine that you weren't looking for a relationship on her show last night?'

'Who said anything about relationships?' Larry quipped, lighting a cigarette and rolling the window part-way down. 'I've only just met the girl.'

Uttering a throaty 'Hmph!' Georgie swung out into the traffic, saying, 'And may I ask how you happened to bump into her again?'

'Why?'

'Humour me,' Georgie said, tapping her fingers on the steering wheel as they waited for a set of lights to turn green. 'Did she slip you her number at the studio?'

'No.'

'Was she at Raine's party, then?'

'No.' Getting irritated now, Larry turned and peered at her. 'What's with the Spanish Inquisition, Georgie?'

'Just one last question,' she replied, keeping her eyes on the road as they started moving again. 'Was yesterday the first time you saw her?'

'Yes. And . . . ?'

'I'm sure I've seen her before, that's all. Three weeks ago, when you opened that supermarket in Sale, she was hanging about in the car park.'

'Don't be ridiculous,' Larry scoffed. 'How could you possibly know it was her?'

'Because I'm observant,' Georgie told him. 'And now here she is again. So what does that tell you?'

'If you're trying to make out like she's some kind of stalker, forget it,' Larry chuckled. 'I've already accused her of that, and she was really offended.'

'Oh yes? And why would you accuse her unless you suspected her?'

'Maybe I did for a split second,' Larry admitted. 'But then I spoke to her, and she didn't have a clue who I was.'

'Oh, *please*,' Georgie muttered, shaking her head. 'And *you* fell for that? I thought you had more sense. She's been following you, and now you've given her exactly what she was looking for. At least, I presume you did. I take it that *was* the grand farewell after a night of fun with Number One Fan?'

'I think you're way off,' Larry said flatly. 'But so what if she *is* a fan? She's obviously not a nutter, 'cos I'm still alive, aren't I?'

'Sure she didn't make prints of your keys in the soap, or anything?'

'You're just being stupid now.'

'So long as you don't follow suit,' Georgie said quietly. 'Fans who pretend not to be should not be encouraged.'

Sighing heavily, Larry told her to shut up now because she was boring him. She was obviously convinced that she *had* seen Stephanie before, so she was only looking out for him. But even if she was right, he didn't care. It wasn't like he was planning on marrying the girl, or anything. She was already spoken for, for one thing. But he wouldn't bother telling Georgie that, because she'd only tell him off for encouraging her to be unfaithful – like that mattered in this day and age.

Driving on in silence, Georgie made a mental note to keep an eye on the situation. Larry obviously wasn't concerned, but she'd seen *Play Misty For Me* enough times to know how dangerous obsessive fans could be when they saw their man talking to another woman. And a man like Larry, who flirted relentlessly and bedded indiscriminately, would bring out the hidden lunatic in this one in no time.

Craig Woodburn was on the phone when Larry and Georgie were shown into his office. Waving for them to wait, he said, 'Okay, Tezza, I'll think about it. But I'm not making any promises, so don't go quoting me on that.' Rolling his eyes now as his caller carried on talking, he said, 'Yeah, yeah, I've said I'll think about it. Gotta go now. Bye-ee.'

Hanging up, he exhaled loudly and stood up. 'Sorry about that. Wogan's pressing for a meet, but I'm trying to avoid it because . . .' Pausing, he flapped his hand dismissively, saying, 'Not your concern, so I won't bore you with the details.' Extending his hand now, he said, 'Good to meet you, Larry.'

'You, too,' Larry said, shaking it.

'And you must be Georgie of the lovely voice?' Craig said, turning to her and kissing her hand. 'She's a keeper, this one, Larry. Balls of steel, voice of velvet.'

'*Right*,' Larry murmured, raising an eyebrow at Georgie who looked like she was on the verge of blushing.

Jerking his head now, Craig said, 'Come and meet the team, and let us run you through the set designs. I think you're gonna like it.'

'You've already started designing?' Larry asked, amused by his presumptuousness. 'That sure I'm going to sign, are you?'

'Positive,' Craig replied confidently, putting a hand on his shoulder and walking him to the door. 'You'd have to be stupid to turn me down when I've got the biggest budget in the industry.' Shrugging now, he added, 'But if you prove me wrong, I'm sure Wogan would jump at the chance, so I'm not really concerned.'

'Nice to know you think so much of me,' Larry snorted, thinking that the man had a lot to learn about the subtle art of persuasion.

'Hey, I'm all for you,' Craig told him, showing him down the corridor. 'But I'm not kissing rump for anyone, my friend. You want it, you got it. You don't, I move on. Simple.'

'Fair enough,' Larry said, respecting him for his honesty.

Winking at Georgie who was walking a couple of steps behind, Craig said, 'Your lovely agent here seemed happy enough about it when I approached her a couple of weeks back.'

'A couple of weeks back?' Larry repeated confusedly, having heard nothing about this until an hour ago.

'Yeah, I had to make sure you hadn't already committed to something else before I started putting my plans into action. And I wanted to see you in action on Raine Parker's show before I made a definite decision. But you were great, so here we are.'

Turning, Larry gave Georgie a dark look, unimpressed that she'd been discussing him behind his back, and keeping it from him in order to give Craig time to screen-test him. That was an outright insult, and she of all people should know that he'd be offended.

Reaching the boardroom, Craig pushed the door open and waved Larry and Georgie in ahead of him.

Grinning when he saw Larry, Gordon Jones stood up and came around the table to greet him. 'Hello, stranger. Bet you never thought you'd see *me* again?'

Peering at him, it took Larry a couple of seconds to recognise him. Then, smiling widely, he reached for his hand, saying, 'Gordon! Christ, how are you?'

'Great,' Gordon said, glad that Larry seemed pleased to see him, because he hadn't been sure that he would be after the telethon. In fact, he had wondered if Larry might be blaming him for Frank Woods finding out about the drinking that night. But Larry didn't seem to be holding any grudges, which was as good a start as Gordon could have hoped for.

'So, you're on the crew, are you?' Larry asked him now.

Nodding, Gordon waved him to take a seat. 'I'm the director.'

Raising an eyebrow, Larry smirked. 'Proper this time, or still assistant?'

'Proper,' Gordon assured him. 'Took a while, but I got there in the end. And Jez was a big help, believe it or not. I think he felt a bit guilty about sacking me that night, so he put a good word in for me with Craig. And the rest, as they say, is history.'

Nodding, not really sure what he was talking about – because he'd been so wrapped up in his own misfortune at that time and hadn't thought to wonder if anyone else had been affected – Larry sat down and crossed his legs.

Pulling a chair out for Georgie, Craig gestured towards the other man who was sitting across the table from Larry, saying, 'This is the producer, Tom Reed.'

Leaning forward, Larry shook the other man's hand. 'Nice to meet you, Tom.'

'Who's for a drink?' Craig asked now, going over to an ornate lacquered Chinese cabinet and opening the door to reveal bottles of every kind of alcohol. 'Larry?'

'Scotch,' Larry said, giving Georgie a defiant look when she frowned at him. Serve her right if he got pissed out of his head – make her think twice about going behind his back again.

Pouring everybody a drink, and ordering a coffee for Georgie, Craig joined them at the table and reached for a large portfolio which was sitting between them. Flipping it open, he turned it so that Larry could see the sketches inside.

'They're only prelims,' he explained. 'But we're pretty much going to go with them. Now, as you'll see, we're planning on separating the stage area into two sections: one for the chat element, the other for live performances from musical guests.'

'Why so many chairs?' Larry asked, peering at the pictures. 'I got the impression it was going to be one-on-one?'

'No, we're thinking more along the lines of Jerry Springer meets Oprah.'

'Are you kidding me?' Larry frowned. 'That sounds like Jeremy Kyle.'

'Hey, you can't knock Kyle,' Craig countered, unconcerned by Larry's sudden dip in enthusiasm. 'He's the most successful of his kind over here. But he's sticking it to his guests in words they understand, whereas you'll be charm personified. The Afghan hound to his bulldog – so to speak.'

'Like Trisha, then?' Larry said sarcastically.

'Not at all.' Craig shook his head. 'Look, you're the star, and this is all about you. The viewers loved you before, and they're already falling in love with you all over again. But we all know you need a vehicle to rocket you right to the top and keep you there – and this is it, my friend. Last time, you were dealing directly with the public, so the viewers felt close to you, but this time you'll be interviewing the stars. And because you're on their level, the viewers will feel like *they*'re mixing with them, too. Does that make any sense?'

'I think what he's trying to say,' Gordon chipped in, leaning forward and resting his elbows on the table, 'is that it won't matter *who* your guests are, because the public will feel such an affinity with you that they'll tune in, whoever you've got on.'

'Paul O'Grady,' Larry muttered, folding his arms now.

'In a way,' Gordon conceded. 'But straight, so the women will still feel they've got a chance with you.'

'And it's well known that viewers always check who's appearing before they decide which show to watch when they've got a choice,' Tom interjected. He'd stayed quiet for the first few minutes in order to get the feel of Larry, and had decided that he'd do. 'With our budget, we can afford the best of the best, so there'll be no contest. Unmissable guests *and* you. Match made in heaven.'

Chewing this over for a minute, a little mollified by the thought of having star guests rather than scummy Joe Public, Larry said, 'Can you guarantee it'll be different enough to attract attention? Because it's still sounding like a bit of a bastardisation of everyone else's shows to me.'

'They're *all* a bastardisation,' Craig pointed out. 'That's why there's so many of them, because the public love this shit. Our special ingredient is *you*,' he went on, his gaze burning with conviction. 'And that's the one thing that none of the other channels can give to the women who make up the mass majority of the viewers for this kind of thing.'

'You're the bad boy they all want to tame,' Gordon chipped in. 'The dangerous, drop-dead handsome guy with a past, who they think they stand a chance with in the future. The man who's going to make every woman in the country cream her knickers at teatime, and make every young girl dream about growing up and marrying him. *The* man – full stop!'

Flattered that they all seemed to have such faith in his powers of remote seduction, Larry smiled wryly, and said, 'So, more like David Beckham, then?'

'And he gets it!' Craig declared, exhaling exaggeratedly.

'So, do I get my own lovely little Vicky to dress me?' Larry teased.

'Do you bloody hell as like,' Craig exclaimed with mock horror. 'You'll be out there by yourself. No Angelinas,

Victorias, or Jennifers squeezing the juice out of your bollocks. Just pure, accessible, love-god you.'

Larry glanced at the beaming Georgie, who was nodding her head at the other end of the table. He was still pissed off with her for keeping secrets, but her instincts were second to none, and if she thought this was a good bet it was bound to work.

'Okay,' he said, looking back to Craig. 'Let's do it.'

'Good boy,' Craig said, standing up to shake his hand. 'Glad to have you on board.'

'Glad to *be* on board.' Larry grinned. And he meant it – because now that he'd agreed to do it, he would make sure that *The Larry Logan Show* wiped all the other chat shows off the map.

# 13

Lying on his bunk with his prison-gym-thickened arms behind his head, Dex sneered as he watched the screws tear his cell apart. He knew exactly what they were looking for, but they were stupid if they thought he would keep it in here. It was laughable, really. They went to such pains to launch these surprise raids, but his tame screw guaranteed that Dex – and anyone else who had the fifty quid a week to keep him on side – knew exactly when to stash his gear in someone else's cell. Well worth the expense, in Dex's opinion, if it saved him the hassle of constantly having to replace the goods they'd have otherwise confiscated – the mobile phone, for example.

It had cost him three hundred to have the phone and charger smuggled in, and there was no way he wanted to lose them, because that was his only contact with the outside world while he was between visits. It was bad enough being stuck in this shit-hole, knowing that life was still going on as normal for every other cunt out there, but it would kill him if he couldn't hear his mother's voice. He needed to hear how Molly was getting on, and be kept up to date about their Patrick. And it was his only way of keeping tabs on Gaynor, too.

She was really pissing him off at the moment, because she was getting a bit lax with her phone calls, and there was no excuse for that – not when she knew how hard it was for him stuck in here. Dex knew she was doing her best to hold everything together for him, and it wasn't easy for her having to lie to his family so that she could deal with his business without their interference. But they weren't smart enough to be trusted with it, so he didn't want them knowing anything. Gaynor hated it, but she was struggling on for his sake, and he had to thank her for that – and when he got out, he would make sure he thanked her *properly*. But, in the meantime, the least she could do was keep in regular touch, because there was too much time to let your imagination run away with you in here, and he'd already spent too many sleepless nights with his guts churning, wondering exactly what she was doing.

Dex knew that Gaynor loved him with all her heart and would never fall for anyone else. Still, he couldn't help but wonder if she could maintain that same degree of devotion and loyalty for fifteen years. And it didn't help that his mam never stopped going on about her, either; always complaining that she was acting like a free woman now that he was off the scene, coming and going as she pleased, and tarting herself up like she was looking for a replacement in his bed – just like Jane had done the last time he'd been banged up. And every time she said it, it made being locked up feel a million times worse, so that the frustration that was relentlessly gnawing at his brain turned to white-hot rage.

But he just had to keep reminding himself that Gaynor wasn't like Jane, and trust that she was working as hard as she said she was to ensure that they had a fantastic future when he finally got out of here.

His cell search was almost done now. Still sneering when one of the screws jerked his thumb and told him to get off the bunk, Dex stretched languidly before sitting up. Then, taking his own sweet time, he swung his legs around and dropped down to the floor so that he was standing nose to nose with the screw.

'Looking for anything in particular, Mr Jenkins?'

'You really think you're funny, don't you?' Officer Jenkins said quietly, his gaze unwavering.

'I think I can smell a pussy, that's what I think,' Dex replied, sniffing softly. 'Give the missus a tonguing before you came to work, did you?'

'If I was you,' Jenkins warned, 'I'd keep my mouth shut before someone shuts it for you.'

'Oh yeah?' Dex grinned, challenging him to go for it, knowing that Jenkins would wait until there were more than the three screws he had with him now to back him up.

'You'll keep,' Jenkins hissed.

'Can't wait,' Dex hissed back, his grin pure evil now.

Shoving him out of the way, Jenkins yanked Dex's mattress off the bunk. Waving one of his fellow officers over to help him, he slipped a pair of latex gloves on and felt his way over every inch of it, scrutinising the seams for slits or holes through which contraband could be shoved into the padding. Dumping it on the floor when he'd finished, he trampled over it and headed for the door, pushing the other officers out ahead of him.

'You forgot to sniff me sheet for spunk,' Dex called after him. 'Give you summat to fantasise about when you're slip-ping the missus one tonight.'

Turning back with a smirk on his face, Jenkins unzipped his fly and aimed his dick at the mattress. Pissing on it, making sure he got a good spread, he zipped himself up again, and said, 'Sleep well, dickhead.'

'Oh, I will,' Dex replied quietly, making sure that the other screws couldn't hear him. 'Hope *you* can, though, when you go home and find your missus bleeding from the arse.' Pausing to let that sink in, he whispered, 'I know where you live.'

Flinging the door wide now, to make sure he had witnesses if anything happened, Jenkins said, 'You threatening me, Lewis?'

'Don't know what you mean, Boss,' Dex replied calmly, looking as innocent as it was possible for a villain to look.

Narrowing his eyes, Jenkins said, 'I'll be seeing you later.'

Winking at him, Dex held his gaze until he turned and walked away. Then he wandered out onto the landing and rested his elbows on the railing, watching until the screws had gone all the way down the stairs. Strolling into the neighbouring cell, he jerked his chin at Tommy West who was lying on the bottom bunk, and said, 'Shift. I'm having your mattress.'

'Aw, come on, lad,' Tommy groaned, his tired old eyes pale and watery as he looked up at Dex. 'I heard what just happened in your gaff, and I ain't sleeping on his piss. I've got me joints to think about.'

'Rather sleep in your own blood, would you?' Dex said coldly.

Feeling no guilt when the sixty-three-year-old man dragged himself wearily off the bunk and flapped his hand for him to take what he wanted, Dex raised his eyebrows.

'I know you ain't expecting *me* to carry it, you lazy auld shite. I think you're mistaking me for one of your fucking care workers, or summat.' Shaking his head now, he walked back out.

Sighing, Tommy leaned down and grasped the edge of the mattress. He was in no fit state to be moving furniture, but he'd be in no fit state to do *any*thing if he didn't – Dex would make sure of that. Lewis had only been transferred here a month ago, but he'd already sprayed his scent all over the landing, and nobody dared refuse when he asked for a 'favour'.

Standing in the doorway of his cell until his neighbour had swapped the mattresses and put his new one up on his bunk for him, Dex told him to clear off. Then he went to the next-but-one cell to retrieve his phone. Kicking the lad who'd been looking after it out onto the landing to keep watch, he closed the door and sat down on the bunk, helping himself to some tobacco from the lad's pouch while he waited for his mother to answer his call.

'About bloody time,' Nora grumbled when she heard his voice. 'I've been waiting for you to call for ages. How come you took so long?'

'Screws keep doing spot raids, trying to catch me out,' Dex told her, lighting his roll-up.

'They don't know about your phone, do they?'

'Course they do. But they won't catch me with it, so I don't give a toss.'

'Yeah, well, just make sure you don't go and lose your rag,' Nora warned him. 'You don't want to end up in solitary again.'

'Don't worry about me. I can look after myself.'

'Yes, I know, but I can't help worrying. You're too much of a snapper for your own good, you.'

'Ma, you're wasting time,' Dex cut in irritably. 'I've only got a few minutes, and I want to know what's going on.'

'Huh!' Nora grunted, the sound of the washing machine going into a loud spin behind her. 'What *ain't* going on, more like. Your Molly's been in trouble at school again, and Jane's threatening to have her put in care if she carries on 'cos she reckons it'll be her who gets done for it.'

'Tell the slag I'll rip her fucking head off if she even thinks about it,' Dex spat, wondering why he craved these calls so much when they always wound him up so bad. 'Fetch Molly on your next visit, and tell her I don't care what excuse she comes up with, 'cos I want to see her. And if she don't behave, tell her I'm sending her back to you, where we can keep a proper eye on her.'

Nora sighed loudly, the thought of having her wayward granddaughter back under her roof making her feel worn out before it had even happened. Dealing with her own lads was one thing, but teenage girls who had no manners was another, and she didn't see why she should be expected to put up with that little mare's moods and tantrums at her age. It was bad enough having their Christine's little one, Lyla, to look after. And *she* was a retard, so she was more than enough for an old woman who wasn't getting any help from anyone to cope with. If their Christine ever dared show her face round here again, Nora would tear the hair right out of her bloody head for dumping the kid on her like that. And that was nothing to what her brothers would do to her, the crack-addled whore.

'Where's Gaynor?' Dex demanded now, interrupting his mother's thoughts.

'You tell me,' Nora grunted disapprovingly. 'She didn't show her face again last night, even though she *knew* I was waiting on that money. I'm giving her till three, then I'm going round there myself. And she'll get what bloody for if I do, I can tell you – making me troll all that way with me leg playing up! You should never have left her in charge of that money, son. I don't know *what* you was thinking, I really don't. I was only saying to—'

'I'm not going over all that again,' Dex interrupted before she could get into her stride. 'I don't want my money at your place 'cos there's too many bent bastards round there.'

'So you'd rather leave it with that slag, knowing she's helping herself while your mam's scrimping and bloody scraping?'

'Belt up, Ma,' Dex said tetchily. 'If you don't see her in the next couple of hours, tell our Jimmy to go round and get it off her.'

'I'm not sending him nowhere,' Nora blustered indignantly. 'He'll probably end up giving her a slap and get himself into trouble. And I can't have that – not now he's the only one I've got left to look after me while you and our Jason are locked up, and our Pat's living it up in prozzie-land. I'm on me tod here, and now them Hannons are sniffing about.'

'What do you mean, sniffing about?' Dex demanded.

'I keep seeing them walking past, clocking the house,' Nora told him. 'I'm sure they're getting ready to break in.'

Breathing heavily as a wave of rage swept over him, Dex gritted his teeth. Lee, Noel, and Stuart Hannon were a mob of shit-arsed junkies who lived on the roughest part of his mam's estate. They'd never have the bollocks to come within pissing distance of the house if Dex and the rest of the Lewis lads were still around, but everyone knew that Dex was doing fifteen, and that their Jason was doing two for burglary, while Pat had skipped to the Dam. Word was obviously out that there was only Jimmy left, and the Hannons might just be stupid enough to think they could take him.

'I know they're planning something,' Nora went on, a worried edge to her voice now. ''Cos I saw Wally Phillips down the doctor's yesterday, and he lives next to their mam, and he reckons he heard them over the fence, discussing all the stuff you must have stashed in here before you got carted off – drugs, and money, and that.'

'And what's Jimmy saying about it?'

Hesitating, because she hadn't wanted to tell him this, Nora said, 'He's not been home for the past few nights, son. But don't get mad, because he's got his kids to think about, and you know how hard it's been for him getting that ex of his to give him access. But she's finished with that bloke she was seeing, so she rang him the other night and told him he could come and spend the week with them. He didn't want to leave me,' she added quickly, so that he couldn't accuse Jimmy of abandoning her. 'But I made him, so don't be blaming him, will you, son?'

Thinking that he'd do more than blame Jimmy when he saw him, Dex bit down on his anger and said, 'Right, here's what you're gonna do, Ma. Soon as you put the phone down, ring Mark Butcher and tell him I said to get the lads together and pay the Hannons a visit. And I want *you* to go with them – so's they know you've got back-up, yeah?'

'All right, son,' Nora agreed, chuckling softly because it felt good to know that, even locked up, their Dex was still looking after her.

'And when you see Lee Hannon,' Dex went on, 'tell him from me that I'm going to slice his fucking throat open and hang him upside down from the top of his mam's stairs when I get out.'

'Oh, now, hang on a minute,' Nora said worriedly.

'No, Ma, I don't give a shit,' Dex grunted. 'I want him running scared so every other fucker who's thinking about getting clever knows to stay clear of you.'

'Eeh, I *am* glad I've got you,' Nora said, sighing softly. 'Oh, by the way,' she said then. 'You'll never guess what I read in the paper about that little bastard Larry Logan. You know how he's been getting his ugly face all over the telly again, bragging about how he got you banged up? Well, he's only gone and got himself a new bleedin' show now, hasn't he?'

'Has he now?' Dex muttered darkly, his cheek muscles spasming at the mention of Logan's name.

'*The Larry Logan Show*, if you don't mind,' Nora went on scathingly. 'Reckons he's going to have all the big movie stars and what have you as guests, 'cos he's such a flaming big shot nowadays. Tell you what, Derek, if I see him on the streets he'll soon know about it.'

'You just keep your neck in and your nose out,' Dex told her firmly. 'I'll deal with him, don't you worry about that. And when I take him down, he's gonna *stay* down – believe me.'

Opening the cell door just then, the lookout hissed that Jenkins was on his way back up.

Telling his mother that he had to go, Dex disconnected and tossed the mobile down the side of the bunk. Then, dashing out of the cell and into his own, he was lying on his bed as if he'd been there all along when Jenkins strolled by.

Hesitating in the doorway, Jenkins narrowed his eyes. There was no way Lewis would be touching that mattress if it was still wet, so the smart-arse must have swapped it for someone else's dry one. Grinning slyly now, he shook his head and walked on. It was all right. Fifteen years was time enough to break the cunt.

Back at home, Nora put the phone down and poured herself a cup of tea from the pot. It was barely tepid now, but she needed to wet her whistle before she rang Dex's mates because she'd be doing a lot of talking once they got here. It'd be lovely to see them, though, because it had been way too quiet since her lads went and she'd really started to feel her age of late. Especially since her niece had sent that cow Christine's little Lyla home. She really could have done without that, but she could hardly expect their Fiona to take the kid on full-time when she had her own brood to see to.

Lyla was sleeping just now, which was good, because Nora didn't really want to have to take her along when she went with Mark and the lads to warn the Hannons off. And, fingers crossed, she'd be out of it for a good few hours yet, after the double dose of medicine that Nora had given her. She knew she shouldn't have, really, because the doctor had warned her that it could cause liver damage further down the line. But he didn't have to cope with Lyla when she was having a fit, did he? All that screaming and foaming at the mouth, with her eyes rolling round in the back of her head, was enough to send you round the bend. Still, Lyla should be okay if Nora didn't double her up again for a few days – tempting as it would be to do so.

Lighting a cigarette now, Nora drank her cool tea down in one and wiped her mouth on the back of her hand. Then she reached for the phone to call Mark. It had just started to ring when the doorbell rang. Shuffling out to get it, she glared at Gaynor when she saw her, saying, 'What time do you call this?'

'Sorry,' Gaynor murmured, following her back to the kitchen. 'I got held up at my mum's.'

'All bleedin' night?' Nora snapped, sitting back down.

'She's not well,' Gaynor snapped back, wondering why she was explaining herself.

'Yeah, well, she's not the only one,' Nora grumbled, her eyes darting to the money that Gaynor had just taken out of her handbag. Snatching it off her, she pocketed it, saying, 'It'd best all be there, or our Dex is going to want to know why.'

'Course it's all there,' Gaynor told her irritably. 'I'm not a bloody thief.'

'Yeah, right,' Nora snorted meanly. 'Certainly making sure you get the lion's share, though, aren't you? I practically have to beg you to hand my keeps over, and it ain't even *yours*.'

'Hey, none of this was my idea,' Gaynor reminded her, glaring right back at her now because she was sick to bloody death of getting it in the neck from the ungrateful old bitch. 'Dex wanted it this way – so if you've got a problem have it out with him and quit getting at me.'

Drawing her head back, Nora gave her an evil look. 'Who the hell do you think you're talking to like that? 'Cos I'll tell you what, lady, you're on thin ice now. If our Dex was here, he'd—'

'But he's not, though, is he?' Gaynor interrupted, adding, 'I wish he bloody was, 'cos then I wouldn't have to see *you*.'

'Carry on, and see what happens, lady,' Nora hissed, her eyes flashing a clear warning. 'I've only just been telling Dex about you and your shenanigans, and he ain't best pleased, I can tell you. Don't make me have to add this to the list, an' all, 'cos he's already getting set to have our Jimmy pay you a visit.'

Inhaling deeply, Gaynor bit her tongue. She'd been up half the night and she was absolutely knackered, so she could really do without fighting with Nora. But one of these days she was going to snap and, when she did, Nora would hear exactly what Gaynor thought of her and her precious lads. They made out like they were so superior, but they were every bit as stupid and as nasty as the rest of the bastards who lived on this estate. And if it wasn't for Dex, she'd happily kill the lot of them.

Dex was the only one of the Lewises she had time for, and not just because she was still deeply in love with him after three years – although God knew he didn't deserve it sometimes, after all the grief he'd given her. But also because he was the only one who actually had something about him. Yes, he was a criminal, and yes, he had an evil temper, but there was a brilliant sense of humour behind the scowl, and he could be really affectionate when he wasn't coked-up or spliffed-out. And her heart still beat faster whenever she saw him, because she loved his rugged good looks, and his sexy blue-grey eyes never failed to make her stomach flip.

'You still here?' Nora's cold voice cut into her thoughts.

Sighing, Gaynor said, 'All right, I'm going. Anything you want me to do?'

'Yeah – get your arse round here when you're supposed to in future.'

Nodding wearily, Gaynor turned and walked out without saying goodbye. There was no point; she wouldn't get an answer. Turning along the hall just as Molly let herself in through the front door, she stepped back and waited for the girl to pass before continuing on her way. Another one there was no point talking to.

'What was *she* doing here?' Molly demanded, going into

the kitchen and dropping the bulging rucksack she was carrying onto the floor.

'*She* was doing what she should have done yesterday,' Nora said, peering at her coolly. 'What's *your* excuse for being here?'

Flopping down onto a chair, Molly shrugged. 'Just needed a break from me mam, 'cos she's doing me head in.'

'Well, don't think you're stopping here, 'cos I've got enough on me plate,' Nora said, stubbing out her unsmoked cigarette. Picking up the phone again, she pressed the redial button, saying, 'I've just had your dad on the phone, and he wants to see you at his next visit.'

'Great,' Molly muttered, folding her arms sulkily. 'What have I done now?'

'Don't play the innocent,' Nora snapped. 'You know full well what you've done.

Blushing, wondering if her grandmother had found out that she was seeing an Asian lad, Molly gave her an innocent look, saying, 'Don't know what you mean, Nan.'

'Bunking off, for starters,' Nora said sharply. 'And your mam told me you got nicked for shoplifting, so don't think I don't know about that, an' all.'

Relieved that it wasn't about Saeed, Molly shrugged. 'It was only a box of Tampax. And I had to nick them, 'cos she wouldn't give me any money. What was I supposed to do? Bleed me way round school?'

'Don't be so disgusting,' Nora scolded, covering the phone's mouthpiece even though Mark hadn't answered yet. 'And you can only bleed your way round school if you actually *go* to school, so don't try that one. If you needed money, you should have come to me. How come your mam wouldn't give you none, anyhow?'

'Reckons she's *skint*,' Molly said sarcastically, getting up and going over to the kettle. Switching it on, she came back to the table to get the teapot. 'Want a fresh one?'

Peering up at her narrow-eyed, Nora said, 'Yeah, I'll have one. But don't think you're buttering me up like that, 'cos it won't work. Soon as the lads get here, I'm off out, and you can get yourself back home.'

'Aw, please, Nan,' Molly moaned. 'Just let me stay. I won't get in your way.'

'You can't *help* but get in the way, you,' Nora grumbled.

'I'll do the pots,' Molly told her earnestly. 'And I'll cook your dinner for you, if you want.'

Chuckling softly, because Molly *must* be desperate if she was offering to do housework without being dragged kicking and screaming from chore to chore, Nora said, 'You bloody won't, thank you very much. I haven't got three days to spare puking me guts up with food poisoning.'

'I'll go for the takeaways, then,' Molly persisted, putting her arms round Nora now and giving her a tight hug. 'Please, please, *please* . . . ?'

'Bugger off before you strangle me, you soft get!' Nora chided, laughing now.

'Only if you say I can stay.'

Shaking her head, because she couldn't deny that the child was poured from the same jug of blood, Nora said, 'All right, you can stay – God help me. But first time you step out of line, you're out – and I mean it.'

Kissing her nan on the cheek, Molly let go and bounced back to the kettle.

Wiping her cheek and grimacing, although she was secretly delighted that Molly had shown her some affection instead of her usual petulance, Nora gave up on Mark and called one of the other lads instead.

'Hiya, Pete,' she said when this call was picked up within seconds. 'It's Dex's mam, Nora. Have you got a minute? Only Dex said I had to call you . . .'

'Everything all right, Nan?' Molly asked, bringing the filled teapot back to the table when Nora had finished her call. 'What are that lot coming round for?'

'Them Hannons are trying it on,' Nora told her, glancing at her watch. 'But your dad's mates are gonna sort it, so don't worry. Good job you're here, actually,' she said then. 'You can stop with our Lyla while I nip out with them – make sure she doesn't puke in her sleep and choke to death. That'd be all I need, that would.'

Narrowing her eyes suspiciously, Molly said, 'You haven't been giving her too much medicine again, have you?'

Sighing, Nora dipped her gaze guiltily and reached for another fag. 'Only a bit, but she was doing my head in.'

'You've got to stop doing that,' Molly scolded her sharply. 'I mean it, Nan, you're gonna kill her one of these days. And it's not that hard to keep her quiet. You've just got to be patient with her.'

'Hark at Mother Teresa,' Nora sniped, resenting that she was being taken to task by her own granddaughter – even if it was deserved. 'Where do you get off pretending you care, anyhow? You're always calling her a mong.'

'Yeah, well, she is,' Molly retorted defensively. 'But that don't mean I don't love the silly little cow. And so do you, so quit overdosing her or you're gonna feel terrible when something bad happens.'

Tutting, Nora flapped her hand to shut Molly up. But she was right; the overdosing had to stop before it went too far. And Nora did love Lyla – Molly was right about that, too. She loved all her flesh and blood with a passion. Apart from her daughter Christine. That was one bitch she truly *did* hate.

'I'll go and check on her,' Molly said now, reaching for her rucksack. Hesitating, she gazed down at Nora. 'Can I still put me stuff away, or are you gonna send me packing for telling you off?'

Shaking her head, Nora said, 'No, you can stay, pet.'

'Will you tell me mam, or shall I?'

'I'll tell her. *And* your dad – though I'm sure he'll be happy to know you're back under control.'

Grinning widely, Molly said, 'Thanks, Nan.' Skipping out of the room then, she ran upstairs to unpack her things. Her grandmother couldn't be more wrong if she thought that Molly had any intention of being controlled. She'd only come back because Saeed lived closer to Nora's place than to Molly's mam's flat. That, and the fact that it was so much easier to get cash off her grandmother than off her tight-fisted mother. And it didn't hurt that her nan actually cooked proper dinners, either. Her mother was so lazy, Molly hadn't eaten anything but butties and biscuits since she'd been staying there, and she'd put on almost a stone – which *so* wasn't good. Not with all those skinny slags hanging about outside Saeed's dad's off-licence every night, trying to get off with him.

Reaching for her tea, Nora gazed up at the ceiling when she heard the sound of Molly's music and gave a contented little smile. She'd been dreading her coming back, but now that she was here, things actually felt a bit more normal again.

Now all she needed was for all of her lads to come home, and everything would be perfect.

# 14

It took six long months from signing the contract to recording the launch show, and Larry had spent the entire time fluctuating between wild exhilaration and sheer terror. Doing interviews and guest appearances on other people's shows was nothing compared to fronting your own, because at least if anything went wrong with those he could walk away and let the host take the blame. But this was all on him. If he fucked up, there was nobody to hide behind.

But Craig Woodburn obviously had no such doubts, and that helped to soothe Larry's nerves a little as things began to come together in the later stages. Determined to ensure that it eclipsed every other show of its kind, Craig had splashed the cash like there was no tomorrow, building the best set ever, and inviting the biggest international A-listers to take part. And when some seemed reluctant because they'd never actually heard of Larry, Craig simply chartered a private jet and sent Larry over in person – to meet them on their own turf and schmooze them over mega-expensive dinners.

And it had worked.

Having charmed his way to securing for his launch show the most impressive guest list the country had ever seen and clawed his way back to the top of every party guest list in town, Larry truly was king of the hill when the big night finally came around. He was looking better than ever, his bank account was more than healthy, and he had an

ever-growing list of mega-celebrity friends' numbers clog-
ging up his phone.

Money, star status, and his own prime-time self-titled show
– everything Larry had ever wanted in life, and more. But
Stephanie hadn't arrived at the studio yet, and that was really
pissing him off.

Contrary to Georgie's suspicions that she was a stalker
who'd manipulated herself into his life in order to further her
own aims, Stephanie was as skittish about being seen in public
with him as ever. At first she'd wanted to avoid it because
she felt guilty about cheating on her dickhead boyfriend.
Then, when Larry had finally persuaded her to finish with
the guy, she'd wanted to avoid upsetting his parents, claiming
that she'd known them for too long and liked them too much
to disrespect them by coming out in a new relationship so
soon after splitting with their son. But it was a good four
months now, and she was *still* holding out, going to hardly
any of the parties Larry had invited her to and outright
refusing to go clubbing with him in case they got papped.

Larry knew that her shyness was a major part of the
problem; that Stephanie hated being stared at, and would die
if she had to face all the attention she'd get when people
realised they were a couple. But surely she could brave it for
one night? And she should be grateful that he *wanted* her to
share his big night, anyway, considering there were so many
other women throwing themselves at his feet and begging
him to walk all over them. But not *Stephanie*, who had not
only not turned up yet after promising faithfully that she
would, she'd now switched her fucking phone off!

Tossing his own phone down onto a cluttered ledge, Larry
lit his zillionth cigarette in an hour and paced the length of
his dressing-room floor, furious with himself for letting her
get to him at a time like this. He knew it was probably more
to do with injured pride because no woman had ever resisted

him before, but Stephanie had got under his skin like an itch that he couldn't reach to scratch. And the more she resisted, the more determined he was to break her down.

Stopping in his tracks when a tap came at the door, he looked up hopefully, half expecting to see Stephanie. Pissed off when Georgie's smiling face appeared instead, he said, 'You took your time, didn't you?'

Saying, 'Sorry, darling, I'd have been here ages ago if it hadn't been for the traffic,' Georgie rushed to him and gave him a hug. 'Then when I got here, it took for ever to get in, because the security guards are being so thorough. But you'll be glad to know that the queue is *tremendous*,' she went on, hardly pausing for breath as she peeled her gloves off and slotted them into her handbag. 'They're four deep at the door, and I really can't see how they're going to fit them all in. More fool those who've turned up without a ticket, because they've got no chance.'

Wishing she'd shut up, Larry turned his back on her and poured himself a large Scotch.

Noticing, Georgie tried to keep a casual tone as she asked, 'Is that your first, dear?'

'No, it's my second,' Larry told her snappily. 'But don't worry. I'm nowhere near drunk.'

'Maybe you'd like to pour me a small one?' Georgie said, sitting down on one of the two easy chairs and crossing her legs. 'Then we can have a little chat, if you like.'

'About what?' Larry asked, slopping a small shot into a glass and topping it up with ginger ale. Handing it to Georgie, he leaned back against the ledge and peered at her, saying, 'Well, chat, then.'

'There's obviously something wrong,' Georgie replied calmly. 'And I just thought you might like to get it off your chest before you go out there. Is it nerves? Because I brought some Kalms if you'd like one.'

'There's nothing wrong with my nerves,' Larry shot back, holding his hand out to demonstrate. 'See? Steady as a rock.'

Frowning, Georgie peered into his eyes, wondering if he'd lied about the amount of Scotch he'd had. They looked clear enough, but his belligerence spoke volumes, and if he *was* on his way to getting pissed, tonight would be a disaster.

Glancing quickly around when somebody else tapped on the door, Larry jerked his chin up questioningly when Ayshia, one of the pretty young runners, came in. 'What?' he barked.

'Sorry to disturb you,' she said, blushing because he always made her feel funny inside. 'But some girl's been ringing the switchboard all week asking to talk to you, and, obviously, Sue told her that she should write if she wanted to contact you. But now she's turned up, claiming she's got a date with you.'

'It's not Stephanie, is it?' Larry asked, fearing that she might have got caught up in the security cordon, like Georgie had.

Having met Stephanie, albeit it only once and fleetingly at that, Ayshia shook her head. 'No, this is a blonde called Tania.'

'Great,' Larry muttered, having no recollection of ever dating any blondes called Tania. 'Just what I need on a night like this – a bloody psycho fan. Have they got rid of her, or do I have to watch my back all night?'

'Security are keeping an eye on her,' Ayshia told him. 'But she's threatening to smash the windows, and Mr Woodburn's concerned that someone might get hurt because the audience are queuing up out there.'

'So tell him to have the silly cow arrested,' Larry suggested coolly, wondering why they were bothering him with this.

'He doesn't want the police involved, because he doesn't want any bad publicity or hold-ups,' Ayshia told him, smiling nervously at Georgie – another one who intimidated her, because she always looked like she was sizing you up and warning you off. 'He said to ask if you'd sign a picture for her.'

'Are you supposed to do that with psychos?' Larry turned to Georgie. 'I thought you were supposed to stay as impersonal as possible.'

'I'm sure it will be all right to sign a picture,' Georgie told him. 'Just don't put love or kisses, or anything she can misinterpret.'

Thinking it over for a second, Larry said, 'Okay, but when you give it to her tell her I don't do dates, and not to bother ringing again because I'm not allowed to take private calls. Okay?'

Nodding, Ayshia waited until he'd signed one of his publicity pictures, then hurried out of the room.

Shaking his head, Larry lit another cigarette and flopped down onto a chair, saying, 'You'd think they'd have better things to do than fantasise about me, wouldn't you?'

Chuckling softly, Georgie said, 'My dear, you've obviously forgotten that this is *all* some of these girls do – all day, every day. And now you're going to be back in their lives as a permanent fixture, I suggest you get used to it, because it's going to get much more intense.'

'Can't wait,' Larry drawled dully, wishing his so-called girlfriend had been here to witness how badly some other women wanted to be in her ungrateful shoes.

Having guessed from the look in his eyes when Ayshia had opened the door that he'd been expecting Stephanie, and suspecting that her absence was at least partially to blame for his mood, Georgie asked, 'Stephanie not here yet?'

Grunting, 'Doesn't look like it, does it?' Larry sucked on his cigarette. Then, looking at her challengingly, he said, 'Not going to say I told you so?'

Staying quiet, Georgie sipped at her drink. In all honesty, she had to admit that Stephanie had done nothing to

warrant her initial suspicions in the time she'd been seeing
Larry, neither pushing herself into his limelight nor trying
to curtail his social life. But there was still something about
her that Georgie didn't quite trust. She couldn't put her
finger on it, but she felt a little undercurrent of *some*thing
not quite right about Stephanie's relationship with Larry.
If she'd known about the ex-fiancé situation she'd have
understood, but Larry's pride had prevented him from
telling Georgie about that. Mainly because he'd been too
embarrassed to admit that Stephanie had taken so long to
decide that he was the one she wanted, when any other
woman would have dumped her boyfriend in a heartbeat
if he'd so much as looked at her. So, with nothing else to
guide her, Georgie could only go on her instincts. And they
told her that Larry liked this one more than he'd liked any
of the others, which put him in a vulnerable position – and
exacerbated Georgie's already overly protective streak.
Stephanie might well be the sweet shy girl Larry claimed
her to be, but if Georgie saw the slightest sign that she was
up to something – like waiting to see if his show was a
success before making her intended move – then she
wouldn't know what had hit her.

'What's *this*?' Tania Baxter gasped, peering down at the photo,
which was signed: *To Tanya . . . Best wishes, Larry Logan!* Glaring
at Ayshia now, she said, 'Is this supposed to be a joke?'

'Not at all,' Ayshia assured her calmly. 'Larry just signed
it for you not two minutes ago. Oh, and he said to thank you
for supporting him, but he doesn't date fans, and he's not
allowed to take personal calls, so could you please stop
phoning.'

Nostrils flaring, Tania drew herself up to her full height,
which was only actually an inch or two taller than the young
runner. But she looked more imposing because her breasts

were so much larger. Perfectly painted eyes flashing with indignation now, she said, 'Do I *look* like a fan?'

'Yes,' Ayshia replied evenly, a little bemused now, because most of the women who were watching from the queue were equally as tarted up as this girl in the hopes of catching Larry's eye when they got inside.

'Well, I'm *not*,' Tania spat, flapping the picture in Ayshia's face as she added, 'And he knows you don't spell my name with a Y. *You* signed it to try and get rid of me. Well, forget it, because I'm not going anywhere till I've seen him.' Balling the photograph up now, she aimed it at Ayshia's face, but missed.

'You can't see him,' Ayshia told her, glancing around to make sure that the security guards were close enough to intervene if the girl went for her, as she looked like she was about to.

'Just go and tell him that I'm here,' Tania demanded, infuriated that they were trying to keep her and Larry apart. She'd been ringing all week, and she just knew that they hadn't passed her messages on, because he'd have contacted her if he'd known she was trying to reach him. She'd been to his flat loads of time, too, but he was never there, so she'd had to catch him at work. Only now she was here everyone was getting in the way, and she was so mad about it that she was going to hit someone in a minute.

'Oi, you,' one of the women in the queue said just then, stepping forward and prodding Tania in the arm. 'Stop holding things up and get to the back of the line.'

Telling her to get lost, Tania carried on glaring at Ayshia. Then, almost losing her footing on the steps when the woman grabbed her arm and yanked her around, she said, 'Get your hands off me, bitch! Me and Larry have got a date, and he won't appreciate one of *you* lot manhandling me!'

'*Me* and Larry have got a date an' all,' the woman informed her angrily. 'And so have the rest of these girls. Only we've got tickets, and we've been waiting for two bleedin' hours in the queue to see him, but *you*'re holding us up. So, if you haven't got a ticket, I suggest you shift out of the way before you *get* shifted.'

'By *you*?' Tania sneered, looking her up and down.

'Yeah, by me,' the woman spat, looking more than capable of carrying out the threat.

'And me,' another woman called out. She was joined immediately by several more angry voices.

Sensing that it was going to kick off, Ayshia asked Tania if she had a ticket.

'I don't *need* one,' Tania informed her, furiously eyeballing the women behind her. Most of them were laughing at her now. But they wouldn't be laughing when Larry found out that she was here and came to get her. Turning back to Ayshia now, she said, 'Just stop messing about and tell Larry I'm here.'

'I've already told him,' Ayshia said coolly. 'And I'm sorry, but he doesn't know anything about a date, and he won't be seeing you. So, if you haven't got a ticket, I'm going to have to ask you to leave, because you really *are* holding things up.'

'*Liar!*' Tania gasped, tears of frustration springing to her eyes now as the women behind her started jeering at her to get a life and stop making up fairy tales.

Shrugging, Ayshia called the security guards over and told them to escort Tania off the premises.

Yelping with indignation when the two burly men grabbed her arms and marched her down the steps, Tania screamed at them to get their hands off her.

'This is illegal! I'll do you for assault! And you can't make me go, 'cos this is a public road.'

'*This* is,' one of the guards informed her as they deposited her on the actual road. 'But that,' he pointed back up to the steps, 'is private property, and if you set foot on it again, you'll be arrested for trespass.'

'*Bastards!*' Tania yelled after the men as they returned to their posts – getting slapped on their backs and cheered along the way by the women in the queue. 'This is a conspiracy! You're just trying to keep me away from Larry, but it won't work! I'll see him when he comes out, and then you're *all* gonna get the sack!'

Back inside, as the women in the queue were finally being filtered through reception, Gordon came to Larry's dressing room to let him know that they were close to the kick-off.

'Fifteen minutes to get the audience seated,' he said, rubbing his hands together excitedly. 'Another fifteen for the warm-up guy to do his bit, then you're on. How you feeling?'

'Like shit,' Larry muttered, stubbing out his cigarette and downing his drink in one.

Terrified that they were heading for a repeat of the telethon when Larry got up and uncapped the bottle to pour himself another, Gordon cast a worried glance in Georgie's direction.

Surreptitiously shaking her head to let him know that she thought it would be okay, she said, 'Right, then, Larry, I suppose I'd better get to my seat before somebody takes it. You'll be marvellous – as always – so please stop fretting and make that your last drink. Oh, and don't forget to ask Liz about that *thing*.' Winking at him now, she headed for the door, calling back, 'Break a leg.'

'Am I missing something?' Gordon asked as the door closed behind her.

'She wants to know if Richard Burton was as well hung as they say he was,' Larry murmured, putting his glass down and scrutinising an invisible blemish on his chin in the mirror.

'I hope you're joking!' Gordon croaked. 'Please tell me you're not going to talk to Elizabeth Taylor about *sex*?'

Grinning at him in the mirror, Larry said, 'I thought you wanted a controversial show?'

'Not *that* controversial. And not with *her*.'

'Relax,' Larry laughed, patting Gordon on the back. 'Me and Liz had a nice chat in her dressing room earlier, and she's not as fragile as people think.'

'Maybe not,' Gordon conceded. 'But what she chooses to confide in private might not be what she wants revealing to ten million viewers.'

'We'll see,' Larry drawled unconcernedly.

Taking her seat front-left of set, from where she'd have a clear view of Larry and his guests, Georgie glanced around at the audience, not at all surprised to see that they were all women. Larry had male fans, too, of course, but they'd obviously been too slow off the mark when it came to bagging one of the precious tickets for tonight's eagerly awaited show, which had reportedly gone within minutes of the phone line being opened up.

Pity Stephanie wasn't quite as eager to be part of Larry's big night as these adoring women were. But Georgie wasn't complaining as she folded her coat and laid it and her handbag on the chair beside her own – the only empty seat in the house.

Crossing her fingers tightly when the house lights went down and the floor manager called for quiet, she settled back in her seat and prayed that everything would go smoothly as the warm-up man stepped out onto the set and went into his routine.

Fifteen minutes later, he said his goodbyes and bowed out to a chorus of cheers from the audience – brought on more by the realisation that him going off meant that Larry was about to come on than by actual appreciation of his talents.

The theme music started up then, and the excitement was

palpable as women all around the studio held their breath waiting for Larry to appear. When he did, Georgie literally ducked as every woman leapt to her feet and exploded into wild, raucous cheering and whistling.

Looking more handsome than Georgie had ever seen him look before, and far happier than when she'd left him in the dressing room – and, thank the Lord, still sober – Larry stood centre-stage and gazed around with a modest *I-can't-believe-this* smile.

'Wow!' he exclaimed when the women finally gave him a chance to speak. 'This is incredible . . . Thank you *so* much. It's really fantastic to be back.'

Wincing at yet more cheering, Georgie exhaled loudly as all the tension she'd been hiding from Larry evaporated. She'd had to maintain an air of absolute positivity for his sake, but she couldn't deny that she'd been worried about how he would cope when it came to the crunch. But he was obviously in his element, so she could relax and enjoy the show – like the proud old momma she felt like right now.

Grinning sexily now, making each and every one of them think that he was directing it at them alone, Larry looked slowly around the audience and said, 'So many beautiful women, so little time to appreciate you all . . . But, hey, we've got a show to do, so what say we get started by welcoming my first guest . . . the most stunningly *gorgeous* Grande Dame of all time . . . the woman who inspired some of my finest teenage dreams . . . let's have a huge *Larry Logan Show* welcome for Miss . . . Elizabeth . . . *Taylor*!'

It took Georgie almost an hour to get backstage after the show, and almost as long to get past the security guards who were guarding every door from there to the executive board-room on the fifth floor to prevent audience members from sneaking into the after-show party. If she'd stayed in Larry's dressing room she'd have had no problem, but coming through from the public side put her in the position of having to prove that she really was who she said she was at every point of entry. And with a building as enormous as this studio complex was, that took some doing.

Pushing her way through the crowds milling about inside the boardroom when she finally made it, Georgie raised up on her toes and scanned the room. Spotting Larry sharing drinks and jokes with that night's guests in a far corner, she made her way across to him, keeping her ears pricked up along the way. No doubt everybody would be pouring praise over Larry to his face, but it was always good to hear their real opinions when they thought they were out of earshot.

Unsurprisingly, no one seemed to have a bad word to say about him, and Georgie was so proud that she could have burst. But Larry truly deserved the acclaim, because he'd been utterly tremendous out there tonight. Warm, witty, sexy, intimate, probing, empathetic . . . everything you could want from a host and more, as he charmed his guests – who were some of the biggest and most notoriously reclusive stars on the planet – into revealing far more of their inner selves to the enraptured audience than any interviewer had ever managed before. Pity he hadn't asked Liz Taylor about her ex's manhood but, oh, well . . .

Catching Larry's eye now as she neared his table, Georgie gave him the thumbs-up to let him know that she was thrilled with his performance, then pointed to the bar to indicate that she would be over there if he wanted her. Turning then, she put her head down and manoeuvred her way back through the crowd.

Bumping into somebody almost halfway across the room, she was about to apologise when she saw that it was Stephanie. Forcing herself not to frown, as was her immediate inclination, she smiled, and said, 'Oh, hello. I didn't realise you were here. Does Larry know?'

'Not yet,' Stephanie told her, glancing nervously around. 'I promised to get here for the show, but I was held up, and my phone ran out of charge so I couldn't let him know I was going to be late.' Pausing then, she flapped her hands, as if she knew that Georgie didn't believe her. 'There's still loads of people outside,' she went on, aware that she was babbling now. 'It looks like some of them are trying to lie their way into the party, though, so the security guards are being really strict. I'm just glad I was on the guest list, or I'd never have got in.'

'They have to be vigilant for Larry's safety,' Georgie told her, feeling a little guilty because the girl was obviously struggling. 'Somebody's already tried to get to him tonight.'

'Really?' Stephanie frowned worriedly. 'What happened? He wasn't hurt, was he?'

Flapping her hand to indicate that it had been something and nothing, Georgie said, 'Just some delusional girl claiming she was supposed to have a date lined up with him. But he didn't know anything about it, so she was escorted off the premises. Anyway, I'm sure he'll be delighted to see you now that you're here.'

Smiling uncertainly, because she always got the impression that Georgie was scrutinising her, Stephanie asked where Larry was.

'He's over there,' Georgie said, pointing to his table. 'Talking to his guests.'

Sensing from the pointed way she'd said that last bit that Georgie was telling her not to disturb him, Stephanie glanced around for a quiet spot where she could hide herself away. Seeing a reasonably secluded alcove off to the side of Larry's group, between the locked drinks cabinet and the window, she said, 'I'll just let him know I'm here, then I'll wait over there. See you later.'

Hurrying away before Georgie could stop her, she paused by Larry's table and, catching his eye, gave him a little wave and was about to point out where she would be sitting when he'd finished when he jumped out of his seat and called her over. Blushing when all the famous faces turned her way, Stephanie shook her head and backed away.

Telling his guests that he'd be back in a minute, Larry edged out from behind the table and followed her to the alcove. Grabbing her arm, he pulled her around to face him and gave her a questioning frown.

'How come you didn't want to sit with me? And what took you so long to get here, anyway? You missed the whole show. And I've been trying to ring you for hours.'

Glancing around, sure that everybody must be staring at them, Stephanie pulled her arm free and rubbed at it, murmuring, 'I'm sorry. I got held up.'

'Convenient,' Larry drawled, with a nasty edge to his voice. 'What was it this time? Taxi break down again? Or maybe it was a national emergency, like you laddered your tights or something?'

Drawing her head back when the distinctive scent of Scotch wafted over her face, Stephanie said, 'Have you been drinking?'

'*Obviously*,' Larry sneered. 'It *is* a party, and that's what people *do* at parties.'

Peering up into his eyes and seeing the glint of something she didn't like there, Stephanie said. 'I think I'd better go.'

'What, running out on me already?' he hissed. 'Got someone waiting outside for you, have you?'

'No, I'm going home – *alone*,' Stephanie told him truthfully. 'I said I'd come, and I did. I'm sorry I'm late, but it's not my fault. And I've got a massive headache already without you shouting at me.'

'You've got a headache,' Larry snorted. 'And there was me

thinking *I* had it tough, doing my first big show in front of a live audience. How d'y' think that made me feel?'

'*Drunk*?' Stephanie replied coolly.

'Well, that's where you're wrong,' Larry snapped. ''Cos I haven't even had all that much yet. But you'd know that if you'd bothered to get here on time.'

'I've said I'm sorry,' Stephanie told him, knowing that he was lying about the drink because he only ever got this nasty when he'd had too much. 'Anyway, you were enjoying yourself before I came, so why don't you just go back to your friends? You can call me when you get home, and I'll come and see you when you've sobered up.'

Larry wanted to carry on arguing, but peering into her dark, sexy eyes, he was overwhelmed by a sudden urge to hold her instead; to feel her silky hair against his cheek and taste the sweetness of her lips.

Tipping his head to one side, he gave her a penitent smile, and said, 'Want to start again.'

Inhaling deeply, Stephanie shook her head and murmured, 'You're going to be the death of me, Larry, you really are.'

Putting his arms out now, Larry pulled her to him and kissed her softly.

'I'm glad you got here,' he said when she pulled back after a minute. 'And I'm sorry for having a go at you. But it's doing my head in that I always have to fight to get you to come out with me.'

Stiffening, Stephanie dropped her gaze. 'I can't help it, Larry. I'm not a celebrity, and I don't want to be seen as one of those women who'll do anything to be famous.'

'I know,' Larry murmured, tilting her chin back up with his finger so that he could see her eyes. 'And I don't want to force you to do anything you don't want to, but I need to know you're not just messing me about.'

'How?' she asked, amazed that someone who had so much

going for him could be so riddled with insecurities. This was a side of him that the public never saw, and they wouldn't believe it if they did.

'I don't know,' Larry murmured, his eyes searching hers for signs of deception. 'I know it's stupid, but I can't help thinking you're still seeing that idiot behind my back.'

Jerking her chin away from his touch, Stephanie sighed wearily and said, 'Don't be ridiculous, Larry. That's over.'

'And you don't still have feelings for him?'

'No. I love *you*,' Stephanie said, wondering why she was bothering to try and convince him when he obviously didn't believe her.

'So why won't you move in with me?'

'Because it's too soon.'

'Still?' Larry gazed down at her. 'We've been shagging each other's brains out for six months.'

'Yes, but it's only four since I split with him.'

'Don't talk about *him*,' Larry spat. 'You know it'll only make me mad again.'

Shrugging, because there was really nothing she could say to that, Stephanie gazed back at him and waited to see what he would throw at her next.

Peering back at her tipsily, Larry said, 'It's a good job I trust you, or you'd be history. But if you keep messing me about, it might just happen anyway. I could have my pick of any of these women, you know.'

Embarrassed when a couple of heads turned their way, Stephanie said, 'Lower your voice, Larry. People are listening.'

'Who cares?' he drawled. '*They* might have nothing better to do, but *I* have. And if you want to do it with me, it's time you got over this *shy* business, 'cos you're gonna get snapped with me sooner or later. I'm a star. It comes with the territory.'

'I know,' Stephanie murmured, sounding less than

impressed at the prospect. 'But I'd sooner it wasn't just yet, if you don't mind. You've just got to give me a bit more time.'

'So long as you mean it,' Larry said, letting her go now but still reaching for her hand. 'Anyway, you've kept me away from the party too long already. Least you can do is come and meet my guests. Guaranteed none of *them* will have a camera.'

Shaking her head, Stephanie pulled back. 'No, I can't. Honestly, Larry, I'd be terrible company, and it'll reflect badly on you. You go back to them. I'll be fine here.'

Nodding, Larry said, 'Okay, but don't sit by yourself. Go and find Georgie. She'll keep you company till I've finished.'

'Er, no, I think I'll just get myself a drink and wait here,' Stephanie said quickly. 'I don't think Georgie likes me very much.'

'Rubbish,' Larry lied. 'She loves you.'

'I'd still rather not,' Stephanie insisted, dreading the thought of having to make small talk with the woman.

'Okay, whatever you want,' Larry said, giving her one last kiss. 'But make sure you have a few drinks, 'cos we'll be having a party of our own when we get out of here and I want you nice and relaxed.'

Saying that she couldn't wait, Stephanie pushed him gently away, then went to get herself a drink – staying well away from Georgie, who was talking to a couple of people at the other end of the bar.

Which suited Georgie just fine, because she'd been keeping half an eye on Larry for the last ten minutes, and had guessed from his body language that he and Stephanie had been having words. And that worried her, because he should be concentrating on his career right now, not letting emotions get in the way. Especially not when he'd only just got his first show out of the way and everything was going so well for him.

Unless this was what Stephanie had been waiting for all along?

Well, she'd better *not* be a kiss-and-tell tramp, or she'd have Georgie to deal with – and it wouldn't be pleasant, because Georgie had no intention of letting any little slut ruin things for Larry ever again.

Standing in the shadows across the road from the studios, where she could keep an eye on both the front entrance and the car park at the rear, Tania hugged herself tightly, wishing that she'd thought to wear something more sensible – it was absolutely freezing. But she'd chosen this outfit specially, to knock Larry right off his feet when he saw how much she'd grown up since he last saw her.

And, boy, *had* she changed. The last two years felt like they'd crawled by as she'd counted the days, hours, *seconds* until she would see Larry again. But what a difference that time had made. No longer just a pretty girl, Tania was a woman now, with defined bone-structure and real curves – even if the tits *were* a job. Model material, in fact, although she hadn't had any actual offers that didn't require getting her kit off – yet. But the serious offers would come pouring in soon enough, she was sure. In fact, it wouldn't have hurt her to approach some of the photographers who were hanging about across the road right now. But she'd wait until Larry came out, and let them catch the big reunion instead.

It was almost one a.m. before the guests began to filter out of the party. Staying well hidden as the small group of women who were still waiting outside the studio rushed forward for autographs, Tania stamped her feet to keep them awake and flicked her gaze between the entrance and the exit, determined not to miss Larry if he sneaked out of one while the fans were occupied with the other celebrities at the other.

A good ten minutes and several false starts later, Tania saw movement by the studio's back door, and a familiar glint of dark-blond hair as Larry stepped out and was momentarily bathed in light from the security spots. In the middle of a group of other people, he moved off to the side and into the shadows so that Tania could only see his silhouette. But she knew it was him – her pounding heart was telling her so.

The sound of laughter floated across the road as the group said their goodbyes. Tania braced herself when a car pulled up alongside them and she saw another flash of Larry's hair as he climbed inside. Unable to see if anyone else had got into the car with him because the photographers were crowded around the exit road now, she stood stock-still and watched as it drove slowly towards the barrier. Then, just as the barrier was raised and the vehicle nosed its way out, she made a mad dash across the road and pushed in front of the photographers, forcing the driver to brake hard as she practically spreadeagled herself on the bonnet.

Rolling his window part-way down, he yelled, 'What the bloody hell are you playing at? I could have killed you, you silly cow.'

Ducking her head, trying to peer in through the blacked-out windows that concealed Larry and Stephanie in the back, Tania said, 'I need to see Larry.'

Muttering, 'Don't they all,' the driver flapped his hand at her, waving her out of the way. When she didn't move, he said, 'Come on, love, you're causing an obstruction and everyone wants to get home.'

'I've got to see him,' Tania repeated desperately, oblivious to the flashing cameras capturing her humiliation. 'Larry!' she yelled now, banging on the window. 'You missed my birthday!'

Inside the car, unable to hear anything, Larry was all set to wind the window down to see what was going on. But Stephanie stopped him, reminding him about the psycho

Georgie had told her about, and pointing out that she could have a knife, or anything.

His mood softened by expensive booze and thoroughly deserved praise, Larry reached out and stroked her cheek, saying, 'Nice to know you care. So, how about a quickie?'

'What, *now*?' Stephanie gasped in horror. 'You've got to be joking. Georgie's right behind us in her car, and our driver could turn round at any minute. And there's too many photographers. And the girl's staring right at us.'

'No one can see us,' Larry assured her, moving closer and sliding a hand up between her thighs. 'The windows are mirrored; they'll be looking at themselves.'

'What about the driver?' Stephanie said breathlessly as Larry reached her panties and eased a finger under the elastic.

'Don't need him,' Larry purred, kissing his way down her neck. 'This is a one-man job.'

'I didn't mean that,' she protested, unable to stop him as he pulled her down on the seat.

'Sshhh,' he said, easing his zip down and climbing on top of her. 'You've got to learn to live dangerously.'

Biting her lip hard as he pushed himself into her and forced her legs up by slipping his arms beneath them, Stephanie put her hands over her eyes and prayed that nobody would open the door. The fear of being photographed with him fully clothed and on her feet was bad enough, but flat on her back with her legs in the air and him pumping away at her would be too embarrassing for words. And it would be guaranteed to make the front page of every national newspaper, making her not just one of his tarts but the biggest tart of them all.

Holding her breath as the car began to move off a couple of minutes later, Stephanie kept her face hidden as the lights from the camera flashed dully through the windows as they passed the paps. Larry had said they couldn't see through the treated glass. But who knew what their lights would do? She dreaded to think what tomorrow's papers might reveal.

Driving slowly out of the car park as Larry's limo took off down the road, Georgie pulled up alongside the sobbing girl, who was screaming at the photographers to leave her alone now as they tried to find out who she was. Disgusted by the callous way they were closing in on her seeking their pieces of flesh, and all too aware that it wouldn't look too good that Larry had ignored one of his clearly distraught fans, Georgie leaned across the seat and pushed the passenger door open, telling her to get in.

Blinded by tears, and desperate to hide because she could feel that her mascara was smeared all over her face, Tania stumbled into the car and pulled the door shut. Putting her foot down, leaving the photographers behind, Georgie drove off in the direction opposite to that in which Larry's car had gone.

'Wasn't that Larry's agent?' one of the paps mused, watching the car's tail lights as it turned the corner. 'Why's she picking the girl up? Does she know something we don't?'

'Anyone know who that girl was?' one of the other paps asked the women who were still milling about.

'A bloody idiot,' one of them called back. 'She nearly had us locked out of the show, and now she's screwed it for us getting his autograph. I'll bloody kill her if I see her again.'

'Me, too,' one of her friends agreed, with a sneer. 'Stupid bitch, going on like she's got a date with him, and how he's missed her birthday. She should be so lucky he'd remember her stupid birthday. I should have punched her bloody lights out while I had the chance!'

Listening to all of this, Sam Brady's mind was ticking over. The girl had looked familiar, but he couldn't quite—

Snapping his fingers when it suddenly came to him, he turned and started running for his car which was parked at the far end of the street.

'Where's the fire?' one of his fellow paps yelled after him.

'My mum's ill,' Sam called back. 'Got to go and change her bedpan.'

Hopping into his car, he tore off, determined to be long gone before any of the other reporters took it into their heads to follow. He could be wrong, but he was sure that the girl was Tania Baxter. Different hair and decidedly bigger breasts than last time he'd seen her, but it was almost exactly two years since he'd caught Logan with her, and she'd just turned sixteen then, so she would have changed a lot in that time.

But if it *was* her, it raised a lot of questions. Like why his agent had picked her up like that, unless – as the other pap had suggested – she knew something that they didn't. And why had Tania been claiming she was supposed to have a date with Logan – and on her birthday, which presumably would be her eighteenth. Unless that was the agreement Larry had made with her back then – to keep whatever they had going on secret until she was of a more acceptable age!

Reaching into the recess under her car's CD player when they were clear, Georgie pulled a handful of tissues out of the pack she kept there and handed them to the girl.

'Better?' she asked when the sobs began to subside.

Nodding, Tania blew her nose, croaking, 'Yeah. Thanks.'

Telling her it was no problem, Georgie asked where she wanted dropping off.

'Anywhere,' Tania said, pulling the sunshade down and glancing at herself in the small mirror. Groaning, she used one of the tissues to try and repair the damage to her make-up.

Too kind to put the girl out on the street in this condition, Georgie said, 'Where do you live, dear?'

'Hulme,' Tania told her, sounding as miserable as Georgie had ever heard anyone sound.

'Not too far, then,' she said, and sighed gently, chiding herself for being so soft-hearted. It was never a good idea to get involved with the fans – especially not the crazy ones; and she had no doubt that this was the same girl who'd been causing trouble outside the studio earlier.

Casting a sidelong glance at her now, Georgie sized her up to assess how much of a danger she might actually be. If she had a weapon she didn't exactly have too many places to hide it, given that she was so scantily dressed. But her acrylic nails would cause some serious damage if she lashed out with them, so Georgie would have to keep an eye on her hands.

'Bet you went to his party, didn't you?' Tania said suddenly. Tutting when Georgie nodded, she said, '*I* should have been there too, but they wouldn't let me see him, so he probably didn't know I was there.'

Murmuring, 'I see,' Georgie frowned. The girl sounded as if she truly believed what she was saying, but Georgie had been in the dressing room with Larry when he'd been told about her and he hadn't seemed to know anything about her. But then, he could have just said that to get rid of her because he was expecting Stephanie.

'Can I ask how you know him?' Georgie said now, curious to know if Larry had been messing around behind Stephanie's back.

'We used to go out with each other a couple of years ago,' Tania told her, embellishing the truth because she'd had to keep it to herself for so long now that it had become much more in her mind than it had ever actually been in reality. 'We were in love, but we had to agree not to see each other for a while because there were some problems with other people. We were supposed to be getting back together for my birthday last week, but the studio people won't let me get near him. And he's never in when I go to his flat, and the stupid doormen won't let me in to wait for him.'

Instincts prickling, Georgie said, 'What were those problems that you mentioned?'

Narrowing her eyes, Tania gave her a furtive side glance. The woman sounded a bit weird all of a sudden, and Tania suspected she might be another spy from the studio. She'd read about this kind of thing, and knew how they operated. They didn't like their stars to be seen to be in love because it put the female viewers off, so they'd do anything to keep the girlfriends away. That was why so many stars were single or divorced. And they'd really want Larry to look single right now, because they were desperate to make his new show a hit. But they were wrong if they thought they could keep her away from him.

Folding her arms now, letting the woman know that she'd sussed her out and wasn't playing the game, Tania said, 'You can drop me off here. I'll walk the rest of the way.'

Taking a shot in the dark, even though the girl looked so different now with long blonde instead of short black hair, and with a much more voluptuous figure, Georgie said, 'It's okay, Tania, we're nearly there. It *is* Tania, isn't it? Tania Baxter?'

Pursing her lips, Tania said, 'You obviously know, so why play the innocent?'

'I'm not playing anything,' Georgie replied calmly. 'I'm just interested to know about this relationship you claim to have had with Larry.'

'Like I'd tell *you*,' Tania retorted bluntly. 'Do you even *know* him?'

'Rather better than *you* do, I suspect,' Georgie murmured.

'Yeah, right,' Tania sneered, looking her up and down. 'Like he's ever slept with an old bag like *you*.'

'And he slept with you, did he?' Pulling in to the kerb when they reached the first block of houses on the run-down estate, Georgie turned to look the girl in the eye. 'Is that what you're telling me?'

Grimacing now, sure that the woman was jealous, Tania reached for the door handle, saying, 'I'm not telling you *anything*, you fucking weirdo.'

'I'm his agent,' Georgie informed her as she opened the door. 'And it's my duty to protect him from damaging stories.'

'Yeah, but who protects him from *you*?' Tania shot back. 'Making out like you've got something going with him at your age. That's just disgusting.'

Ignoring the childish insults, Georgie said, 'Look, I know you're upset with Larry because you think he snubbed you, but he genuinely didn't remember you, so you shouldn't take it personally.'

'It *is* personal,' Tania snapped. 'Very personal, actually – not that it's got anything to do with you.'

'Maybe not, but I shouldn't think his girlfriend would be too happy to hear you talking like this.'

'What are you talking about?' Tania scoffed. 'Larry hasn't got a girlfriend.'

'Yes, dear, he has, and they're very happy,' Georgie insisted, wanting the girl to understand that it was futile to chase Larry. 'Whatever you've been thinking would happen between you, I guarantee you it won't,' she went on kindly. 'I know you don't want to hear this, but I think you should put the dreams away and find yourself a nice boyfriend of your own age, because you're a pretty girl, and you must have—'

Hissing 'Get lost, you lying old bitch!' Tania leapt furiously out of the car and flounced away down an alley between the houses.

Sighing, Georgie reached over and pulled the door shut. Doing a U-turn then, she set off for home, going over the conversation in her mind. Larry had always denied sleeping with that girl, and Tania's own denials had backed him up at the time. But she was telling a different story now, and if it was true, then Georgie had unwittingly supported Larry through two years of lies – and she would not be pleased with him for deceiving her like that.

Tania's bare arms and legs were covered in goose bumps as she stalked angrily through the estate, but a boiling pit of rage was simmering in her gut. Girlfriend? Since when did Larry have a fucking *girlfriend?* There had been nothing about it in any of the papers or magazines, and he hadn't mentioned it in any of his radio or TV interviews either. And she'd have known if he had, because she'd read, listened to, and watched every single one.

There had been plenty of pictures of him coming out of parties and clubs with women since he'd got back on telly after getting attacked by that criminal. But Tania hadn't been worried about them, because – just like before – it had never been the same one twice, and she put them down to his needing sex while he was waiting to get back with her. But the word *girlfriend* implied something more serious than a one-night stand, and that bothered her. If it was true, and he'd given up waiting for her and let some other bitch into his life, he'd be sorry.

Very, very sorry.

Yanking the heavy communal door open when she reached her block of flats, Tania marched past the gang who were hanging about in the stairwell with her nose in the air. Yelling 'Fuck off!' when one of them called after her, asking if she fancied a shag, she hurried up the next two flights. Key already in hand in case they followed her, she jabbed it into the lock when she reached her door and had just stepped inside when the lads caught up with her.

Gritting her teeth when she saw that the leader, Chappo, had stuck his foot in the door, Tania stuck a defiant fists-on-hips pose and said, 'What do you want?'

'An apology,' he drawled, smiling slyly. 'Not nice being told to fuck off when you ain't done nothing.'

'You started it,' she retorted indignantly. ''Cos it's not very nice being asked for a shag like that, either, you know.'

'You wasn't so fussy last week,' Chappo said, sucking on his spliff and blowing the smoke into her face. 'So, you letting us in, or what?'

'Or what,' she said, trying to close the door. Furious when he didn't move his foot, she said, 'Look, just piss off, Chappo. I can't be doing with stupidness tonight. I've got a raging headache, and I need to go to bed.'

'Don't let me stop you,' he quipped, trawling his gaze down her body now, leering at her breasts and her pierced belly button, which was on display in the uncovered section between the hem of the top and the waistband of her short skirt. 'Where've you been, all tarted up like that, anyhow? You look like a right slag.'

Wanting to punch him, but resisting because she knew full well that she'd get it right back, Tania folded her arms, letting him know that he wouldn't be getting an invite into her bed again any time soon. She'd made that mistake once, prac-tising to make sure that she was on form for Larry, but he'd been way too rough and crude for her liking, so she wouldn't be repeating it.

'You're pissing me off now,' Chappo said darkly as his mates sniggered behind him. 'I'm talking to you, so the least you can do is fucking answer. Think you're too good for me now, or something?'

Knowing that she'd offended him, and that none of the

neighbours would come to her aid if he kicked off, Tania was just wondering if she might have to give him what he wanted to get rid of him when her mobile phone began to ring. Jumping because she hadn't expected it, she pulled it out of her purse and got a shock when she saw that it was her dad calling. Scared that something might be wrong with her mum, but more scared of what Chappo might do if she didn't get rid of him, she answered the call as if she'd known it was coming.

'Hi, Dad, you nearly here? Two minutes? Yeah, that's fine. Just come straight up; the door's open.'

Hopes of a shag dashed, Chappo gave her the two-finger down-pointed-gun salute, saying, 'Catch you later, bitch.' Then, jerking his head at his mates, he turned and walked away.

Sticking two fingers up at their backs, Tania shut the door and pushed the bolt firmly across, saying, 'Sorry about that, Dad. I was trying to get rid of someone.'

'Never mind "sorry",' Phil Baxter snapped back at her furiously. 'I don't know what's going on in that head of yours, Tania, but I don't find you at all funny. And me and your mum don't appreciate being woken up at this bloody time of the morning, either.'

'Er, *you* rang *me*,' Tania reminded him, walking through to her tiny living room and wrinkling her nose at the musty smell of damp wallpaper and soggy carpet. 'Have you been having a nightmare, or something?'

'Yeah, I'm having a flaming nightmare,' her dad replied sharply. 'Wondering what the hell you think you're playing at, chasing after that bloody Logan again after all the trouble it caused last time.'

Frowning, Tania perched on the edge of the sofa, wondering how on earth he'd heard about her and Larry.

'Well?' her dad demanded. 'What have you got to say for yourself?'

Irritated that he was talking to her like she was still a child, despite the fact that she was eighteen now *and* he'd kicked her out, forcing her to move into the first dump the council had offered her, Tania said, 'I don't have to explain myself to you. If I want to see Larry again, it's my business.'

'Don't you bloody *dare* talk to me like that, you ungrateful little bitch!' her dad yelled, audibly slapping his wife's hand away when she reached out to try and calm him down. 'You might not think it'll affect us if you end up in the papers again, but the neighbours already think we've bred a slut and a liar, so what the hell do you think they'll say when they see you acting like an idiot again?'

'It might help if I knew what you were talking about,' Tania retorted defensively.

'That bloody reporter,' her dad informed her tersely. 'Turning up here at this time of the bloody night, trying to interview you. He's lucky I didn't do more than kick his arse off the path!'

'Reporter?' Tania repeated, excited to hear that she was being sought out by the press after running away from them earlier.

'The same smarmy little shit who exposed you for what you really are the last time you made a bloody fool of yourself over Logan,' her dad spat. 'And I'm warning you now, Tania, if you—'

'Did you get his number?' Tania interrupted.

'No, I bloody well didn't! What the hell do you think I am, Tania? Your flaming secretary?'

'Oh, thanks a lot, Dad!' she snapped petulantly. 'You've always hated me. If it was *Cindy* they were looking for, you'd have told them fast enough. But you'd do anything to stop me from getting anywhere.'

'And where exactly do you think it's going to get you if you keep getting yourself in the papers for being a stupid obsessed little girl who can't leave well enough alone?' her dad demanded. 'If he wanted to know, he'd have kept in touch with you after that last nonsense.'

'Who said he didn't?' Tania sniped, wanting to wipe the sneer out of his voice.

'You'd better be lying,' Phil Baxter said angrily. 'If I find out he was messing around with you behind my back all along—'

'You'll what?' Tania hissed. 'I'm eighteen now. There's nothing you can do to me. You can't even *ground* me, and I bet that's really killing you, 'cos you're nothing but a big control freak and everyone hates you – even my mum, 'cos you're a shit husband, and an even shittier dad!'

Hanging up then before her father had a chance to explode, she hurled her phone across the room, where it bounced off the wall and landed in three parts on the floor. Groaning, she dropped her face into her hands. Well, that was it: she'd totally burnt her bridges with her dad now. She just hoped she hadn't got her mum into trouble by dragging her into it like that – even if it had been true. But it was her mum's problem if she wanted to stick around and put up with him. Tania had escaped, and she had no intention of ever going back – not that he'd let her, but she wouldn't even if she could. Now all she wanted to do was get herself to where she should be in life: at Larry's side, gracing the front pages of the papers and magazines, the pair of them like David and Victoria.

Only her selfish bastard dad had gone and ruined her big chance by sending the reporter packing. And with no idea how to get in touch with the journo concerned, all she could do was sit and wait and hope that he would track her down.

# 15

Larry was already up and dressed when Georgie arrived at his apartment the next morning. Looking relaxed and happy, he hugged her when she came through the door, then waved her through to the kitchen, saying, 'Great night, wasn't it? Got to admit I was a bit drunk, so it's taken a while to put the pieces together in my head. But I think it went really well.' Nodding at the newspapers she was carrying now, he said, 'I was just about to send out for mine to see what the critics are saying. So, go on . . . what's the score?'

'Rave reviews, as expected,' Georgie told him, pulling one of the tall stools out from under the breakfast bar and sitting down. 'You'll particularly like the write-up in the *Mirror*. But take a look at these pictures first.'

Looking over her shoulder as she laid the newspapers out, Larry smiled when he saw all the shots of his limo at the studio gates, taken from various angles to highlight the blonde girl in the too tight top and *way* too short skirt who was sprawled over the bonnet in one, looking suspiciously knickerless; trying to yank the door open in another; and kicking out at the photographers in another, with black mascara streaks running from her eyes to her chin.

'Jeezus, she's a mess,' he snorted, shaking his head. 'I had no idea any of that was going on.'

'Notice anything familiar?' Georgie asked.

Wondering if Stephanie had been right to worry after all, and the camera flashes *had* exposed them at it on the back seat, Larry peered at the car's blackened windows. Satisfied that nothing was visible, he said, 'Nope.' Then, laughing, 'Unless you're talking about you in your car behind? Christ, look at your eyes. You're like a rabbit in headlights.'

'I'm not talking about me,' Georgie said, impatiently jabbing a finger down on a shot of the girl. 'I'm talking about *her.*'

'What about her?' Larry asked, moving away to fill the kettle. 'Coffee?'

'Yes, please. So you don't recognise her?'

'Should I?' Switching the kettle on, Larry reached into the cupboard and took out three cups.

Guessing that Stephanie must have stayed the night – or maybe he'd picked someone else up after dropping her off, because who knew what he got up to when he thought nobody was looking? – Georgie said, 'I'd say you should, considering you slept with her.'

'Did I?' Larry looked thoughtful for a moment, then shrugged. 'Can't say I remember.'

'Tania Baxter?' Georgie persisted, watching his face for signs of recognition. Tutting when she saw none, she said, 'Oh, for goodness' sake, Larry. It's the girl from the telethon. The one who destroyed your career, and almost ruined your life. Remember now?'

Frowning as he spooned coffee into the cups, Larry said, 'No, it's not. She had dark hair and small tits.'

'Oh, so you remember that much about her,' Georgie said disapprovingly. 'Well, maybe you'll remember sleeping with her as well, then. Because *she* certainly does.'

'Bullshit,' Larry snorted. 'You know nothing happened.'

'So you both said. But now she's saying different, and I'd like to know why.'

'*I* don't know.' Larry shrugged. 'How do you know what she's saying, anyway? Is it in the papers, or something?'

'No, I had a chat with her last night when I gave her a lift

home, and she told me you'd been seeing each other a couple
of years ago but had agreed to take time out while you sorted
out some *problems*. Now, I'm assuming that those problems
were to do with the bad publicity about her age. And I'm
also assuming that it was *your* idea to take a break. Am I
right?'

Irritated now, Larry said, 'My, we have been digging, haven't
we?'

'So it's true, then,' Georgie said quietly, disappointed
because she'd sincerely wanted him to deny it.

'Not in the way *you* mean,' Larry replied tersely, pouring
hot water into the cups. 'I never slept with her, and I can
swear on that. Not that it's any of your business if I did, by
the way.'

'You weren't the one who had to rescue her from those
reporters last night,' Georgie reminded him bluntly. 'So I'd
appreciate a bit more *gratitude* and a bit less *attitude*, if you
don't mind.'

'What's that got to do with anything?' Larry grunted,
bringing the cups to the bar and putting hers down hard, so
that some of the coffee slopped out onto the top paper.

'If I'd left her there to tell *them* what she more or less told
*me* we'd be looking at some pretty damning headlines right
now,' Georgie pointed out, moving the papers out of the way.

Telling her that she was overreacting, Larry sat on the stool
beside hers and looked at the pictures again, saying, 'Oh,
come on. She's a mess. You can't really think I'd be interested in her?'

'You were that night,' Georgie reminded him. 'You took
her clubbing and were caught snogging the face off her, if I
remember correctly.'

'Snogging?' Larry grimaced. 'Don't you think you're a bit
old to be using words like that? It sounds so wrong coming
from someone like you.'

Ignoring the jibe, Georgie said, 'You obviously had some attraction for her, and now she's saying that things went further than either of you admitted. And I'd hate to think what damage she could cause if she said it to anyone else.'

'She can't hurt me,' Larry scoffed dismissively, shoving the offending pictures away. 'She's already told everyone what really happened that night. She didn't stay the night with me, and we didn't have sex.'

'But *some*thing happened,' Georgie said perceptively. 'And please don't lie, because I can see it in your eyes.'

Adamant that he genuinely hadn't had sex with the girl, Larry admitted, 'But I might have promised to take her out to dinner, or something. I'm not sure.'

'For her birthday?'

'Yeah, I think so. But only to get her off my back.'

'Wonderful,' Georgie groaned, flapping her hands. 'How could you be so stupid?'

'*I* don't know,' Larry retorted, feeling as though he was being told off by his headmistress. 'You know what I'm like. I say stuff like that to girls all the time, but it doesn't mean I'm going to do it. And they don't usually try and hold me to it.'

'Yes, well, this one isn't quite like the rest,' Georgie told him, sighing wearily. 'I get the feeling she's a wee bit *unbalanced* when it comes to you.'

'Well, that's her problem, not mine. And I've got no intention of taking her out, so that's the end of it.'

Saying, 'I certainly hope so,' Georgie smiled at Stephanie who'd just walked in, wearing Larry's dressing gown and with her hair wrapped in a towel. 'Morning, dear. You're looking better today. Sleep well?'

Taken aback by the friendly tone, Stephanie said, 'Er, yes. Very well, thanks. I think I was just a bit stressed out yesterday, with all the running around trying to get to the studio.'

Peering at Georgie bemusedly, having also picked up on her seeming change of attitude, Larry looked at Stephanie and raised his eyebrows in a *whaddyaknow?* gesture.

Aware that she'd surprised them both, Georgie reached for her coffee and gazed around the kitchen as they kissed each other good morning. Given what Larry *could* have hooked himself up with, Stephanie suddenly didn't seem so bad. Maybe it was time to stop treating her like the enemy, Georgie mused. She was a nice-looking girl with no airs and graces, and Georgie had to admit that she was having a good effect on Larry, because he was so much more relaxed when she was around. And, despite drinking last night, which was quite acceptable given the occasion, he'd managed to stay relatively clean so far.

Looping an arm around Stephanie's waist now as she sipped her coffee, Larry said, 'Georgie's just been telling me about that girl last night. You'll never guess who it was.'

'Who?' Stephanie looked from him to Georgie.

'Remember I told you about that trouble a couple of years ago with the girl who lied about her age to get onto my show? Well, it was her,' Larry said, adding sarcastically, '*Apparently* we were having a relationship, and agreed to not see each other for a while.'

'Oh, really?' Stephanie gave a wry smile. 'And I take it she's ready to pick up where you left off?'

'Guess so.' Larry shrugged. 'You can't believe the crap some people come out with, can you? And Georgie reckons she really believes it.'

'Scary,' Stephanie murmured, shaking her head.

'Very,' Georgie agreed. 'But I told her to stop chasing him because he's very happy with you, and suggested that she get herself a boyfriend her own age.'

'Oh, I bet she loved that,' Larry chuckled, delighted that Georgie had recognised that he was happy with Stephanie and seemed to have accepted it at last. 'What did she say?'

'Nothing. She just jumped out of the car and stomped away like a sulky little girl.'

'Is that her?' Stephanie asked, leaning forward to peer at the newspapers.

'Yeah,' Larry said, his tone sneering again. 'As if I'd look twice at someone like *that* when I've got you.'

'About that,' Georgie interjected thoughtfully. 'I was wondering if it might not be time you were seen together – as a couple.'

'You what?' Larry snorted. 'Craig would cut your tongue out if he heard you suggesting something like that. He'd freak out about losing all the viewers if they realise I'm off the market.'

'I don't care what Craig thinks,' Georgie said dismissively. 'But I *do* care about you, and I think it would be a good preventative measure – to stop any silliness with girls like that one last night cropping up again in the future.'

Stiffening, Stephanie was about to protest that she really wasn't ready to put herself in front of the cameras. But Larry saved her the trouble, saying, 'That wouldn't be fair. It'd feel like we're just using Stephanie as some kind of besotted-fan shield. We'll come out when we're good and ready – eh, babe?'

Smiling when he squeezed her around the waist, Stephanie mouthed a grateful thank-you. Then, reaching up to touch the towel, she said, 'I'd better go and dry my hair before it sets like this.'

'You're not still going to work, are you?' Larry gazed up at her disappointedly. 'I wanted you to come with me today.'

'I've got to,' she told him, reaching behind him to put her cup down. 'I'd get out of it if I could, but I've got a heads-of-department meeting at ten, and I've really got to be there.'

'What is it that you do, dear?' Georgie asked, taking an interest in her for the first time.

Shrugging modestly, Stephanie said, 'Nothing very exciting. Just retail.'

'I keep telling her she should pack it in and move in with me,' Larry said, looking to Georgie for support. 'There's no point her working so many hours when she could be a lady of leisure.'

'I don't want to be kept,' Stephanie murmured, wishing he wouldn't do this in front of his agent, because she'd probably think that Stephanie was after his money now.

'Quite right,' Georgie said approvingly. Then, to Larry, 'And you shouldn't be trying to take her independence away from her, because we women need to be able to stand on our own two feet. Too many of us rely on men only to find ourselves up the creek when they decide to trade us in for better models.' Back to Stephanie: 'Not that I'm suggesting for one minute that he'll trade you in, my dear, but I'm sure you know what I mean.'

Giving the most genuine smile Georgie had seen from her so far, Stephanie said, 'Yes, I do. And I've got to admit that I had no idea what I was getting into when I agreed to go out with Larry, or we might not be having this conversation right now. But I don't want the fame, or the money, I just want him. And if we do ever get caught out, I want to be able to hold my head up, knowing that no one can accuse me of being a gold-digger.'

Peering up at her, Georgie pursed her lips and nodded slowly. Then, turning to Larry, she winked, and said, 'She'll do.'

Laughing when Georgie had finished her coffee and gone, Larry pulled Stephanie into his arms and said, 'See, I told you she liked you.'

Exhaling with relief, Stephanie said, 'Took her long enough.'

'Ah, yes, but she had to put you to the test before she gave us her blessing.'

'Bit late for that,' Stephanie said, biting her lip coyly as she peeled Larry's hands from around her waist and backed away from him. 'If she had any idea what we've been getting up to behind closed doors, she'd have had me burned at the stake months ago.'

Loving that she was being so playful, Larry reached for her again, saying, 'Don't go to work. Phone in sick and come back to bed.'

'No,' she said firmly, sidestepping him. 'You heard your mother . . . I need my independence.'

Rolling his eyes now, Larry said, 'I think I'm already regretting letting you two get to know each other. Now there's two of you to gang up on me.'

'Two of us to love you,' Stephanie corrected him softly, stroking his cheek. 'Now, stand aside, Mr Logan, and let me get ready for work.'

'Only if you promise to meet me at the studio when you're finished and let me introduce you to George Michael,' Larry said, following her when she headed for the bedroom. 'Craig's arranged for us all to go out for dinner, and I'd like you to come.'

'I can't,' Stephanie said, flicking her head forward and rubbing her hair briskly with the towel.

'It's a really safe venue,' Larry told her, thinking she was refusing because of the publicity shit again. 'Definitely no paps, or George wouldn't have agreed to come.'

'I still can't,' Stephanie said, moving him out of the way so she could reach the hairdryer she kept in his drawer. 'I'm being sent to Milton Keynes on an over-nighter straight after the meeting.'

'Again?' Larry moaned, frowning now. 'Why didn't you tell me?'

'Because they only told *me* yesterday, and you were too busy celebrating when I saw you, so I didn't want to put a downer on things. But it's only one night, and it sounds like you'll be having fun with your pop-star friend.'

'I wanted you to come,' Larry said, watching as she started to style her lovely hair. 'Even Georgie thinks it's a good idea for us to be seen together.'

Gritting her teeth, Stephanie forced herself to smile at him in the mirror. As much as he was – light-heartedly – regretting her and Georgie making friends because it meant they could now henpeck him together, it was going to make things even more difficult for *her* now that Georgie seemed to have accepted her. Now she'd have *two* of them pressuring her to go public.

Knowing there was no point trying to persuade her because she had that stubborn-pursing-of-the-lips thing going on, Larry shrugged and said, 'Fine. You go off on your important business trip, and leave me to suffer the company of my favourite singer on my own – see if I care. But don't let me find out you've been flirting with any other men behind my back, or there'll be trouble.'

Knowing that he was only half-joking, Stephanie blew him a reassuring kiss and carried on with her hair. Larry was an exceptionally gorgeous man, and she knew that she was in a privileged position, given that every woman in the country would probably kill to be where she was. But the more she got to know him, the more she realised how insecure he really was beneath the Mr Smooth and Handsome façade. He was nowhere near as arrogant as the press had made him out to be, although there were definite traces of it. He expected everything to go his way, and everyone to bow down to him. But that was understandable, considering that most people toadied around him like he was some kind of god.

Stephanie had no intention of becoming one of his lackeys, and had told him so in no uncertain terms on a couple of occasions when, pissed out of his head, he'd tried pulling the

*I'm-the-star-and-you-should-be-grateful-I'm-giving-you-the-time-of-day* routine. She'd nipped that *right* in the bud, letting him know that she wasn't like his previous women and wouldn't tolerate his shit just to stay in his bed and share his limelight. And – surprisingly, because she'd actually expected him to tell her to sling her hook – it seemed to have made him respect and like her all the more.

Unfortunately, the more Larry grew to like her, the more possessive and insecure he became. Stephanie found herself having to spend hours reassuring him that she wasn't still seeing her ex behind his back, or sleeping with every man on the train or at the hotel when she went on business trips.

But there was no way she was going to give up her independence to satisfy his insecurities. And no way was she giving up her flat and moving in with him, because then she'd have nowhere to go when she needed time on her own.

# 16

*The Larry Logan Show* rocketed straight to the top of the ratings and stayed there, going from strength to strength over the next few months as the stars queued up to get an invite to appear.

Larry was delighted that he'd totally blitzed Raine Parker's long-held ratings record, and was also spitefully thrilled when *Star Struck* slid so far out of favour that it was axed by Oasis and shunted off to a rarely watched Sky channel. He never stopped trying to persuade Stephanie – who he now admitted to 'liking a *lot*' – to move in with him. But she was still too camera-shy, and he was too busy to keep hassling her about coming out as a couple, so they settled into a mutually agreeable routine of getting on with their individual day-to-day lives while spending nights together whenever they could – albeit always at his place, because she didn't want to risk him going to hers and being followed.

Happier than he'd ever been in his life before, Larry completely forgot about Tania Baxter.

But she hadn't forgotten him. And he was about to feel the full force of her ever-growing obsession for him.

Tania was frustrated that she still hadn't been contacted by the reporter several months down the line. She was also infuriated that no matter how many times she called the studio, using different names and accents, they still wouldn't put her through to Larry. So when she finally got lucky and managed to get one of the highly sought-after tickets to be in the audience for his show, she thought she'd finally cracked it, and formulated a foolproof plan to thwart his people.

Still sure that all it would take for them to be together was for Larry to see her, Tania decided she would sit in the audience and watch the show. Then, when Larry was saying his goodbyes and everyone thought it was all over, she would rush onto the set while no one was expecting it and let him know what had been happening behind his back.

Convinced that the old bitch who'd claimed to be his agent had been lying about the girlfriend – because there had been absolutely nothing about it in the papers – Tania took extra-special care with her appearance on the night of the show, wanting to ensure that Larry would be completely wowed when he saw her. Then, excited at the prospect of getting back together with him, she made her way to the TV station and waited in line with the rest of the women – sneering at their stupidity as she listened to them all fantasising about him spotting them in the crowd and whisking them away. She felt like telling them all to shut their stupid mouths, because there was only *one* woman he would be whisking anywhere, and that was her!

Keeping her head down as she passed the security guards standing on either side of the main doors, Tania reached the desk and handed her ticket over. But then, just as she was about to follow the women who were already making their way into the studio, she felt a hand on her shoulder.

'This one?' the security guard asked, looking at Ayshia for confirmation.

Nodding, Ayshia said, 'Could you escort her out, please – and make sure she doesn't come back.'

'What's going on?' Tania yelped as the guard took a firm grip on her arm and marched her towards the door. 'I've got a ticket! You can't do this to me!'

'You're barred,' the guard told her, marching her down the steps and pushing her firmly into the road. Folding his arms then, he glared at her, challenging her to try and get past him.

Fully aware that she stood no chance of physically forcing her way back inside, Tania folded her own arms and glared right back at him, determined not to leave just because he'd told her to. But he obviously liked the staring-out game because he didn't turn and walk away after a few minutes as she'd expected. And in the end, it was *her* who couldn't take any more.

Screaming that she was going to come back and blow the station up, Tania finally gave up and stomped away with as much dignity as she could muster – which wasn't much, given that she was already crying uncontrollably.

Running almost all the way home – which, fortunately, was only a mile or so away if you used the subways – she let herself into her flat and threw herself down on the couch to cry some more.

Everything was hopeless. She'd tried so hard, but she was never going to get to Larry. And if she couldn't be with him, she didn't see any point in living.

Filled with self-pity, Tania dragged herself into the kitchen and rooted through the drawers and cupboards. There were plenty of knives she could have used to slice her wrists, but she was far too beautiful to do that to herself. When she was found, she wanted to be as flawlessly perfect in death as she had been in life. And the only way of ensuring that was an overdose.

Gathering together every tablet she could find – including an old packet of paracetamol that the previous tenant must have left behind, because it was absolutely filthy when she dragged it out of the gap it had slipped into at the back of the cutlery drawer – she poured herself a glass of cheap flat cola, and carried it into her bedroom.

In full tragic-heroine mode by now, Tania wrote a letter to Larry, telling him all about how his so-called friends and colleagues had conspired to keep them apart, and saying that she was truly sorry she wasn't strong enough to keep on trying, but that she would wait for him in heaven. Folding it neatly when she'd finished, she stood it on the bedside table where it would be easily spotted when they broke in and found her body. That done, she pulled her suitcase out from under the bed and took out her precious newspaper clippings. Selecting the one which most clearly showed her and Larry kissing at Bone that night, she sat on the bed with it and cried his name as she touched his beautiful face with her fingertip.

Still clutching the clipping, she tipped all the tablets into her hand – blissfully unaware that there were nowhere near enough to kill her but more than enough to irreparably damage her internal organs. Then, just as she raised the pills to her mouth, she took another look at the clipping – and could have kicked herself.

The reporter's name was right there in the story! She'd wasted all this time waiting for him to find her when *she* could have contacted *him* all along. All she had to do was ring the *Herald*.

Rushing back into the living room, she rooted around for last week's *Herald*, which she'd bought for the picture of Larry on the cover. She'd had to cut him out carefully, though, because he'd been kissing some stupid bitch who'd claimed to have cancer and reckoned that meeting him was her dying wish – although Tania suspected she'd probably shaved her own hair off just to get his sympathy. Finding the paper under a pile of clothes, she located the switchboard number and jotted it down. Then, cursing herself for having thrown her mobile at the wall that time, because she hadn't been able to afford to replace it, she pulled her coat on and rushed out to the payphone around the corner.

Telling the switchboard operator when she finally got through that she wanted to speak to Sam Brady, Tania was gutted to be told that he was on holiday at the moment.

Saying, 'You must have his mobile number, so can't you just give me that?' she was irritated when the woman said that she couldn't give out that kind of information. 'But he's looking for me,' she told her desperately. 'He went to my mum's house trying to find me, but my dad wouldn't tell him where I've moved to. Please, you've got to help me. It's a matter of life and death!'

Thinking that the girl was being a tad over-dramatic, the operator said, 'Look, love, I really can't give you his number. But I'll take your details, if you like, and pass them on to another in-house reporter. If they think you've got a story, they might contact you.'

Annoyed, because she'd really wanted the man who was interested enough in her to come looking for her, Tania mulled this over for a moment. Then, deciding that any reporter was better than no reporter, she gave the woman her name and address.

'And what's the nature of your story?' the operator asked when she'd jotted them down.

Narrowing her eyes when it suddenly occurred to her that if she gave her story away to this woman she might go and sell her own version, Tania said, 'It's about me and Larry Logan. But I'm not telling you any more than that. Just make sure a reporter contacts me, or I'll go to the *News of the World*.'

Hanging up then, she bit her lip, wondering if that might not actually be a good idea anyway. But she didn't have any more change and, anyway, she'd have to get a copy of the *News of the World* to get the number, but it wasn't out for another four days and she couldn't wait that long. So she'd wait and see if the *Herald* contacted her first. At least it was local, so Larry would be guaranteed to see it. And she was pretty sure that all the other papers would soon come begging for interviews.

Sam Brady had shoved Tania Baxter to the back of his mind by the time he got the call from Hannah telling him that the girl was looking for him. After being threatened by her dad that night, he'd hit a complete dead end trying to track her down. He didn't know any of her friends' names, so he couldn't ask them if they'd seen her; and she wasn't on the electoral register, so he couldn't find her from that. And after driving round and round Stretford for several nights on the off chance of spotting her on the street, he'd finally given up, because he had better things to be getting on with – like *earning* money, instead of spending it on petrol chasing wild geese.

Perking up when Hannah told him about Tania having called them looking for him, Sam asked if the other operator who'd taken the call had passed it on to another in-house reporter yet. He was relieved when Hannah told him no.

'I know you're on holiday,' she said. 'But the girl specifically asked for you, so I asked Jen to let me get hold of you first and see if you were interested.'

''Course I'm interested,' he said, already getting his pen ready to write down the address. 'How long ago did she call?' he asked then, wondering if she'd have had time to follow through with her threat to contact the *News of the World*.

'About ten minutes,' Hannah said, laughing when Sam hissed a jubilant '*Yes!*'

Tania frowned when she heard the knock on her front door just half an hour after making her phone call and coming back home. It was hard and fast, like a copper's knock. Or, worse, her dad's.

Afraid that it might be him, even though they hadn't spoken

since their last argument, she tiptoed to the door and pressed her ear against it. There was no spyhole, so she'd have to listen instead. But there'd be no mistaking it if it *was* him because he had a distinctive way of breathing through his nostrils that made him sound like he was perpetually furious.

Hearing nothing but the shuffling of feet, and a deep, weary sigh, Tania jumped when a note suddenly came through the letter box. Wondering now if it was a debt collector or some other official she was trying to avoid, she eased herself down and picked the note up as quietly as possible in case the person was still standing there, waiting to catch her out. Unfolding it, she gasped when she saw Sam Brady's name and mobile number.

Fumbling with the lock, she yanked the door open and rushed out onto the communal landing. Finding it empty, she galloped down the stairs and shoved the heavy outer door open. Seeing a man making his way to a car across the road, she called out to him.

Turning back, Sam Brady looked her over and smiled, saying, 'Nice to see you again, Tania. Must say you've changed a bit since last time, though. I almost didn't recognise you at the studio that night.'

'Were you there?' Tania asked, leading him back up to her flat. 'I didn't see you.'

Chuckling softly, Sam said, 'Don't think you were paying too much attention to anyone, that night. Too busy throwing yourself on Larry's car.'

'God, did you see me?' she murmured sheepishly. 'I made a right fool of myself, didn't I?'

'Not at all,' he lied, waving her into her flat ahead of him when she opened the door. 'Wasn't sure it was you at first, to tell you the truth. Then it clicked, and I thought, hmmm . . . wonder what that was all about. Hope you're going to tell me all about it?'

'Yeah, 'course,' Tania said. Then, blushing when she took him into the living room, she said, 'Sorry about the mess and the smell. It's damp, but the council are dead lax about coming out to fix stuff.'

Telling her that he'd close his eyes and breathe through his mouth, Sam looked around and nodded approvingly. 'Cool flat. Is it all yours, or do you share?'

'It's mine,' Tania told him, thinking that he was nothing like any of the other adults who'd come in here since she'd moved in and who had all looked down their noses. Like her dad – whose fault it was that she was here in the first place, because he'd kicked her out just for *borrowing* some money out of her mum's savings jar. He'd only been here once, and had refused to sit down or touch anything; just stood there looking around with a disgusted sneer on his ugly face. And the cheeky-bitch social worker who'd helped her to get the flat, and then thought she had a licence to come round every week to check that she was keeping it tidy.

'Love a tea, if you're brewing?' Sam said, sitting down on her couch as if he'd been there a thousand times before. 'Unless you fancy something stronger?'

'Oh, sorry, I haven't got anything,' Tania admitted, blushing as she added, 'I haven't even got any tea bags, to tell you the truth. The social's been kind of messing me about with my money.'

'Lucky I brought this, then,' Sam said, bringing a half-bottle of white rum out of his pocket. 'Not that I make a habit of carrying booze around, you understand, but I was supposed to be going to a mate's to watch the footie when I got the call to say you were looking for me.'

'Oh, sorry, I didn't realise you had things to do,' Tania said, hoping that he wasn't going to leave in a hurry.

'Hey, the footie can wait,' he reassured her, twisting the cap off the bottle. Looking up at her then, he grinned and said, 'Come on, girl – what you waiting for? Get some glasses.'

Running into the kitchen to fetch two glasses and the bottle of flat cola, Tania said, 'This'll have to do, I'm afraid.'

Telling her that owt was better than nowt, Sam poured two large shots of rum, topped them up with cola, and handed one to her. Then, reaching into his pocket for his cigarettes, switching his Dictaphone on in the process, he offered one to her. Settling back in his seat when they'd both lit up, he said, 'So, you and Larry, eh? What's that all about, then?'

Relaxing, because he sounded genuinely interested – and in the way a friend would be, not a reporter – Tania said, 'Long story.'

'Hey, just how I like them,' Sam said. 'Can't beat a good girly gossip. Not that I'm girly, or anything,' he added with a chuckle. 'But when you grow up with five sisters, it's kind of cool to get roped in for the opposing opinion.'

'Five sisters?' Tania repeated, shaking her head. 'Wow! That must have been horrible. I've only got one, and she's a bitch.'

'Cindy?' Sam said, nodding understandingly as he added, 'I kind of got the impression she was like Little Miss Perfect when I spoke to your mum and dad that time. Bit of a daddy's girl, is she?'

'You can say that again,' Tania spat, taking a large swig of her drink. 'Couldn't do any wrong, her. But *me* . . . I couldn't do any right.'

'Larry Logan obviously doesn't agree,' Sam reminded her smoothly. 'I mean, if there is a you and him, you've got to be doing something right, haven't you?'

Smiling coyly as she took another sip of her drink, Tania nodded. 'Yeah, I suppose so. But that was then, and I haven't really seen him since I turned eighteen.'

'Then? As in two years ago when you said you *weren't* seeing him?' Sam probed, his eyes twinkling as if he was totally on her side as he added, 'I always *knew* he had a thing for you.'

'Did you?' Tania gushed, delighted that he'd seen it for himself and wasn't going to tell her that she was imagining things – like everyone always did when she tried to tell them about herself and Larry.

''Course, man,' Sam drawled, really latching onto her vibe. 'Everyone else was like, nah . . . he's too old for her; he wouldn't look twice at her. But, me . . . I was just like, you know what, she's a good-looking girl, why the hell *wouldn't* he be interested?' Taking a drink himself now, he gestured for her to do the same, intent on loosening her tongue. 'Anyway, go on . . . tell me all about it.'

'Well, we kind of had an agreement not to see each other again till I was eighteen,' Tania admitted. 'And then he was going to take me out for dinner.'

'Wow,' Sam murmured admiringly. 'That must have been fantastic. So where did he take you? Bet it was somewhere really expensive.'

'Well, yeah, it probably would have been,' Tania said. She sighed as she went on to admit, 'But it hasn't happened yet, 'cos I moved out of my dad's, so he wouldn't have known where to find me.'

'Dad not too hot on him?' Sam ventured, guessing that Logan hadn't even bothered to go looking for her or she'd have heard, just like she'd heard that *Sam* had been round there.

'No, but *he* just wants me to be miserable for the rest of my life,' Tania said, swallowing the last of her drink.

Refilling her glass before she had a chance to put it down, Sam said, 'Did he know about you and Larry, then?'

'God, no!' Tania snorted. 'He's the reason I lied about it in the first place, 'cos he would have battered me if he'd found out that I stayed at Larry's flat that night.'

'For real?' Sam gave her another admiring grin. 'You really stayed at his place?' Then, 'Nah, you're having me on now. You stayed in your mate's garage.'

'That's what I *told* everyone,' Tania confided, biting her lip, already feeling the effects of the strong alcohol. 'But I didn't really. I was at Larry's all night.'

'What's his place like?' Sam asked, watching her closely for signs of hesitation: she would have to take time to think about this before she spoke if she was lying.

'Oh, it's gorgeous,' Tania said wistfully – and truthfully; remembering it all too clearly, having mentally relived that night and morning many times over the last two years. 'Everything's just really fantastic,' she said now, kicking her shoes off and drawing her legs up onto the couch. 'Like, he's got this massive bed, with a TV built into the wall opposite. And his windows go right down to the floor, with no nets or anything, so you can see all the tops of the buildings when you're lying there. And his kitchen's *amazing*. Everything's built-in, and it's all kind of dark red and black. You'd just *die* if you saw it. And the shower's incredible. It's got this huge nozzle in the ceiling, and there's no curtain, or glass doors, or anything.'

Sure that she was telling the truth, because she'd never have described it in so much detail if she were lying, Sam said, 'So, what happened?'

Giggling shyly, thinking that he was asking for details about the sex, Tania said, 'I can't tell you *that*! It's private.'

'Aw, go on,' Sam urged. 'I won't tell anyone. Was he, like, a once-a-night man, or a keep-it-up-all-nighter?'

Laughing, Tania slapped out at him, saying, 'You're terrible!'

'And you're gorgeous,' Sam replied, winking at her. 'No wonder Logan's gone on you. Bet he couldn't keep his hands off you.'

Biting her lip, Tania wondered whether she ought to tell

the truth at this point. But Sam was so sure that Larry must have been crazy about her, and *she* was sure that he *would* have been if he'd been conscious. Anyway, if she admitted that nothing had actually happened, he'd think she was lying about everything else.

'*Well . . .*' she said after a moment, glancing up at Sam through her lashes. 'He was very romantic.'

'One way of putting it,' Sam laughed. 'And was that your first time?'

'God, no,' Tania snorted, thinking that he was asking if she'd been a virgin before Larry.

'*Really?*' Sam said, thinking that she was talking about having been with Larry before that night. 'So, when was your first time?'

'God, *months* before that,' Tania said. She grimaced as she added, 'But don't tell my dad, or he'll kill me.'

Giving her a sly smile now, Sam said, 'You're not telling me you were only fifteen, you naughty girl?'

Nodding, Tania giggled. 'But you've got to swear you won't tell anyone, 'cos that bit's a secret.'

'Hey, we're just mates having a chat,' Sam drawled, shifting a little closer to make sure that the Dictaphone picked up every word. 'And if you can't trust a mate, who *can* you trust?'

# 17

'You've got to be fucking joking,' Larry gasped, staring at the headline on the paper that Georgie had woken him up to show him.

'You'd better read it,' Georgie told him. 'It's not good.'

*LOGAN MADE GIRL LIE!* the headline said. It was followed by:

*Almost two years to the day since we exposed love-rat Larry Logan for turning his lustful attentions to girls young enough to be his daughter – a claim he strenuously denied – we can now reveal the truth behind the lies he coerced his young victim into telling in order to cover his tracks.*

*Tania Baxter, who, at just sixteen years of age was sacrificed on the altar of Logan's ego and vilified by the press and public alike for the crime of falling in love with her hero and lying her way onto his show, last night spoke to our reporter Sam Brady about the impact this episode has had on her young life.*

*Contrary to what she said at the time – as dictated to her by Loathsome Logan, we now know that Tania Baxter DID spend the night with Logan at his luxury apartment that night. DID have sex with him. And DID think that he would honour his word when he promised to resume their relationship on her eighteenth birthday – providing she took the blame and allowed him to rebuild his tarnished reputation with a cloak of innocence acquired at her expense.*

*And, worse, we can also reveal that the night our reporter caught them was* NOT *the first time they had been together. In fact, the tawdry affair began some months before the fateful night when Tania appeared on Logan's then game show* Star Struck *and walked away with the jackpot. And she was just* FIFTEEN YEARS OLD *at that time, making Logan both a liar and a paedophile!*

The phone started to ring just then. Seeing from the look of horror on Larry's face that he was in no fit state to talk to anyone as he carried on reading the story, which went on to tell the woeful tale of a young girl abandoned by her older lover, rejected by her own family and forced to live in squalor, Georgie answered it.

It was Craig Woodburn, wanting to know if they were watching the news.

'No, why?' Georgie asked, already turning in circles, looking for the remote for the kitchen TV. Finding it, she switched it on, and said, 'Oh, good Lord, *no*,' when she saw what was happening on the screen.

Alerted by his agent's grim tone, Larry looked up from the paper. Following Georgie's gaze, his jaw clenched when he saw a blonde girl whom he wouldn't have recognised in a million years if her name hadn't been splashed along the bottom of the screen being interviewed at her own front door by an ITN news crew.

'Is it true you're claiming to have been in a relationship with Larry Logan since you were fifteen years old?' the presenter was saying, shoving a microphone into her face.

Looking shocked and confused, Tania shook her head, murmuring, 'No, I was sixteen.'

'Sixteen at the time you were caught,' the presenter persisted. 'But you were quoted in the *Herald* today as having admitted that it started some months earlier.'

'It's in the paper already?' Tania gasped, casting a nervous glance at the camera.

Confirming that it was, the presenter said, 'And in it you claim you *were* having a relationship with Larry Logan two years ago, when you actually made a statement at *that* time denying it.'

'Well, yeah, but I only lied 'cos I didn't want to get in trouble with my dad.'

'Not to keep Larry Logan out of trouble because you knew it would come out that he'd slept with you when you were still a minor?'

'I *wasn't*! I was sixteen, and me and Larry really liked each other, but the papers made it sound dirty, so I lied to make them shut up about it.'

'And Larry Logan asked you to do that?'

'Yeah, but not because he'd done anything wrong. We just knew that people would try to make trouble, so we agreed to wait until I was eighteen before we started seeing each other properly.'

'So, you *are* seeing each other again?'

Frowning, sure that the presenter was trying to trip her up, Tania said, 'No, but only because the people at the studio won't pass my messages on.'

'And you don't think it's possible that they're just trying to protect him from what could be perceived as an over-imaginative fan who'd do anything to get near her idol?' the presenter asked smoothly.

'I'm not a *fan*,' Tania spat, the anger flaring in her eyes. 'Fans don't sleep in stars' beds, do they? But *I* did, so get lost!' Stepping back into her flat then, she slammed the door shut.

Turning to camera, the presenter raised a knowing eyebrow and said, 'Whatever the truth of this continuing mystery, this reporter, for one, will be reserving judgement until we've had a response from the man himself. Until then, I guess it's a case of lock up your daughters.' Pausing now, he adopted a serious expression, and said, 'James Reed, reporting from Hulme, for *ITN News*.'

'That was fucking bullshit!' Larry barked when the reporter went off screen and the studio presenter came on in his place.

Flapping her hand to keep him quiet because Craig was talking to her again, Georgie said, 'Yes, I'll get on to him right away. But I must say I feel a bit better after seeing that.' Nodding then, she said, 'Yes, I will. Soon as I know what's happening.'

'What did he say?' Larry demanded when she disconnected. 'And what do you mean, you feel better after seeing it? It was fucking awful!'

'Let's just try and stay calm,' Georgie told him, switching the kettle on to make him a strong coffee, because he looked like he could really use one right then. 'I feel better because it was quite obvious that she was lying. The only thing I *am* concerned about is her description of your apartment in the paper. She couldn't possibly know what it was like unless she'd actually been here, so how do you explain that?'

Dropping his head into his hands, Larry groaned and said, 'She *has* been here.'

'You brought her here?' Georgie said flatly. 'The night of the telethon?'

Larry nodded guiltily. 'Yeah, but I was pissed out of my head, and when I woke up I didn't even know who she was. And then I got that call from you telling me it was all over the papers and I'd been sacked, so I just panicked.'

'And asked her to lie?'

'Well, yeah, kind of. Actually, I only asked her not to admit that anything had happened if anyone asked, but then she told me it hadn't, anyway.'

'And you didn't know?' Georgie asked sceptically.

'No. I had no idea. I was unconscious.'

'But you believed her?'

'Yeah, 'cos I could see it in her eyes how gutted she was. She said she *would* have slept with me if I'd been awake, but I was out of it, so she just undressed me and slept next to me.'

'Bloody hell,' Georgie muttered, instinctively believing him but knowing that others might not be so willing to give him the benefit of the doubt. 'This won't be good if it gets out.'

'How the hell am I supposed to keep it quiet now?' Larry croaked. 'The stupid bitch is making out like we're lovers, or something. I'll have to admit what really happened and hope to God people believe me.'

'You'll say nothing for the time being,' Georgie told him firmly. 'I'm going to set up a meeting with your solicitor so you can talk it through and find out exactly where we stand.'

'What about Craig?' Larry asked, dreading the thought of losing yet another show because of this stupid bitch.

'He wants you to carry on as normal, because it'll look worse if you hide away. But he'd rather you didn't do any interviews until we've had a chance to get the solicitors involved, so leave the reporters to me. You just concentrate on your show. And for goodness' sake, do *not* make contact with the girl.'

'Oh, yeah,' Larry muttered sickly. 'Like I was going to run out and try to find her!'

'Well, she obviously thought you were going to do exactly that,' Georgie said, bringing his coffee over to him. 'Hate to say it, but I almost wish you'd taken her for her stupid birthday dinner. At least you'd have known what she was thinking and could have nipped it in the bud.'

Groaning again, Larry shoved the coffee aside and reached into the cupboard for a bottle of Scotch, aware that his hands were shaking as he poured himself a large glass. This was the worst thing that had ever happened to him. Tania Baxter had already ruined his career once. And now, just because he'd forgotten a stupid promise to take her out for dinner on her birthday, she was trying to destroy him. And he *knew* he hadn't done anything to her that night, no matter what she was saying now.

Allowing him his drink without nagging, Georgie said, 'Look, I know you don't like me talking about this, Larry, but don't you think it might be time to come out about you and Stephanie? It's your longest relationship to date, so you're obviously serious about her. And she's a beautiful, independent woman, as opposed to a silly girl with a crush, so people would know that you couldn't possibly have *those* kind of feelings going on.'

Muttering 'Shit!' because he hadn't even thought how all this was going to affect Stephanie, Larry reached for the phone, saying, 'I'd better warn her before she sees it in the papers. And no, by the way,' he said then, tapping in the number. 'I don't want her involved. In fact, it's a bloody good job no one knows about her yet, or they'd be harassing her right now.' Tutting when he heard that Stephanie's phone was switched off again, he said, 'She must be in a meeting.'

'Give me her number,' Georgie said, reaching into her handbag for her own mobile. 'Craig wants you down at the studio by twelve, and I want to see if Doug can fit you in before that. You might not get a chance to speak to her until tonight, so I'll keep trying for you.'

'Okay, but make sure she realises that it's absolutely not true,' Larry said. 'And you'd best tell her not to come round tonight, either. Until I speak to her, actually, because I've got a feeling I'm going to have reporters crawling all over the place after this.'

★

An hour later, and just a couple of miles away from Larry's apartment, in the visiting hall of Strangeways Prison, Nora Lewis was busy telling Dex all about the latest scandal.

'Didn't I always say he looked like a bloody pervert?' she sneered. Then, tutting loudly when Dex pointed out that, no, she'd actually said quite the opposite, she said, 'Yeah, well, I didn't think so *straight* off, obviously, 'cos he was such a bloody convincing liar. But, soon as I knew what he was up to with you, I said it. And I've been saying it ever since. And now look.'

Lighting another cigarette now, she surreptitiously shoved the pack across the table, flapping her hand for him to pocket them before the screws spotted him. Taking one, he lit it and shoved the pack back to her, because there was no way he was going to give the screws an excuse to strip-search him.

'Anyhow, I reckon he needs a damn good kicking,' Nora went on, with a nasty glint in her eye. 'And I know you keep telling me he'll get his comeuppance without me interfering, Derek, but even *you*'ve got to admit he's long overdue.'

Groaning, 'Give it a rest, for fuck's sake,' Dex glanced at Gaynor, who looked more drained than he'd ever seen her before. Jerking his head at Nora now, he said, 'Why don't you go get yourself another brew while me and Gaynor have a chat, Mam?'

Sniffing loudly, because she didn't see why Gaynor should get preferential treatment when she was still messing Dex around, Nora said, 'I don't want another brew, I want to talk to *my son*.' Emphasising the words to remind Gaynor that Dex was her blood and always would be, she sucked deeply on her cigarette.

Leaning forward, Dex rested his elbows on the table and said, 'Lay off, Mam. She's doing nowt to you.'

Snorting softly, Nora muttered, 'No, but she's probably doing plenty to *you* behind your back. She's never at home when any of us try to get hold of her. And she never comes on time when she's supposed to fetch my keeps round.'

Saying, 'I know exactly where she is and what she's doing, 'cos she's keeping things running for me,' Dex gave his mother a long, hard stare, letting her know that he meant it when he added, 'So just lay off, 'cos there's no one else who could hold it together like she has.'

'Bollocks,' Nora spat, furious that he was giving Gaynor credit for running his business in his absence. All she had to do was pick up the gear, weigh it out and drop it off, then go round collecting money. Hardly rocket science. Even their Lyla could do it – at a push.

'Go and get a tea,' Dex growled, afraid that he might lose it if she carried on with her sniping. And wouldn't the screws just love an excuse to haul his arse down the block for a kicking.

Pursing her wrinkled mouth so hard that it almost turned her face inside out, Nora shoved her chair back and stalked over to the small snack bar at the rear of the hall.

Reaching for Gaynor's hand when she'd gone, Dex said, 'You all right, babe?'

Nodding even though her eyes were already brimming with tears, Gaynor took a tissue out of her pocket and dabbed at her nose. 'Sorry, I didn't mean to get upset, but she's been so bloody horrible all morning. I knew I shouldn't have let you put her on my VO. She doesn't let *me* come on *her* visits.'

'She only wanted to see me because it's the anniversary of me dad's death,' Dex reminded her. 'Don't worry, you won't have to bring her again.'

Murmuring, 'Good,' Gaynor gazed into his eyes and bit her lip when her chin began to wobble. 'God, I hate this.'

Squeezing her hand, Dex said, 'Me too. But it won't be for ever, and I'll make it up to you when I get out.'

'It's so *hard*,' Gaynor sobbed, unable to stop the tears from escaping now. 'I miss you so much, and every time I see you it gets harder to walk away. And then I've got to go home and put up with your mum moaning and quizzing me. And all the other stuff is *killing* me.'

'I know, babe, and I hate putting it all on you like this,' Dex said, reaching out to wipe away a tear that was rolling down her cheek. 'But me mam and our Jimmy would fuck everything up if I left it to them, and I don't trust no one else but you. You're doing this for our future. Don't give up on us now.'

Sighing softly, because she knew that she really was the only one who could do this for him, Gaynor said, 'I'm only doing it 'cos I love you, so don't you dare blame me if I mess it up.'

'You won't,' Dex said with certainty. Then, 'How's it going, anyway? Any of the guys trying it on?'

'Felix is getting a bit naughty,' Gaynor told him. 'I had to go round to his place twice last week, and I know he was in the first time but he wouldn't open the door. I waited round the corner the second time and caught him on his way out, but he said he didn't have the money so I had to give him another week.'

'Cunt,' Dex snarled, his nostrils flaring. 'You should have told him to get to fuck and made him pay.'

'Er, *how*?' Gaynor asked. 'I'm not you, you know. I can hardly kick the shit out of him for taking the piss.'

'Christ, Gay, I hope you're not talking like this in front of them or they're gonna think you're a right soft touch. You're my bird, for fuck's sake. Front it.'

'And what if they get nasty?'

'I'll kill 'em.'

'From here?' Gaynor raised an eyebrow.

Shaking his head irritably, Dex said, 'Jeezus, Gaynor, why d'y' have to be such a soft shit? You're making me wish I'd left fucking Jane in charge. At least she'd have no trouble keeping the cunts in line.'

'Ex*cuse* me?' Gaynor said quietly, her eyes narrowing as the blood drained from her face. 'What the hell has *she* got to do with this? You'd better not be messing round with her behind my back again, Dex, because I'm warning you now, I'll never forgive you if you are.'

Chuckling softly, Dex said, 'Chill out, you jealous bitch. 'Course I ain't messing with her. She's nowt to me but Molly's mam. And what would I want with a slag like her when I've got you?'

Staring at his hard expression, looking for even the remotest flicker of guilt in his eyes, Gaynor snatched her hand away when he reached for it, hissing, 'You'd better mean that, Dex.'

'Course I do,' he reassured her, amused that she could get so pissed off with him yet couldn't tell one of his punters to pay up on time. But she had a point about that, he supposed. So, sighing, he said, 'All right, I know I can't expect you to heavy the guys. But when you get out of here, I want you to go back round there and tell Felix from me that if he messes you around again I'll be sending some visitors round, and he won't have no kneecaps left at the end of it. Oh, and make sure you remind him that I know where his mam and his baby-mother live, so it could come any time, anywhere.'

Nodding, Gaynor felt a fresh set of tears building up behind her eyes when Dex reached for her hand again and raised it to his lips, saying, 'I do appreciate what you're doing for me, babe, and when I get out I'm gonna treat you like a queen. I know I've been a bastard in the past, but that's all gonna change now.'

'I don't want *you* to change,' she told him earnestly, pressing her knees into his under the table. 'I just want *things* to change. I never want to hear you mention that bitch again. And I've had enough of you always being on the run so I don't know if you'll be home from one night to the next.'

'Keep the money turning over, and I won't have to do anything too strenuous when I get out,' Dex said. Then, glancing quickly around to make sure that his mother wasn't on her way back yet, he said, 'Subject of money: I've had an idea how to get a big wedge fast . . .'

Narrowing her eyes as she made her way back to the table a couple of minutes later and saw Dex and Gaynor with their heads close in conversation, Nora deliberately ruined what she took to be a tender moment by plonking herself down in her chair, saying loudly, 'Even the bloody tea woman's talking about that pervert. Apparently, that girl was on the news this morning as well as in the paper. Must have missed that when we was on our way here – eh, Gay?' She gave Gaynor a sharp dig in the ribs with her elbow.

Sitting wearily back in his seat, Dex said, 'Mam, I know exactly what's going on out there. We *have* got a telly, you know. And we get the papers every morning, so I don't need a running commentary every time I see you. It's bad enough when I call you, 'cos you waste most of me time waffling on about shit.'

'I like talking to you,' Nora said, looking hurt by his dismissive tone. 'And Logan's got my goat over what he did to you, so excuse *me* if I can't help but dream about getting the lads together to give him a going-over.'

'Will you just *leave* it?' Dex moaned. 'We both know he'd end up dead if they went steaming in, and then I'd never get my bleedin' hands on him.'

Folding her arms, Nora said, 'I don't know what the bloody hell's up with you since you got in here, but you ain't yourself, I can tell you that for nowt. There *was* a time you'd have had him strung up for this, but now you're acting like you want to protect him, or something.'

'Behave,' Dex snarled, angry with her for making out that he'd lost his bottle. 'All I'm saying is there's plenty of ways to skin a rat, and he's gonna get his. But it's gonna be *me* who sorts him. Till then, you just keep your neck in and your nose out. And quit hassling Gaynor, 'cos she's the one who's bringing the money in now. Got that?'

Giving a grudging nod, Nora let it drop and spent the last ten minutes of the visit telling Dex about Molly's upcoming school trip to Austria.

''Course, she'll need spending money on top of the cost of the trip,' she said at the end, smiling sarcastically at Gaynor now as she added, 'If that's all right with your ladyship? Only I wouldn't want to be begging for handouts or nothing.'

Telling her that Gaynor would make sure she got whatever she needed, and that he wanted to speak to Molly later so she should make sure that she stayed in to wait for his call, Dex was relieved when the bell rang to signal that visiting time was over. Staying in his seat until his mother and Gaynor had gone, he narrowed his eyes and cracked his knuckles sharply, enjoying the dull spears of pain which shot through his hands.

Which was nothing to the pain *Logan* was going to feel when Dex got hold of him. And it looked like fate might just be conspiring to orchestrate that reunion a little sooner than he'd hoped. Fate, and a little *persuasive* interference from Molly.

# 18

Tania hid in her flat after the news crew had gone, refusing to answer the numerous knocks on her door in case it was more reporters. She'd been horrified to hear that Sam Brady had taken her comment about having sex at fifteen and turned it into an admission that it had been with Larry. She couldn't blame him for misunderstanding, but she felt really stupid for letting her guard down like that and confiding in him. He'd made out like they were just having a chat, but he'd obviously been interviewing her all along, and now everyone thought that Larry was a paedophile. She just hoped that Larry understood it had been a mistake when she got a chance to tell him what had really happened, because she would *never* have dropped him in it if Sam hadn't got her drunk and twisted her head up.

Venturing out cautiously when it got dark, Tania slipped through the caretaker's tool-room door at the pitch-dark rear of the flats to avoid the reporters who were still hanging about outside the front entrance. Putting her hood up and her head down, she dashed to the shops with the money that Sam Brady had slipped her the night before.

As soon as she got there, some girls spotted her and came rushing over to tell her that they'd seen her on the telly and in the paper. Feeling a bit like a movie star as they gushed all over her, telling her how fantastic she'd looked and asking her about Larry, Tania played it cool. Now that she'd had the exposure she needed to get Larry's attention, she didn't want to risk doing any more damage by telling people things he'd rather they didn't know. So, giving the girls – and the rest of the customers who'd wandered into the shop in the meantime and were hanging around listening – a secretive smile, she told them that she'd promised Larry not to say anything else until they'd had a chance to get together for a private chat, but that they'd be the first to know if there was any news after that. Then, buying a paper, cigarettes, and the few groceries she needed, she rushed out, leaving them to speculate about whether she'd been hinting about news of the wedding or baby variety.

Making her way home now, alternating between feelings of wild joy at having achieved the fame she'd dreamed of for so long and guilt that she'd said something potentially harmful about Larry again – which needed rectifying if she was to stand any chance of getting him to see her – Tania didn't notice the girl and the woman on the other side of the road. Dressed in dark clothes, with their own heads covered, they were carefully staying just a step behind her so that she wouldn't spot them. But even if she did and decided to run, they weren't worried, because she wouldn't get too far.

Sneaking back in through the caretaker's door, which she'd wedged ajar with a brick, Tania was about to close it behind her when it was pushed roughly open again and two shadowy figures came in. Stepping nervously back as they approached her with just the whites of their eyes visible as they stared out from under their hoods, she scraped her hand on the rough brick wall, searching for the door back into the flats. But just as she reached it, one of the figures lunged at her.

Crying out, Tania was immediately silenced by a vicious punch in the stomach. Slumping down to her knees as a wave of nausea washed over her, she raised her hands to protect her face as the attacker grabbed at her hood, yanking her by it and her hair back to her feet.

'Please don't hurt me,' she whimpered, sure that she was about to be raped. 'Please . . . I'm a virgin.'

Laughing nastily, Molly said, 'Hear that? Reckons she's a virgin.'

Coming towards them now, having made sure that the door was secured, Jane gripped Tania by the front of her jacket and slammed her back against the wall. Lowering her face until they were eye to eye, she hissed, 'You ain't no virgin, you lying little bitch, but you'll wish you was dead and buried if you don't do as you're told. Got that?'

Nodding quickly, her stare darting from the woman to the girl, Tania was terrified. She'd thought they were men, but at least men would only have raped her. Girls were much more vicious, and there was no telling what they would do to her – or why. Although it was a pretty good bet that it had something to do with Larry.

She was right, but not in the way she'd imagined. Because Molly and Jane weren't there to give her a beating for getting off with their hero; they were there to take Dex's plan for revenge to the next stage.

'You told them on the news this morning that you was lying about only being fifteen when you shagged Logan,' Molly said now, gripping Tania's face and squeezing it so hard that Tania felt like her jaw was about to break.

'Yeah, 'cos the papers got it wrong,' Tania croaked painfully, misunderstanding again and thinking they were annoyed with her for getting Larry into trouble. 'They said I'd said it, but I hadn't. And that's what I told them on the news.'

'Quit fucking spitting on me,' Molly hissed, giving her a slap.

Crying now, because her face was hurting and she was so scared, Tania said, 'I'm sorry, I didn't mean to. And I'm going to tell everyone I never said that, I swear it.'

'No, you ain't,' Molly snarled, squeezing even tighter. 'You're gonna say you *did* sleep with him when you was fifteen. And you'd better make sure they believe you, or you're dead.'

Squealing with pain when Molly shoved a hand between her legs now, grasping and twisting her crotch, Tania cried, 'I don't understand.'

'You don't *need* to understand,' Jane told her, peering darkly into her eyes. 'You just need to do as you're told, or we'll be back. And if you was scared when you thought you was about to get raped just now, you ain't seen nothing yet, 'cos we've got some guys lined up for you who'd split your arse in half, then lick the blood off it for fun – *and* pay us for the privilege!'

'And if you think this is a joke,' Molly chipped in, 'just try us and see what happens, 'cos we know where to find you. And we know where your mam and dad live, an' all. So pull any stunts, like calling the police, and you'll all be dead. And you'd better believe it won't be fast,' she added nastily, giving another sadistic twist to Tania's crotch. 'It'll be slow and really painful, like this.'

Sobbing now, Tania said, 'I'll do whatever you want, but please don't hurt me or my mum. *Please* . . . I'm begging you!'

Looking at each other, Jane and Molly nodded simultaneously. Then, turning back to Tania, Jane said, 'So, what you gonna say?'

'That I was fifteen the first time I slept with him,' Tania gasped, the pain from her crotch and her face searing her entire body.

'And why are they gonna believe you this time? 'Cos you're gonna have to be convincing after all the lying and taking it back you've done so far.'

Tears pouring down her cheeks now as she betrayed the man she loved for the sake of her own skin, Tania howled, 'I know about the b-birthmark on his dick.'

Sneering, Molly said, 'So you *did* sleep with him, you dirty little slag. You wanna be ashamed of yourself for letting an old man like that touch you! Aren't you ashamed, eh?'

'Yeah!' Tania sobbed.

'And what are you?'

'A dirty slag!'

'That's right. And no one cares about dirty slags, so don't think no one will care when they find you dead with your arse ripped open.'

'Just one more thing,' Jane chipped in, getting an irritated look from Molly for ruining her fun. 'You don't say nothing for a week. And I don't care how many reporters come knocking, you keep your gob shut for one full week from today. Then you go and tell them all about you and Larry when you was fifteen. Understand?'

Giving Tania one last winding punch in the stomach when she nodded, Molly said, 'Just make sure you do as you're told, or we'll be seeing you again – soon.'

Leaving Tania in a heap on the floor, Jane and Molly snuck back out the way they'd come and ran across the field behind the flats.

Laughing as they stumbled against each other in the dark, Jane said, 'You're your dad's daughter, all right, you. Where d'y' come up with all that mafia shit?'

'You,' Molly retorted amusedly. 'Me dad always said you was a nutter.'

'Like hell,' Jane chuckled, pleased that Dex still saw the spark in her.

Climbing through the gap in the fence at the far end of the field, they ran to Patrick's car and climbed in, relieved to have made it so far without being seen. Turning the key in the ignition, Jane cursed under her breath when it spluttered like an old man after a lifetime on Woodbines. She had wanted to use Dex's Jag but Nora had vetoed that again, even though she knew that they were doing this for him. She reckoned he'd forbidden her to let anyone touch it, but Jane knew she was just being selfish because she wanted to keep all of his stuff to herself. Still, Dex would regret letting her keep such a tight grip on his motor because it was going to be a rust bucket by the time he got out if no one had been allowed to maintain it.

'I could kill your nan sometimes,' she muttered after her third unsuccessful attempt.

'Funny, that's what she says about you,' Molly retorted cheekily, reaching into the glove compartment for her mum's cigarettes.

'Light me one, an' all,' Jane told her, finally getting the car started. 'And your nan loves me, for your information.'

'In your dreams,' Molly snorted, passing Jane's cigarette to her. 'She can't stand you.'

'Yeah, well, she'd best get used to me,' Jane muttered, pulling out onto the road and setting off for Nora's house. 'When your dad gets out I'm planning on spending a lot of time round at your nan's. Till I persuade him to come home where he belongs.'

'Behave,' Molly sneered. 'He ain't gonna leave Bitchy-Poo for you.'

'Is that right?' Jane replied, a knowing half-smile on her face. 'Just shows what you know, then, doesn't it? 'Cos me and your dad have never stopped loving each other. He was round my place all the time before he got banged up.'

'Yeah, whatever,' Molly drawled, sure that her mother was making it up. Her dad might well have gone round there for the occasional shag, but that was all it was. Much as Molly and the rest of the family loathed Gaynor and wished that he'd bin her, they'd long ago resigned themselves to the fact that he must have some sort of feelings for her. Though God only knew why. Unless, as Molly was beginning to suspect, he was just using her to keep his business going till he got out.

Driving on in silence, Jane wondered why Molly found it so hard to believe that Dex still found her attractive. All right, she might have exaggerated how often he went round, but he *had* been popping in throughout the whole time he'd been with Miss Frosty Knickers, so he obviously still wanted her. And Gaynor might well suit his craving for a respectable front, but she'd never be able to give Dex what Jane gave him. She wasn't smart enough to survive in his world, for starters. And she definitely wasn't sexy enough to keep him satisfied.

Jane and Dex had history, and no bitch could ever take that away from her. While she might have messed it up by grassing him up and shagging his mate behind his back that time, he knew she'd only done it for revenge because he'd hurt her one time too many. She'd regretted it ever since, but there was no way you came out and laid yourself at Dex Lewis's feet with an admission like that. You had to know how to play the game *his* way, and that meant never admitting you were wrong while leaving the way open for him to come back into your life when he was ready.

And much as Nora professed to hate her, Jane had her number, too. She might be a vicious old bitch, but behind the snarl she had a damn sight more respect for Jane than she would ever have for Gaynor. And she would get used to Jane being around sooner or later. It was just a different kind of game you had to play with that one.

As usual, Nora was in the kitchen when Molly and Jane arrived back. She was on the phone to Dex, who had chanced keeping his mobile in his own cell for the night so that he could find out if things were going according to plan.

Saying, 'Here they are now, son,' she looked up at Jane expectantly. 'How did it go?'

'Like a dream,' Jane told her, pulling the fridge open without asking and helping herself to a bottle of beer.

Nora would usually tear a strip off her for being so cheeky, but she let it go this time. Grinning, she said, 'Hear that, son? They pulled it off, no trouble. You wanna speak to them?'

Flipping the cap off the bottle, Jane grabbed the phone before Molly could get it and said, 'Hiya, babe, were you missing me?' Turning her back now, she giggled and whispered, 'Yeah, me too. And I told you I'd pull it off. I've never let you down, have I?' Tutting softly when he reminded her that she'd let him down plenty of times, she said, 'Yeah, but I'm making up for it now. Anyway, I'll love you and leave you, darlin', 'cos our little girl wants to talk to you.' Blowing him a noisy kiss, she handed the phone to Molly, giving her an *I-told-you-so* smile.

Plonking herself down in a chair, she winked at Nora and said, 'Coming together now, eh, Ma?'

'No thanks to that dozy mare Gaynor,' Nora grumbled, checking her watch. 'She's supposed to be fetching some money round, but she's late, as per.'

'Want me to drive round to the flat and get it off her?' Jane offered, determined to make herself indispensable.

Saying, 'Ta, but you'd best not or his lordship might kick off,' Nora took her cigarettes out of her pinny pocket and tossed one to Jane – a sure sign that she was thawing, at long last.

Finishing the call now, Molly put the phone down and turned to her mother and grandmother with a sneer on her face. 'He says to tell you thanks for coming with me,' she told Jane, pissed off with her for making a show of shoving herself back into the family. Then, to her nan, 'And he says you're to tell the other one to fetch an extra five ton for *her*.'

She jerked her chin towards her mother. 'Only you're not to tell her who it's for.'

Hurt that her own daughter didn't seem to want her to be a part of the Lewis side of the family, Jane's eyes glinted with something indefinable as she swigged her beer straight from the bottle. But who gave a toss what *they* thought? Molly, Nora, Patrick, Jimmy, Jason – they could all go to hell if they thought she wasn't worthy of Dex's love. And as for Gaynor, that bitch better live it up while she could 'cos her reign was coming to an end – if Jane had anything to do with it.

# 19

Tania felt like a prisoner in her own flat during the week after the women had attacked her. She was terrified of them coming back with their rapist friends and killing her, and furious with herself for getting into this position in the first place. If she'd only had a little patience, fate would surely have brought Larry to her door sooner or later. But no . . . she'd had to go wading in like a bull in a crystal factory, trying to force his hand. And now look what had happened.

Two police officers had turned up the morning after to talk to her about the under-age sex claims in the paper, and for a moment Tania had contemplated telling them about the women and begging them to put her into witness protection, or something. But she'd bottled out in the end, because she was terrified that the women would find out that she'd grassed them up. Anyway, she'd known from the way they were talking to her that the officers already didn't believe a word she said, so why would they help her if she came out with something that sounded as preposterous as that?

Too scared to ask for protection, but unable to lie and say that she *had* slept with Larry when she was fifteen because the women had warned her not to until the end of the week, she'd ended up telling the police that she'd made the whole thing up. But then she'd had the worry of wondering what they would do to her when she completely contradicted herself in the papers a week later, claiming that she *had* slept with Larry when she'd been under age, after all. They would

probably lock her up for perverting the course of justice –
and lock Larry up for rape.

Already in a complete state about all of that, it almost
tipped Tania right over the edge when she got the letter from
Larry's solicitor midway through the week, telling her that
she would be sued if she spread any more lies about him,
and that she wasn't to try to contact him ever again. She
totally didn't understand how he could be so cold after everything she'd been through for him. And she wouldn't have
minded, but she hadn't even done the *worst* bit of damage
yet, so he had absolutely no reason to be so horrible.

But if Tania was hurt that Larry had set his solicitor on
her like that, and frustrated that she couldn't get to him to
explain how it had all gone so wrong, she was absolutely
furious that there had been moments during the last few days
when she'd actually considered killing herself to protect him
and it was so obvious now that he didn't give a toss about
her. He still hadn't admitted that she had slept in his flat that
night, or apologised for leaving her to take all the flak. He'd
just had his solicitor send her a nasty letter threatening to
sue her – the bastard!

Screwing up the insulting letter, she'd tossed it into the bin
and had spent the rest of the week veering between regret
that it had turned out like this and anger that Larry had hung
her out to dry again. But Tania's overriding emotion was fear
of what the women would do to her if she didn't do what
they wanted.

Which proved to be justified, she soon discovered, when
an unwelcome visitor broke into her flat on the night before
she was due to go to the papers with her latest story.

Sleeping fitfully, Tania was shocked awake by someone shaking
her shoulder. Opening her eyes with difficulty only to find
that it was still pitch dark, she thought she must have been

dreaming. She was just drifting off again when she got a stinging slap across the face.

Eyes wide now, she was barely able to breathe as she peered up at the shadowy form standing over her.

'You listening?' a man's voice growled, his tone every bit as dark as his face, which was covered by a scarf. Grunting 'Better had be' when Tania nodded, he leaned right over her, saying, 'You remember what you've got to do tomorrow, right? And you know what's gonna happen if you fuck it up?'

Nodding again, Tania squealed with terror when he lowered his face so close to hers that she could feel the heat of his breath through the scarf.

Telling her to button it before he shoved his dick in her gob to shut her up, the man said, 'After you've done what you've been told, you're gonna forget any of this ever happened, 'cos we'll be watching, and if we hear one word about you being forced to lie, you're dead. And we'll find you – no matter where you are. Got that?'

Tears streaming down her cheeks now, Tania nodded again.

'Right,' the man said. 'There's been a change of script. You're still gonna say what you was always gonna say, but now you've got some new shit to add to it. So listen up, 'cos you need to get this dead right . . .'

Unable to go back to sleep after the man had gone, Tania turned all the lights on and checked all the windows and the door to see how he'd got in. More scared than ever when she found no visible signs of a break-in, she bolted the front door and wedged her floor brush between it and the wall, terrified that they had somehow got hold of a key.

Keeping the TV on for the comforting sound of voices for the last few hours before dawn, she was a nervous wreck by the time she went to the phone box and called Sam Brady, asking him to come round immediately, because she had something really important to tell him.

Surprised to hear from Tania again, because he hadn't expected to after her reaction to his last story, Sam said, 'You *are* joking, right? You've already denied half of what you told me last time, so what's the point?'

'I lied to the news people,' Tania told him, sounding desperate as she added, 'but I wasn't lying to you, Sam, I swear it. And now I need to tell you what *really* happened with me and Larry.'

'I'm not sure I can be bothered,' Sam said wearily. 'You're a nice girl, Tania, but you've got yourself so hung up on this bloke, I don't think even *you* know what's what any more.'

'I *do*,' Tania insisted, terrified that the women and their friends would kill her if she couldn't get Sam to listen to her. 'Look, I know you think I'm messing about 'cos I keep changing my story, but it's really important that you listen to me now.'

'Why?' Sam asked, thinking she'd better have a really good reason for him to even *think* about getting involved again. He'd already been questioned by the police, and had voluntarily relinquished the Dictaphone recording of his last interview with her for their inquiries. He wasn't concerned about that, because he knew he'd done nothing for which he could be prosecuted or sued. He'd merely reported what he'd been told, and any judge would be sure to say that he'd acted on a reasonable assumption of truth. But he couldn't risk his reputation by doing yet another piece if she was going to deny it again.

'I can't explain over the phone,' Tania told him now. 'But I need to tell you something I haven't told anyone else. It'll prove that I really did sleep with Larry, and there's no way he'll be able to deny it. *Please*, Sam – you've got to come.'

Intrigued, despite his instincts telling him that he was already perilously close to losing his credibility because of her constantly changing story, Sam agreed to come straight round. The whole thing was getting a bit twisted, even for him, and he wasn't holding out any hope of getting anything spectacularly new or usable from Tania now. But she'd said she had definite proof this time, so he'd have been an idiot not even to check it out. Still, he thought, it had better be really convincing, or there was no way he'd be committing a single word to paper this time.

Stopping off on the way to buy tea bags, milk, biscuits and cigarettes, Sam handed them to Tania when she opened her door. Frowning when he saw how pale she was, and how outright scared she looked as she nervously scanned the corridor behind him, he said, 'Are you all right, sweetheart?'

Nodding quickly, she flapped her hand at him to hurry up and come in, then bolted the door and put the brush back in place.

Really worried now, Sam followed her into her musty-smelling living room and peered at her, saying, 'You're *not* all right, are you? I thought you sounded odd on the phone, but you look terrible. And what's with barricading yourself in?'

Looking on the verge of tears now, Tania shrugged, and said, 'I'm just nervous in case they come back.'

'Who?' Sam asked, his frown deepening when he noticed how badly she was shaking. Taking the groceries off her, he said, 'Right, sit down and have a fag while I make the tea. Then you can tell me what's really going on here.'

Already lighting her second cigarette by the time Sam came back with two cups of tea and handed one to her, Tania drew her knees up to her chest and peered over them at him like a frightened child.

'So, who are you trying to avoid?' Sam asked, cutting straight to the chase.

'I don't know them,' Tania admitted. 'But there were two of them, and they broke in last night while I was in bed.'

'Oh, Jeezus,' Sam muttered. 'Are you all right? Did they do anything to you?'

Shaking her head, Tania said, 'No, they just threatened me.' Pausing now, she inhaled shakily. 'They said if I didn't stop telling people about me and Larry they were going to kill me.'

'Are you sure?' Sam peered at her, wondering if this was yet another lie to add to her growing catalogue.

'Honest,' Tania murmured, biting her lip now as the tears started to trickle down her cheeks. 'It started when I got a letter from his solicitor a few days ago, saying he was going to sue me if I did any more interviews and telling me not to try and contact him again.'

'Have you still got it?'

Nodding, Tania got up and went to fetch it out of the bin.

Uncrumpling it, Sam read it, then shrugged, and said, 'Good news is it's only a letter of intent, to scare you into behaving yourself. I'd keep well away if I was you, though,' he advised her. ''Cos it'd be pretty easy for them to get a restraining order after all the exposure you've had recently from claiming to be in a relationship with him when he's obviously denying it.'

'But he's the liar, not me,' Tania said plaintively.

Feeling sorry for her, because she'd obviously taken a huge knock by seeing it in black and white how little she meant to her hero, Sam said, 'Did those men really break in, Tania, or are you just saying it to get back at Larry for rejecting you? I'd understand if that's what this is all about, sweetheart, and I promise I won't write a thing about it. But I'd rather help you through this than go through a load of bullshit again.'

'It's true,' she told him earnestly. 'And I *want* you to write about it. I want everyone to know what he's really like. I used to think he was fantastic, but now I know he was just using me, and I want him stopped before he does it to anyone else. Please, Sam – you've got to help me.'

Still sure that she was just a hurt little girl seeking revenge, Sam nodded. He reached into his pocket for his Dictaphone, saying, 'Okay, here's what I'll do. I'll tape what you say and take it home and listen to it. And if I think you've got anything significant on him, I'll write about it. But I'm telling you now, there's no mileage in another "he loved and left me" story. You said you had proof, and that's where we'd best start.'

Nodding, Tania waited until he'd switched the recorder on. Then she said, 'Larry's got a birthmark on his . . .' Pausing, she dipped her gaze before murmuring, 'On his thingy. It's right underneath, and you can't see it unless it's – well, you know.'

Guessing that she meant it was only visible when he was erect, Sam felt his interest stepping up a notch. Pretty good evidence of intimacy, if it was true.

'That's my proof that I really did sleep with him,' Tania went on, lighting another cigarette and sucking on it hard. 'Because it's there and he can't get rid of it to say it never was. And now I'll tell you about the *other* stuff.'

'What "other stuff", Tania?' Sam prompted gently when she fell silent.

'He *did* know I was only fifteen,' Tania said quietly. 'And I've been thinking about that a lot lately, and I've realised I wasn't the only one.'

'Are you telling me you know of other young girls he's slept with?'

'No, but I know he's into all that, 'cos he let me use his computer one time, so I could look something up for my homework, and that's when I saw the . . . *stuff*.'

Raising an eyebrow, Sam waited.

Looking thoroughly embarrassed, Tania lowered her gaze and said, 'Kids. I saw pictures of kids on his computer. Dirty pictures . . . with men . . .'

'And did Larry know you'd seen it?'

'Yeah. He freaked and turned the computer straight off. He reckoned they'd come through by accident and he'd just forgotten they were there. But you wouldn't leave something like that on your machine, would you? Not if you thought it was disgusting – and it was, 'cos these were *little* kids.'

Muttering 'Shit!' Sam shook his head. Then he asked, 'Is that everything, Tania?'

Nodding, she said, 'Yeah, but I reckon that's why he's threatening me. I swore on my mum's life I'd never tell, but he must have known how pissed off I'd get if he kept ignoring me. And I'm not a kid any more, so I don't have to stick with stupid promises, do I?'

Sam was stunned. He'd been so sure that she was just lashing out, but this was heavy shit. And it would be easy to prove, because you couldn't erase stuff like that from a computer's internal memory, no matter how hard you tried. If it had ever been there, the police would find it.

'Are you going to write it?' Tania asked him quietly, sounding thoroughly drained – as she actually was. She'd done what the women had ordered her to do, so they wouldn't kill her. But she'd practically killed herself in the process by destroying any last shred of a chance of ever getting Larry to even talk to her again. But oh, well . . . he obviously hadn't had any intention of contacting her anyway, or why would he have sent that nasty solicitor's letter?

'I'll write it,' Sam muttered, switching the Dictaphone off and slotting it back into his pocket. 'But I've got to do something first.' Looking at Tania now, he said, 'You know that when this comes out you might have to go to court and say it all again if there's proof that it's true. Are you up to that? Because you'll get questioned over and over, and they'll try to rip you to pieces and make you out to be a liar.'

Inhaling deeply, a light of pure sadness in her eyes, Tania nodded.

Leaving her, Sam went straight home and made a copy of the recorded conversation with Tania for his own future use. Then he went to the police station and handed the original in. There was no way he was messing with this shit until it had been dealt with properly.

# 20

'Wanna hear the good news?' Gordon chirped, bursting into Larry's dressing room that evening. 'We've just had Robbie's manager on the phone, and they've finally found a window in the tour schedule! He's flying over for next Friday's show, and he's agreed to sing two tracks!'

'Really?' Larry laughed delightedly. 'Wow! That's brilliant.'

Saying, 'Isn't it, though!' Gordon gave a guilty grin when he saw that Larry's shirt was still unbuttoned, showing off his toned chest, and that he only had one leg in his suit trousers. 'Sorry, mate . . . guess I should have knocked, eh?'

Shaking his head amusedly when Gordon backed out of the room with a hand over his eyes, calling back that the warm-up man was just getting started so he had fifteen at the most, Larry finished getting dressed with a lighter heart.

He'd had a shit week, waiting to hear if that stupid bitch Tania had any more tricks up her sleeve. After her last piece of bullshit, he'd had to play hide-and-seek with the paparazzi who'd camped outside his apartment to follow him from there to the studio and back each day – hoping to catch him with another under-age girl, no doubt. It had damn near killed his social life, because there was no way he was risking going to a club while the heat was on. And he'd had to tell Stephanie to stay away, so he hadn't even had sex for a full week and his balls were getting bigger by the day.

Larry really hadn't appreciated having to go with his solicitor Doug for a voluntary interview with the police that first day, either, during which he'd had to come clean and admit that Tania Baxter *had* been in his apartment that night, after all. Feeling like a criminal, even though he knew he'd done nothing wrong, he'd told them exactly what had happened in the morning, and admitted that he *had* asked her not to say anything. But he'd still strenuously denied that anything sexual had occurred between them.

Fortunately, because of Tania's age on that particular occasion, plus the fact that there was no actual evidence to prove that Larry had been involved with her previously as she'd alleged, the police had told him that he was free to go. But not before they'd warned him that they would be interviewing Tania as a matter of course, and that he should expect that they might want to speak with him again at some point, depending what she said.

But the fear of waiting for something else to crop up as a result of that was nothing to the fear he brought on himself when he looked up some erotomania websites on the internet.

He'd never actually heard the word 'erotomania' before Georgie had mentioned it at his solicitor's office that morning. She'd asked Doug if he thought that it might help Larry if they could prove that Tania Baxter was a sufferer, because then they could discredit everything she'd already said, or was likely to say in the future. Intrigued, Larry had gone home that night and looked it up on the internet, and had been shocked by how many people – particularly famous people, like himself – had almost had their lives destroyed by over-obsessive fans. And not just by common-or-garden stalkers but full-on whackos who – like Tania – seemed to think they had a special relationship with the object of their delusional affections and would do anything to get near them – often taking out anyone who got in the way.

Larry had had a couple of sleepless nights after that, listening out for the sounds of crazed female assassins shinning up the side of the building in the middle of the night. But both Georgie and Stephanie had told him to get a grip when he'd started checking his apartment whenever he got home, claiming that a cup had been moved, or a door left ajar when he could have sworn he'd closed it. And, knowing that they were probably right, that he was just freaking out over nothing, he gritted his teeth and struggled on, praying that Doug's letter would do the trick and make Tania Baxter disappear.

And it seemed to have worked, because a full week down the line there hadn't been another peep out of her. And Larry was beginning to feel good again. Not least because he now had definite confirmation that the elusive Mr Williams was coming onto the show at last.

Still on a high about that when he walked out onto the set to do his show fifteen minutes later, his smile was genuine as opposed to the forced grin he'd been wearing all week, as he thanked his packed audience for their continued support.

Blissfully unaware that his words were about to turn right back and bite him on the arse, he said, 'I can't go into detail, folks, but let's just say I've got a good feeling that every-thing's about to work itself out. And I'm touched to my *heart* that you guys had faith in me all along, so thank you all sincerely.'

Bowing his head modestly as loud cheering and whistling erupted around the studio, Larry held up his hands for silence, saying, 'Hey, quit before you get me going. It took my make-up girl three hours to get me looking like I can survive without a drip, and she'll kill me if I ruin it all by crying.' Rolling his eyes now, as if embarrassed to have his vulnerability exposed, he said, 'Anyway, without further ado, let's have a huge *Larry Logan Show* welcome for my first guest of the night . . . the outrageously talented . . . Miss . . . Reece . . . *Witherspoon!*'

★

Outside the studio just then, Ayshia was heading for reception with a worried look on her face. She'd been told that a vanload of police officers had just pulled up out front and, fearing that they'd come as the result of a hoax call, she wanted to make sure that they didn't disrupt proceedings now that the show was on air. Live filming was so much more intense than pre-recorded, and there was only a tiny time-delay available if they had to pull it for any reason.

Approaching a plain-clothes officer who seemed to be in charge when they all trooped in, Ayshia asked if she could help him.

'We're looking for Larry Logan,' he informed her brusquely. 'Can you direct us to him, please?'

'I'm sorry, but he's on set,' Ayshia said. 'And we're already on air, so I'm afraid you'll have to wait.'

'This can't wait,' the officer grunted, waving his men on towards the door she'd come through.

'You can't go in there,' Ayshia protested, a note of panic in her voice now. 'If you disturb them now, they'll have to black-screen, and that will be disastrous.'

'Not my problem,' the plain-clothes man snapped, brushing past her as he followed his men.

Ayshia followed at a trot, feeling helpless. She couldn't ask security to throw them out, and she couldn't even call the police to deal with the intrusion, because they *were* the intruders.

Struck by how amazingly pretty Reece was in the flesh, Larry was just getting into his stride with the flirtatious banter when he heard the sound of raised voices coming from the rear of the auditorium. Sure that it was nothing to worry about, because security would make sure that no one made it all the way onto the floor, he was just about to make a joke about over-zealous fans when a man's voice called out: 'Larry

Logan – I am arresting you for engaging in unlawful sexual acts with a minor, and the possession of indecent images of children . . .'

Feeling as though the sky was crashing down around his ears, Larry shook his head as several uniformed officers surrounded him and handcuffed him in full view of the cameras and the audience – who had gone into a mobile-phone frenzy, ringing everyone they could think of to relay this latest shocking news.

'No, you've got this all wrong!' he protested as the officer finished reading him his rights. 'I never had sex with her. And I never took any pictures of her, so if you've found any she must have planted them on me. Everyone knows she's a nutter. I'm in the process of *suing* her, for Christ's sake! And you lot have already interviewed me, so you must know what's going on.'

'Oh, we know all about it,' the officer told him, pushing him roughly out through the door as Gordon screamed at the cameramen back on set to quit fucking filming. 'But she's only part of this now that we've got all the other shit on you.'

'What are you *talking* about?' Larry gasped, just about managing to duck his head to save it being bashed as he was marched outside and shoved into the back of the police van. 'I haven't done anything wrong!'

'How about all the dirty downloads we found on your computer?' the officer asked, his cold tone and flinty eyes telling Larry exactly what he thought of him – and what he'd like to do to him. 'Think they're normal, do you?'

Frowning deeply and assuming that he was talking about the erotomania articles, Larry said, 'That's research for my case!'

'You sick fuck!' the officer snarled, looking at Larry with contempt now, as if he couldn't believe that he'd actually come out and admitted it just like that. Lowering his voice so that none of the audience members who'd rushed out to take yet more pictures of Larry being arrested could witness it and call it police brutality, he hissed, 'Tell you what, mate, I can't *wait* to see what they do to you when you reach the nick. You're not gonna last a fucking *minute* when they hear what you've been up to. And they *will* hear, 'cos it's gonna be all over the papers again tomorrow. Then everyone's gonna know all about you and your kiddie-porn collection.'

Staring at the door, open-mouthed with shock when the officer slammed it in his face, Larry sat in stunned silence all the way to the police station, only speaking when he got there to verify his name and ask for his solicitor.

He'd truly believed that the worst was over. But the real nightmare was only just beginning.

# 21

Sitting on the other side of the dividing window in the visiting room of the remand wing in Strangeways Prison, where Larry was being held until they had a court date, Georgie said, 'You've lost weight. Please tell me you're not doing anything silly, like going on hunger strike or something.'

Attempting to lighten the atmosphere, because he would break down if he didn't, Larry snorted softly and said, 'I'd defy even a gannet like *you* to eat the shit that passes for food in here. But *no*, I'm not starving myself. I need to keep my strength up to fight this – right?'

'Right,' Georgie murmured, smiling sadly because this was obviously killing him. 'We're all working really hard on our side to get you out,' she told him now. 'I was talking to Doug just before I came in, and he doesn't seem to think you'll have too much to worry about with that stupid girl's testimony, considering she's changed her story so many times already.'

'You reckon?' Larry replied cynically. 'Even though she'd described my birthmark to a T? I can't tell you how much fun it was trying to explain how she knew about *that* when the flaming doctor examined me to verify it was there. And do you think they believed me when I told them she must have been messing about with me when I was unconscious? Did they hell!'

'Mmm, well, it *does* look suspicious if you don't know the whole story,' Georgie conceded. 'But Doug still thinks we might get lucky with that one. It's the other stuff that's going to be tricky.'

'That's another bloody lie,' Larry said tersely, his eyes sparking with frustration and anger. 'I don't know where the hell she got all that shit from, or how it came to be on my computer, but I swear to *God* I've *never* downloaded child porn in my life. I didn't even know you still *could*. I thought they'd clamped down on all that shit ages ago.'

'Yes, well, unfortunately it *can* still be accessed, as we now know,' Georgie replied. 'And because it's recently downloaded, Doug's working on the theory that it might have got through without your knowledge via links from the erotomania websites.' Sighing heavily now, she added, 'He did say that it might be difficult to get a judge to believe it, though, given that it was paid for with your credit card.'

Sickened by the mere thought of what he was being accused of, Larry closed his eyes and shook his head slowly from side to side. Looking up after a moment, his eyes brimming with tears, he said, 'I swear to God it wasn't me, Georgie. I've been set up, but I don't know how to prove it. I just keep going over it all in my head, but it doesn't make any sense. I *know* she must have planted it if she knows that it was there – but it's two years since she was in my place and it's a different computer from the one I had then, so that would be impossible. And how could she have got hold of my credit card? Unless she took my number when I was asleep that night and somehow found my spare door key.'

Wishing that the dividing-window glass wasn't there so that she could give him a hug, because he looked so lost and desperate, Georgie said, 'Stop upsetting yourself, Larry. Doug will make sure that these things are all brought to light, and we'll get to the truth in the end. We all believe you, so now we've got to concentrate on building a defence that the judge and jury will believe.' Pausing, she bit her lip and said, 'Look,

I know you won't like this, but Doug says we need to look at every possible means by which somebody could have gained access to your place without your knowledge. So do you think there's any chance that Stephanie—'

'Don't be ridiculous.' Larry cut her off, his eyes dark and intense. 'You know as well as I do that she wouldn't do something like this to me. Even if she could – which she *couldn't*, because she's never in my apartment without me being there too. No one is. Someone must have broken in while I was out.'

Holding up her hands, Georgie said, 'I know, and I'm sorry for even voicing it, because I know how much Stephanie loves you. But these are the questions the prosecution will be asking if you deny it when you get to court.'

'Of course I'm going to deny it,' Larry snapped. Then, rubbing a hand over his eyes, he said, 'Sorry. But they can ask what they like. I'm innocent, and that will have to come out in the end – won't it?'

Sincerely hoping that justice *would* be done, although she doubted it was going to be anywhere near as easy to prove his innocence in light of the evidence as everyone was trying to make out, Georgie said, 'I'm sure it will, dear.'

Nodding now, when the screw who'd been standing guard at the door told her that her time was up, she stood up and smiled at Larry through the glass, saying, 'I'll be back as soon as I can, Larry. But in the meantime, will you *please* think about what I said the other day, because even Doug agrees that it would be a good time to do it if you're ever going to.'

Nodding, Larry gritted his teeth to keep from bursting into tears as she walked out.

A few minutes later, having been escorted back to his tiny cell in the segregation wing where he was being kept to protect him from the other prisoners who, having heard what he was being charged with, had already threatened to kill him the

first chance they got, Larry lay on his bed as the key turned
noisily in the lock. He thought about what Georgie had said.
And the more he thought about it, the more he thought she
might be right.

Feeling as nervous as a teenager on a first date when Stephanie
came to visit a few days later, Larry leant forward in his seat
and pressed his hands up against the glass. Smiling when she
returned the gesture, he said, 'You look beautiful. But can
you take the shades off? I really want to see your eyes.'

Slipping the dark glasses off, Stephanie folded them and
put them to one side. Then she clasped her hands together
in front of her. Larry looked awful: she felt terrible for him,
because this whole thing was obviously taking a massive toll
on him. But Georgie had told her to try and keep his spirits
up so, forcing herself to smile, she said, 'How are you doing?'

'Not great,' he admitted. Then, shrugging, he said, 'But
hey – I'm not going to be here for ever, am I?'

'God, no,' Stephanie said, sounding much more positive
than she felt. 'You'll be out in no time.'

'And will you still be waiting for me?'

'Of course.'

'Good,' Larry said, taking a deep breath. 'Because there's
something I wanted to ask you . . .'

# PART THREE

# 22

'He's asked me to marry him.'

Raising his eyebrows, Dex gave a soft, incredulous laugh. 'Fucking hell! I didn't expect *that*.'

'Neither did I,' Gaynor murmured, not looking half as happy about it as he obviously was. Shrugging dismissively, she said, 'Well, that's it. I can't go and see him again after this.'

'Don't be stupid,' Dex hissed, lowering his voice and peering at her across the table as if she was crazy.

'I'm not being stupid,' she hissed back. 'It's really hard, having to pretend I've got feelings for him when all I can think about is you.'

'Stop whingeing,' Dex sneered. 'Why's it always got to be about you, eh? I'm doing fifteen fucking years because of that cunt.'

'You're doing fifteen years because you committed a serious crime,' Gaynor reminded him coolly. 'All he did was set you up to get arrested for it.'

Narrowing his eyes, Dex gritted his teeth and said, 'You'd better tell me you ain't defending that cunt. 'Cos I swear to God—'

'Don't be ridiculous,' Gaynor snapped, pursing her lips furiously. 'I wouldn't have gone anywhere near him in the first place if you hadn't made me, so don't you dare try and turn this round.'

'You sure as fuck don't sound to me like you hate him,' Dex snarled, the fires of jealousy leaping in his eyes.

Gaynor was about to say that she'd never said that she *did* hate Larry. But then she thought better of it, because the screws were too far away to reach Dex if he went for her throat. She actually *didn't* hate Larry, but she certainly didn't love him, either. Having spent all these months with him, she'd seen a side to him which few others probably ever saw, and she felt more sorry for him than anything because he was so insecure. She also felt a little bit guilty, she had to admit, for playing such a large part in putting him away for something that he hadn't done. But he *had* screwed Dex over, so she supposed Dex was entitled to his revenge. And, loving Dex as she did, she'd done everything she could to help him in his quest. Not that he seemed to believe it.

Sighing heavily now, she looked at Dex and said, 'You're driving me crazy, Derek Lewis. You know how much I love you, and how much I've hated doing what I've done. But if you're still going to act like this and accuse me of rubbish, it makes me wonder why I bothered.'

Pushing his own lips out now, Dex peered back at her hard, trying to suss out if she meant what she was saying. Because if she did, she ought to be willing to go that one step further, instead of bleating about it.

'I'm very fucking grateful,' he said now, getting a scowl from Gaynor for sounding so facetious. 'But I just don't get why you're bailing out at the winning post, because this is working out way better than we planned. Christ, I only wanted you to get in with him while I figured out a way to get him banged up, so you'd know how to tap into his bank account, and that. But this is perfect, 'cos you'll be able to get at everything if you're his wife. And if he has a little *accident* when he gets put through to the proper block, you'll inherit the lot *and* get the life insurance.'

Peering at him as he went on about the money, Gaynor

shook her head and said, 'You don't get it, do you? I *can't* marry him, because I want to marry you.'

'Yeah, and when it's all over, we will,' Dex said blithely, wondering why birds always had to complicate everything with emotional claptrap.

'I don't want to marry you as a divorcee or a widower,' Gaynor persisted, tears brimming at her eyes again. 'When I get married it's got to be real – and *for ever.*'

Peering at her, Dex shook his head and sucked his teeth. 'You're really pissing me off now, Gay. What the fuck's it matter who got there first, so long as it's me you end up with?'

'It matters to *me*,' Gaynor sobbed, dabbing at the tears which were flowing freely now.

'Fucking Catholics,' Dex sneered, more concerned by the thought of losing out on some easy money than with comforting the soft bitch. 'Always got to do everything by the bleedin' book, haven't you?'

'You're a Catholic, too,' she reminded him tearfully.

'Yeah, right,' he snorted dismissively. 'And when was the last time you caught *me* sniffing round a fucking church? Never, that's when! Anyhow,' he went on, sparking a cigarette and blowing the smoke in her face, knowing full well that she hated that, 'I've already been married, so what difference does it make if you do it an' all? Kind of evens the score, don't you think?'

'It's not the same,' Gaynor muttered, not wanting to think about that. 'That was before you met me.'

'Yeah, well, if it makes you feel any better I'll remarry Jane, then we'll really be evens, won't we? We can have a double, if you want. Me and her, you and him.'

'I can't believe you said that,' Gaynor hissed, the blood completely drained from her face now as she glared at him across the table. 'I always knew you were a bastard, but that's low, even for you.'

'Sit down,' Dex said when she reached for her bag and stood up.

Shaking her head, she said, 'No! I'm going. And I won't be coming back till you've apologised.'

'Sit . . . *down*,' he repeated slowly, his teeth gritted. He glanced quickly around as if checking to see where all the screws were situated.

Seeing that he'd balled his hands into fists and fearing that he just might blow if she didn't, Gaynor did as she was told. Folding her arms, she flopped down onto the chair.

'Right, let's get something straight, you dozy cow,' Dex said, peering intensely back at her. 'I only said that about Jane to wind you up 'cos I'm sick with fucking jealousy about you and that cunt. But now he's locked up there'll be no more funny business, so it'll be easier. All you've got to do is drop the holier-than-thou bullshit and marry the twat, and that's us made for life. I love the tits off you, and I thought you loved me, but if you can't do this one last thing I guess you're not as committed as you made out.'

'That's not fair,' Gaynor muttered. 'I love you more than I've ever loved anyone in my life.'

'So prove it,' Dex said, pleased with himself for manipulating her into seeing things his way just by giving it to her in the kind of soppy words she understood.

Sighing resignedly, she said, 'How are we supposed to explain it to your family?'

'What's it got to do with them?' Dex said dismissively. 'Anyhow, they haven't sussed you out so far, have they?'

'No, but it'll be a bit harder to hide once I'm Mrs Larry bloody Logan. He *is* kind of famous, in case you'd forgotten.'

'And he'll also be a convicted paedophile any day now,' Dex reminded her. 'So I hardly think *Hello!* magazine's gonna be in any rush to buy the wedding pictures, do you?'

'No, I suppose not.'

'There you go, then,' Dex said, slapping his hand palm down on the table. 'Just do what you've got to do, then carry on as you have been all along. If you're smart, no one will ever know. And you *are* smart, I've got to give you that. 'Cos I'm fucked if I thought you'd ever pull this off as good as getting him to marry you.'

'Okay, I'll do it,' Gaynor said reluctantly. 'But you'd best tell your family what's going on – I'm not having them calling me a traitor when they find out, just because they think I went behind your back with the bloke who had you put away.'

'The less they know the better,' Dex said quietly. 'And trust me, they ain't *gonna* find out – so long as you don't fuck it up.'

'I won't,' Gaynor murmured, feeling tearful again as she looked at his handsome face.

She would never in a million years have expected him to give her his blessing to marry another man, and she actually felt a bit betrayed that he was willing to sacrifice her dreams for money and revenge. But she supposed she just had to accept that he wasn't the sentimental kind, and that this was nothing more than a business deal to him. And at least he'd finally said that he *would* marry her, instead of skirting round the houses like he usually did.

So, yes, she would do this last thing for him. But God help him if he forgot his promise when he finally got out.

# 23

Larry looked worse than ever when he stood beside Stephanie in front of the visiting registrar three weeks later. He had a nasty scab on his cheek, which he claimed was the result of a shaving cut, although Stephanie, Georgie and Doug very much doubted that because they all thought it looked a little big for a simple razor nick. And the suit that Georgie had brought in was hanging off him because he'd lost so much weight. But at least he was smiling, which made them all feel a bit better, because he'd been sinking lately and they were afraid that he might be becoming depressed.

Saying, 'I will,' when the registrar asked if he, Larry Logan, took Gaynor Stephanie Lloyd to be his lawful wedded wife, he turned to her and smiled lovingly when she was asked the corresponding question.

Murmuring, 'I will,' she swallowed hard to keep herself from bursting into tears, her gaze focussing anywhere but on Larry because she just couldn't bear to look at him. Although the view she was confronted with instead did nothing to make her feel any better; just this awful starkly furnished room, with gloss green walls and one filthy heavily barred window.

Signing the register when it was all over, Larry held her in his arms and kissed her, whispering, 'You look beautiful, Mrs Logan.'

Smiling sadly, Stephanie averted her gaze again, unable to muster the energy to return the compliment. She knew she looked lovely in her cream silk dress and jacket, with her hair tied in a French pleat and her make-up immaculate. But this was not how she'd envisaged her wedding day, and that was upsetting her more than she'd imagined it would now that she'd gone through with it.

She'd always dreamed of the full white gown and veil, with her family on one side of the church and her groom's on the other, all joining together as one at the lavish reception afterwards. Not that her family would have come, knowing that her dream groom was a man they loathed. And Dex's family would only have come under sufferance. But it had been her dream nonetheless, and now she'd trashed it by exchanging meaningless vows in a horrible prison room, with a man she didn't love and right now actually resented.

Thanking her for believing in him and standing by him in his hour of need, Larry turned to his solicitor and rubbed his hands together, saying, 'Have you got the paperwork?'

'Yes, it's all here,' Doug said, taking a sheaf of papers out of his briefcase and laying them on the table. Looking Larry straight in the eye, letting him know that this was the time to pull out if he was going to, he said, 'Absolutely sure about this?'

'Positive,' Larry said, sitting down and smiling up at Stephanie, who was looking down at the small posy of cream roses she was holding as if they were riddled with greenfly. 'She's the one who's got to live there, so she needs to know she's secure until we know when I'm getting out of here. Not too long now with any luck, though, eh?'

Saying, 'Absolutely. Any day,' Doug exchanged a hooded glance with Georgie. Things were nowhere near as positive as Larry seemed to imagine, and Doug was struggling to build any kind of plausible defence against the overwhelming weight of evidence against his client.

In truth, Doug knew that, based on the evidence alone, even *he* would have been hard pushed not to think that Larry was as guilty as sin, and if it hadn't been for Georgie's passionate conviction to the contrary he might well have written him off a long time ago. But the judge wouldn't have the benefit of Georgie's unswerving belief to sway him, and Doug truly didn't hold out any hope of Larry getting an easy ride of it once it reached court. In fact, Larry was looking at a pretty hefty sentence, in Doug's professional opinion.

Looking lovely in her powder-blue suit, with her unruly grey hair tamed into a chignon, and a rare coat of pink lipstick, Georgie was well aware of Doug's opinions, because they were pretty much the same as her own concerning the probable outcome of Larry's case. But she was grateful to Doug for maintaining a confidence he obviously didn't feel, because that allowed her to keep her own negative thoughts at bay.

Acting as witness now when Larry signed his apartment and control of his bank accounts and various other financial interests over to Stephanie, she pushed all thought of his case aside and struggled to quash her misgivings about the matter at hand. She'd tried to talk Larry out of doing this when he had first proposed it, fearing that he was making rash decisions which might adversely affect his future should anything go wrong with Stephanie. He'd been adamant that it was what he wanted to do, so she'd had to accept it in the end, but she was still nervous about it.

Signing the forms now, she sighed, trying to convince herself that it wasn't such a bad thing. Negative instincts aside, Stephanie obviously loved Larry dearly to stand by him like this in his hour of need. And Georgie had to admit that she wasn't like any other woman he'd ever dated, because she'd never once tried to wheedle money out of him or use his fame to further herself. And as Larry had said, who better to make sure that he still had something to come out to than his lovely, legal wife.

★

Hustling Stephanie straight into her car after the short soul-less ceremony, keeping a keen eye out in case any paparazzi had got wind of the proceedings, Georgie waited until the new Mrs Logan had covered herself with the blanket they'd brought along for the occasion, then set off.

'You can come out now,' she said after a while, when they were completely clear of the prison and she was sure that no vehicles were following. Smiling at Stephanie when she uncov-ered herself and pulled the sunshade down to repair her hair in the vanity mirror, she said, 'That went as well as could be expected, didn't it?'

'Mmm,' Stephanie murmured, not looking half as happy as Georgie would have expected her to, given that she was now the proud wearer of Larry Logan's rather impressive platinum and enormous-diamond wedding-cum-engagement ring.

Sensing that Stephanie was just sad because she'd had to leave her new husband behind so soon after exchanging her vows, and that she wasn't looking forward to the lonely honey-moon period she was facing, Georgie said, 'Don't worry, dear. Doug's determined to get him as light a sentence as possible, so, fingers crossed, you'll be back together before too long.'

'Hope so,' Stephanie said, gazing out of the window.

Looking at her as she sighed and gazed the next couple of miles away, Georgie clutched for something to talk about because the silence was pressing in on her. Clearing her throat after a while, she said, 'Can I ask why you don't use your real name, dear?'

'It *is* my real name,' Stephanie told her, folding her arms as if she really didn't want to talk about this. 'Well, my middle name, anyway. I just don't like Gaynor all that much.'

'Your mother obviously preferred it,' Georgie said. Then, afraid that she'd offended her when she saw Stephanie's jaw clench ever so slightly, she said, 'Sorry, my love. I'm just too nosy for my own good sometimes. You're entitled to call your-self whatever you like.'

'I know,' Stephanie muttered, turning her face even more towards the window so that Georgie wouldn't see the tears that were clouding her eyes again.

Gaynor was her name when she was living her *real* life, as Dex Lewis's woman. But Stephanie was the insignificant part of herself which she had given to Larry Logan. And that was how it would stay until this was all over. And the sooner it came to an end the better, because she felt sick inside knowing that she was someone else's wife. And it might have been Dex's idea, but it still felt like she'd betrayed him in the worst possible way.

She just thanked God that the press hadn't caught on, because there was no way she could handle the shame of other people finding out what she'd done.

# 24

Nora was woken by loud, continuous knocking on the front door below, interspersed with annoying blasts on the bell, which echoed through the hall and up the stairs and curled itself around her head until her eyes popped open.

Yelling, 'For fuck's sake, pack it in, whoever you are!' she shoved her quilt aside and dropped her feet down to the floor. Sliding them into her slippers, she winced as she stood up and hobbled across the room to get her dressing gown off the hook on the back of the door.

Molly was just coming out of hers and Lyla's room when she reached the landing. Brushing past her, Nora said, 'Shut that flaming door, before she wakes up an' all.'

Grumbling her way down the stairs then, she grumbled some more as she struggled to slide the heavy bolts back. Then she yanked the door open, snarling, 'Don't you bloody dare!' when she caught Jane raising her hand to ring the bell again. 'You could hear me unlocking it, so why couldn't you just bloody wait like any normal person?'

'This can't wait,' Jane said, brushing past her into the hall and pushing the door shut. Grabbing Nora's arm, she shoved a newspaper under her nose. 'Look!'

Wrenching her arm out of Jane's grip, Nora headed for the kitchen, muttering, 'What's the point of telling me to bloody look when you can see I ain't got me flaming glasses on?'

'Where are they?' Jane asked, rushing after her. 'Are they in your bedroom? I'll get them for you.'

'Belt up, for gawd's sake,' Nora snapped, reaching for the kettle. Then, as if she was talking to someone else, she said, 'First she wakes me up in the middle of the flaming night by trying to hammer me flaming door down. Then she's after going into me bedroom. Liberty, that's what she is . . . a flaming liberty merchant.'

'Nora, just quit fucking moaning and get your fucking *glasses*!' Jane yelled, losing patience. 'You need to see this picture!'

Coming into the room just then, Molly glared at her mother and said, 'What you doing round here so early? Not like you to crawl out of bed before teatime.'

Snatching up the newspaper which Nora had tossed onto the table, Jane thrust it into her daughter's face, and said, 'Look at that, and tell me what you see.'

Narrowing her eyes, Molly looked at the picture on the front page. It was really grainy, and she couldn't make it out properly. But there was no mistaking the headline.

'Larry Logan's got fucking married!' she squawked, her young voice filled with indignation.

Barking, 'Mind your language, you!' Nora pulled her glasses out of her pocket where they'd been all along and shoved them on. Snatching the paper out of Molly's hand now, she looked at it and said, 'Well, the cheeky bloody bastard! And look at him grinning his flaming head off like butter wouldn't bloody melt, and all the time he's been fiddling with kids! They shouldn't have allowed it! I'm gonna make a flaming complaint about this, you watch!'

'Shut up spouting off, and look who he's *with*,' Jane said, leaning over both of their shoulders now and jabbing a finger down on the bride's partially hidden face.

Bringing the paper up close to her own face, squinting her eyes, Nora peered at the face. Then she literally staggered back against Jane, spluttering, 'Holy Mary, Mother of God! I don't fucking believe it!'

'What?' Molly asked, looking at her nan and mother as they stared at each other, both shaking their heads. 'Who is it? What's going on?'

Flopping down onto her chair at the table, Nora lit a cigarette with shaking hands, and said, 'It's that bloody Gaynor, that's who.'

'Don't lie!' Molly scoffed, reaching for the paper to see for herself, sure that they were imagining things. It took her a few seconds, but when she saw it she said, 'Fucking hell! It *is* her, an' all!'

'Didn't I just tell you that?' Nora snapped, giving her granddaughter a hefty whack on the arm. 'Now quit shouting before you wake Lyla up, and get them brews made while me and your mam figure out what to do about it.'

'No figuring out to be done,' Molly snarled, her eyes flashing with hatred and thoughts of revenge as she stomped across to the cupboard and dragged three cups out. 'I'm gonna smash her fucking face in!'

'If I have to tell you one more time about your language,' Nora warned her, 'it'll be me smashing *your* face in!' Shaking her head now, she turned to Jane, and said, 'No wonder you sent her packing, if this is how she carries on in front of you.'

'Nowt to do with me,' Jane retorted indignantly. 'It's you lot who've brought her up, so it's down to you if she swears like a docker.'

'Like bloody hell!' Nora snorted.

'Shut up, the pair of you,' Molly snapped, folding her arms and glaring at them. 'I'm nearly sixteen, for God's sake. I can talk how I like.'

Narrowing her eyes, Nora said, 'You'd best not let your dad hear you talking to me like this, lady, 'cos nearly sixteen or not, he'll kick the crap right out of you!'

'Can we just stop arguing and get back to the important thing,' Jane suggested, sensing that they were going to get nowhere if they carried on like this. 'We need to decide what we're going to do about this before Dex gets the shock of his life.'

'Mmm,' Nora murmured grudgingly, a worried frown creasing her already furrowed brow. 'I suppose we're going to have to tell him. But he ain't gonna like it, and I dread to think what'll happen if he kicks off. They're always looking for an excuse to put him in solitary and give him a beating, them screws.'

'Well, he's gonna kick off either way,' Jane said quietly. 'We all know that. Least if we tell him, we can break it to him gently.'

Nodding her agreement, Nora looked up when Molly brought the teas to the table, saying, 'Ta, pet. You're a good girl.'

Sitting down, Molly reached for her nan's cigarettes and slid one out of the pack. Lighting it, she said, 'I reckon he's better off without the slag, and we should go round there and beat the living shit out of her – make sure she don't get any ideas about blagging him that it wasn't her, or anything. 'Cos you know what me dad's like. He'll probably believe her.'

Eyes narrowed and glinting with hatred, Nora said, 'Oi, you! I hope that ain't the lighter Logan give you what I just saw you using. 'Cos if you're still hanging on to that after everything that's happened, you're no granddaughter of mine, and that's a fact!'

Blushing, because she hadn't meant to take it out in front of her nan, Molly put it down on the table as if it had burned her, and said, 'Shit! I'd forgot he give it to me.' It was a lie, because she'd never wanted to get rid of it. But how was she supposed to explain to her vengeful family that, much as she hated Larry, she still felt perversely proud to own something that had once belonged to a famous person? She'd kept it hidden for so long, but now she'd lost it through her own stupidity.

Picking it up now, Nora pocketed it, saying, 'Yeah, well, think on next time, 'cos your dad would have had a fit if he'd caught you with that.

'Will you shut up about that, and get back to this,' Jane said, slapping her hand down on the picture of her rival as if slapping her in her actual face. 'What we gonna do about it?'

'I don't get it,' Nora murmured thoughtfully, gazing down at it. 'She wasn't even here when Logan come round that day, so how did she meet him to end up marrying him?'

'You know what a slag she is,' Molly sneered, flicking her ash agitatedly. 'She's always out since me dad got banged up, and she's always tarting herself up, an' all. She probably bumped into him at some club when she was looking for men to shag.'

'You could be right,' Jane agreed, pursing her lips as she mulled it over. 'But it doesn't make sense that she'd go for *him*, though. I mean, she must have known who he was and what he did to your dad, so wouldn't she have told him to sling it?'

'Well, I wouldn't have thought she was the kind to go with his enemies behind his back,' Nora said. She gave Jane a pointed look as she added, 'That's more your line, that,' letting her know that she'd neither forgotten nor forgiven her for shagging Dex's mate behind his back that time.

Eyes glinting with irritation, Jane said, 'He knows why I did that, and so do you, so get off your high horse. It was revenge for what he did to me.'

'And this might be *her* revenge,' Molly chipped in, giving her mother a defiant look. 'She must have found out about you and me dad, eh?'

Looking from Molly to Jane, Nora said, 'Oh, don't tell me you and him have been at it again?'

'Never stopped, according to her,' Molly said.

'Well, how come I never heard nowt about it?' Nora demanded. 'Dex tells me everything.'

'Apparently not,' Molly muttered smugly.

'All right, pack it in,' Jane snapped. 'Me and Dex have been seeing each other, Nora, yeah . . . and there's nowt you can do about it, so you might as well quit worrying. You know I never stopped loving the idiot, so I don't see why you're so surprised. And even *you*'ve got to admit I'm better for him that that treacherous slag.'

Nora wasn't happy about this latest revelation at all – but, as Jane had said, there was nothing she could do about it. Not right now, anyway. But she'd have a damn good go when she got her hands on that bloody son of hers!

'So, are we agreed?' Molly said now. 'We're gonna get the bitch and give her a kicking?'

Sighing heavily, Nora nodded. 'Yeah. It's what she deserves, I suppose.'

'No "suppose" about it,' Jane muttered. 'She's gone too far this time, and the Lewises have got to show her what's what.'

Gaynor was still sleeping when Molly used her key to let herself, her nan, and her mother into the flat an hour later. Georgie had dropped her at Larry's place straight from the prison yesterday, but she'd had no intention of staying there. Waiting until the nosy bitch had gone, she'd called a cab and had it bring her home, where she had spent the entire night sobbing into Dex's pillow.

Exhausted now, having finally cried herself to sleep just a couple of hours earlier, she thought she was dreaming when she felt a violent punch in her stomach. But then the pain hit, and she knew it was real. Opening her eyes to find the three Lewis women standing over her, their faces wreathed in hatred as they smashed their fists down on her head and body, Gaynor could do nothing but try to protect her face as the blows rained down on her. Afraid that they were going to carry on until she was dead, she closed her eyes and prayed to God to make it quick.

Then, as suddenly as it had started, it stopped, and Nora yelled, 'Look at me, you bitch!'

Afraid that they would start hitting her again if she didn't, Gaynor forced her eyes open and looked up at them fearfully.

'What have you got to say for yourself?' Nora demanded, pulling the by now tatty newspaper out of her pocket and flapping it open to show Gaynor the proof of her betrayal.

Groaning, Gaynor opened her mouth to explain, but coughed instead as blood trickled down her throat.

'Don't you try and get out of this by fucking choking yourself!' Jane snarled, grabbing her by the front of her pyjama top and hauling her into a sitting position. Tossing her back against the headboard then, she wiped her hands on her jeans as if they were dirty, and said, 'You've got a fucking cheek lying here in my Dex's bed after what you've done to him!'

'I'm not trying to get out of anything,' Gaynor croaked, slurring over her words as her lip swelled painfully. 'And Dex knows about it. It was his idea.'

'Don't make me laugh!' Nora snorted disbelievingly. 'My Derek would never put up with something disgusting like this! You know what he did to her when she did him over like that,' she said, jerking a thumb in Jane's direction. 'Anyhow, he's banged up, so how the hell's he gonna know about you and your bloody fancy man?'

'I swear!' Gaynor yelped, wincing as Molly raised a hand to hit her again. 'He planned it from the start. Almost as soon as he got banged up, he started thinking up ways to get back at Logan—'

'Isn't that *Larry, baby* to you?' Molly mocked.

'I've never had any feelings for him,' Gaynor muttered, resenting Dex for putting her in the position of having to explain herself to his bitch brat of a daughter. 'And I didn't want to do it, but Dex begged me to.'

'Why?' Nora peered down at her questioningly. 'It doesn't make sense. What could he possibly gain out of doing something like this?'

Careful not to mention the money, because she knew they'd be all over her in a flash if they thought they could get their hands on it, Gaynor said, 'Revenge. If I could get Logan to trust me, I'd have access to his flat, and that made it easy to do all that stuff with his computer.'

Slapping Molly out of the way when she leaned forward to ask how long it had been going on, Nora frowned as she struggled to put the pieces in place.

'So, he sent you to get off with Logan? And then encouraged you to sleep with him, just so's you could get at his computer?' Nora murmured, wondering how all of this could have happened without Dex telling her a single thing. 'And what about that girl?' she asked now. 'Was that all his doing from the start, an' all?'

'No.' Gaynor shook her head, wondering how Nora could be so stupid as to ask something like that when she already knew that Tania had met Larry way before he met Dex. 'She just popped back up and started trying to get to Logan,' she explained now. 'But he didn't remember her, so she must have got mad and tried to make him look bad by saying she'd been under age when it started. But it wasn't true.'

'Oh, yeah, and how would *you* know?' Molly spat.

'I just do,' Gaynor replied coolly, not wanting to appear to be defending Larry by explaining how she'd seen him tear himself up about it. And not wanting to let them think that she had had feelings for him by telling them that she knew him well enough by now to know that he simply wasn't capable of what he'd been accused of.

'So, when he had me and Molly batter that girl,' Jane chipped in – not noticing the glint in Gaynor's eye at the mention of Dex having spoken to her recently – 'he'd already had you working on the kiddie-porn shit at Logan's place?'

Hissing 'No' between her teeth, Gaynor made a determined effort to keep a lid on the rage which was flaring in her bruised gut.

'So how did he manage it, then?' Nora asked confusedly.

'He had Mark break in when Logan was out,' Gaynor told her. 'But Dex didn't tell me how he was going to do it, because he didn't want me involved in that bit so I couldn't get dragged into it if it went wrong.'

'More like he knew you'd fuck it up,' Jane sneered. 'That's why he came to *me* to sort the girl out.'

'And me,' Molly reminded her, refusing to let her mother take all the credit.

'Okay, I get all that,' Nora said quietly, still mulling it over. 'But I totally don't get why he wanted you to marry the bastard. Surely it was enough to get him banged up, so he'd be able to get at him?'

'Probably wanted to get her married off so he'd be free of the silly bitch when he got out,' Jane said, smiling down at Gaynor nastily as she saw her words hit home like poisoned darts. 'We all know how bleedin' clingy she is, don't we, Mam? He was only saying it the last time we went on a visit, wasn't he – how he can't stand the way she talks like she's posher than the rest of us, and can't stand to see her preening herself like she's something special.'

'You're lying,' Gaynor croaked, tears spilling down her cheeks now. 'Dex loves me.'

'Sure he does, darlin',' Jane spat back. 'That's why he's still been coming round to my place the whole time he's been with you, eh? God, it must *kill* you to know he still prefers me.'

Listening to her mother gloating, Molly began to feel uneasy. It might well be true what her mum was saying, but her dad must have had his reasons for keeping it from Gaynor, and she guessed that it had something to do with this plan of his. Gaynor was obviously crucial to its success, so it would be disastrous if her mum ruined it all now by making Gaynor pull out.

That in mind, she gave her mother a sharp dig in the ribs with her elbow and said, 'Right, shut it, Mam! You know I can't stand this bitch, but I'm not having you lie about me dad like that.'

'You what?' Jane spluttered.

'You heard,' Molly said, jutting her chin out and flashing her eyes at her mother, trying to warn her to go with her on this. 'He got shut of you years ago and told me himself that he'd never go back to you,' she went on, 'so quit making out like you've got something going with him, 'cos you haven't, and it's pissing me off. I lived with you for long enough, so I think I'd know if he was coming round or not, and he wasn't – not once!'

Nostrils flaring with fury, Jane glared at her daughter. But she didn't retaliate as she'd have liked to. Molly must have her reasons for saying what she was saying in front of the bitch but, by God, she was going to get a slap round the face for it when they got out of here.

'I'm going home,' Nora said suddenly, feeling faint from her exertions. Age was no longer creeping up on her, it was hitching a lift on her back and riding her like a mule, kicking the shit out of her every step of the way. Looking down at Gaynor again now, she said, 'You got a visit coming up?'

Nodding, Gaynor said, 'Tomorrow.'

'Right. Well, don't you say a bleedin' word about none of this, or you'll get more of the same. Understood?'

'Be a bit hard to hide, won't it?' Gaynor said cynically, all too aware that she must look a mess, because she could already feel how big her lip was, and one of her eyes was slowly closing.

'You can tell him one of your new hubby's fans jumped you,' Molly said sarcastically.

Telling her to button it, Nora said, 'Dex has been working on this for too long for us to wade in and screw it up now. He'll tell me what he's up to in his own good time, but till then I don't want no one saying nothing to him. Everyone got that?' Jerking her head at Jane and Molly when everyone agreed, she said, 'Come on, you two. I need to get home and make sure our Lyla's all right.'

Waiting until she'd heard the front door close behind them, Gaynor gingerly eased the quilt back and hobbled into the bathroom to survey the damage. Standing in front of the mirror, she groaned. She looked a mess, all right, although it wasn't quite as bad as she'd imagined. Her lip would prob- ably go down a fair bit overnight, but her eyes would be badly bruised for a while. Fortunately, most of the bruising was on her body, so it would be hidden by her clothes. But it was going to hurt like hell to move around for a week or so.

But the physical pain was nothing compared with the emotional pain she was suffering right now. She'd excused Dex's lack of sensitivity for so long, putting it down to him being a man – and one dragged up by the emotionally void witch that was Nora, at that. But if Jane was telling the truth he'd been lying to her all along, and she just couldn't bear that. Although it would certainly explain why he'd been so blasé about her marrying Larry.

But why should she believe Jane, when all of the Lewises

from the time Dex first took her home to meet them had done nothing but slag the woman off? And Molly had actually called her mother a liar to her face, and she certainly wouldn't have done that to defend Gaynor because she'd never made any secret of the fact that she hated her guts. But had she only done that to cover for Dex? Because *he* obviously didn't want Gaynor to know, or he'd have told her by now. And Molly would defend her dad no matter what, even if she had to humiliate her own mother in the process.

There was something not quite right about all of this, but Gaynor just couldn't put her finger on it. And there was no way she could ask Dex, because then he'd know that his mother and the other two had been hassling her. And Nora had already warned her what would happen if she did that.

It was going to be really hard to face Dex tomorrow with all of this going through her mind. But she couldn't not go, because he'd go crazy. Gaynor desperately didn't want to think that he'd been using her all along, but she would have to wait and see what her instincts told her tomorrow.

'What the bloody hell was all that about?' Jane demanded, crunching Patrick's car into gear and pulling away from the kerb with a squeal of tyres. 'Me own fucking daughter, talking to me like that in front of that stuck-up bitch!'

'Are you thick?' the girl retorted, knowing that she could say what she liked because her mum couldn't reach her while Molly was sat in the back. 'That stupid cow is doing something for me dad, and you could have messed it up with your bleedin' bragging.'

'It's time she knew the score,' Jane muttered, still bristling. 'She'll know soon enough when he gets out and runs to me instead of her.'

'Over my dead body,' Nora interjected, lighting a cigarette

without offering them round. 'He'll be coming to his mam before he comes to either of you two, and that's a fact.'

'He might come to you for your cooking, Nora,' Jane sniped. 'But you're no use to him in the other department, are you? And I'll kill that bitch with my bare hands if I have to, because I'm sick of her lording it up in his flat, splashing his money around like the queen bloody bee. I've given Dex chance after chance, but if he doesn't make up his mind once and for all when he gets out I'll make it up for him and get rid of her.'

'Oh, behave,' Molly snorted. 'If you start scrapping over him, he'll just sack the pair of you off and find some other tart. He's probably already got someone lined up waiting, knowing him.'

'You don't know your dad like I do,' Jane said unconcernedly. 'He'll be stringing Frosty Knickers along till she's done what needs doing, then it'll be "See ya, wouldn't wanna be ya" time.'

'And you and him will head off into the sunset and live happy ever after?' Molly sneered. 'Yeah, right!'

'You two are giving me a flaming migraine,' Nora grumbled, wishing she'd thought to pick up her painkillers on the way out. 'I just want to get home and have a brew, and think this out.'

'Do you think she'll tell me dad what we did?' Molly asked, sounding a bit worried now.

'Not if she's got any sense,' Nora replied. 'Whatever my Dex is up to, he's given her a job to do and she ain't gonna want to admit she screwed it up, is she?'

'He'll know soon enough when he sees that picture in the paper,' Jane reminded them.

'Weren't you listening, you thick bitch?' Nora snapped. 'That was *his* idea. He already knows.'

'Yeah, I know that,' Jane snapped back. 'I mean, if he's kept this from us lot for a reason he'll realise that we know, 'cos we're bound to have seen it.'

Shaking her head, Nora said, 'Not necessarily. Not if we don't mention it. He'll assume we didn't recognise her. It didn't mention her name, did it?'

'No, I don't think so.'

'Well, there you go, then. We all keep schtum, and it'll be old news by tomorrow. Soon as Dex is ready, he'll tell us what he's up to. But till then, I reckon we should back off from the funny one, 'cos I've got a feeling we nearly messed it all up back there.'

'That's what *I* said,' Molly piped up indignantly. 'So how come I got told to button it?'

''Cos you're a kid, and should know better than to interfere when the grown-ups are talking,' Nora told her, sucking on her cigarette and going into an immediate coughing fit – tutting when she'd eventually recovered, because neither Jane nor Molly had lifted a hand to pat her on the back.

# 25

'Jeezus, what happened to *you*?' Dex asked, peering at Gaynor's face with concern as she sat down carefully in the chair across the table from him the next day.

'I got jumped,' she told him, glancing nervously around to see if anyone was looking at her. Fortunately, nobody was, because they were all too busy chatting to their own loved ones.

'By who?' Dex growled, thinking she was going to tell him that it was one of the guys she was dealing to in his absence. If it was, there would be no warnings for the cunt, just instant death as soon as Dex got back to his cell to arrange it over the mobile.

'One of Larry's fans,' Gaynor told him quietly, mentally thanking Molly for giving her a perfectly feasible explana-tion. 'I take it you saw yesterday's paper?'

'Yeah, but you can't tell it's you in the picture. I wouldn't have recognised you in a million years, and you're my bird.'

'Well, someone obviously did. And she wasn't very pleased about it, as you can see.'

'Fucking bitch,' Dex muttered angrily. Then, 'My mam didn't recognise you an' all, did she?'

'Obviously not, or she'd have probably beaten the girl off to get at me herself,' Gaynor lied. Pausing then, she tapped her nails on the table top before saying, 'Can I ask why you're so desperate for her not to know about this, Dex? I thought you told her everything, so why all the secrecy?'

'I've already told you,' he replied irritably. ''Cos I don't want them sticking their noses in and messing it up. You know what me mam's like for gossiping. All she'd have to do is let it slip to that Hilda, and the next thing you know the police will be all over us for setting Logan up. Soon as we're in the clear with the money, I'll tell them – if that's what you want,' he said then, grinning as he added, 'Who knows, it might even make them respect you a bit more if they see what you were willing to do to help me get revenge.'

'Yeah, whatever,' Gaynor said flatly, knowing full well that there was no way she was ever going to get respect from Dex's family, no matter what she did. He could fool himself if he liked, but she wouldn't be letting her guard down any time soon.

Reaching for her hand now, Dex curled his huge fingers around hers and said, 'Hey, I had a bit of good news this morning. They've given me the go-ahead for an appeal, and my brief reckons she could get up to half me original sentence hacked off because of the entrapment shit. And she's raising the issue of reasonable doubt about the DNA evidence on the rape an' all, 'cos it could just as easy be our Pat as me. Anyway, take time served off that, and add good behaviour, and she reckons I could be looking to be out in three to four.'

'Really?' Gaynor gasped, her eyes lighting up at the prospect. 'That would be fantastic.'

Wincing as he looked at her, Dex said, 'Whoa! Don't smile that much, babe – that lip looks like it might split.'

'I don't care,' Gaynor said happily, the news that he might be back in her arms much sooner than anticipated eclipsing the pain – *and* the suspicions that had been eating away at her. 'I just want you home, and if it's that much faster than we thought I can put up with any amount of pain.'

'Only if the appeal comes off,' Dex reminded her, not wanting her to get too carried away, because then *he* might get carried away, and it would feel like double shit if his appeal failed.

'Do you love me?' Gaynor asked suddenly, holding his gaze across the table.

A flicker of a bemused frown twitching his brow, Dex said, ''Course. Why?'

'Just wanted to hear it,' Gaynor murmured, relieved because he'd answered without having to think about it. And his eyes hadn't so much as flickered away from hers, so he'd obviously been telling the truth. Whatever game his slut of an ex was playing, Dex had just told Gaynor everything she needed to know.

'You all right?' Dex asked, sensing that she wasn't quite herself today.

'Me?' Gaynor said, still smiling. 'I'm absolutely fine, thanks. How about you?'

Grunting amusedly, Dex said, 'Not too bad, considering me missus just got hitched to another bloke. How was the honeymoon, by the way?'

'Solitary, and filled with thoughts of the man I love,' she purred, feeling her heart melt as Dex gazed at her with that certain twinkle in his eye.

'Good job, too.' He grinned, knowing full well that she was talking about him. Then, 'So, have you checked the bank accounts yet?'

Jerked out of the misty moment and deposited back in the here and now with a bang, Gaynor frowned.

'Bloody hell, Dex, I only married him yesterday. And then I got jumped, so it would have been kind of difficult to toddle off to the bank and say oh, excuse me, I want to draw all of my new husband's money out in one lump sum, please.'

'Obviously not,' Dex said, chuckling softly. 'But you can always check it out on-line, can't you? See exactly what kind of amounts we're looking at. There's a guy in here who used to work for a bank and he reckons it's dead easy. You can even move all the money out of one account and into another without talking to a single person or filling out a single form. You've just got to have all the right numbers and passwords – and Mark can hack into all that shit, so that won't be a problem. He'll just need you to pass on the account details.'

'Are you *crazy*?' Gaynor said, drawing her head back and squinting at him. 'There's no *way* I'd trust Mark with all those details. He'd have the lot out of Larry's account and into his own before you could blink.'

'*Larry*'s account?' Dex repeated, narrowing his eyes.

Mentally kicking herself for slipping up when she'd tried so hard to remember to call him Logan, not Larry, Gaynor dipped her gaze. She was about to apologise when Dex chuckled and said, 'Don't you mean *your* account, Mrs Logan? Or should that be *mine*, considering I did all the graft to get it.'

'Ex*cuse* me?' Gaynor peered up at him incredulously.

'Yeah, I know you've done your bit an' all,' Dex conceded, waving his hand dismissively. 'But that was nowhere near as hard as what I've been doing. I mean, what's so hard about drinking champagne and getting your leg over? And we all know how much you like your sex, don't we, babe?'

'With *you*,' Gaynor gasped, hardly able to believe what she was hearing. 'It damn near killed me having to do it with someone I don't love.'

'Well, you obviously did the trick for Logan.' Dex grinned. ''Cos he was quick enough to try and nab you for himself, wasn't he? And, boy, is he gonna *pay* for the privilege.'

Gaynor couldn't speak – she was too numb. She'd never been entirely comfortable with the thought of stealing Larry's money, and had had to remind herself constantly that he deserved it in order to carry on doing what she was doing. If she'd had her way, she'd have walked away as soon as they'd got Larry arrested. Job done. But Dex had to keep pushing for one more bite of the cherry, and she really didn't like the fact that he seemed not to care what she'd been doing with Larry.

So maybe Jane *had* been telling the truth, after all. And maybe that was what her instincts had been trying to tell her since her little visit from the three witches yesterday morning.

Letting Dex natter on about the money for a while, Gaynor waited for a lull in the conversation, then said, 'I saw your Molly the other day.'

'Oh, yeah?' Dex said, looking interested suddenly. 'Where was that, then? Round at me mam's? Was she behaving herself, or being a little madam, as per?'

Irritated that he could muster genuine warmth in his eyes for the brat, Gaynor smiled and said, 'No, she was driving past, actually – with Jane. I'm sure they were in your Patrick's car, though.'

Saying, 'Oh, yeah?' again as if he saw nothing wrong with that, Dex reached for a cigarette.

'Don't you think that's a bit funny?' Gaynor persisted. 'That they should let Jane use his car, considering how much they hate her?'

'She's family,' Dex said, shrugging as if it was no big deal.

Inhaling deeply to keep at bay the tears that were stinging the backs of her eyes, Gaynor said, 'Does she ever come to see you?'

'Does she fuck,' Dex lied. Then, 'Anyhow, shut up about her. I wanna know when you're gonna get stuck into those accounts, 'cos we need to start shifting it before anyone catches on.' Smiling evilly now, he cracked his knuckles loudly and said, 'I'm gonna do that cunt like he did me, then sit back and watch him disintegrate when he realises you've cleaned him out – legally.'

Careful not to let him see how hurt and confused she was

when the bell rang a few minutes later, Gaynor said goodbye and walked away, almost certain now that Dex *had* been playing her for a fool; that she was just another Jane in his eyes – there to be used as it suited him.

All she had to do was wait two weeks to see if Jane came on Nora's visit. That would be all the proof she needed.

Sure enough, she got it.

# 26

'Who should I say wants to see him?' the sergeant asked, looking over his desk at Gaynor.

'Mrs Logan,' she said, raising her chin a notch as she added, 'Mrs *Larry* Logan.'

It killed her to use the title, because it wasn't real, and she resented the fact that she'd had her real dreams of being a wife shattered for ever by a man who had purported to love her. But it was the only guaranteed way of getting the inspector's attention without having to jump through hoops, because he had apparently been quite friendly with Larry and had been instrumental in bringing Larry into Dex's life in the first place.

Taking a seat against the wall while she waited for her message to be passed on, she kept her eyes straight ahead as various lowlifes came in and out of the door. There was a time when she'd have felt comfortable among them, but she was no longer a part of that world. That was Dex and Nora and *Jane*'s domain, and they were welcome to it.

After almost ten minutes, a door opened to her left, and an elderly-looking man with thinning red hair and searching brown eyes came out. Looking at her, he said, 'Mrs Logan?'

Standing up, Gaynor said, 'Inspector Keeton? Thanks for seeing me. I know this is a bit presumptuous, just turning up like this, but I really need to talk to you about Larry.'

'I'm sorry, my dear, but I don't really think there's any point,' Keeton said, giving her a regretful smile. 'I'm in no position to pull strings for him – even if I wanted to, and I'm sure you'll understand if I say I don't.'

Glancing around, aware that people might be listening in, Gaynor lowered her voice and said, 'Could we please go somewhere more private? I'm sure you'll change your mind when you hear what I've got to say.'

Very much doubting that, Keeton gave a little shrug and said, 'Okay, five minutes.'

Promising not to take too long, Gaynor followed him through the door he'd come out from and into a small office behind the scenes.

Waving her into the visitor's chair, Keeton strolled behind the desk and heaved himself into his chair. Then, resting his elbows on the desk, he said, 'So, what have you got to tell me, Mrs Logan?'

Telling him to please call her Gaynor, she took a deep breath and said, 'Larry's completely innocent.'

Sighing wearily, Keeton said, 'I thought I just told you I couldn't pull strings, Mrs— *Gaynor*. And I'm sorry but I meant it. This case has got nothing to do with me – I actually resent Larry sending you to try and get me involved, based on a fleeting acquaintanceship.'

'He knows absolutely nothing about this,' Gaynor assured him.

'Well, then, I admire your loyalty,' Keeton said, already beginning to stand up. 'But you're still flogging a dead horse.'

'He was set up,' Gaynor persisted. 'And I can prove it, because I was involved.'

Frowning now, Keeton pursed his lips. 'But you're his wife.'

'That was part of the set-up,' Gaynor said, feeling every bit as guilty as she looked when she added, 'I'm – I *was* Dex Lewis's girlfriend.'

Not speaking for several moments, Keeton cleared his throat and reached into his pocket for his cigarettes.

Remembering that he was no longer allowed to smoke on the premises, he put them back, and said, 'So, can I take it that you're no longer with Lewis?'

'You can,' Gaynor murmured, her nostrils flaring ever so slightly as she struggled to keep the tears at bay. She still loved Dex too much to brush off the scorching pain of his betrayal, but there was no use pretending that things could ever go back to how they had been before. Or, rather, how she'd *thought* they were, because she'd obviously been walking around in blinkers the whole time, believing Dex's lies and ignoring the glaring truths. And all he'd had to do was tell her that he loved her every now and then, and she'd been putty in his lying, cheating hands.

But no more. He reckoned he'd shafted Larry, but it had actually been *her* he'd been shafting all along. And now it was payback time.

Seeing the pain in Gaynor's eyes, and sensing that she was finding this really difficult, Keeton said, 'Shall we start off with an informal chat over coffee? Only I'd like to hear what you've got to say before I start any official balls rolling. And, to be honest, I could really do with a fag.'

Getting two steaming coffees from the canteen, he carried them both out into the yard and led Gaynor to a bench in a quiet corner away from the uniformed officers who were milling about among the cars and vans.

Handing Gaynor's coffee to her when she'd sat down, Keeton sat beside her and lit his cigarette, sighing with contentment. Then, turning to her, he said, 'So, what's a nice girl like you doing getting yourself hooked up with a thug like Lewis?'

'You tell me,' Gaynor murmured, holding the vision of Jane tarted up to the nines as she arrived arm in arm with Nora and Molly at the prison that morning firmly at the forefront of her mind. She wanted to keep any sentimental ideas about letting Dex off the hook at bay. She'd started, and now she would finish – him.

Looking into Keeton's eyes now, she said, 'I just need to know if there's any way you can keep me out of this when I tell you what I know. Because the Lewises are going to come after me with everything they've got, and I won't be safe – not even in prison, if you decide to arrest me for my part.'

'I'm sure we can work something out,' Keeton replied, sensing that Gaynor was about to give him enough rope to hang Dex Lewis once and for all. 'This is just an informal chat,' he reminded her, giving her a very pointed look. 'So if I were to hear things in passing which lead me to go away and start digging, who's to say where it came from in the first place, eh?'

'Can you do that?' Gaynor asked, a note of sheer hope in her voice.

Smiling, Keeton said, 'Depends if you're about to confess to murder, I suppose, 'cos obviously I couldn't ignore that, could I? But I don't suppose you *are* going to confess to anything like that, are you?'

'Definitely not,' Gaynor told him earnestly. Then, taking a deep breath, 'Well, not committed by me, anyway . . .'

# EPILOGUE

Peering over his glasses, the judge raised his gavel and then brought it down with a short, economical *clack*!

'Case dismissed. You're free to go, Mr Logan.'

Gasping loudly, Larry turned and looked up at the spectators' gallery. Sitting right at the front, her eyes red and swollen, with a tissue clutched tightly in her hand, Georgie nodded, and mouthed, '*You did it!*'

Wide-eyed with shock and disbelief, Larry spun around when he felt a hand on his shoulder. Seeing it was his solicitor, he grasped his hand and pumped it, saying, 'Thank you so much, Doug . . . You don't know what it meant to have you in my corner. I couldn't have got through it without you and Georgie, I really couldn't.'

Telling him that he'd been glad to help, Doug said, 'There's a ton of reporters outside. Do you want me to get them to open the back door so that we can slip away?'

Taking a deep breath, Larry shook his head. 'No, I'll have to face them sooner or later. Might as well get it over with.'

Georgie was waiting in the hall outside the door by the time Larry and Doug came out. Pulling Larry into a warm hug, she said, 'I'm so pleased for you, darling.'

'Christ, you don't know how good this feels,' Larry murmured, holding her tight. 'Every time you visited me and we had that glass window between us, I just wanted to smash it down and get one of these hugs!'

'Good job you didn't, or they'd have had a *real* case against you,' Georgie chuckled, not even trying to stop the tears from streaming down her cheeks.

'Ready?' Doug asked.

Composing himself, Larry nodded. 'Yeah, I'm ready. Let's do it.'

Cameras flashed like fireworks as soon as Larry stepped out of the court and into the daylight. Taken aback by the sheer number of reporters and photographers, not to mention the TV crews, Larry clutched at Georgie's hand and whispered, 'Shit! I hope they realise I was acquitted.'

'How's it feel to be a free man, Larry?' one of the reporters called out to him.

Laughing, Larry raised his face to the sun and said, 'Better than you could ever know, mate.'

'And how do you feel about Dex Lewis now that you know he did all this for revenge?' another asked.

'I don't feel anything,' Larry lied, smiling to cover the hatred that was still burning away inside him. 'He's never going to feel what I'm feeling right now, is he?'

'Did it shock you to hear that he was responsible for four gangland murders?' one of the TV presenters asked now. 'And that you nearly became his fifth victim when he tried to slice your throat open?'

'Nothing about Dex Lewis could shock me,' Larry said. 'I'm just glad it's all over.'

'Must be a relief to know the brother's been caught and brought back from Amsterdam for sentencing?'

'Yeah, that *is* pretty good,' Larry agreed. 'At least I don't have to keep looking over my shoulder now that I know where they all are.'

'What about your wife, Larry? How do you feel about her now you know she was Dex Lewis's girlfriend?'

Spirits dropping like a stone at the mention of her, Larry turned to Doug and said, 'Can we go now?'

Nodding, Doug held up his hands and said, 'No more questions, gentlemen . . . Mr Logan needs to go home and relax. There'll be a press conference at the Lowry Hotel in a week, and you'll all be welcome to come and talk to him there. But for now, we thank you for your support, and say goodbye.'

Larry inhaled deeply when he walked into his apartment a short time later. The air was stale, but all the old familiar scents lay in wait underneath. Dust motes rose as he moved through into the lounge, settling on him along the way as if to welcome him home.

'Never thought I'd see this place again,' he said quietly, looking around. 'Doesn't look like anybody's been living here while I've been away.'

'Even *she* couldn't be that cheeky,' Georgie muttered disapprovingly, heading into the kitchen with her shopping bag. Emptying milk, coffee and sugar onto the ledge, she filled the kettle and swilled it out, then refilled it and switched it on. 'Everyone having one?'

Grinning sheepishly, Larry came up behind her and put his hands on her ample hips. 'Not for me, babe. I need a *real* drink. Kissing her on the cheek now, he reached past her and pulled the cupboard open, delighted to find his Scotch where he'd left it.

Rolling her eyes, Georgie smiled fondly and said, 'Go on, then. But try to make it a small one, because you need to get showered and changed. There's no way we're being seen in public with you in this state.'

'Seen with me where?' Larry asked, pouring himself a large shot and Doug a smaller one.

'We're taking you out to dinner,' Georgie told him. 'So drink that and let's get you cleaned up. And I sincerely hope you've got a shaver in the bathroom, because that stubble has *got* to go.'

'It's prison chic,' Larry quipped, glad to see that she obviously had no intention of pussyfooting around him.

'Yes, well, you should have left it in the prison where it belongs,' Georgie chided, stirring a sweetener into her coffee. 'I've had to look at that miserable face through the glass for long enough without comment, but you're out now, and we want the old Larry back.'

The doorbell rang just then. Tutting softly, sensing that this was just the start of an endless round of visitors coming for a gawk at the returning hero, Georgie flapped her hand to tell Larry to stay put and, wiping her hands on a tea towel, bustled out to answer it.

Her smile slipped when she saw who it was.

Stepping out into the corridor, she pulled the door almost to behind her so that Larry wouldn't hear who she was talking to, and said, 'What do you want?'

Embarrassed, Gaynor dipped her gaze, and said, 'I know I shouldn't be here, but I need to see Larry.'

'Why?' Georgie peered at her incredulously. 'Don't you think you've done enough damage? That man did nothing but love and respect you, and you damn near destroyed him.'

'I know,' Gaynor admitted, sighing heavily. 'And I want to say I'm sorry.'

'Bit late for that,' Georgie huffed, folding her arms.

Looking her in the eye now, Gaynor sighed again. The older woman had every right to be angry with her, but this was between her and Larry.

Fortunately, Larry himself came to the door just then, curious to know what was keeping Georgie. As shocked to see Gaynor as Georgie had been angry, he just stood and looked at her.

Saying, 'Hello, Larry, you're looking well,' Gaynor put her hands in her pockets and gave him a nervous smile.

Murmuring 'Stephanie,' Larry gave a tight half-smile of

his own, confused that he was neither furious nor filled with hatred as he looked at her. She'd betrayed him in the worst possible way, yet there was still a spark of something preventing him from telling her to get lost.

'Can we talk?' she asked now, trying to ignore Georgie who was glaring at her.

Inhaling deeply, then exhaling resignedly, Larry nodded and stepped back into the hallway.

Raising her eyebrows incredulously, Georgie had no choice but to step aside and let Gaynor enter. Going in after her, she closed the door, then went back to the kitchen, waving her hands in a *what-can-you-do?* gesture to Doug as Larry and Gaynor went off into the bedroom.

Standing behind the door when he'd closed it, Larry didn't even look around despite the fact that he hadn't been into this room yet since arriving home. Folding his arms as if to defend himself from his own mixed emotions, he looked at the only woman who had ever claimed any part of his heart and said, 'So, talk, then.'

'I'm sorry,' Gaynor said calmly, determined not to let her nerves get the better of her and make her forget what she had to say. 'And I know you probably don't believe me, but it's true.'

'Why?' Larry asked, his eyes dull with disappointment. 'I thought you'd achieved your objective, so why regret it now?'

'I *did* achieve what I set out to achieve,' Gaynor admitted. 'And I didn't regret it at the time, because I was doing it for the man I loved. But I don't expect you to understand that.' Pausing, she gave him a tiny, sad smile. 'Believe it or not, I started out hating you and thought you were getting exactly what you deserved. But then I got to know you, and—'

'Oh, please!' Larry interrupted, frowning cynically. 'And then you fell in *love* with me, I suppose?'

'Absolutely not,' Gaynor replied truthfully. 'I still love

Dex – stupid as that sounds. But I'm under no illusions any more, and I realised that what he and I did was wrong. That's why I went to see your friend Inspector Keeton.'

Sighing, Larry ran a hand through his hair, which was in desperate need of conditioning and a good cut. 'Well, I guess I've got to be grateful to you for *that*, haven't I?' he said. 'So, thanks. At least it proves you're not all bad, I suppose.'

Shaking her head as she felt a sting of tears behind her eyes, Gaynor said, 'Please don't thank me. I don't deserve it.'

'Listen, Stephanie,' Larry said, immediately correcting himself. 'Sorry, *Gaynor* . . .'

Interrupting him before he could go on, she said, 'Actually, I prefer it when you call me Stephanie. Sounds stupid, I know, but that's who I was when I was with you. Anyway,' she went on, smiling shyly, 'I always did like the way you said it.'

'So, that part of it wasn't a lie, then?' Larry said softly. 'And the *other* stuff?'

Gaynor shook her head.

Frowning, Larry said, 'I'm sure there were times when you enjoyed it as much as I did. It couldn't *all* have been an act.'

'No, and I hated myself for that,' Gaynor admitted. 'But can we not talk about it, please, because I'm not exactly proud of myself.'

'Sure,' Larry said, shrugging off the last remnants of hope. 'Anyway, I *am* thanking you, because you've taught me a lesson. And I know I should hate you for what you did, but I don't. I feel sorry for you. I just hope you don't stay with Lewis, because you're way better than him.'

A tear escaped now, and Gaynor swiped it away with her finger and blinked rapidly. He was being kind, and she couldn't handle it, because he should be calling her all the bitches under the sun.

Sniffing softly, she shrugged and said, 'Well, that's all I

wanted to say, so I'll get out of your way. Oh, and please don't worry about your accounts and the apartment, by the way, because I won't be trying to lay claim to anything. Same with your name – that's all yours again, and I won't contest whatever you say to get a quick divorce. *Which*,' she added sadly, 'is my real punishment, as it happens, because I'm Catholic and it's a sin. But oh, well . . .' Another shrug. 'My family disowned me years ago over Dex, so what difference will it make if I don't make it into heaven with them?'

Tapping softly on the door just then, Georgie popped her head around it and said, 'Sorry for interrupting, Larry, but Craig's on the phone.' Casting a hooded glance in Gaynor's direction, wanting to let her know that she hadn't destroyed Larry after all, she added, 'He wants to come to dinner with us tonight . . . to discuss your new series.'

'Sorry?' Larry frowned.

'*New series*,' Georgie repeated, grinning broadly. 'Of *The Larry Logan Show*!'

Thanking the doorman for looking after her suitcase a few minutes later, Gaynor walked out of the building, leaving Larry and his real friends to their celebrations in his apartment above.

She was glad that things looked like they were going to work out for him, because he was a lot nicer than anyone had ever given him credit for. And she should know, because even after everything she'd done to him he'd *still* offered her money to help her out when she'd told him she was moving away to start over in a place where Dex and his family couldn't find her.

The men of the family were in for the long haul, but the police wouldn't be able to hold Nora, Molly and Jane for too long on the assault charge she'd brought against them once their solicitor got things moving. Gaynor had to be gone by

the time they got out and came looking for her, or she'd be
dead.

But she hadn't needed Larry's money anyway, because she
had every penny Dex owned in her bag. And why not? He
was never getting out again, and Nora and Molly certainly
didn't deserve it. And don't even get me started about *Jane*
getting her hands on it, she thought bitterly.

Anyway, it was hers, not Dex's, considering that she'd
earned the bulk of it while he'd been inside. Whatever he'd
had before he went in had long ago been gobbled up by his
greedy family.

Heading out towards the kerb now to look for a cab, Gaynor
noticed a figure huddled in the darkened shop doorway across
the road. Doing a double take when she caught a glimpse of
blonde hair beneath the hoodie, she narrowed her eyes,
thinking, *Surely not?*

A black cab came by just then and idled to a stop beside
her. Shaking her head, Gaynor waved him on his way and
made her way over to the girl.

Squatting down in front of her, she said, 'Hello, Tania.'

Not recognising her as the woman in the picture that she
had of Larry getting married, and wondering how she knew
her name, Tania drew her knees up to her chest, terrified that
she'd been sent by the Lewises to get her.

'I'm sorry . . .' she whimpered. 'I did what I was told, but
they knew I was lying.'

'Hey, it's all right, sweetheart,' Gaynor said softly, sensing
that she was every bit as much a victim of the Lewises as
she and Larry had been. 'You only did what you had to . . .
same as me.'

Reaching out to give Tania a reassuring touch on the knee,
she frowned when she noticed the rucksack in the shadows
behind her, on top of a dirty folded blanket.

'Have you been sleeping here?'

'I can't go back to my flat,' Tania muttered, clasping her knees still more tightly. 'And my mum and dad don't want to know me 'cos of what I did.'

'Isn't there a hostel you could go to?' Gaynor suggested, concerned for the girl's safety. She might be eighteen, but she was obviously still a child.

Shaking her head, Tania said, 'No. But I'm all right. Soon as the social stop messing me about with my money I'll get somewhere else to live.'

Sighing, Gaynor reached into her bag and took out her purse. Taking out two twenty-pound notes, she pushed them into Tania's pocket. She could have given her much more, but she had a feeling that it wouldn't really make any difference; that the girl would probably stay right here no matter how much she gave her, because it was as close as she could get to Larry.

Glancing down at her hands now, Gaynor gazed at the ring Larry had refused to take back and bit her lip thoughtfully. Slipping it off her finger on an impulse, she held it out to Tania.

'What's this for?' Tania asked, taking it and gazing at it as if it was the most beautiful thing she'd ever seen.

'To remind you that it's not good to love people too much,' Gaynor told her softly. 'Because you only end up hurting them – *and* yourself.'

Getting up then, she turned and walked away.